ARRIVAL

CHRISTOPHER GALLAGHER

Mesen Publishing
Mesen@gmx.co.uk

ISBN:151887343X
ISBN-13:9781518873430

In memory of my mother, Marjorie Gallagher,
for inspiring me with a love of books.

'...knowing that Christ, having been raised
from the dead, dies no more.
Death no longer has dominion over Him.'

Romans 6:9 NKJV

BEFOREHAND

THIRTY THREE YEARS AGO.
BATLEY. NORTHUMBRIA.

'Oh my God.'

Breathing, puffing, panting.

The midwife, an experienced middle-aged woman, moved about her business without unnecessary fuss. She checked for dilation and mopped the sweat from the girl's brow, then looked at Joe as though to say, you could have done that.

A few seconds silence, then…

'Oh my God.'

Breathing, puffing, panting.

'Oh my God. Oh my God. Oh my God.' One continual wail building to a crescendo, then…

'OH MY GOD.'

Joe looked away, embarrassed.

'Believers, are you?' The midwife, Angela on her name badge, said.

Joe nodded, he hoped it wouldn't an issue.

The woman sniffed. 'Sun worshipper myself. Me and the old man, every year, Majorca, two weeks in the sun, lovely.'

Joe smiled warily, he didn't want to encourage her too much, she'd have the holiday snaps out next.

'Long way from home though?' Angela said, waiting for the next wave of contractions. Just another job, another bairn on an overcrowded planet.

Joe shrugged. 'We're all a long way from home. None of my people has ever set foot in our land. We've been here centuries.'

'It's alright here.' Angela said in a pleasant tone.

'Yeah.' Joe agreed, but it wasn't home.

'Here for the census, then?' Angela asked.

'Yeah.'

All the states in the Union took an annual digital census where everyone declared their present status. But every ten years, all citizens were obliged to travel to their hometown, to be counted and prove they were who they said they were. It was the biggest mass movement of people on the planet.

'It's a pain.' Angela said, her hand below, checking Mary.

'Yeah.' Joe said again, looking away.

Angela squeezed Mary's hand, smiled, and checking her watch, said encouragingly. 'Won't be long now. You're doing ever so well.'

Joe squeezed his fiancée's hand.

She gave him a wan look. 'I don't like this Joe...' She broke off as a spasm of pain swept through her body. 'Oh, noooooooooooo.'

Joe didn't like to remind Mary that none of this was his doing. It was strictly between her and God.

The contractions were coming closer and closer together. Joe instinctively knew it wouldn't be long. There was more wailing, puffing, and panting. He glanced at the portable gas and air mask and wondered what kind of hit it would be.

At the next break in the contractions, Angela looked round at the dark interior of the shed. 'What brought you here then?'

'We tried everywhere for a room.' Joe explained. 'Travelodge, Ibis, Holiday Inn.' He shrugged. 'All full.'

'No room at the Inn?' Angela queried. 'That's a wonder. They've always got room there.'

It didn't matter Joe decided. He'd been grateful for the offer of the hotel tool shed. Had been overjoyed when the night porter had insisted on calling for an ambulance. The ambulance hadn't turned up, but Angela the midwife had.

A short while later, after more screaming, shouting, swearing, the baby came, sliding into the world, almost without warning, it seemed to Joe. Mary lay back weak and exhausted as the midwife wrapped the child in a white cloth, and placed it on Mary's chest.

'Here you are dad,' she said to Joe, 'we've finished down that end now, come and have a look at your son.' She paused, unsure, 'you are the dad?'

Joe half smiled. 'Sort of.' It was too difficult to explain.

Angela nodded. It was the way of the world these days. But they looked a decent enough couple. She hoped they'd make a go of it. 'Do you have a name for baby?'

'Jesus.' Mary said, glancing at Joe who nodded.

Angela smiled. 'Don't get too many of them round here. Still,' she paused in her cleaning and tidying. 'It's nice enough.'

Thirty minutes later, with Mary comfortable, Angela completed her paperwork. She presented Joe with her phone. 'If you could sign in the box on the screen I'll be on my way.'

Joe took the device, didn't look at the amount, just signed, knowing the money would be gone from his account instantaneously. He prayed there would be enough to cover it. He didn't like being in debt to the Union, the interest they charged was diabolical.

Seconds later, Angela was at the door. 'Now, don't forget your post-natal checks when you get home.' She left, closing the door.

Joe breathed a sigh of relief. It was done, and as lovely has Angela had been, he was pleased that she'd gone. He was so proud of Mary. It hadn't been easy for her since she'd announced her pregnancy. As devout adherents of the ancient faith they strongly believed in the sanctity of marriage and that women should remain virginal until their wedding night. Such a view was at odds with the liberality of the modern world and had only increased the ridicule that had come her way, and his too, since he'd decided to stick by her.

Joe looked at the child suckling contentedly at Mary's breast. How on earth was a child, any child, this child, going to change the world?

The door swung open, Joe looked up in annoyance. Was it too much to ask for a quiet moment with Mary and his son? He shielded his eyes against the light that flooded through the door. How could it be as bright as day in the middle of the night? He could just about see it was the midwife back again. 'Hope you don't mind,' She said, 'but you've got some visitors. I found them wandering round the car park looking for you.' She pulled a face, lowered her voice. 'They look a right scruffy lot.' She smiled. 'Well, all the best then, tarra.'

She left, leaving the door open. Joe looked in amazement as a man peered in, took off his cap and bowed low.

Joe and Mary exchanged glances.

It had begun.

ONE

THREE YEARS AGO.
LEEDS. NORTHUMBRIA.

Sir?

Thud.

Sir?

Thud.

Sir?

Thud.

Would the little bastards never shut up? Beaumont stalked the classroom peering over shoulders, pointing out errors, suggesting amendments, all the while his head thumping; an incessant throb of pumping blood. Throughout the day, every day, the swine never shut their whining voices. Sir this. Sir that. He sighed, checked the clock. It must be time to cane one of them, thrash the little bastard, see if he could make him squeal, always the highlight of the day.

There must be more to life than this, he thought, not for the first time.

'Sir?'

'Yes, Jennings?'

'Why do we have to learn about the exodus from Egypt, sir?'

Beaumont paused. 'Because Jennings, I say so.'

'It's not history, though, is it, sir?'

'Oh?' Beaumont replied. He glanced at a few of the grinning brighter boys. Predators sensing blood.

'Well, sir.' Jennings didn't seem to realise he was heading into dangerous waters. 'It's more Religious Education, isn't it?'

Beaumont decided to play along for a while. 'Well Jennings, as a religious, historical event, it could be either.'

'Can we be sure it happened, though, sir?' Another youth, Baxter was it, chirped into life.

Was it a conspiracy, Beaumont wondered. 'Something puzzling you, Baxter?'

'Exodus, sir. Did it happen?'

'Have you not been listening, Baxter?'

Baxter decided to take the question as rhetorical.

Beaumont took a deep breath. 'As you know, the Jews left Egypt, and managed to flee through the desert, keeping just ahead of Pharaoh's army. They went across the Red Sea into what they thought would be their promised land. However, once there, their leaders decided they didn't feel that safe, so they kept on travelling, all the way across Europe, arriving here in Northumbria forty years after they left Egypt. Where they've lived ever since.'

'All of them, sir?

'No, Jennings, not all of them. In every country they journeyed through, a few stayed and made lives for themselves. There's a remnant of the Jewish people in practically every country in the Union. But by far the biggest population is here in Northumbria.'

'Excuse me, sir.'

Beaumont sighed. 'Yes Schulz?'

'Why can't we study the Union sir, how it came about?'

'Is it true, sir that we used to have a king in this country?'

'What would happen, sir, if the four kingdoms joined together, sir, declared independence from the Union?'

Beaumont had often wondered that. There had been talk over the years of uniting the four kingdoms of Northumbria, East Anglia, Wessex, and Mercia within the Union. It would make administration easier, but like many such initiatives it had come to nothing. There had never been a genuine option to leave the Union, despite the 1975 referendum posing that exact question. That vote had been rigged in favour of remaining within the safety of the Union. The financial ruin that would have followed an exit had been too much to contemplate for most of those eligible to vote. In any case, the present Fuehrer was known to oppose the idea. She didn't like the possibility of a potential rival power on her doorstep. There was enough trouble with the Slavs to the east.

'Sir?'

'Sir?'

'Sir?'

'Silence.' Beaumont screamed. 'One at a time. If you wish to speak, raise your hand. Yes, Baxter?'

Before Baxter could speak, Beaumont became aware of Schulz muttering, decided it was time to make an example.

'What was that, Schulz?' He barked.

'My father thinks we should make God's so called chosen people fight the animals in the Arena.'

'Does he now?' Beaumont lowered his voice.

A throwback to the Roman days, the games in the Arena had been reinstated by the first Fuehrer. A three day jamboree incorporating among other spectacles, trials of strength, man against man, animal against animal, and by far the most popular, man against animal, where it was rare for man to come out alive.

'Yes, sir. That would show them who's in charge?'

Beaumont, the vein in his temple throbbing, nodded. 'And then, what of the survivors?'

'They should be shipped back to their so called promised land.' The youth sneered.

Beaumont nodded.

'And what do you think Schulz?'

'I agree with him, sir.' The boy paused, full of youthful confidence. 'In fact, I think we Saxons are God's chosen people. What do you think, sir?'

Beaumont smiled. 'I think you should come out to the front Schulz, and bend over my desk.'

Later, after laying the cane across Schulz's backside three times, Beaumont wondered whether direct action might not be such a bad idea.

✝

WHITBY, NORTHUMBRIA.

'"Look, I will send to you Eliyahu the prophet before the coming of the great and terrible Day of the Lord. He will turn the hearts of the fathers to the children and the hearts of the children to their fathers. Otherwise I will come and strike the land with complete destruction."'

Brian rolled up the scroll and regarded his congregation in silence. He could just about count them on the fingers of both hands. He wondered again, why he bothered. Better to pack it all in, get a proper job. Heathens the lot of them. As much heathens as the new agers, the druids, the sun worshipers, rain dancers, the tree huggers, the child sacrificers and they were just the ones Brian could recall off the top of his head. He could tolerate most of the offbeat, strange practices that people indulged in, apart from child sacrifice. That was the only religious practice banned by the Union, but it still happened, out there in the wilderness. He shivered, took a deep breath, said.

'This is the word of the Lord.' He glanced round for eye contact with someone, anyone. An old woman in the front row looked away. A man near the back held his eye as though to say, 'Go on, amaze me.' Brian continued,

'These are the final words from the ancient scriptures.'

Didn't they care?

Apparently not.

Well, Jesus apart, a keen young man, who one day would make a fine teacher of the law, if he would concentrate more, listen once in a while, stop thinking he knew more than his teacher. He scanned the room, no sign of Jesus today. It was rare for him to miss a service.

'The last words spoken to His people by the Lord of the universe. We are his people. He is our Lord. And we are still waiting for Eliyahu to point the way to Messiah.'

So, if anybody sees him, send him my way.

There was silence

Brian blessed his flock, dismissed them. As the congregation shuffled out into the evening sunset, Brian smiled at the thought of the ancient prophet turning up here in Whitby. More chance of winning the lottery.

He stacked the chairs away, thought again how things had changed since his people had left the Promised Land. Then, back in the day, there'd been dedicated synagogues, holy places, not draughty village halls, civic centres, and, he looked round with disdain, Multi Faith Worship Centres aka MUFWOCS.

Trouble was the Jews had been waiting too long for God to speak, to send Messiah, to free them from oppression. Most had drifted. Brian considered them secular followers. Seldom seen at worship, visiting the Temple in York once a year, because to stop, would be a step too far.

Brian felt a draught, his notes on the lectern shifted. Typical, some of them couldn't even get here at the right time. 'The service is over for today,' he called out without looking, 'come back tomorrow.'

No response, but Brian, aware of a presence, turned and saw a figure framed in the doorway, the setting sun forming a halo round his head, his first thought. Eliyahu? He tensed as the figure moved towards him but relaxed when he saw it was Baptiste. A local nutter who lived on the moors for months at a time. He'd started immersing people in the sea. Preparing them for Messiah, he claimed. A small, barrel of a man, wild tangled hair - birds could nest in that hair Brian always thought. He was said to be harmless, but Brian wasn't taking any chances. His fingers touched the personal attack alarm on his waist.

Baptiste noticed the movement. Amusement flickered over his weathered face. 'You've no need for that lad. I don't mean you any harm.' He chuckled in his thick local accent.

Brian continued clearing chairs, keeping a close eye on Baptiste.

'He's coming.' Baptiste said. 'Messiah.'

This was new. For all his ramblings, Baptiste had never come out with a definite statement before.

Brian waited.

'He's with us now. Messiah walks with us.'

'Is that right?' Brian asked, sceptical.

Silence.

'And who is this Messiah? Does he have a name?'

'Soon. It'll be revealed soon. I just wanted you to know, what with you reading that passage from Malachi.'

Brian smiled. 'And that makes you, what, Eliyahu?'

Baptiste shook his head, 'Nay lad, that's not me. I'm just a voice crying int' wilderness.'

'You want to be careful,' Brian warned, 'there's some that might think you're serious.'

Baptiste nodded, 'That's the idea,' he turned to leave. 'Why don't you come down to the beach in the morning hear what I have to say.'

Baptiste left and Brian carried on clearing the chairs, strangely unsettled by the encounter. It was some time later before he stopped, and wondered how Baptiste knew he'd read from Malachi.

LEEDS, NORTHUMBRIA.

Bocus idly watched columns of figures flicker their way across his screen and dreamed of a day when the four kingdoms of Northumbria, Wessex, Mercia, and East Anglia joined together and became free of the Union and its Saxon overlords. Perhaps joining together with Scotland, Wales, and Cornwall, to form one glorious nation.

Bocus was a member of a small but determined group working to make it happen. He used his position as an analyst for Northumbrian Water to insert corrupt data into the figures for water availability. His intention was to make the current water shortage appear a lot worse than it was. Soon there would be a hosepipe ban but his ultimate outcome was standpipes in the streets, long queues for water, just like back in '76, well before his time, of course, but remembered with horror by some older employees. There was a small element of risk involved, the authorities always watching, monitoring, for any sign of dissent, but they were more concerned with groups of armed rebels that sprang up from time to time. These groups were hunted down with ruthless efficiency, and survivors, if any, were executed by being nailed naked to wooden crosses in the Arena at York.

The Saxons were, for the most part, benign oppressors, but could demonstrate a ruthless streak when it was required to keep order. Crucifixions, while not common, occurred often enough for it to be a constant reminder. Bocus shuddered at the thought.

Life was good for the majority of citizens, there was

no incentive to agitate for separation, and it was always a risky business, raising the subject of the Union. It was a long, slow process, a word here, a hint there, reactions gauged, assessed. A word out of place to the wrong person could lead to a visit from the Polizei.

There had been tentative contact between some members of the ancient faith and the underground Northumbrians. A reaching out, see if they could join together and help each other. A strange bunch, Bocus thought, despite being here for the best part of two thousand years they still kept themselves apart, with their odd customs. Live animal sacrifices to appease their god, their annual pilgrimage to the Temple at York.

A message box popped on the screen. It was from his manager, Mayer, another Saxon. A summons - my office, now!

Bocus read it with a faint feeling of disquiet. Was this it? No, first indication wouldn't be a summons for a chat, more like a snatch squad would lift him on the street, whisk him away to State Security HQ in York.

Mayer, a neat, precise man, close-cropped hair, middle aged, was at his desk, writing notes on a pad. Smoke from a cigarette curled up from the ashtray. He waved at Bocus through the glass, beckoned him to a seat. Bocus sat, waited, resisted the urge to fidget, and wondered if cameras were recording. He looked around, couldn't see any.

After a while, Mayer placed his pen on the blotter, took a last pull from his smoke, stubbed it out, and looked at Bocus over his glasses. He picked up a piece of paper, 'Memo from State Security.' He explained, waving it at Bocus, then placed it on the desk, squared it up. 'There's been a threat from a dissident group,' he shrugged, 'apparently they're threatening to cause disruption to the water supply.'

Good.

'How?'

'Non-specific.' Mayer shook his head, frowned. 'We're already struggling without this,' he gestured to his screen. 'But, of course, you know the levels are way down.' He shrugged. 'Climate change, global warming, call it what you will. It's having an impact.' He paused. 'What do you think is causing it?'

Not enough rain you Saxon cretin.

'Too many sun worshipers, not enough rain dancers.' Bocus said.

Mayer stared.

Bocus, feeling uncomfortable, said, 'I am joking.'

'No, no.' Mayer said, lighting another smoke, 'you may have something. Do you know, according to the last census returns, twenty percent of the population of the four kingdoms put sun worshipper as their official religion compared to five percent as rain dancer.'

Bocus, surprised it was that high, said as much.

Mayer, broad grin, pointed his finger at Bocus, 'Gotcha.' He chuckled. 'You Northumbrians are so gullible.' He blew smoke, continued, 'I've got a little project for you.'

Bocus nodded, tried to look eager, failed. As if he didn't have enough to do.

'Yeah, I want you to make a tour of all our facilities, check the security procedures at each one, and make recommendations.'

'Why me?' Bocus asked, surprised.

Mayer spread his hands, his mind made up. 'Why not? Someone has to do it. Why not you?'

Why not arse-licking Grauber?

'I don't know anything about security.' Bocus protested.

'Now's your chance to learn.' Mayer stood. The meeting was over. 'I'll expect your report on my desk within four months.'

'That's a lot of sites to get round in that time.' Bocus protested. 'What about my day job?'

'Relax Bocus,' Mayer told him, 'I've got Grauber to cover for you.'

†

WHITBY, NORTHUMBRIA.

Andrew watched as the congregation left the MUFWOC. He'd been intending to go in, sit at the back, be anonymous, but there hadn't been enough of a crowd to hide him. He waited till everyone had left, before walking away. He headed for the seashore having some vague notion of looking for Baptiste, perhaps he could talk to him, see if he could throw any light on the way he was feeling. Andrew wandered up and down the beach without seeing any of the crowds that the prophet attracted. Disappointed at not finding Baptiste, he stood at the edge of the sea for a while, staring, and thinking. Twenty-eight years old, what had he achieved. A successful self-made man, part owner with Peter, his brother, of Whitby Fish. He was married to a beautiful, loving woman. They had three children, who Andrew adored, but, it just wasn't enough, and he didn't know why. There was something missing. It wasn't money. It wasn't stuff. It was just a vague gap that needed filling. Truth be told, he was lost.

It might be worse mind, he thought with a wry smile. He could be living Peter's life of dissolute debauchery. Peter, drunk every night, sleeping with a different woman every few days. A lifestyle understandable in your late teens shouldn't be the same when you reached maturity. It was all too prevalent though. There were a lot of broken, empty people in the world, necking anti-depressants by the ton.

Andrew searched for a suitable pebble, skimmed it, pleased as a bairn to make six bounces. That's what he found so exciting and refreshing about Baptiste. So what if most folks thought him a nut job? He had something, a vision, a hope, an idea, call it what you will. And if he was right, there was an even greater one to come.

Andrew stood on the beach until the last rays of the sun faded, then skirted that day's sand castles and climbed the steps to the road. It was still early season, not many holidaymakers about, the cafes, pubs and restaurants all with a trickle rather than floods of customers. He walked through the narrow streets, avoiding people, made his way to the pub where he knew he would find Peter.

✝

The Rising Sun, an old-fashioned pub, beer on draught, was full to heaving. Peter was buzzing. It'd been a good day. A reciprocal fishing rights agreement had been signed with representatives from East Anglia, Mercia and Wessex. It would ensure work for the Whitby Fish processing plant for years to come. Well, as long as there was fish to be caught, but that, Peter thought, was a problem for another day.

He signalled to the barmaid. Why couldn't Andrew have come for a drink to celebrate, instead of going off on his own? Wouldn't put it past him to go along to the service at the MUFWOC. Load o' nonsense that was. What had God ever done for him?

The barmaid set his drink down, Peter looked her up and down, 'Keep the change love,' he said, slipped her a note and forgot all about his brother as the woman in the flame red dress he'd been eyeing for most of the evening came out of the ladies. She looked familiar, where had he seen her before? Did she work at the plant?

'Hey.' He touched her arm.

The woman paused, saw a man in his thirties, not unattractive, but far from sober. 'Yeah?'

'Do I know you?'

She smiled. 'Is that what passes for a chat up line round here?'

Peter grinned. 'No, I do know you from somewhere.'

Shrug. 'Maybe you do.'

'Where do you work?'

'If you need to ask you don't know me.' She turned to go.

'That dress you're wearing.'

The woman half turned, stopped, 'You like it?'

Peter gave a crooked little smile. 'Look better on

my bedroom floor.'

The woman leaned towards Peter, her perfume sweet, subtle. He anticipated her lips. She whispered in his ear. He drew back amazed. 'How much?'

The woman shrugged.

'That's way more than NorPro.'

'I'm sure you can afford it.' The woman lingered.

'What's your name?' Peter asked, enjoying the flirtation.

'Maggie. Yours?'

'Peter.'

'Well, Peter, the ball's in your court.'

'Why should I go with you rather than use NorPro?'

Maggie smiled. 'Because I'm worth it.'

'I bet you are.' He stepped back, gave her his full attention. She was what, early twenties, slim figure, full breasts, and her legs, bare beneath the short red dress held much promise. She had dark hair with highlights that framed her regular features. Brown mischievous eyes, unfazed by the inspection, held his.

His verdict, well worth it.

Decision made. He drained his drink. 'Okay, let's go.'

'Not so fast.' The man appeared from nowhere. He was of medium height, thinning hair. He held Maggie's arm, his small piggy eyes blinked behind round spectacles.

Maggie wriggled free of the man's grasp. 'Levi. Where did you spring from?'

Peter struggled to work out what had happened. 'Who the fuck are you?'

'Private arrangement, Maggie?' Levi asked, ignoring Peter's outburst.

'No. Peter's an old friend, we were just talking.'

Even to Peter her denial sounded less than convincing.

'Is that right?' He turned to Peter. 'Known her long have you friend?'

Peter shrugged, he didn't need this shit. There was always NorPro.

Levi took Peter's arm, moved him to one side. 'Look friend, I'm Maggie's manager, she's not supposed to make private arrangements. If you want to spend time with her, you have to pay the going rate.'

'Which is?'

Levi mentioned a sum that was a lot lower than Maggie's. It was even less than the official NorPro price. Peter smiled, opened his wallet, and pulled notes. 'It's a deal mate.'

Levi took the money, smiled. 'Enjoy.'

Leaving the pub, Peter, Maggie on his arm, bumped into Andrew. 'Can't stop bro, the meter's running. See you in the morning, yeah?'

✝

After Peter and Maggie had gone, Andrew bought a drink, found a corner seat with a good view of the TV. The rolling news was rolling on. Same old, day after day. He watched fuming as Baptiste immersed people in the sea. Knew he was being stupid and irrational, knew Peter screwed prostitutes on a regular basis, and knew Maggie opened her legs for men every day of the week. She meant nothing to him.

Nothing.

Why then, was he so bothered? He brooded for a

while, sipping his beer, making it last. Bloody Peter. Always been the same. Andrew could never have anything, but Peter had to have it. His phone rang, he answered.

It was Marje.

They had a brief conversation. He told her he'd be home soon. He cleared the call, finished his beer, got another, and felt himself beginning to calm down. He tried to rationalise his feelings. Why wasn't he happy with just one woman? Why this thing for Maggie? A prostitute of all people. A mad prostitute at that, with her talk of the voices in her head. Okay, she was beautiful, good in bed, but then, so was Marje, why on earth wasn't he satisfied? All his thoughts led him back to the Garden of Eden and the temptation of the forbidden fruit.

He'd been immersed though, prepared for Messiah, he shouldn't still be sinning, should he? What was the matter with him? He switched his attention to the screen. There'd been a crucifixion in York. The pictures gruesome. Andrew read the writing on the bottom of the screen as it scrolled along. The serial killer Sutcliffe took seven hours to die watched by a jeering crowd.

Andrew shuddered, looked away. What a horrible way to die. Bloody Saxons. There was supposed to have been an opt out clause for crucifixions when Northumbria joined the Union. That hadn't lasted long.

The Governor, Pilate, appeared on screen, appealing for calm, promising rewards for people with information on terrorists. A Freephone number displayed, anonymity guaranteed.

Andrew thought again about Peter. Jayne, his wife, had left him not long ago, running off with an estate agent from Mercia. Andrew knew he should be more understanding of his brother's troubles. Knew also that his troubles were largely of his own making. The wonder was that Jayne had stayed as long as she had.

He gave the TV a final glance before he left for home. It was showing pictures of the first Fuehrer. A funny little man, toothbrush moustache, slashed haircut. He was standing in the back of an open top Mercedes giving that curious salute he'd favoured. He'd come to prominence in the early part of the last century before the formation of the Community which had quickly morphed into the Union.

He was known to have hated the Jews, blaming them for any and every problem. At the time there'd been a lot of talk of forcibly resettling those of the ancient faith in specially built facilities. With the Fuehrer's early death the threat had come to nothing, but still...' Andrew shivered. Those had been dark days on the mainland.

The picture changed to rain dancers doing their thing. The scrolling text informing that the hot spell was set to continue, that an announcement about declaring drought conditions would be made in due course.

Andrew drained his beer, thought about another, decided against it. He had a sudden urge to go home and make love to Marje.

†

Maggie, wide-awake, lay on her back staring at the ceiling. Her phone buzzed, Peter, beside her, stirred, turned over. 'Wassat?'

That, my love, Maggie thought, is your meter running out. She turned over, smiled at the sight of her dress on the floor, answered her phone in a low voice, listened, and said, 'Okay.' Maggie slipped out of bed, dressed, and paused at the bedroom door. Peter was watching her. She shrugged. 'Sorry, gotta go.'

'I thought I had you for the night?' Peter grumbled, his voice thick with sleep.

'That was my price,' she shook her head, 'not Levi's.'

Peter nodded, slumped down, and closed his eyes.

It being a calm night, Maggie decided to walk home by the sea. The tide was coming in, the water making shushing noises as it crept up the beach. She found it relaxing, looking into the black of the night, listening to the waves. The embers of a campfire could be seen below the sea wall, just above the high water mark. Dark shapes huddled together, voices carried on the night air. She listened to a guitar strumming, a male voice singing.

> 'Messiah's coming soon,
> Messiah's coming soon,
> Oh Messiah, you're coming soon.
> Messiah, walk with us,
> Messiah, walk with us,
> Oh Messiah, you'll walk with us.'

Maggie stood still, straining to hear, enjoying the moment, feeling a part of something, but then a squad car came crawling along and broke her mood. She sensed the occupants, young male Polizei officers, looking at her, and was conscious of her short dress, her bare legs. Maggie weighed her options, run and they'd chase. They'd catch her and take her somewhere for their enjoyment. Of course, she could always head down the steps to the beach, could lose them down there, but the voices wouldn't like that. There were always the voices, draining her life. The one she called Terror sparked off now, stirring up anxiety, 'There's nothing for you down there.'

She affected an air of casual ease. It must have worked, as, after a few minutes the car moved off at a leisurely pace. Rooting in her bag she found the remains of a recent spliff, lit it, drew the intoxicant deep into her lungs, exhaled, relaxed. Maggie stood for a while longer, enjoying the peace, the sound of the sea. The guy on the beach had stopped singing, was strumming his guitar. They'd never accept her, she told herself, but desired it still. Maggie nipped out the spliff, blow was all right, but was nowhere as good as the Morph. She should have got some from Levi when she saw him last night.

Maggie set off for home, replaying again the shock she'd felt at bumping into Andrew as she'd left the pub with Peter. Andrew, one of her regulars, had masked it well, but she'd seen the look of annoyance pass over his face before his features relaxed, accepting that for once she wasn't available for him. Maggie thought of the brothers sharing notes, boasting, bragging who'd satisfied her most, when in truth, neither had. It would take a very special man to satisfy the deep longing that she craved.

TWO

WHITBY, NORTHUMBRIA.

Early morning on the beach, the fire about gone. The sun, just breaking. Tom turned over in his sleeping bag, tried to get comfortable, who'd have thought sand could be so hard? He groaned as he heard the first few notes of Phil's latest composition. Did the guy never rest? Tom buried his head in the bag, tried to block out the sound of Phil singing the same lines. Okay, the guy had a reasonable voice, wrote some decent songs, even if they were all about the promised Messiah, but Tom didn't need to be part of the creative process.

Phil began singing in a low voice.

'This is the day, Lord that you gave.
You sent Messiah for him to save,'

Then discordant chords, a key change, led into a louder,

'Us from the pit of eternal hell.'

The strumming stopped. Phil muttered something inaudible, laid the guitar to one side.

'What do you think Nathan?' Phil asked.

An answering grunt from Nathan told Tom he was

equally unimpressed.

Tom thought about Nathan. A quiet man, who would speak when he had something to contribute but beyond that, was silent. Tom wondered what he did for a living. He seemed to have lots of free time to spend with Baptiste. He'd so far resisted Tom's gentle probing questions, deflecting all enquiries with a disarming smile. They seemed an odd match, the straight, buttoned up Nathan, and Phil, the dreamy not quite on the same planet, unemployed singer songwriter. What was the connection? It was a spiritual gig and one that would attract Phil. But what was it with Baptiste that attracted Nathan?

For Tom himself, the jury was still out on Baptiste and his prophecies of Messiah. It seemed so unlikely that God would send an emissary to bridge the gap between heaven and earth. He wondered how long to give it as an undercover reporter before abandoning his dream of landing a major story to augment the mundane pieces he contributed to the Northumbrian media. A while longer, he thought, before turning over, and slipping back into an uneasy sleep.

†

After the early morning catch up at Whitby Fish - hot bacon rolls and black coffee - the brothers tended their separate workloads until they had another chat at the end of the day.

This morning Andrew lingered in the doorway. 'That girl?'

'What girl?' Peter frowned. 'I know lots of girls.'

'Last night, you were leaving the pub with her as I

came in. Dark haired, attractive, red dress.'

'Oh,' Peter smiled. 'That girl.'

'Known her long?' Andrew tried for casual, fell some way short.

'Nah, met her last night.'

'Quick work.'

'Andy, bro, she was a whore. Gave me an excellent shag. End of. Now,' he rustled the paperwork on his desk, 'if there's nothing else.'

'Not a new girlfriend then?'

Peter sat back in his chair, regarded his brother. 'Why the sudden interest in my activities?'

Andrew shrugged. 'Just wondered if you'd got yourself a proper woman at last.'

'No, no, no.' Peter grinned. 'I don't think so. I think you fancy a piece of the action. Why didn't you say? I can get you her pimp's number. Just don't put it through the books as entertaining.'

'No thanks, I'm quite happy with Marje, I don't need another woman.'

'Don't fancy a change?' Peter teased.

'That's how it started with you. Fancying a change. Now look at you. Jayne's gone. You're pissed every night, throwing your money away on cheap whores.' Andrew toyed with the idea of telling his brother about Baptiste, the prophecy of Messiah. As always, the fear of ridicule kept him silent.

'I'm living the dream bro, and you're just jealous.' Peter scooped the buzzing phone off the desk. 'Hello?' He listened in silence, then, 'Send him in.' He replaced the phone. 'Jim from Whitby Builders, come to give us a quote for the office extension.'

Andrew nodded. 'I'll catch you later.'

Jim settled behind the wheel of his battered pick-up, Whitby Builders just visible through the grime. He was scribbling a few notes when his phone rang.

He looked at the screen, Jude the Dude calling.

This had better not be trouble. He didn't need trouble, not the Dude kind anyway.

'Yeah?' He answered the call with a growl.

'Hey Jimbo, it's the Dude.'

'I know who it is, whaddaya want?'

'It's Jesus.'

'And?'

'He's vanished.'

Jim sighed, trouble it was. 'Whaddaya mean vanished, are we talking puff o' blue smoke or alien abduction?'

'Nah Jimbo, nothing so exciting, he's walked off the job.'

Jim frowned. Didn't sound at all like Jesus. His best worker by far, the most renowned, sought after chippie in all Northumbria. 'Did he say anything? Perhaps he's ill.'

'Nah, he just said, it's time, and then he walked.'

Silence, then, 'Just thought I'd let you know.'

'Time for what?' Jim asked.

'How should I know?'

'Tea? Shop? Dump?'

'Dunno.'

'When was this?'

'Two hours ago.'

The Dude's knowledge exhausted, Jim cleared the call, found Jesus' number in his phone contacts, called and got voicemail, 'Hello, and thanks for calling Jesus, of Whitby Builders, I can't take your call at present, please leave a message.'

✝

Phil meandered along the beach strumming his guitar, desperately trying to come up with more lyrics. He thought of himself as a wandering troubadour serenading the crowds. Someone nudged his arm. It was a woman in her fifties. A bored looking man of a similar age hovered at her elbow.

'What's going on here love?' She asked. 'I mean, who are all these people?'

'It's a religious gathering.' Phil said.

'Oh, religion?' The man sneered. 'We thought it might be summat interesting. 'Come on Mavis, we've no business here.' He turned to go, and stopped when he realised the woman wasn't behind him.

'What religion is it?' Mavis asked.

'We're Jewish.' Phil told them.

The man rolled his eyes.

'The one where God created the earth in six days and will one day send a Saviour.' Phil explained.

'What brought you here, like?' Mavis asked.

'Must be our green and pleasant land.' The man muttered.

'Shut up Ted. Sorry love,' she smiled at Phil, 'carry on.'

'There's loads of information on the internet about it.' Phil said, strumming a chord change.

Ted looked about to speak, but a glance from Mavis silenced him.

'We thought we might have seen that feller immersing people.' Mavis said.

35

Phil looked along the beach. He could see Tom scribbling away in his notebook, Nathan was moving around the gathering crowd, chatting to people. 'That's Baptiste. We believe he's a prophet preparing the way for the Messiah.'

'Messiah?' Mavis raised her eyebrows.

Phil sighed. He was asked the same thing countless times a day. 'Messiah is the Saviour that God will send to save his people and lead them out of captivity. He'll set us free.'

Mavis looked around, lowered her voice, 'That could be dangerous, couldn't it? I'm not sure the authorities would welcome this Messiah.'

Phil smiled, shrugged. He didn't care one way or the other.

'Mavis.' Ted tugged at her cardigan. 'Mavis, let's go. I don't want to miss the brass band'

'You and your blessed brass bands.' Mavis snorted.

'Mavis, this is the Northumbrian and they do a fine rendition of Blaydon Races.'

The sounds of instruments tuning up could now be heard. Phil smiled, strummed his guitar.

'They'll be starting soon.' Ted complained.

Mavis rolled her eyes at Phil. 'But why does he dip people in the sea?'

'It's a symbolic act of repentance in readiness for the Messiah's arrival.' Phil was always happy to discuss elements of his faith. 'It's a public acknowledgement that despite how clean we might look on the outside, on the inside we're just dirty. It's a declaration that we recognise that we need cleansing and that's a job for the Lord.'

Mavis chuckled. 'Are you listening Ted, happen you

could do with some o' that.'

Ted gave a tight smile, turned, head cocked like a bird. In the distance the band started to play.

The conversation tailed off. Phil turned towards the road, people were still streaming down to the beach and behind him, he could hear Ted and Mavis chuntering away.

'Ted, it's not every day you get to hear a genuine prophet.'

'Mavis, I am not missing that brass band concert for a prophet, or a Messiah.'

Phil tuned them out and watched as the crowd continued to grow.

†

'Repent, repent. The kingdom of heaven is near.'

Baptiste was in full flow proclaiming and denouncing in equal measure. Nathan stood at the water's edge, waiting for the preaching to stop and trying to estimate the size of the crowd. Between seven hundred and a thousand was his best guess. Nathan had heard it all before, and reckoned he could deliver it just as well as Baptiste. He was good though, Nathan admitted.

'You immoral generation, you bend like trees in a gale.'

The crowd lapped it up. They seemed to like being insulted and came from all over the kingdom for the privilege. Nathan had already spoken with folks from Newcastle, Leeds, Sheffield, York, and they all told him the same thing. They were here to be dipped by Baptiste.

Nathan yawned, stretched. He'd been detailed to help Baptiste with the immersions, along with Phil - that is, if Phil could be arsed to put his guitar down.

'There is no conscience anymore. And what of the commandments handed down by our forefather, Moses? Those instructions carved in tablets of stone by God Himself, are ignored.' Baptiste paused, the crowd were silent, hanging on every word, then, arms held high, he continued, 'You must confess and repent. The Lord is watching, He will judge. He will burn with unquenchable fire.'

Nathan didn't think anybody had sussed he was a State Security officer working undercover. Tom was always asking questions though, maybe he was undercover as well. Nathan wouldn't put it past the authorities to have infiltrated more than one person into Baptiste's circle.

Nathan watched as Baptiste worked himself to a fever pitch, and then dropped his voice to a whisper.

'You people, you think that I am Messiah.'

Silence.

Anticipation.

'I am not Messiah.'

The crowd let out a collective groan.

'I have come to prepare the way for Messiah.'

The official line on Baptiste was: low level agitator, harmless, if not a little mad, with his message of the coming Messiah. Now though, with the growing crowds, TV and internet exposure, Nathan wouldn't be surprised if the decision makers were getting a little anxious.

'I am not the light.'

Nathan wondered about the promised Messiah,

what might happen if he did arrive. It could be a right bloodbath.

'I have come to bear witness to the light.'

'You people, you believe that Messiah is an earthly warrior, that he'll come to overthrow earthly powers. Think again. He's more, much more. The coming kingdom will not be of this world. The Lord's kingdom will be established here on earth.'

Wild cheers erupted from the crowd. This was close to sedition, Nathan realised. He scanned the area towards the road, wondering where the riot Polizei was. They'd be close, waiting, and ready to move in if it all kicked off.

Baptiste must have realised he was getting close to what was acceptable as he finished his preaching soon afterwards. He rubbed his face on a towel, had a quick drink, and then took his place between Nathan and Phil, ready to begin immersing.

To Nathan's surprise, the first man in the queue was someone he knew. A riot control officer. Was he here for genuine reasons, or was he too working undercover? The officer gave no indication that he knew Nathan. Nathan and Phil stood just behind him, held him at elbow and shoulder, waited for the signal.

'Do you believe in the one who comes after me?' Baptiste asked.

'I believe.' The man replied.

'Do you repent?'

'Yes, yes, I repent. ' The man replied. Nathan could feel him shaking, whether from the cold or emotion, he couldn't tell.

Baptiste placed the palm of his hand on the man's chest, pushed.

They lowered the man into the sea, and then raised him back to a standing position. The crowd cheered.

'You are ready, for the kingdom is near.' Baptiste told him. 'Go, tell others.'

The man tried to speak, Phil urged him to move away. Nathan, watched as the man stumbled up the beach and prepared himself for the next person in line.

The afternoon wore on and hundreds of people were dipped. The line of people waiting eventually getting shorter. Phil was replaced by Tom, but Nathan carried on.

They were down to the last dozen when it happened.

Baptiste had just finished an immersion when he stood stock still and stared along the beach. It was late afternoon, Nathan, tired, hungry, wanted a curry and a pint. He tried to make out what Baptiste was looking at, and decided it was the lone man walking towards them. As he got closer, Nathan could see the man, early thirties, above average height, clean-shaven, was wearing a light pair of chinos and a long sleeved blue shirt. The shirt was tucked in, the collar open. On his feet, he wore grey canvas deck shoes.

The man stopped a few metres away, smiled at them both. Nathan had an incredible feeling of peace sweep over him. The hairs on the back of his neck stood on end.

After a moment's hesitation, Baptiste said, 'Jesus, it's you.'

The two men embraced.

'Did you know?' Jesus asked.

Baptiste shook his head in amazement, smiled. 'I've always had an inkling, a mere suspicion that it might have been. But just now, when I saw you walking towards me, I knew.' He paused. 'Jesus, will you baptize me?'

'No,' Jesus replied, 'you must baptize me.'

'I'm sorry, I can't.' Baptise was apologetic. 'I'm not fit to lace your boots.'

'If the ancient scriptures are to be fulfilled you have to baptize me.' Jesus said. He stood waiting between Tom and Nathan.

Baptiste hesitated for a second, before touching Jesus on his chest. They lowered Jesus into the water, then back up again. There was an instant rumble of thunder. It went on for several minutes, Tom and Nathan looked at each other in amazement. It was a clear, cloudless sky, no hint of rain. The thunder faded away and as it did Tom could see that Jesus' countenance had changed. A blanket of compassion, utter kindness, and unconditional love seemed to be resting on him.

It seemed to Tom as though time stopped, it could have been hours or seconds, he had no way of knowing. The angelic, dreamlike atmosphere was broken when he realised that Baptiste was lying in a crumpled heap on the wet sand. Tom couldn't be sure, but it looked as though Baptiste had diminished, was smaller, as though part of him was missing.

Jesus stood before Nathan, looked him in the eye. Confused, Nathan looked away. It was as though Jesus had x-ray vision. He felt the layers of his existence peeled away, his every thought and deed exposed. Jesus smiled. 'Nathan, Tom,' he said, 'I must go now, but we'll meet again, soon.'

Jesus turned and walked back the way he'd come.

Tom and Nathan watched in silence until he was out of sight. At their feet, Baptiste lay sobbing.

Jim answered the phone warily. It'd been a long day; he didn't need any more shit.

'Jimbo. It's the Dude.'

'I know. Whaddaya want?'

'Jesus is here. He wants some camping gear.'

'And?'

'What shall I do?'

'Give him what he wants.'

'How long's he gonna be off? You know we've got that big job coming up.'

Jim sighed, a weary sound that lasted a long time. 'Jesus no longer works for me.'

'You've sacked him?' The Dude was stunned.

'No, he resigned. Apparently he's got other more important stuff to do.'

'Do you reckon he's setting up on his own?'

'No idea.'

'How do you feel about that?'

'Dude.' Jim answered with feeling. 'I am not my brother's keeper.'

The call ended and Jude returned to the garage. He would have liked to question Jesus about his plans, but didn't feel he could. Something had happened to the guy between him walking off the job in the morning and reappearing a while ago asking about camping stuff. He'd changed. Perhaps Jim hadn't been too far off the mark when he'd joked about alien abduction.

Jesus looked at him and smiled. That was another thing. His smile seemed different. It had some kind of brilliance to it.

'What did Jim say?' Jesus said.

'Jim?'

'You just spoke to him on the phone, didn't you?'

Jude thought about lying for a split second, realised he couldn't. 'Yeah, he says you've resigned.'

Jesus nodded. 'That's right. It's time for me to be about my father's business. I'd like you to be part of it.'

Jude was flattered, wondered if there'd be a pay rise.

'We'll talk more when I return from my trip.'

'Where you going?' Jude wanted to know.

'I'm going to spend some time alone out on the Northumbrian moors.'

'Communing with nature sort of thing?'

Jesus smiled. 'I wouldn't say that.'

'Tent, sleeping bag.' Jude ticked them off the list, looked at Jesus, seated on an old camping chair, eyes closed in an attitude of prayer, either that, or sleeping. 'Camping stove, spare gas, matched, rucksack, sleeping mat, clothes, I'll let you sort your clothes Jesus. I'm not your mum.'

He couldn't be sure, but a faint smile seemed to flit across Jesus' face.

'Water, food,' He looked at the mound of camping gear he'd accumulated, convinced he had a stack of meals ready to eat that he'd acquired from a contact in the Northumbrian civil defence. Not here now. He sighed, 'Jesus, you need food.'

'No food.' Jesus replied his eyes still closed.

'That's what I'm saying, you need food, but we can pop down the shops, get you sorted.'

'I'm not taking any food.'

'You can't go camping on those moors without food, you won't last a week.'

'No food.' Jesus was insistent. 'My father will

supply all I need.'

Jude shook his head in disbelief, didn't like to say that Joseph had been dead over ten years. Fell off that roof, big house in Redcar. Not his problem, Jesus seemed to know what he was doing. Couldn't help wondering: what had happened to him today?

'How you getting out there?' Jude asked. He removed the camping stove, spare gas, and matches from the pile.

Jesus opened his eyes, gave the Dude a brilliant smile. 'I thought you might give me a lift.'

✝

LEEDS, NORTHUMBRIA.

Bocus weaved his way back from the bar.

Beaumont watched him, wondered, not for the first time, why he continued these meetings. It wasn't like they had a great deal in common, apart from their hatred of the Saxons.

Bocus set the drinks down, offered a smoke, Beaumont declined. Bocus lit his own, blew a thin plume. Beaumont took a sip of his beer, savoured the taste, watched in fascination as Bocus took a long pull, and demolished half his pint.

'Seems like an ideal opportunity.' Beaumont ventured. And it was. Bocus given the keys to all the Northumbrian water facilities, remit to improve security. Fox invited in by the chickens.

''Kin' right mate, show these bastards a thing or two.' Bocus declared, voice a notch too loud.

Beaumont gave the bar a quick scan. 'Keep your

voice down.' He advised.

'Couldn't believe it when he called me in, told me what he wanted.' Bocus continued, 'thought it was a bollocking at first, but no,' he shook his head in amazement. 'Just the job, eh? Get all the info. Pass it onto comrades who can make use of it.'

'Shh.' Beaumont urged.

'What?'

'You never know who might be listening.'

'So what?' Bocus shrugged. 'Bunch o' pillocks these Saxons, coming over here, taking our jobs, screwing our women.' He belched. 'It's about time we fought back.' He lapsed into a moody silence.

Beaumont thought back over the Union, how it had evolved. Way back in time, the Germanic tribes had, after decades of warfare, finally subsumed the Roman Empire. A power vacuum ensued, filled only when the first Reich was established. That empire, a loose collection of small independent territories, had lasted the best part of a thousand years before falling apart in the early years of the 19th Century. The second Reich followed in 1871, lasting until the early 20th century, after which, the first Fuehrer seized power and established the third Reich. He quickly expanded his territorial empire to the north, south, and west before turning his attention to the Slavic nations to the east. A disastrous war lasting six years followed, during which, both combatant empires fought themselves into the dust. With the death of the first Fuehrer in 1945 an uneasy peace ensued, both sides turning inwards to recover and rebuild.

And over all those centuries, Beaumont marvelled, the peoples of this small island at the western edge of

Europe had kept their own council, co-existing peaceably with each other, and ignored the strife on the continental mainland.

Out of the ashes of the third Reich a new approach to nationhood was formed. All the countries of Europe met in a great council and decided to join together as a trading community where all borders would be open and there would be completely free movement of people. The four ancient kingdoms of Northumbria, Wessex, East Anglia, and Mercia, along with Scotland, Wales, and Cornwall were invited to join. All declined. That state of affairs couldn't last, didn't last. Scotland, Wales, and Cornwall stood firm, but the four kingdoms were eventually assimilated into the Community in the early 1970's.

Big mistake.

The inevitable had happened. Over decades of incessant erosion the trading community had morphed into the Union. In the early days nations were bullied into staying by the threat of financial ruin, latterly the threats had been more militaristic. To all intents and purposes the Union was a fourth Reich, ruled by the Fuehrer, from Berlin. The more astute citizens had realised what was happening but their warnings had been ignored. And now, like Bocus said, there seemed to be more Saxons over here than there were over there.

'It's them and us.' Bocus stirred himself. 'Never been invaded, this country, mate. That Norman bloke gave it a go. William the Bastard, wasn't it?'

Beaumont nodded.

'Aye. Thought you'd know.' Bocus suppressed a burp. 'History teacher knows things.' He stubbed his cigarette out in the overflowing ashtray. 'Good King Harold met him on the beach, threw him back in the sea.' Bocus swigged his beer, set the glass down, 'We shall fight them on the beaches.' He nodded in approval, 'sounds good that, eh?'

It was true, Beaumont thought, apart from the Romans, they'd never been conquered by military might but King Harold hadn't lasted long after his triumph on the sands at Pevensey, and the fledgling nation had soon returned to the old fiefdoms of Northumbria, Mercia, East Anglia, and Wessex. Who knows what might have happened if the concept of England had taken hold? Might even have built our own empire. He smiled at the thought.

'And now what have we got?' Bocus chuntered on. 'These tossers in Berlin telling us what to do, what to think. It's no longer a free country.'

Beaumont looked round warily. Nobody was listening or taking notice, but you never knew. All it took was somebody with a grudge, anonymous call to State Security, next thing, dark room, lamp in your face, answering impossible questions with electrodes attached to your genitals.

There was a sudden commotion by the door, the room fell silent as a routine six-man patrol came into the bar, took up position by the doors. Somebody close to Beaumont muttered, 'Sodding Polizei.'

The patrol leader came round checking ID cards. When the man reached Beaumont and Bocus, they were ready. Their cards were scanned into a hand held terminal. The machine beeped once for each card. The sergeant thanked them, moved on. Beaumont watched the patrol leader continue round the bar, a succession of single beeps accompanying him. It wouldn't be long before some bright spark thought it a good idea to implant the citizens with a microchip same as they did with animals.

A quick, smooth operation, the patrol was gone from the crowded bar inside ten minutes. Beaumont and Bocus exchanged glances, didn't speak. Beaumont watched as Bocus extended the middle finger of his left hand, pointed it towards the door. He thought back to a time in his lifetime when there might have been a possibility of breaking the ties with the Union, couldn't think of one.

It was too late.

It had been too late for a long time.

THREE

Swanger eased her shoes off, rubbed the soles of her feet, thought about the meeting she'd just had with her boss. Heathersedge had been edgy, no doubt about it. Swanger wondered how far up the line the edginess went. To the top, beyond? There was a very short command structure in State Security. The field agents, of whom Swanger was one of many, reported to Heathersedge, who then reported to the Governor, who in his turn reported to Berlin. Four steps to the Fuehrer. Swanger smiled. According to the old song, there were only three to heaven.

Still, at Swanger's level, it didn't matter who above was pulling the strings. Didn't matter to whose tune she danced. All Swanger knew, all she needed to know, was that somebody somewhere was anxious about the religious nutter out at Whitby, dipping people in the sea, and raving about a Messiah. This talk of kings coming from heaven to establish earthly kingdoms was unsettling.

Heathersedge wanted a close eye kept on the situation. Swanger snorted. What the hell did the weasel-eyed pillock think she did all day? She'd been keeping a very close eye on Baptiste and his cronies for months, in anticipation of this request. Even had an ex-Polizei officer embedded in Baptiste's circle, giving regular reports. His opinion. No need to panic, Baptiste was no threat to the regime.

Swanger could have told Heathersedge that earlier, but didn't see the point of letting him know she was ahead of the game. Still, it would be as well to check again, see if anything had changed. She smiled at the thought of a day at the coast, closed her eyes, and daydreamed of sea air, ice creams, a walk along the beach, fish and chips.

†

THE MOORS, NORTHUMBRIA.

Hungry. Starving. Nauseous.

By his reckoning, this was the fortieth day he'd been out here camping on the Northumbrian Moors. A vast untamed area that stretched practically unbroken from the east coast to the west.

Forty days where his entire sustenance was water.

He'd never been so hungry in all his life.

Jesus had been thinking what his first meal would be back in Whitby. Fish and chips definitely, lashings of salt and vinegar, pot of tea, bread and butter.

A proper Northumbrian meal.

Jesus bowed his head, spoke aloud, 'Father, how much longer?'

Silence.

Thinking about food had sent his senses haywire again. Yesterday it had been a sizzling steak, now it was freshly baked bread and, was that a hint of roasted coffee beans.

Stop it.

It was tantalising.

In fact, it was so real it had to be real.

He opened his eyes. Saw he had a visitor.

An old man, dressed in rags, long straggly hair, wild eyes, stood before him, chewing on a piece of bread.

At last.

'Satan.' Jesus acknowledged.

The man changed into a younger incredibly handsome version, film star looks, and a twinkle in his eye. 'You recognised me.' He complained.

'You haven't changed a bit.' Jesus replied.

Satan produced a packet of cigarettes, flipped the lid, and offered one to Jesus, who shook his head. Satan shrugged, put an unlit cigarette in his mouth, drew breath, the end of the cigarette glowed red. He inhaled, blew smoke at Jesus who raised an eyebrow. 'What are you doing here Jesus?'

'I wasn't sure, but I am now.' Jesus said.

Satan adopted a puzzled look. 'I'm not getting it. You've put your majesty to one side, stepped out of heaven, come down here,' he gestured with his arms, 'for what? I mean, what do you hope to achieve?'

Jesus shrugged.

Satan blew smoke rings into the clear morning air. 'The earth is my realm, my playground. You've no business here.'

Jesus was silent.

The cigarette in Satan's hand morphed into a thick wedge of bread spread with golden butter. 'Like a piece?' he offered.

Jesus declined.

'Why do you do it Jesus? Why starve yourself like

this? Who benefits? You still insist you're the son of God?' Satan shrugged. 'You're not acting like you are.' He frowned in disappointment. 'Anything you desire could be yours for the asking.'

Jesus watched as Satan ate the bread, licked the butter from his fingers.

'That was good.' He teased. 'Come on Jesus, if you were the son of God you could have food at any time, you should be able to produce bread like that.' He snapped his fingers and more bread appeared in his hand.

'Man does not live by bread alone, 'Jesus replied, 'but by every word that comes from the mouth of God.'

Satan smiled, went back to smoking. 'Ah, the old quoting the ancient scriptures trick. Back in the day when God's people were stumbling around in the wilderness, led by that cretin Moses.'

'My Father will provide what I need.'

'But will he? And is your precious Father going to provide food?'

'It is written.' Jesus replied.

Satan raised his eyebrows.

'Do you remember the garden?' Jesus asked.

'Garden?' Satan looked puzzled.

'Of Eden.' Jesus said, 'The man and the woman?'

Satan clicked his tongue. 'With you. That was so easy. They wanted to believe they could become like God.' He laughed. 'Fools.'

'Yes, that was a mistake,' Jesus replied. 'And one that humanity has paid for ever since. But no more, I've come to pay the full price for that mistake, once and for all.'

Satan smiled. 'We'll see.'

Jesus closed his eyes for a moment. When he opened them again, Satan had vanished.

†

NORPRO, WHITBY, NORTHUMBRIA.

Maggie gave into the loudest voice, as she knew she would. It was futile to resist the voice that told her to have the Morph, that she needed it, couldn't live without it. She placed the small lump of black tarry substance on the flat piece of foil, heated the underside with her lighter. As the wispy vapour came off, she inhaled it through a straw.

Her friend Poppy came into the restroom, kicked off her shoes, poured a red wine, lit a cigarette. 'You'll get a better rush injecting.'

Maggie nodded. 'I hate needles. This is okay for me.'

Poppy shrugged, blew a perfect smoke ring. 'Drink?'

'Yeah, thanks.' Maggie packed away her gear, took the glass from Poppy, sipped, and waited until the voices were subdued, peace for a while. She sighed. 'And relax.'

'Busy night?' Poppy asked, blew smoke, and wafted it away.

'Not too bad, you?'

'Four straights and a light spanking,' Poppy grimaced, 'oh, and another, "my partner doesn't understand me".'

Maggie laughed, holding her glass against Poppy's,

'Cheers.'

'Cheers.' Poppy echoed, drank half her wine in one go. 'I should be grateful all he wanted to do was talk.'

'You or him?' Maggie asked.

'What?'

'The spanking. You or him?'

Poppy laughed, drained her glass, and offered it. 'Him, thank the Lord.'

Maggie gave her friend a sideways glance. 'Do you believe then?'

'Nah.' Poppy gave a brief shake of her head. 'Just a saying, innit? Why, do you?'

'Dunno.' Maggie refilled the glass, handed it back. 'I'd like to.'

'Don't believe in anything, me.' Poppy declared.

Maggie sipped her wine, enjoyed the peace of the Morph. 'Have you seen that feller down on the beach? Dipping people in the sea, preparing them for a Messiah.'

Maggie thought back to the night she'd heard the voice on the beach singing about a coming Messiah. 'What is a Messiah?' She asked.

Poppy shrugged. 'Dunno, some kind of all-powerful king, I think. The Jews believe he's gonna turn up and save them from the Saxons, get them back to their ancient homeland.'

'Don't you ever dream of someone coming along, take you away from all this?' Maggie smirked, 'The daily grind.'

Poppy laughed, choked on her wine. 'Ya bin watching too many films pet.'

Maggie sighed. 'I expect so.'

'It's just us against the world love.' Poppy said.

Maggie frowned, was that true? 'I'm thinking of going down to the beach. See what they're all about.' The voices stirred, but were silent, listening for treachery. 'I have this feeling Poppy.'

'Lucky you, I wish I did.' Poppy laughed. It was a harsh sound.

Maggie smiled, acknowledged the quip, and continued, 'It's time for change Poppy. There's something in the air, can you feel it?'

A soft buzzing sound started, both girls looked at their phones. Poppy shook her head, pressed the mute button on her phone, 'No love, I can't.' She sniffed, laughed. 'Your dreams and stale smoke, that's all I can smell,' She slipped her shoes on. 'Tomorrow will be the same as today,' She placed her half-smoked cigarette in the ashtray, finished her drink. 'Just like today was the same as yesterday.' She paused at the door, 'Don't touch that ciggie, I'll be back in three minutes.'

Maggie watched her go, miffed it was Poppy that had been summoned She ignored the voice in her head telling her not to bother, there was no point, she was past it, that nobody would want her ever again.

†

THE MOORS, NORTHUMBRIA.

York.

The roof of the Temple at night. A dream? It didn't feel like a dream, he could feel the wind on his face. A vision then.

Jesus looked over the rooftops at the lights of the

capital, wondered what was coming next. He peered over the edge of the roof at the ground. He felt a chill, became aware of a presence.

'It's a long way down, isn't it?' A soft, soulful voice, whispered.

Jesus turned, and looked at the beautiful woman stood at his shoulder. She was wearing a gold dress, had long black hair. She was a vision of feminine beauty.

He nodded in reply.

The woman moved even closer, Jesus was conscious of her perfume, the red of her lips, her jet black eyes.

'Any person falling from here is bound to die.' She said.

Jesus didn't respond.

'Just you and me, Jesus.' The woman said. 'It would be so easy to push you off.'

'If you had the power and the authority,' Jesus replied, 'which you don't.'

The woman changed into the familiar form of the handsome young man.

Satan, again.

'Don't push your luck, Jesus.' Satan said. 'This is my realm. I'm the prince of the earth.' He raised his hands as though to push Jesus in the chest but stopped, laughed. 'Just kidding.'

Jesus stood impassively. 'What is it you want?'

'You're puzzling me, Jesus. You say you're the son of God, but you're not willing to prove it. I wonder why that is?'

'I don't need to prove anything.' Jesus replied.

'Of course not.' Satan agreed, 'but,' he shrugged,

'you might find people unwilling to believe unless you give them some proof. Don't you think?'

'No.' Jesus responded.

'I don't believe you are who you say you are. You're an imposter. You couldn't produce bread when you were starving. I bet you're still hungry now.'

Jesus was silent.

'Let's settle it right now. Why don't you jump from this great height, see what happens? If you were the son of God, you could jump from here, Jesus, and be saved. It is written, "For He will command His angels concerning you, to guard you in all your ways. They will lift you up so that you will not strike your foot against a stone".'

'Oh, Satan,' Jesus replied. 'It is also written, you shall not test the Lord your God.'

'Aren't you curious though,' Satan said, half smile, 'to see if he means it? Your constant thought on the way down. Will he, won't he? A bit like bungee jumping. Is the rope too long?'

'Satan, I know what you're about.'

'You do?' Satan tried, failed to look innocent.

'I don't have to jump to prove my trust in the Father. I trust His word. If I were to jump, I'd be putting myself in danger in order to force Him to save me. I would be trying to manipulate Him. You, with your experience of the Lord, know that God is sovereign. If I jump, I will be telling my Father that I doubt Him. We both know this is not the case.'

Satan pulled a face. 'You're no fun, Jesus.'

'The kingdom I bring has no place for your kind of fun.'

'We'll see.' Satan said, before fading from Jesus'

sight.

†

NorPro, Whitby, Northumbria.

Levi checked the roster in the manager's office, running his finger down the list of names. The youngest girl on duty today was Sally, a sixteen-year-old blonde, and the eldest, a vivacious, experienced forty-three year old redhead, Samantha.

Levi had been with Sam before, she was good, but today, he fancied a younger model, someone new, different. He finished his coffee, wandered through to the bar-come-waiting area where the girls were seated at tables waiting for clients. He stood in the doorway letting his eyes adjust. One of the things he loved about his job was seeing so many women lounging around in varying states of undress and NorPro catered for all tastes. Every town throughout the kingdom had a branch, and Levi, employed as a hygiene inspector, was always busy. He sat at an empty table, picked up the printed card. Joanne, twenty-seven. The passport-sized photo, showing an unsmiling woman with lank hair, didn't do her any favours, but Levi knew from experience not to rely on the selection cards.

A waitress, eighteen, nineteen, maybe, bright eager smile, offered him a drink. Levi declined, asked for Maggie.

The girl scanned the room. 'With a client, sir. Was it just Maggie, or would you like to choose another girl?'

'It was, but now I've met you...' He didn't disguise

58

his interest, his eyes roamed over her body.

The girl shook her head, smiled uncertainly. It was well known the waitresses were off limits, serving drinks their only function.

'You new?' Levi asked in a friendly tone.

The girl nodded, nervous all of a sudden. He liked that. Shy little virgin no doubt.

'What's your name?' Levi asked.

'Trudy.'

'Working girl?'

'No sir, just waitressing.'

'Job important to you?'

'Yes, sir, very important.'

Levi nodded. 'Wouldn't like to lose it then, would you?'

Trudy had stopped smiling.

'Why don't you find us an empty room, Trudy?' Levi suggested. 'I fancy spending some time alone with you'

Trudy's hand moved to the panic alarm she wore on a chain round her neck.

'You can do that if you like, love, your call,' Levi shrugged. 'This place gets shut down within the hour.' The turmoil showed on her face. Would she call his bluff? He wasn't that worried. A simple case of misunderstanding. He could sense her distaste. It increased his excitement.

She toyed with the alarm for a minute before saying. 'I don't suppose I have much choice, do I?'

Levi grinned, 'You're right love. You don't.' He stood, adjusted his trousers, and then patted her plump little arse before following her from the bar in urgent anticipation.

THE MOORS, NORTHUMBRIA.

'You sir. Yes, you sir, take a card, any card.' The well-known TV magician fanned the cards in his hand, offered them.

Jesus looked at the cards. Not normal playing cards, these bore the names of countries and states. The Union, The Oceanic Federation, The Combined States of America, the Slavic States, the African Federation, among others.

Jesus shook his head. This was all so pathetic. He was weak, in a pitiful state, no food for forty days. His blood sugar was way down, off the scale. Wasn't sure how much more of this he could take.

Why Father?

The magician fell silent, watched the inner turmoil, relished the moment of surrender. 'In fact, don't take one, take them all,' he continued, 'you sir, yes, you sir, could be the ruler of all these great states, The Union, empires, federations, countries large and small. The greatest ruler the world has ever known.' He looked at Jesus, 'So, what do you say?'

'And the catch is?' Jesus asked.

'No catch, sir, well...' The magician paused, all injured innocence. 'Maybe there is a small teeny weeny condition.'

Jesus waited.

The magician shrugged. 'You have to bow down, worship me, confess me as your Lord and Master, then all this and more will be yours. A one-time offer, unbeatable value. Of interest, sir? The magician asked, looked expectant.

Jesus clapped his hands together. 'Go away Satan,'

he said, 'you've given it your best shot, but I can't be bought like a naive mark at a country fair. It is written, "worship the Lord your God, and just serve Him".'

The magician cursed, changed once more into the handsome star of the silver screen. 'You do know Jesus, don't you, that you'll come to a horrible end? These people down here, these corruptible created beings. They won't understand what you're trying to do. They won't want your help. You, the word made flesh, they'll destroy you.'

'And what good will it be,' Jesus scorned with the little strength he could muster, 'for someone to gain the whole world at the cost of losing their soul?'

Satan shrugged. 'Your loss Jesus, but yours won't be an easy task. I'll be watching and waiting at every turn, and when you do crash and burn, I'll be there having the final laugh, when they lower you into the earth.'

'Satan,' Jesus said with the last of his energy. 'I command you to go, bother me no more.'

Satan vanished. Jesus slumped to his knees, exhausted by the ordeal. He gave thanks to the Father for the strength he'd received to withstand the three temptations. Drained, he rested his forehead on the ground, was aware of spiritual beings moving around, ministering to his needs. They provided food. He ate, regained strength.

He slept for what seemed a long time, awoke refreshed, revived.

It was time to head back to Whitby.

It was time to be about his Father's business.

It was time for his mission to commence.

✝

WHITBY, NORTHUMBRIA.

Nathan finished his glass of ice-cold lager, signalled the waiter for a refill. Say what you like about the Saxons, they brewed a nice drop of lager.

Across the room, he could see his handler, Sal, making her way back from the ladies. She was a small rotund woman, barrel of a figure, with a haircut resembling a coalscuttle. There was nothing feminine about her, she didn't often smile, but Nathan noted, as she skipped past a waiter bearing a tray of steaming food, she had dancer's feet.

Sal picked up her empty glass and looked at Nathan's. 'Another?'

'Sorted.'

'Good.'

Nathan looked around the restaurant, conscious of Sal's gaze. Not my real name she'd said at their first meeting, a casual encounter in a local pub. He'd always assumed it was his old skipper on the job who'd pointed him out. Had never asked.

Nathan didn't think Sal was native Northumbrian. There was a slight accent there. He suspected Saxon, in which case she must be State Security. The service being predominately staffed by them. Again, he hadn't asked. Truth was he didn't care, less he knew the better. Just another job, another way of putting food on the table, means to an end.

She opened her bag. 'Do you need money?'

Nathan saw the pistol, thought it looked incongruous alongside the detritus of a woman's bag. He wondered if she'd intended him to see it. 'I always need money.' Nathan smiled, watched as she pulled

Euros from her purse, pushed them across the table. He picked up the notes, toyed with them. The waiter came, left their drinks, eyed the money, and departed.

'I'm thinking of pulling the plug.' Sal said.

'Oh?' Nathan raised an eyebrow. He'd been wondering why she'd turned up out of the blue. There was a set procedure for meets. Just arriving wasn't one of them.

Sal shrugged. 'Don't want you getting too cosy out here. Anyway, it's been quiet for the last few weeks. This Messiah Baptiste was banging on about hasn't come to light. Same as usual, fart in a gale.' She shook her head in frustration. 'It's a lot easier when they take up arms, plant a few bombs.' She took a sip of her soft drink. 'Least then you know what you're dealing with, but these religious nuts with their threats of spiritual kingdoms, it's just a load o' bollocks.'

She set her glass down, looked at Nathan. 'What do you reckon, fancy coming in from the dark side?'

Was this a trap, Nathan wondered. If Tom was also undercover for the authorities and had told Sal about this Jesus character and Nathan didn't, she would wonder what was going on. Be careful lad, he told himself. For all her bluster Sal was a shrewd operator.

'I think I should stick it out a bit longer.'

'Why?' The challenge was immediate.

'Just a feeling.' Nathan replied, casual.

Sal shrugged. 'Your call, you're the man on the inside.' She grinned, 'you reckon this Messiah is still gonna turn up?'

Nathan shrugged. 'Hard to say, but if he does it'd be a shame to miss him for the sake of a couple o' weeks.'

'Okay.' Sal agreed, 'let's give it another two weeks. First sign though, I need to know.'

Nathan nodded in agreement. He thought again about the new guy, Jesus, who'd appeared from nowhere. What had Baptiste called him, the Lamb of God, who takes away the sins of the world. That had been a funny old business. Baptiste hadn't gone through the, believe, repent, and confess routine when he'd dipped Jesus. Almost as if he knew this Jesus had no sins to confess, but that was impossible, everybody had some kind of shameful secret, impossible not to have.

Nathan knew one thing. Baptiste was finished, drained. After his encounter with Jesus the guy had been left a crumpled heap, mumbling incoherently. Okay, he was back, immersing in the old routine, but he wouldn't last.

And what had Jesus done?

Done a runner.

Strides on the stage, gets dipped, goes on his merry way.

Like the feller in the film, I'll be back.

And it was that promise of a further meeting that was keeping him close to Baptiste. This Jesus, Messiah or not, he had something, and Nathan wanted more of it.

FOUR

WHITBY, NORTHUMBRIA.

Baptiste had soon regained his equilibrium after his encounter with Jesus. He'd been back the following day immersing the thousands who flocked to him from all over the kingdom. He was puzzled though. Couldn't understand why having identified Jesus as the Messiah, he should then disappear. Still, he reasoned, it would all be revealed in the Lord's good time.

That had been six weeks before and Baptiste was still waiting, still immersing, still asking the people who came, to confess and repent. This afternoon he was being assisted by Andrew and John, followers who'd decided their lives were worthless and without purpose. It was mid-afternoon, the sun blazing, light breeze off the sea, a salt tang in the air. Sounds of early season holidaymakers drifted down from the road, bingo callers competed for attention with electronic voices from the arcades.

Baptiste looked past the long line of folks queuing to be immersed, his gaze drawn to the road, where a convoy of cars had just arrived. An official looking delegation came down the steps to the beach and trudged across the sand. They pushed past the queue of people and came to a halt at the head of the line. All men, they wore black three quarter length suit jackets with open neck white shirts, along with a black hat. They all sported a thick bush of facial hair. It was the modern style for the orthodox Jewish male and looked totally incongruous on the beach. Their appearance prompted much laughter and good-natured catcalling. Baptiste eyed them and continued immersing.

Andrew looked at John, raising his eyebrows.

'From the Temple in York.' John said.

'I'd never have guessed.' Andrew said with a smile.

Baptiste received two more people, heard them confess and repent, before turning to face the waiting group.

'My name is Brotherton.' The leader of the delegation spoke. He was a tall, thin man, with hollowed cheeks and a disapproving look permanently etched on his face. When Baptiste didn't respond, he followed it up with, 'sent by Caiaphas the High priest.'

Baptiste shrugged, and looked at one of the other smart suits, phone held to his face, filming the encounter. 'And?'

'Who are you?' Brotherton demanded.

'Baptiste.'

'Yes, yes,' the official said, frowning. 'I know that, but who are you?'

Baptiste was silent. He'd answered that question.

'Are you Eliyahu?'

'No.'

'Are you the prophet?'

'No, I'm not.'

'Are you the Messiah?'

Baptiste chuckled. 'No.'

'I must give an answer to Caiaphas. What do you say about yourself?'

Baptiste looked at Brotherton, his delegation, the phones recording his every word, his every facial expression. He took a deep breath and it seemed as though boldness came upon him. 'I am the voice of one crying in the wilderness,' he declared, 'making straight the way of the Lord. I am baptizing to prepare people for the Messiah who is coming after me, even though,' he shrugged, 'He is before me.'

'You talk in riddles. On whose authority are you baptizing people?' Brotherton demanded.

Baptiste didn't answer, but pointed to a solitary figure standing to one side. 'Look, look,' he roared, startling everyone within ear shot. 'Behold! The Lamb of God.'

Everybody turned to look at the man indicated by Baptiste. He met their gaze, untroubled by the attention.

'He is the one I am speaking of.' Baptiste continued. 'He was baptized, and then disappeared for a while. He has now returned, the one who takes away the sin of the world. I knew him, but did not know him.'

The buzz of the crowd had died down. Clouds covered the sun. Andrew shivered.

'You snake.' Baptiste hissed. 'You hypocrites. You ask me about authority.'

Startled Brotherton took a step back as Baptiste continued. 'I saw the Holy Spirit fall on this man, I heard the Lord proclaim this man.'

The official group, fearful now, continued to back away.

'Who told you to come here? Are you fleeing the Lord's rage? Come,' Baptiste indicated the sea,

'Confess, repent, be saved.'

The group of men gathered together, conferred, checked video footage, trooped back to the waiting cars.

'This is the Son of God.' Baptiste called after them.

The departing delegation gave no sign of having heard.

Baptiste called again. 'The Messiah.'

Jesus smiled at Baptiste, turned, and walked away.

Baptiste watched as Andrew and John looked at each other, then, without speaking, followed Jesus along the beach.

✝

Peter waited for a quiet moment at work before pulling Andrew to one side, and suggested a stroll along the harbour side. They walked in companionable silence for a while before Peter said, 'What's all this I hear about you being dipped in the sea by that oddball, Baptiste?'

Andrew chuckled, knew there was some reason why his brother wanted his company. 'It's no big deal.'

'It's true, then?'

'Yeah, so?'

Peter held up his hands. 'No matter to me Andy lad, except...'

'What?'

'Well, you don't seem the type to be off following religious crackpots.'

'He's not a crackpot.' Andrew stopped, nudged an old buoy with his foot. 'In fact, we think he's identified Messiah.'

All Jews, whether they were strict adherents of the faith, or just paid lip service, knew about Messiah. He would be a great charismatic leader, a mighty warrior and a wise judge. He would transform the lives of the people, and lead them back to their ancient lands.

'Oh aye, who's that?' Peter asked.

They walked on.

'Jesus.' Andrew said.

Peter frowned. 'I was at a school with a lad called Jesus.'

'It's the same one.' Andrew hesitated. 'In fact, I've decided to get involved with his movement.'

'Have you? Didn't strike me as Messiah material when I knew him.' He shrugged. 'Nice enough lad, never any trouble, kept his head down, got on with his work.' Peter paused, remembering. 'Good opening bat, decent off spinner.' He laughed. 'Crap at rugger.' He shook his head in wonderment. 'Thought he'd gone into the building trade, but Messiah, eh? Wouldn't mind catching up with him sometime, have a jar or two.'

'You'd like that?'

'Sure, why not? Messiah, eh?' Peter laughed. 'Heard it all now.'

†

EAST NORTHUMBRIA.

Bocus, three months into his project was still surprised at how much he enjoyed getting out of the office. He loved spending time in the beautiful Northumbrian countryside visiting the company facilities. He was glad to shake off the bustle and noise of the city. The majority of the sites were miles from anywhere, set in the most remote parts of the kingdom, only accessible by dirt tracks off country lanes.

But now, he was lost somewhere in the wilds of east Northumbria. His first mistake had been pushing himself to get wrapped up in this sector, before spending a few days in the office, by visiting that last installation, a pumping station on the River Ouse. Should have left it till his next visit. As it was he'd been confronted by a buzzing alarm, flashing lights on the display panel. Should have turned round, walked away.

Second mistake, calling it in, result, spending two frustrating hours talking to the tech guys back at base. Push this button, push that button, power down, reset, hold the line, we'll get back to you. End of process, we don't think it's anything serious, but thanks for letting us know. Have a nice evening.

Some chance.

Third mistake was not filling up in Goole.

No signal on the mobile. A soft Gaelic voice on the sat-nav telling him, turn around when possible.

Bocus gripped the wheel, used all the swear words he knew, before assessing the situation. He could either stay put or walk to the nearest house or farm. Trouble was he couldn't recall passing any sign of habitation in the last four, five kilometres. There might be a house full of nubile women waiting round the next bend, or the next, or there might not. Plus, it would be dark soon, so the sensible course was to stay where he was, suss it out in the morning.

He had sandwiches and coffee in his flask, so wouldn't starve. He'd had the foresight to pack a sleeping bag in the boot, so wouldn't freeze, not that there was much chance of that in the warm early summer night.

Once out of fuel, Bocus had coasted downhill for 500 metres, and managed to swing the car onto the grass verge under some trees. He got out. Walked up and down the lane for a short way in both directions, open fields to the right, a copse to the left. He smoked a cigarette, walked into the woods for a little distance. The trail he followed through the trees soon petered out in a small clearing. A few beer cans, tab ends, and used condoms were the signs of recent activity. The light was fading fast as he made his way back. Bocus, trying and failing not to think about horror films set in remote woods, kept glancing over his shoulder for the last 50 metres, convinced he was being watched.

Relieved to reach the car in one piece, he used the last remaining light to get his sleeping bag from the boot along with his heavy-duty torch. Once in the car he locked the doors, placed the torch on the passenger seat.

Pillock.

He ate his sandwiches, drank coffee, thought about his project. Anybody who wanted to gain access to any of the Northumbrian Water facilities would manage to do so without any problem, surrounded as they were by flimsy chain link fences. It would cost millions to get the security to a standard where it would take longer than ten minutes to gain access. Given that the more remote sites were a good two hours from civilisation, Bocus couldn't see how it could be justified. Even if they spent the money on fences, cameras and alarms, a determined group could be in and out long before help arrived. Better to have half a dozen dogs roaming free.

He rubbed his eyes. Not his problem. Enjoy the outings, write the report, and take the pay. He decided against another smoke, the glow would be seen from outside, not that he expected there was anybody out there watching, but still. It was dark outside now. Bocus flicked the interior light to the off position. Didn't want it coming on if he opened the door. He wrapped the sleeping bag round his shoulder, snuggled down. It wasn't that he was scared of the dark, more what might be out there in the dark. He double-checked the windows were closed and the doors locked. He eased the seat backwards and flicked the radio on for some company.

'...concerns are growing over the safety of a four month old baby boy taken from his pushchair outside local shops in Scunthorpe. The child was left outside while his mother was buying cigarettes...'

Irritated, Bocus turned off the radio. Silly cow. Everybody knew you didn't leave children unattended. The chances of them being snatched, of them disappearing, never to be seen again, was just too high. Society placed a high value on the safety of children. The mother of the missing baby would be ostracised by her neighbours for evermore. In the laissez-faire attitude engendered by the Union, the threat of harm to children, real or imagined, was just about the only thing guaranteed to bring a mob out on the streets baying for blood. Which was ironic, he thought wryly, given the official figures for abortions.

Eyes heavy, Bocus fought sleep for a few minutes, but soon gave in, drifted off.

Cawood, Northumbria.

Peter eyed the last drop of beer in his glass. He tilted his glass, drained the dregs, drop o' good stuff that. Another? That was the big question.

The band, playing some kind of heavy reggae rubbish, were coming to the end of their set, it'd be that thumping dance music, flashing lights next. Headache coming on though, didn't want a hangover. He'd set a limit, long since past, another one wouldn't hurt. Just one more though. He looked around morosely, didn't know anybody. Andrew was off somewhere with Jesus and his other mates, having a good time no doubt. Knew he shouldn't have come. Seen the dirty look Jesus' mother, Mary, had thrown at him, when he turned up with four mates, hangers on, none of them invited to the ceremony. Look on her face, a right picture. How could you do this to me Jesus?

He thought back to their arrival a few hours ago, been alright then, been sober then. They'd been met at the front of the O'Deamus mansion by pipers playing the traditional Northumbrian pipes. Dancers in colourful costumes showed the guests to their seats in the chandeliered ballroom. Nobody had made a fuss. The father of the bride had greeted them like old friends. They'd all squeezed in, plenty o' room.

The O'Deamus clan had turned out in full for the wedding and the happy father moved among his guests greeting them with a quiet word, a handshake, a back slap. With the guests settled the processional music commenced. Nice touch that, Peter thought. Fields of Gold by that famous Northumbrian singer. The bride arrived, accompanied by her proud father. Good-looking girl, nice dress. Look better on my bedroom floor mind.

There was a round of applause, Peter dragged himself back to the present, joined in half-heartedly. The band took a bow, trooped off. The DJ slipped into place, started the dance music he hated.

Weddings didn't agree with him, reminded him too much of his own failed marriage. Truth was, he still missed Jayne, wondered where she was. Be easy to track her down, drag her back, scruff o' the neck. But why go to the trouble, bitch wanted out, well she's out.

Another beer?

It was a free bar. What's not to like?

Peter shook his head, tried to get his thoughts straight. Supposed to be having a catch up with Jesus, this Messiah business.

He sighed.

Another pint it was.

He made his way unsteadily to the bar. On the way he promised a dance to the bride's vivacious mother, Maeve, and then stood swaying in line waiting to be served.

†

Mary sipped her wine, watched the youngsters whirling on the dance floor, the children running around causing mayhem, and thought back over the day. The traditional wedding ceremony had been short, simple but moving. The bride, Sinead, beautiful, as all women are, on the day they marry their husband. She'd chosen an elegant full length ivory dress sculpted round the bust, luxuriant red hair pinned above bare shoulders. The effect crowned with a half veil draped coquettishly over one eye. Her face pale, a hint of makeup, lips red, eyes green. She carried a simple bouquet of yellow lilies.

Mary remembered her own wedding. Most of her family had shunned that event. It had taken years for them to come round. Not many people willing to believe that God himself had been responsible for her child. In vain she had pointed to ancient scriptures, where it was foretold that the Messiah would be born of a virgin.

She remembered the scorn, dulled now by the passage of time, but still hurtful. Yes, yes, they'd said, but you Mary, why you? Why don't you confess to having slept with Joe, rather than keep up these fanciful stories of being visited by an angel?

Well, they'd have to change their minds now, whistle a different tune, now that her son Jesus, had been proclaimed Messiah by no less an authority than Baptiste.

She smiled at the thought of herself, Mary, coming from a poor background, mother of Messiah, then her thoughts clouded, such a shame Joe hadn't lived to see it. Would she ever feel happiness again? She was content, sure, but happiness, real happiness, was that now a thing of the past?

Jesus finding a young woman he wanted to marry, grandchildren, that would bring her happiness back, a sparkle to her eye, lift the heavy burden that came upon her each morning. He was thirty now, an age where most men were married with families, but he still didn't seem interested. She'd got sick of mentioning it. Pointing out girls to him, she's nice, or she's suitable. And now, with this Messiah business, would he even have time to find a partner?

Angry voices from the bar drew her attention. Mary looked over and sighed. That drunkard Peter was waving his arms around, complaining about something. What was there to complain about with a free bar?

She caught the eye of a barman as he hurried past. 'What's the problem?'

'They've run out of beer.' The man replied, 'Sure, I'm away to tell the boss. There's a feller in there making an awful fuss.'

He didn't say, didn't have to say, that the man at the bar was one of the uninvited friends that came with Jesus.

Mary watched him hurry away. Now, that's the sort of follower you need Jesus. Well spoken, polite young men like that. She didn't expect he'd listen to her though. He'd always been headstrong, wilful. That time they'd taken him to the Temple at York and he'd slipped away. They'd found him a day later instructing the priests in the ancient scriptures, explaining prophecy. Joe had been so annoyed when Jesus had told him he was about his father's business.

'I'm his father, Mary.' He'd said later, 'and my business is building.'

Mary went to look for her son. It was his friend causing the trouble. He could sort it out. She found Jesus chatting to his friends in a side room. They were talking about the Pharisees. Nick O'Deamus was a member of this select group of religious fanatics. They each took a solemn vow to live their entire lives with reference to the Ten Commandments given by God to Moses on tablets of stone way back in the mists of time. This was all well and good Mary thought, until you realised that the commandments were given in general terms. They weren't specific enough for the Pharisees, so another group called Scribes had evolved. The Scribes studied God's commandments, and devised rules that applied to every single life situation, so Pharisees could follow these rules and thus please God.

Mary sighed. She sometimes wondered if God wanted blind obedience to rules, He hadn't set. Jesus looked up at her arrival, smiled, kissed her cheek, melting her heart as usual. He was such a good-looking young man.

'Mum.' He said. 'You look troubled.

Mary drew him to one side, told him about the beer running out and Peter causing trouble.

'Can you do anything?' She asked. He ought to be able to fix a simple thing like a bar running dry of beer, shouldn't be too much trouble for the Messiah.

Jesus looked at Mary. 'You don't understand, mum.'

She frowned. 'It's not much to ask. I expect it's your friend Peter who's drunk the bar dry in the first place.'

Jesus laughed, replied. 'I expect you're right. Come on then, mother, take me to the bar.'

Mary found the young barman she'd spoken to earlier, told him, 'You might think this an unusual or stupid request, but please do whatever Jesus tells you.'

The man looked at Jesus for instruction.

'The purification jars, are they empty?' Jesus asked.

'Yes, sir.'

'Fill them with water, draw some off, and serve.' Jesus turned to re-join his friends.

'Is that it?' The barman asked, anxious.

'Yes.' Jesus replied.

'Just water from the tap.'

'Yes.'

The barman filled the massive stone jars that were used for the purification ritual used by all strict adherents of Judaism, all the while muttering about fools and nutters. He was amazed when, ten minutes later, he dipped a jug into the first jar, was rewarded with the finest wine he'd ever tasted in his life. Okay, it wasn't beer, but that lot out there would be satisfied with any drink at all.

A few minutes later, a massive cheer told Mary that Jesus had accomplished his first miracle.

†

EAST NORTHUMBRIA.

Bocus, wide-awake, stared through the window, convinced he'd heard a sound. Dreaming? Nah didn't think so. Clock on his phone, two fifteen am.

The moon, high, gave sparse light through the clouds, on, off, on, off, enough to see trees in outline, sinister, metres away, moving towards him, branches waving, running, chasing.

Stop it.

Heart thudding, he waited, watching. Something had disturbed his sleep. He turned the key, the radio came on, early hours request show, soft female voice asking, would you play Misty for me? Bocus jabbed the buttons, muted the sound, lowered the windows a fraction, and listened. Night noises. Soft breeze, rustling leaves, animals hunting, killing, being killed. A white shape floated past the windscreen, knew it was an owl, saw a ghost.

Choice. Run, or wait to be slaughtered.

Calm down.

He'd heard something, some noise. A howl.

Wolves howl.

There are no wolves in Northumbria, apart from the Arena. Maybe one had escaped?

But, a part of his innermost being reminded him - they run wild in the Highlands of Scotland. One could have travelled down this far, could be out there now watching, waiting.

He heard the faint sound of an engine, miles away, next field, no way of knowing. It came nearer, louder, stopped abruptly, silence, a door slammed.

Relief. Wolves don't drive.

But, someone was out there, confident that nobody else was.

Silence. Then laughter carried on the night air, a rising, falling cadence. It slammed into Bocus, demolished the defences he'd spent minutes erecting, left him wanting to curl up, hide under the bed.

Silence again, then through the trees, in the depths of the wood, a flickering light - torchlight. Kids. Just kids messing about, spooking each other, spooking him. Kids getting drunk, getting stoned, getting laid.

Bastards.

Bocus was out of the car racing into the trees before his rational sense kicked in wanting to find the kids, give them an almighty bollocking. Kick seven shades of shit out of them.

Slow down.

Had he locked the car door?

How many kids were there?

Bocus, out of courage, stopped, leant against a tree, listened, dithered. Was about to turn and slink back to the car, when the lights started flashing again. Creeping closer, tree to tree, he tripped over a root, fell, breath exploding with a soft oomph. Picking himself up, he checked for damage, nothing broken. He looked again, the lights were still moving around in the trees.

This is stupid.

Sometime later, in position near the clearing, Bocus watched in fascination as a group of white robed figures wearing head lamps held hands and moved in a circle round a dark object. A mixture of men and women chanting in unison. Not kids. Some kind of worship ceremony.

Bocus knew he should go, leave them to it, not get caught, but thought about the used condoms, and stayed.

After a short while the movement, the chanting, stopped. A male figure broke from the circle, the others reforming around him. He held his arms to the sky, 'Oh, mighty Gaia, mother of all things, we come to pay tribute.'

The circle responded with chants.

Bocus breathed a sigh of relief. Earth worshippers, nothing too sinister. He couldn't remember if they got naked or not, thought they might, stayed, watched.

The priest figure continued, 'Who brings the offering?'

A woman moved to his side. 'I do.'

Even from a distance, Bocus could see she was a good-looking woman, shoulder length blonde hair. Shapely figure beneath the robe. He waited, anticipating the moment she'd drop her robe and the fun would begin.

'You bring the offering of your own free will?'

Get on with it.

'I do.' The woman replied. The circle chanted.

'Bring forth the offering.'

The woman passed a bundle to the priest who took it, held it close to his body. 'Why do you make this offering?'

'To bless mighty Gaia, mother of creation.'

Chanting.

The priest held the bundle aloft. 'Mighty Gaia, we pray that this offering, this token of our love, will be acceptable.' He placed the bundle on the dark object, which in the flickering torchlight looked to Bocus like a wooden butchers block.

More hypnotic chanting. Bocus shivered, wanted to leave, couldn't, watched as the bundle was unwrapped, revealing a small child, a few months old.

The priest picked up a silver object, raised it above his head, over the sacrifice. 'Oh mighty Gaia, mother of creation, accept our offering, release your bounty on the land.'

The chanting grew louder, the robed figures swayed. The priest brought the silver object down in a sudden swift movement. Bocus heard the soft thud as it went clean through the child's body, embedded in the wooden block. The lights went out, a woman screamed. He buried his head into his arm, lay silent, motionless. Didn't move when the rain started falling, didn't move until the sun rose a few hours later, when, soaking wet, shivering, he opened his eyes, looked at the empty clearing, and wondered if he'd dreamed it all.

✝

WHITBY, NORTHUMBRIA.

Salt air, slight breeze, expectation in the air.

One of Peter's favourite activities, now that he no longer went to sea, was to come down to the harbour, wait for one of their fleet of fishing boats to return to port. He liked to do this alone, but this morning Andrew had tagged along. The brothers stood in silence, scanning the horizon through glasses, a throwback to the days when their father offered a token reward for the first sighting.

'There she is.' Andrew said, lowered the glasses, and pointed.

'You're joking man, that's never the Freebooter, look to your left a touch, faint smudge.'

Andrew refocused, grunted, noncommittal, didn't want to concede defeat too soon. Peter had always had the sharpest eye. As boys, the rivalry so intense, sometimes lead to blows, fist on bone, bloody noses, until the old feller stepped in and pulled them apart.

When the faint smudge grew larger, became the Freebooter, no room left for doubt, Andrew nodded in affirmation. Peter chuckled, 'Told ya.'

Andrew, resisting the urge to plant one on his brother's nose, asked, 'What's the catch like, you heard?'

This brought a dour response from Peter who knew what his brother was doing. 'Crap by all accounts.'

Later, with Freebooter tied up alongside, the crew, long faced with disappointment stood around discussing the trip, bemoaning the lack of fish in the sea. Andrew looked past Peter. Saw a familiar figure striding down the jetty, picking his way past fishing nets, lobster pots, buoys, ropes. He nudged his brother who sighed when he saw Jesus approaching.

'Have you set this up?' Peter muttered. Could have done without seeing Jesus quite so soon after the wedding at Cawood. He'd meant to dance with the mother of the bride, not attempt to seduce the woman. Peter had left in disgrace and here was Jesus, no doubt coming to express his disappointment.

'How are you both?' Jesus asked, gave them both a broad smile. He nodded towards the boat. 'Good catch?'

'Rubbish.' Peter replied, lighting a cigarette, 'Absolute sod all. Complete waste of money, what with the wages, the fuel.' He pulled smoke deep into his lungs. 'Never known it so bad.'

'Take the boat out again.' Jesus suggested.

'You're joking.' Peter snorted, 'I've lost enough brass as it is.'

'Just beyond the harbour wall, lower the net, see what happens.'

'Nah.' Peter shook his head.

'Go on.' Andrew urged. 'Let's do it. What we got to lose?'

An hour later, the Freebooter was back alongside again. Peter stared in disbelief at the hold, full to overflowing with cod. 'That's amazing.'

'Now do you get it, bro?' Andrew asked, grinning like a small boy on his birthday. 'Can you see why I'm joining Jesus, becoming one of his followers?'

'And you too Peter,' Jesus said, 'I'd like you to join us.'

Peter shrugged. 'I've got a business to run. Fish to catch, mouths to feed.'

Jesus opened his arms wide, 'Come on Peter, I'll make you a fisher of men, feed their souls, as well as their bellies.'

FIVE

YORK, NORTHUMBRIA.

They arrived in York in the Jude supplied minibus, parked, and walked to the Temple. Jesus stood inside the gates of the outer court of the Temple, gazed on the scene, which had long offended him and the Father.

It was time.

'Peter,' he asked, 'what do you see?'

'Same as usual,' Peter shrugged, not sure what Jesus was looking for. 'Oxen, sheep.'

Jesus looked around. 'Andrew?'

'Cages of pigeons.'

Jesus nodded. 'Jamie?'

Jamie looked around, considered. 'Money changers.'

'Jim?'

'Lots of noise, confusion.'

'John?'

'A market, it's a market.'

'Jude?'

Jude's face lit up with a big smile. 'An opportunity.'

'An opportunity?' Jesus replied, nodding in agreement. 'You're right, and I intend to make the most of it.' He looked at them in turn. 'Watch.'

Jesus moved to the centre of the courtyard, held up his hands. 'STOP.' He shouted. 'STOP RIGHT

NOW.'

A few traders looked, shrugged, continued with their transactions. Some people pointed, sniggered. The vast majority ignored him.

That was never going to work, Peter decided, these people didn't understand sweet reason.

The disciples watched in stunned disbelief as Jesus ran across to a moneychanger's booth, pushed it over. Shouts of anger came from within as the structure toppled to the floor. Pigeons flapped. Coins from the booth, rolled across the ground, people stooped, picked them up, slipped them in pockets, and carried on, one fluid movement. Jesus moved on to the sheep pens, unlatched the gates, urged the animals out, and did the same with the oxen.

In a few minutes, what had been a chaotic but peaceful trading area, was transformed into a scene of utter confusion. Animals bellowing, bleating. Men shouting, swearing, screaming, while Jesus ran round the entire area, knocking over stalls, ordering people to leave, take their goods with them.

Whoa!

Peter took a deep breath, looked at Jim in stunned silence. This was definitely a different Jesus to the lad he'd known at school.

Jim looked round the other disciples, most of who were looking on open mouthed, apart from Jude who seemed to be enjoying the spectacle. 'Get like this often, does he?' Peter asked Jim, who shook his head, his cheeks red, from embarrassment or anger.

'"The Lord whom you seek, shall come to His Temple without warning,' John said, the others looked at him in surprise, 'and He will purify the sons of..."

sorry, I forget the rest.'

'You what mate?' Peter scratched his head.

'Ancient scripture,' John explained, 'Jesus is fulfilling ancient scripture.'

'Oh, right,' Andrew remarked dryly, 'and there's me thinking he's totally lost it.'

'No, not lost it,' John said, 'you can see he's angry, but controlled. He isn't striking out indiscriminately.'

'He's right.' Jamie affirmed. 'Just watch.'

Together they stood, watched as Jesus, using a cattle prod he'd acquired, drove the animals towards the gates. He picked up a tin of change from a stall, poured the coins out. He handed a cage full of flapping pigeons to its owner, pointed to the exit. Startled animals defecated everywhere. The noise, heat, stench overwhelming.

'"The zeal of thy house has consumed me."' John said.

The others exchanged glances.

When the trading area had cleared, a small huddle of angry merchants gathered by the door moaning and groaning. Jesus stopped, his breathing heavy, straw and faeces clinging to his shoes. The others joined him. They formed a protective circle around him and watched in apprehension as a group of priests, robes flapping behind, made their way to the disciples. 'What is this outrage?' The high priest, Caiaphas, tall, thin faced, righteousness bubbling up, 'That you come into the Holy Temple, and...' he flung his arms wide. 'Why?' he demanded. 'On whose authority?'

'Destroy this Temple,' Jesus, mirrored the priest's arm movement, 'and in three days I will raise it up.'

'It has taken centuries to build this Temple,'

Caiaphas retorted, derision evident, 'and you will raise it up in three days?'

Jesus ignored the high priest, looked at his followers, 'Come on lads, let's go.'

There was silence on the way out. Nobody stood in their way, preventing them from leaving. Once outside, the tension relieved, a babble of voices broke out.

Jesus raised his voice. 'One at a time, please.'

They looked at each other, looked at Peter.

'Why now?' Peter said. 'That circus has been happening for years.'

'Everything has a time, no matter how long it's been happening.' Jesus replied. 'As you know, once a year, every Jewish male has to come to this Temple, pay a tax. That tax can't be paid in the normal currency of the land. It has to be paid using a special coin that is obtained from the Temple money changers.'

'And,' Jamie interrupted, 'it's a rip off. It costs ten times what you should be paying.'

'That's right.' Andrew agreed.'

'Sounds like a good business to be in.' Jude smiled, half joking.

Jesus wrapped his arms round the Dude, hugged him, 'I've much to teach you Jude.' He released him, and looked at the others, 'I've much to teach you all.'

'What about the oxen, the sheep, where's the scam there?' Andrew asked.

'What happens to the oxen and the sheep?' Jesus asked.

'They're sacrificed.' Jim replied.

'Why?'

They all shrugged, this was simple stuff. All Jews

knew the answer.

'It's part of the ritual required to atone for our sins.' John said. 'It requires a blood sacrifice.'

'From?' Jesus prompted.

'A perfect animal without blemish.' Peter replied.

'Correct.' Jesus smiled. 'Has anyone ever tried taking along their own animal for the sacrifice?'

'Aye.' Jamie growled.

'What happened?'

'It was found to have a minor blemish that my eye couldn't detect.' Jamie shrugged. 'I had to surrender it. I'm sure they took it inside, sold it back to me at an inflated price.'

The others laughed, but Jesus had made his point.

†

LEEDS, NORTHUMBRIA.

Mercer, the sweaty, overweight Head Teacher pulled Beaumont to one side of the staff room, invited him into the office, a quick word.

'Now?' Beaumont, surprised, but not concerned.

'If you don't mind.'

And if I do?

'There's been a complaint.' Mercer said, wedged safe behind his desk. 'I thought it best to have a quiet word.'

Beaumont looked into the eyes of the Head and as usual, had no indication of what the man was thinking.

'You know I've no intrinsic objection to thrashing the boys,' Mercer continued, 'however, you seem to be concentrating your efforts on the Schulz boy. Nothing wrong in that if it can be justified on the grounds of punishment or keeping order.'

Mercer paused, seeking comment. Beaumont shrugged. 'He's not the sole recipient.' I thrash them all in turn.

'Seven times in a week seems rather excessive.' Mercer raised an eyebrow. 'The boy's father is not happy. He's wondering if you've got some antipathy towards Saxons. I assured him you hadn't, and that his son deserved every stroke that you'd delivered.'

'Thank you.' Beaumont said, surprised at the show of support from the usually spineless Head Teacher.

Mercer waved his hand dismissively. 'We have to stick together. All the same...'

Beaumont nodded, an off-hand dismissive gesture, half rose to go. That wasn't too bad, he decided. He wondered idly whether it might be pushing it to thrash Schulz again before home time. He smiled at the thought.

'There was something else.'

'Oh?' Beaumont sank back on the seat.

Mercer regarded him with interest. 'How long have you been here now?'

'Ten years.'

Mercer nodded in confirmation. 'Quite a while. Have you given any thought to the next stage of your career? You're an excellent teacher. Head of Department in another school would be the logical move.'

Beaumont stared at the Head. You fat bastard.

Anyway,' Mercer stood, opened the door, 'you'd best get back to your class.'

Beaumont squeezed past his sweating Head

Teacher, resisted the temptation to plant one on him.

'Give it some thought.' Mercer's voice floated down the corridor after him.

†

WHITBY, NORTHUMBRIA.

In the kitchen, O'Deamus watched as Jesus made tea, took the mug when it was offered. The two men regarded each other in silence for a moment. 'Thanks for seeing me, Jesus.' O'Deamus said.

Jesus shrugged. 'Are you here seeking God?'

'I came to see you.' O'Deamus replied, toying with his mug, 'Tell me Jesus, what are you doing now you've packed in the building?'

'You could have picked up the phone to ask me that,' Jesus smiled, 'but instead, you come at night, in secret to see me.'

O'Deamus nodded in acknowledgment, ignored the comment. 'What will you do for money, now you're longer working with your brother, Jim?'

'Is that why you're here? Concern for my welfare?'

'In a way, yes. It's a harsh world for those without money.'

'Don't worry about tomorrow,' Jesus said, broad smile, 'tomorrow will worry about itself.'

O'Deamus shook his head in frustration. 'Jesus, it's obvious to even the most casual observer that you're performing powerful signs. That business at Sinead's wedding. That could have been very embarrassing for me. I tasted that wine. It was the finest wine I've ever tasted. I don't know what happened, what you did, but thank you.'

Jesus nodded. 'It was done for my Father's glory.'

O'Deamus continued, 'We on the Sanhedrin believe that you're a teacher sent by God...'

'Are you representing them,' Jesus interrupted, 'or is this a private visit?' The council of seventy Pharisees who made up the Sanhedrin ran the religious affairs of the Jews.

'Well,' O'Deamus hedged, 'it's not that simple.' He paused, set his mug down. 'Let me be straight with you Jesus. Nobody can do the things you do unless God is with him. We can't do them. There are some of us who'd like you to come and teach us all you know about the kingdom of God.'

Jesus smiled, said, 'I tell you now. Unless you're born again, you will not enter the kingdom of God.'

O'Deamus laughed, 'And they say we Irish talk a lot of auld nonsense. Be serious Jesus, how on earth can a man be born again? How can a man be born again when he's old and grey like me? Once a man or woman has popped out the womb, there's no way on earth they'll get back in again.'

'I understand your puzzlement,' Jesus replied, 'but unless you are born of water and the spirit, you cannot enter the kingdom of God. That which is born of flesh is flesh, and that which is born of spirit is spirit. Don't be surprised that I say you must be born again.' He broke off. 'Listen.'

'What is it?' O'Deamus asked, puzzled, all he could hear was a faint breeze.

'The wind blows where it will,' Jesus continued, 'you hear the sound of it, see the effect, but you don't know where it comes from, or where it goes. It's the same with everyone born of the spirit.'

O'Deamus frowned. 'When you say water, you mean the immersing that Baptiste has been doing?'

'That's right, but don't be confused by the water.' Jesus paused, smiled at the obvious puzzlement on his visitor's face. 'The water is purely symbolic. You need to repent, but first you need to realise your need, and then admit it.' Jesus continued. 'This is the problem of you Pharisees. You're living by the law. By your own efforts, you tie yourself in knots. Your own efforts will never be good enough no matter how hard you try.'

'How can this be?' O'Deamus asked, frustrated.

'You're a teacher, a most diligent adherent of the ancient faith,' Jesus said, 'and yet you don't understand? I am astonished. If I tell you earthly things and you don't believe, then how can you believe heavenly things? You have given your life to studying the ancient scriptures and you do not understand what I say. The prophet Isaiah spoke of a new life from God. Jeremiah predicted a new creation would be given. Ezekiel said that God would take out the old heart of stone and give a new heart of flesh.' Jesus smiled in wonderment, 'All through the ancient scriptures there are passages that tell of, a new birth, a new beginning, a new creation, a new life that will come as a gift of God, to those who would humbly, without pride, receive it.'

They spoke for a while longer, until O'Deamus stood to go. 'You seem sincere in all you say, but I can't help feeling you're on the wrong track with this born again business. I would urge caution Jesus, there are others on the council who won't listen as I do, or,' he paused, 'be as sympathetic.'

GRETNA GREEN, SCOTLAND.

Andrew knew he was being a pain. Quiet, morose, hardly the life and soul. Fed up of living a nomadic campfire lifestyle, he was missing home, missing the sea.

It was the fifth week of their tour and he was thinking of packing it in, returning to Marje and the kids. He would have done, had she not encouraged him to stick it out, telling him he was in on something big, something important. She'd met Jesus, been impressed, told Andrew, without a doubt, this was the Messiah.

But still, seven blokes in a minibus, camping in farmer's fields, washing and crapping in pub toilets, was no life for a grown man. The fine weather helped. It was good for early summer in Northumbria, no rain for weeks, farmers watching the sky. TV people forecasting a long dry spell. Climate change deniers gone to ground.

He thought Peter would have cracked long before now, but no, his brother seemed to have shrugged off his former lifestyle of drink and debauchery, had even embraced the open-air existence. For Andrew though, the constant travelling, stopping, starting, meeting people, glad-handing, was wearing him down. Truth was the one thing keeping him going was one man.

Jesus.

Couldn't say no to the guy, none of them could. He was amazing.

He had time for everybody, but seemed to spend most of his time with the dregs of society. The dropouts, the alkies, the druggies, the prozzies. The very people that Andrew would cross the road to avoid, apart from prostitutes he thought guiltily. He'd decided his visits to NorPro had to end, could do without them.

Everywhere they went. Crowds of people would flock to hear Jesus speak. Like a magnet for the masses, they were drawn to him. He'd lay hands on them, absolve them of sin, cure their ailments, straighten broken limbs. He gave sight to the blind, a voice to the dumb, and hearing to the deaf. He'd cast out more demons than Andrew had thought existed.

Not everybody was happy though. The Polizei kept a close eye, albeit from a distance, but they were there, watching. The Pharisees seemed unsure of Jesus, who he was, what he represented. They were always about, on the fringes, asking awkward questions, testing Jesus, looking for a weak link. Jesus though was magnificent, he handled everything with ease. Didn't suffer fools though. He'd answer the questions and move on.

They passed a road sign that read, Welcome to Scotland, the land of the free. Andrew called back, 'Watch out for marauding jocks.'

Laughter from the back. The sun broke through the wispy cloud, another glorious day. Andrew's spirits lifted. He came to a fork in the road, slowed down, looked at the finger signpost, neither name meant anything, called out, 'Which way?'

'Left.' Jesus said, from his seat near the back.

Andrew flicked the indicator, turned left, trundled down another country lane. Apart from being just over the border he hadn't a clue where he was, heading towards another God forsaken village, where the people would turn out, lining the streets, anxious for a sight of Jesus, cameras poised, all wanting selfies with the main man. The Boss, as Peter had started calling him.

'Could you pull over?' Jesus called out above the clamour of the guys playing poker for cents, squabbling like children.'

Andrew cruised to a halt, waited. The side door opened, Jesus got out, the others prepared to follow, but he gestured them back inside.

He came round to the driver's door. 'Carry on into the village, stock up on provisions, meet me back here in an hour or so, okay?'

'Okay Boss.' Andrew saluted, let out the clutch. Watched in the rear view mirror as Jesus sat on the low wall of an old well, then he rounded the corner, heading for the village, feeling strangely empty.

†

Sophia didn't give the minibus a lot of attention as it swept by. She was too busy covering her eyes from the cloud of dust it kicked up, but was conscious of men staring from the windows, assessing. She knew she looked good with her slim, elegant figure. Her long brown hair gathered in a ponytail. Her long legs encased in faded blue jeans were always a magnet for male eyes.

'Bastards.' She muttered, trudged on, pulling the round water barrel behind. Shouldn't have to be using an old well, in this day and age, but when the water company had declared drought conditions, put standpipes in the village, she'd had little choice. The other women had made it clear that her presence was unwelcome, crowded her out, actions just this side of hostile. She'd tried going at different times of day, but there was always some woman there, giving her the evils, muttering about slags.

Well, stuff 'em.

Her choice. Pay the exorbitant price the village shop charged for bottled, or use the old well. It was just her and Dennis, their needs weren't great, so the well it was. The water perfectly drinkable, if a little brackish. She turned the corner, stopped abruptly. There was a man sitting by the well, almost, Sophia thought, as if he was expecting her. He looked respectable, clean, and tidy. Not a threat she decided, carried on, lowered the bucket into the water, the man watching her.

He didn't speak until she'd lifted the first bucketful, was using the funnel to fill her barrel.

'Could I have a drink, please?' He had a polite deferential tone with a slight Northumbrian burr.

Sophia looked at him warily. Was this the prelude to a proposition? Well, what if it was, she was lonely, needed cheering up. 'Bit of a turn up isn't it,' Sophia said, giving him her look. The one that made men melt. 'A Jew from Northumbria asks a Scottish woman for a drink.'

'If you knew about the gift of God,' Jesus said, 'and who it was that asked for a drink, you would have asked me for living water.'

'Well, now,' Sophia replied in a flirtatious tone, 'You have no cup, and I have control of the water, so where would you get this living water?'

'Everyone who drinks water from the well will get thirsty again, but whoever drinks of the water I give will never thirst.' The man looked at her and despite the warmth of the day, Sophia shivered. Who was this man? 'The water that I give will become a spring of water welling up to eternal life.'

'I'll have some o' that.' Sophia said. 'Fancy, never getting thirsty again.'

'Go.' Jesus told her, 'bring back your husband.'

'I'm not married.' Sophia replied and wondered where this was going.

'No, you're not, are you.' Jesus said, in a kind but firm voice. 'The truth is you've been married to five men before and the man with whom you now live is married to somebody else.'

Sophia lowered her eyes, couldn't meet the man's eye. She listened in silence as he spoke, and wondered why she thought it would be any different two kilometres from the village.

'Falling in love is easy,' Jesus said, 'men and women do it every day, they get together, marry with the best of intentions to spend the rest of their lives together, but, after a while the early excitement fades away, leading to a richer, deeper contentment.'

Does it? Sophia wondered. It never had for her.

'But,' Jesus continued, 'that requires an act of will on both your parts. It's impossible to continue with those same feelings of intoxication throughout your days. And when you have given everything in love and the relationship starts to fade, as it will, you feel restless, cheated, deprived. So, it's out with the old, in with the new.'

Jesus paused, waited.

Sophia looked up, searched for the condemnation in the man's eyes, saw pure honest love. 'What are you? Who are you? Some kind of prophet? You've nailed it.' The tears pricked her eyes. 'That's me. You've just described me. The way I am, who I am.'

Jesus continued to look at her.

'Where do I go, what do I have to do to get this kind of life you're talking about? You Jews say it's the Temple in York, my people say it can be found in the Highlands, what do you say?'

Jesus smiled, took her hand. 'Believe me, very soon it won't matter where you worship the Father, whether in the Temple, or in the mountains. God is spirit, and those who worship him must do so in spirit and truth. He has provided all you need in the form of your body, your spirit. That is all you need to worship from the heart. Let your spirit join with His spirit, then you will have your answer.'

Jesus released her hand, stepped back, watched as she dabbed her eyes with a tissue.

'I have heard that a Messiah is coming.' Sophia said after a few moments.

'That's right.' Jesus replied. 'I am he.'

†

ASKHAM BRYAN, NEAR YORK, NORTHUMBRIA.

'The itinerant preacher Baptiste, known for immersing people in the sea on the east coast, and his dire warnings of a coming Messiah, has been arrested.'

Not before bleedin' time. Swanger watched the TV pictures as armed riot Polizei cordoned off a section of beach, and led away a vociferous arm waving Baptiste, watched by a silent, bewildered crowd, held back by officers.

'As yet there is no word from the authorities on any charges that may be brought against Baptiste.'

Being a gobby pillock 'ud be a good start.

'Meanwhile, Jesus, the man who many believe to be the promised Messiah, has been travelling around the northern part of the kingdom. This report, which contains flash photography, is brought to us by our Carlisle correspondent.'

The screen changed to show a silent Jesus addressing an open-air meeting. A voice-over provided the commentary, 'Jesus from Whitby has been meeting and greeting people all over the north during the last few weeks. According to eyewitness reports, Jesus has been healing the sick and giving sight to the blind. In his public speaking, Jesus proclaimed the love of God for all people.'

The TV showed a montage of pictures, Jesus kissing babies, Jesus laying hands on the sick, a blind man throwing away his dark glasses and stick, running down the road, tears streaming down his face. A man with a severe limp, one leg shorter than the other was talking about his cure as the camera showed in close-up his leg growing by 5 centimetres.

Despite her healthy scepticism, Swanger was impressed by some healings, but reminded herself that anything could be faked.

The report ended. Michelle, the studio anchor came back on the screen, 'Jesus hasn't been met with total acceptance. Some of his more controversial activities have been received with anger from some quarters, as in the case that he claims to cure mental illness by the unusual method of casting out demons. I asked a leading psychiatrist if he favoured this method.'

The picture changed to a screen, a man in a white coat, thick glasses, mad look about him, the caption read, Dr Carter, Consultant Psychiatrist. 'No, Michelle, this approach is very dangerous. It has never been established that demons even exist, and,' he shrugged, gave a little laugh, 'even if they do, there's no saying that they mean harm to anybody.'

Michelle in the studio, 'In what way might Jesus' approach be considered dangerous?'

Dr Carter, 'It must be understood that the mentally ill are quite vulnerable. All this talk of demon possession might be giving them false hope.'

Michelle in the studio, 'But if it works?'

Dr Carter, Shaking his head. 'It doesn't work, and even if it did, it wouldn't work for everybody.'

Michelle in the studio, 'Much like psychiatry?'

Dr Carter, 'A one size approach fits all doesn't work very well with mental illness. For some it's medication, others shock treatment, for others again, it could be counselling.'

Michelle in the studio, 'But not casting out demons?'

Dr Carter, 'No.'

Michelle in the studio, 'Would you say that Jesus was acting irresponsibly?'

Dr Carter, 'Without a doubt. We've seen these people come and go before, a quick blaze of glory, spectacular signs and wonders, then, it all fizzles out, leaving people quite bereft.'

Michelle in the studio, 'what do you mean when you say, "these types of people"?'

Dr Carter, 'Well, they're all charlatans.'

After more verbal sparring Michelle wrapped up the interview and addressed the camera, 'Jesus is now back in his home town for a short stay before he heads out on another tour. We asked him for his reaction to Dr Carter's claim that he was a charlatan, but he was unavailable for comment.'

'In other news a kingdom wide search for the terrorists behind a recent bombing campaign has been stepped up...'

Yes, love, I know. Swanger muted the sound, thought over the previous few days. Baptiste's arrest had been a political decision. There hadn't been any real evidence against him. He hadn't been proclaiming against the state, just pointing the way towards the one who would. But, from what Swanger had seen of Jesus, he didn't seem the type to spark a revolution. Too much joy and peace. Lots of talk, too little action, and now he was being discredited on live TV by a psychiatrist. Still, not Swanger's problem, though, to be on the safe side, she was keeping in loose contact with Nathan, who had now attached himself to Jesus, become one of his followers, one of the inner circle no less. Swanger turned the TV off, shooed Max her tabby out for his nocturnal activities and went to bed.

SIX

THE TEMPLE, YORK, NORTHUMBRIA.

Yada, yada, yada.

O'Deamus yawned, stubbed out his cigarette, drained his coffee, and took a quick glance at his watch. Please, not much longer. The meeting, a Sanhedrin subcommittee, chaired by Caiaphas the high priest, was dragging. He ticked off the last but one agenda item as a conclusion was reached that the item be discussed at the next meeting. The chair asked if there was any other business. O'Deamus shook his head, mentally switched off, was on the golf course practising his swing, when he heard Simon, one of Caiaphas' advisors say, 'Jesus.'

The elephant in the room.

'Now,' Simon continued, looking at the others, 'I'm sure you'll all agree that Jesus is a personable young man with some interesting ideas.'

An influential Scribe, David, snorted in derision. 'He's a hothead. Look at that business in the Temple Courts, turning the tables over, releasing the animals. That's no way to behave.'

Nods of affirmation, muttering.

'Is he Messiah?' Somebody asked.

'No.' David responded. 'Definitely not.'

'Sent by God, then?' Another asked.

'He heals the sick on the Sabbath,' David said, 'nobody that God sent would do that.'

Head shaking, tutting, all round the table.

'He has performed some powerful signs, though.'

'But on the holy day.'

'He doesn't follow the recognised way of doing things.'

'He mixes with the lowest members of society.'

'Is he a recognised teacher of the law?'

'He ignores the law.'

'He's getting too much coverage on TV, the internet, the papers.'

O'Deamus listened as the debate raged, noticed that everybody apart from himself and Caiaphas took part. After the arguments were beginning to be repeated, Caiaphas held up his hands. 'I consider this Jesus to be a dangerous maverick who is advocating that the people should be able to access God without the guidance of those in a position to know better. However, he has gained a certain popularity and we can't be seen to be going against him.'

David raised his hand. Caiaphas nodded in his direction.

'Perhaps we should set up a small group to monitor his activities.' David suggested.

'I'm sure the Polizei are doing just that.' O'Deamus responded.

'I'm sure they are,' David agreed, 'but it won't harm if we set up our own group.'

'An interesting suggestion,' Caiaphas said, nodding. 'And of course, we're getting regular reports back from our people on the ground. But,' he paused, made sure he had their full attention, 'what we need to do is puncture his balloon, show the people he's just like other men, that there's nothing special about him.'

One of the Scribes, a well-spoken cultured man, said. 'I think I know just the thing.'

✝

The car came to a halt. What now, Maggie wondered. The passenger door opened, she turned at the noise, couldn't see a thing, knew better than try to lift the blindfold. 'Get out then.' The voice, Levi, her pimp.

Maggie stumbled out of the car. Levi took her arm. They walked a short distance, and then stopped. A door opened, they entered and turned left into a room. Levi, hands on her shoulders 'Sit down.'

She'd assumed this a routine assignment. It happened sometimes. A rich client who didn't want to visit NorPro, arranged for a girl to be brought to him. Levi would wait outside in the car, then, business concluded, would drive her home.

As pimps went Levi wasn't too bad, liked to sample the goods on occasion, but then, didn't they all. At least she got paid on time, and he always had a regular supply of Morph.

She sat, listening as Levi left the room and let her senses work. Somewhere in the depths of the house a piano could be heard. Maggie, no way of knowing if it was a recording or someone playing. It sounded familiar. Classical music from an advert? There was a smell of furniture polish. She had the impression this was a big house. A mansion, many rooms. A movement in the air, then another smell came to her, soft, subtle. Aftershave, expensive. A man had entered the room.

The voices sparked into life.

This is the big one.

Don't mess it up.

Do as you're told.

Morph, ask for Morph.

Maggie shook her head, frustrated, wished they'd be quiet. She was trying to concentrate.

She had a feeling she was seated opposite someone who was studying her. A watcher, a game player. Maggie crossed her legs, was rewarded with a sharp intake of breath. She was wearing the flame red dress that had aroused Peter the fisherman so much.

'You have a lovely body.' The voice was soft, cultured, no hint of an accent.

'Thank you.'

'Do you like what you do, enjoy it, perhaps?'

Maggie had never known a working girl enjoy the life. She shrugged. 'It pays the bills.'

'Could you seduce any man, do you think?'

An odd question. Maggie, in her line of work, didn't need to seduce men. They wanted her, that was a given. 'If he wasn't gay.' Maggie smiled, although she'd managed that once.

'Have you heard of the prophet, Jesus?'

Who hadn't? 'Yes. Is he the one?'

'Could you work your charms on him?'

'Of course.' It would be a pleasure. Jesus was a good-looking man.

'Excellent.' She heard the man stand. 'I'll be in touch.'

'This is a paid job?' Maggie asked.

'Of course.' The man chuckled. 'It's a job for a

whore, and you're a whore.'

✝

WHITBY, NORTHUMBRIA.

A beautiful day, early afternoon, sun high, salt tang in the air, the sea calm. A racket of noise flooded from the arcades, and everywhere Andrew looked, there were people. The beach and seafront heaving with tourists from all parts of the Union attracted by the possibility of seeing Jesus. The beach covered with towels. Saxon towels for the most part, Andrew thought wryly as he mooched through the crowd, happy again, now that he was back home with his family. He didn't know how long before they'd be off again, so, was making the most of it.

Andrew weaved his way through the entertainers drawn by the crowds. The magicians with their sleight of hand tricks, the jugglers, the fire-eaters, the statues that came to life scaring the unwary. And amidst everything, children dashing about, laughing and shrieking.

The hubbub of noise threatened to intrude on his thoughts, but he didn't mind. He was content. He thought back to that morning when Jesus had visited Peter's mother-in-law, Judith, who'd been stricken with a sudden fever. Andrew had gone along with his anxious brother. They'd watched as Jesus laid hands on the woman's brow, both expectant that the fever would vanish. It had, and Judith, raised from her sick bed, restored to health, had insisted on making tea, provided cakes. She'd pronounced Jesus the Messiah and was now a follower. The disciples had been told they could do as Jesus did, including healing the sick, but Andrew didn't think any of their small group had tried it.

Then later, back at the sea front, after Jesus had finished preaching, a man in obvious pain had approached. He was stooped over, with a pitiful appearance, his body thin and obviously wasting. People nudged, pointed, and moved away from him. He was about to be turned away by Peter, when Jesus noticed, beckoned him closer, and listened with compassion as the man explained how, as the result of an unwise sexual liaison, he'd become infected with HIV AIDS. The illness was at an advanced stage and the medical professionals had warned that even a minor cold could cause his death. He finished his account by asking if Jesus was willing to relieve his suffering.

Jesus had raised his hand towards the man, a slight gesture. 'It is done.' He told him.

Andrew had watched in amazement as the years rolled back and he became fit and healthy. The man had suddenly straightened and his complexion cleared. His skin glowed with health and vitality. He thanked Jesus profusely, hugged him, and then, still dazed by his encounter, had sat in the warm sun telling everybody within earshot of the miracle, even though Jesus had asked him to remain silent.

With the afternoon session beginning soon, Andrew noticed the Pharisees had taken up their customary position at the front, ready for any opportunity to challenge Jesus. Later, after a reading from scriptures, a man called out, 'Jesus, I will follow you wherever you go.'

'Foxes have dens and birds have nests,' Jesus replied, 'but the Son of Man has nowhere to lay his head.'

Another man called. 'Lord, I will follow you, but first I have to arrange my father's funeral.'

'Follow me now, and let the dead in spirit bury their own dead.' Jesus told him.

There was a sudden commotion at the edge of the crowd. Andrew saw a group of four young men each holding the corner of a stretcher. On it lay another young man. 'Make way,' they called out, 'let us through, this is urgent.'

The crowd parted, the stretcher party moved through, lowered the stretcher in front of Jesus. 'Are you Jesus?' One of them asked.

'I am he.' Jesus said.

The man gestured to the man on the stretcher. 'This is our friend, paralysed for five years. We believe you can heal him. Will you?'

Jesus addressed the man. 'Son, your sins are forgiven.'

The Pharisees looked at each other, began muttering in low voices.

'This can't be right.'

'He's blaspheming.'

'Only God can forgive sins.'

'Why are you saying these things?' Jesus challenged them. 'Which is easier to say to this paralysed man, "Your sins are forgiven," or to say, "Get up, and walk"? But I want you to know that the Son of Man has authority on earth to forgive sins.'

He turned to the paralysed man and said. 'I tell you,

get up, and walk.'

A gasp came from the crowd, as the man drew his knees up, rolled onto his side and levered himself to his feet, where he stood unsteadily for a moment. Cheering and whistling followed, as the man and his friends grabbed each other and whirling round, set off dancing down the street, calling out their thanks as they went. The stretcher was left behind, forgotten and redundant.

✝

The black Range Rover, tinted windows, over-sized alloys, stopped at the kerb. Levi left the engine running, looked at Maggie, and grinned. 'You know what to do?'

'Yeah.' Maggie answered. 'Been doing it long enough.'

'It's not enough for you to screw the guy, they need the evidence. Make sure the camera is pointing the right way. Yeah?'

'Yeah, course.' Her bag had been adapted to accommodate a small spy camera. Not that difficult to point it in the right direction.

'Don't mess up.' Levi cautioned.

'No.' Maggie answered listlessly. How could she mess up?

'You need to liven up girl.' Levi said, squeezing her thigh. 'Give him a reason to want to screw you.'

'Give me some Morph, and then I'll liven up.'

'Later. Give us a bell when you're done, yeah?'

'Yes.' Maggie sighed, watched as Levi drove away.

She walked around the corner, stood outside the

ordinary three bed semi-detached house in the ordinary street. Maggie wasn't sure what she'd been expecting. A mansion, a palace? She walked up the path, adjusted her dress to reveal more cleavage. Even feeling out of sorts as she was, Maggie was confident in her ability to seduce this man, Jesus. Okay, he was a powerful man of God. The promised Messiah, some said, but she'd screwed plenty of Pharisees, Scribes, Rabbis, and Priests. All men of God. Jesus was just another. One glance at her boobs, her legs, she'd guarantee he'd be all over her in minutes.

The voices in her head were muttering among themselves, she ignored them. A black cat on the front doorstep looked at her. Maggie reached out to stroke it.

'No.' one of her voices screeched.

Silence.

She withdrew her hand away from the cat, it stood, stretched, gave her a knowing look, stalked off, tail in the air.

The voices started babbling again.

'Shut up.' Maggie ordered. 'All of you just shut the fuck up.'

She composed herself, rang the doorbell. The door opened. Jesus stood there smiling, waiting for her to speak. Time slowed, Maggie wanted to turn and run. To run forever and never stop, but didn't. Levi would be so pissed off if she messed this up. Although the voices were quiet, she could sense their restlessness.

Maggie smiled her brightest smile, forced her mouth to work. 'Hello,' she said, 'I'm Maggie.'

'What can I do for you Maggie?' Jesus asked.

Now she was here, Maggie was unsure, her

confidence drained away. In theory it was easy, she undressed, lay down, Jesus did what men do. But then, in that scenario, both parties knew what was expected of them. This was different. Jesus didn't know she was a whore and he wasn't looking at her in a lustful way. His eyes hadn't once left her face, he wasn't uncomfortable, but seemed to be totally in control. She couldn't do this, so did the one thing she could do. She burst into tears.

Maggie expected the door to be slammed in her face but instead Jesus stood to one side. 'Why don't you come in, have a drink?' His voice calm, soothing. 'We can talk about what's upsetting you.'

She followed him into the living room, stood close, wrapped her arms round his body, and snuggled in close. The voices murmured in agitation. Jesus held her close for a few seconds then eased her away.

'What's wrong, Jesus,' she pouted, ready for more tears, 'don't you like me?'

'What do you want from me, Maggie?' Jesus asked.

This was hopeless, she couldn't seduce him and he didn't seem to know what he should do. This is my final option, she thought, releasing the straps on her dress. She let it fall to the floor and stood naked before him. 'I want you to love me.'

'Oh, my child, this is not the way.'

Maggie smiled through her tears. 'Don't you find me attractive?'

'Maggie, you're a beautiful woman.' Jesus replied.

'So, what's the problem?'

Jesus maintained eye contact but didn't speak. The voices went into overdrive.

You stupid girl.

He doesn't fancy you.

Fancy getting your kit off so quick.

You've put him off.

Perhaps he's gay.

You should have taken your time to seduce him.

Bull at a gate.

What's Levi going to say now?

No more Morph.

Maggie felt wretched, even her naked body wasn't good enough for the Messiah, it seemed. 'Shut up, all of you shut up.' Her eyes welled with tears again as she picked up her dress, tried to cover herself.

'How many?' Jesus asked.

'Seven.' Maggie told him. 'They drive me crazy. All the time, jabbering away. I have no peace.'

'You want rid of them?'

'Yeah, course.'

Jesus closed his eyes, was silent for a moment. He seemed to be praying, Maggie thought. He opened his eyes and said, 'Do you know who I am?'

'Yeah.' Maggie replied between the snivels, 'You're Jesus.'

Jesus put his finger against his lips, raised his eyebrows, said again. 'Do you know who I am?'

Silence, then,

'Of course.'

'Jesus.'

'Son of the living God.'

'The Messiah.'

'The Word.'

The voices answered at once, tumbling over themselves, eager to be heard.

'This woman is holy, not to be defiled. I command

you to come out of her. Leave now and go back to whom you belong. Do not return.' Jesus spoke in a low steady voice. Maggie almost laughed. That will never work, she thought. They need something a bit stronger than being told to go. She'd told them to go dozens of times. They just laughed at her. They'd laugh at Jesus too.

Time past, seconds, hours, she didn't know, then almost imperceptibly, her body started shaking. She pressed her feet firmly on the floor, tensed her muscles, tried to stand still but it was impossible. Maggie looked at Jesus. His face was in sharp focus one second, and then blurred the next. She tried to speak, couldn't. The voices in her head were shouting, screaming. She had the sense they were running about in a panic, bumping into each other, falling over. Her abdomen tensed, she was conscious of something rising from the pit of her stomach, up through her throat, into her mouth. She turned her head just in time as her lips were forced apart by the pressure. She watched in horror as a stream of vomit shot across the living room, splatting against the wall.

Puzzled, terrified, she looked at Jesus. He smiled in reassurance. She tried to speak but more vomit spewed out accompanied by a fearful shriek. She looked around in alarm as the sound of an express train thundering down the track filled the room. It brought a smell of ozone and wisps of black smoke hung around at ceiling height before slipping out through the open window.

Silence.

Maggie stopped shaking. Her knees buckled, she fell against Jesus who held her steady, wrapping his arms around her. She felt safe, could have stayed there for the rest of her life. After a while Jesus asked, 'How do you feel?'

'Strange.' Maggie told him. 'Like I'm not me anymore. I feel like a new person.' She looked at Jesus and smiled. 'I feel free, released, and peaceful.'

'That's good.' Jesus said. 'You are free.'

She frowned at a sudden thought. 'What if they come back?'

'They won't.' Jesus replied. 'They've gone for good. Along with all your addictions and sin. Now, go upstairs, run a bath, get clean, while I arrange somewhere safe for you to stay.'

✝

'I won't be a minute.' Jesus said, and slipped away into the crowd.

'Jesus.' Peter objected. 'We'll be late.' He watched in frustration as Jesus skipped across the road, dodging traffic, oblivious to the blaring horns, shouted insults, and hand gestures.

Where was he going?

'Jesus.' Peter shouted. A few heads turned. Peter ignored them, ran after Jesus, caught up with him by the side of a high spec black Range Rover, tinted windows.

A pimp's car, Peter reckoned, had his prejudices confirmed when he saw the driver. It was the guy who'd sold him the girl in the red dress. The window down, Levi, armful of gold jewellery, fat Rolex, his elbow jutting out, was looking at Jesus with a puzzled expression. Peter, late to the conversation, heard him say, 'Follow you? Just like that?'

'Yeah,' Jesus replied. 'Why not?'

Whoa.

Not this bloke.

Please Jesus not this one.

'Okay,' Levi agreed. The window slid up, the engine stopped. Levi got out, grinned. 'Why not, let's do it.'

He can't mean it, Peter thought, he's taking the piss. Why would he give up everything to follow Jesus?

'Where we going?' Levi asked. He was flexing on the balls of his feet and Peter wondered if he was high.

Jesus pointed to the MUFWOC. 'There.'

Levi grinned again. 'Should be interesting. I haven't been to a service since I was a kid.'

Peter couldn't hold back any longer. 'Jesus?'

'I know Peter, we should go. We don't want to be late.' He turned to go. Peter tugged his sleeve. 'Do you know who this man is?'

Levi watched the exchange with a slight smile.

'Yes, of course.' Jesus replied. 'It's...,' he broke off, thought, 'Matthew. Levi is now Matthew.' He looked at Levi.

Levi shrugged. 'Fine with me.'

Peter,' Jesus said, 'this is Matthew, do you two know each other?'

'Boss, you do know what he does?'

'I know what he used to do, Peter. Now he's like you, he follows me.'

Silence.

'Right, let's not keep the people waiting any longer.' Jesus turned, walked away.

Matthew locked the car, made to follow, was brought up short by a tug on his arm. He turned, looked at Peter, grinned. 'Yeah?'

'We give up our worldly possessions to follow Jesus.' Peter said, looking at the Range Rover.

Matthew smiled, unlocked the car and tossed the keys on the seat. 'First one to find it then.' He looked at Peter. 'Happy?'

'What about the watch?'

Mathew stared at Peter for a long moment before sliding the bejewelled Rolex off his wrist. He laid it alongside the keys, then followed Jesus across the road, leaving Peter to trail along in his wake.

✝

The MUFWOC was packed to the rafters. Brian couldn't remember the last time so many of his flock had turned out on the Sabbath. It had seemed a good idea at the time. Ask Jesus to come along, speak to the faithful. Jesus had agreed, would love to come and preach in his hometown. Problem was, no Jesus. He checked the time, knew he should stand, try to explain that Jesus had been delayed, but would be here soon.

Brian looked down at the disciples who were out in force. These were the people who'd given up their jobs and businesses to follow Jesus. All good men, but not steadfast adherents of the faith. Brian would have liked to be called as a disciple, couldn't understand why he hadn't and told himself it was because he was needed here. He sighed. It was time. He couldn't put if off any longer. He stood, waited for the low buzz of conversation to fade.

'Friends, welcome. It is good to see all of you here today. I didn't realise my preaching was held in such esteem.'

Laughter.

Brian milked it for a few seconds, endured some good-natured heckling, then continued, 'Ahh, if only that were so.' He paused, wondering how to break the news, when the outer door opened. Jesus and two companions entered and made their way to the front.

'Seriously, friends,' Brian continued, 'we are indeed honoured to have one of our own speak to us today. This man has been proclaimed by Baptiste as the promised Messiah. Perhaps our guest will be able to tell us more about that. Ladies and gentlemen, please welcome, Jesus.'

Brian was relieved when thunderous applause, whistles, greeted Jesus. A solemn air had descended at the mention of Baptiste, whose recent arrest had stirred the community. Brian didn't want it to overshadow the visit of Jesus.

Jesus stood at the lectern and waited. From his position on the front row, Peter watched with interest.

When it was quiet, Jesus took the offered scroll, unfurled it, and said, 'A reading from the prophet Isaiah.' He waited a second. '"The spirit of the Lord is on me, because he has anointed me to proclaim good news to the poor. He has sent me to proclaim freedom for the prisoners and recovery of sight for the blind, to set the oppressed free, to proclaim the year of the Lord's favour."'

Jesus stopped, rolled up the scroll, handed it to the attendant, paused, and looked at the congregation. All eyes were fixed on him, a few folk toward the back were muttering.

After what seemed an eternity, Jesus said, 'Today

this scripture is fulfilled in your hearing.'

Silence.

Not a good silence, though, Peter thought. Not going to ease into it then? This could get awkward. He glanced at the others. They looked at him, shrugged. Jesus must know what he's doing.

At the front, to one side of Jesus, Brian looked agitated. Peter knew full well the problem lay in Jesus declaring that the prophecy from Isaiah had been fulfilled. Trouble was he'd missed the final line, "And a day of vengeance for our God."

As far as the Jews were concerned, the prophecy couldn't be fulfilled without God having his vengeance on the enemies of his people.

Behind the disciples, the muttering grew louder. It rippled through the crowd, from the back to front, then back again. A Mexican wave of dissent. A few of the comments came to Peter. Funny sort o' Messiah. What about God's vengeance. Thought he'd be getting shut o' Saxons.

Jesus waited until the dissent had all but died away. 'I expect there are some among you who will quote this proverb to me, "Physician, heal yourself!" And you will tell me, do here in Whitby what you've been doing in the northern region.'

He paused for a second. 'I tell you the truth,' he continued, 'no prophet is accepted in his hometown. I assure you there were many widows in Eliyahu's time, when the sky was closed for more than three years and there was a severe famine throughout the land. Yet Eliyahu was not sent to any of them, but to a widow in Coventry in the kingdom of Mercia.'

Jesus paused while the tumult in the crowd grew

loud again. An old man behind Peter muttered to his companion, 'What's he say? What does he mean? Has he come to kick holy shit out o' Saxons?'

Peter wondered the same as he listened to the reply. 'Nay dad, he's a difficult bugger to understand, but it sounds to me as though he's telling us to expect the unexpected.'

'Isn't he Joseph's lad. Joseph the builder what fell off that roof?'

'That's right dad.'

'You can't expect a builder's lad to be a Messiah.' The old man stated. 'It's not right.'

A few people called for quiet. A voice shouted. 'Give the lad a chance.'

'And,' Jesus continued, 'there were lots in the kingdom with leprosy in the time of Elisha the prophet, yet not one of them was cleansed, just a man from Wessex.'

'What ya saying Jesus?' A voice called out. 'Are you here to help your own people or not?'

'He's bloody not, is he?' Somebody else shouted. 'He's here to help everybody else.'

'Bugger that, the Messiah should be helping the Jews.'

Peter looked round at the hostile crowd. These were people he knew, people who'd bought his fish, people he'd drunk with, and, he realised ruefully, some women whom he'd slept with. A few met his gaze, looked away, embarrassed. A slow hand clapping started, followed by a hissing sound, men and women alike showing their disapproval.

Peter turned at someone tugging his sleeve. It was Brian, looking worried. 'Perhaps now would be a good time to leave?' He suggested.

Peter nodded, blew air through his teeth. 'Aye, happen you're right.'

Jesus was still speaking, 'You want miracles? You've come here today expecting to see miracles. I'll give you miracles, not in here, though,' Jesus shook his head sorrowfully, pointed to the door, 'out there, that's where the miracles happen. Out there.'

The tumult increased. Jesus stepped away from the lectern, strode to the exit. The jostling crowd parted, let him through. Peter and the others scurried to keep up.

Outside, Matthew asked of nobody in particular, 'Is it always like this?'

Jesus and the disciples made it to the minibus unscathed. People scattered as Jude drove straight at them. The crowd, emboldened, enraged, began throwing half bricks, stones, anything they could lay hands on.

They left town with a hostile crowd chanting, out, out, out, and bricks bouncing off the side of the vehicle.

Jesus, lying back in a corner seat, seemed unperturbed at the fuss.

Back inside the MUFWOC, Brian gazed in awe at the floor, and wondered how on earth a man wearing shoes could leave a trail of sandy footprints.

SEVEN

TWO YEARS AGO.
THE TEMPLE, YORK, NORTHUMBRIA.

'When was this?' Caiaphas asked in a soft tone.

The man, a well-known local beggar, looked at him for a long moment, considered the question, wondering for a moment if there was anything in it for him. He saw the stony look on the high priest's face, decided not.

Caiaphas waited.

Shrug. 'A few days ago.'

'On the Sabbath?'

'Maybe.' The man twitched his shoulders again, grimaced.

'Tell me again what happened.'

The man sighed. 'I was lying by the pool at Sheep Gate. You know where...'

'Yes, yes.' Caiaphas interrupted. 'I know what happens there.' Everybody knew it was where the lame, the not so lame, the dossers, the dregs, laid around all day begging. 'Just tell me what the man said.'

'This man was walking past with his friends. Just an ordinary man he was, nothing special about him. He noticed me, stopped walking, and asked if I wanted to get well.' The beggar paused.

'And?' Caiaphas prompted.

'I said yes, of course I did. So the man said, "Get up. Pick up your mat and walk." It was amazing. Thirty-eight years I've been crippled. It was like a surge of electricity coursing through my body. And warm, I've never felt heat like it.'

'And then?' Caiaphas urged.

The beggar smiled. 'I got up and walked.'

'Just like that?' Caiaphas snapped his fingers.

The man agreed. It was that quick.

'And the mat. You picked up your mat?'

'Of course.'

'On the Sabbath?' Caiaphas queried. 'You know it's forbidden to do any work on the Sabbath.'

The beggar frowned. 'It's what he told me to do. The man. I thought if I didn't follow his exact instructions it might not work.'

'Do you have a name for this man?'

Hesitation. 'I don't want to get him into trouble.'

'It's not a question of blame,' Caiaphas assured the beggar. 'It's more re-education.'

'Well...'

'His name.' Caiaphas insisted. 'Then I would be prepared to forget your transgression.'

'Jesus.'

'On the Sabbath.' Caiaphas raged a short while later. 'At Passover. It's an outrage. He flits in and out of York, the Temple, as though he owns the place. He comes, he teaches, he heals, he goes. Him, his band of followers, they don't dress like Jews, they're all clean-shaven, scruffs the lot of them. He's making a mockery of us all.' He paused for a second to catch his breath.

O'Deamus nodded, could understand his anger. Passover, when Jews celebrated their liberation from

123

slavery in Egypt, was one of the most important festivals of the year. He wondered if he should speak, didn't get the chance.

'And what happened to that plan one of the Scribes had,' Caiaphas raged on. 'Get a whore to sleep with him, get it on camera, and flood the internet with it. What happened there?'

'The girl was riddled with demons. Jesus healed her, she became a follower.'

Caiaphas clicked his tongue. 'How is it this man always seems to thwart our plans, turn them to his own advantage?'

There was no answer to that, O'Deamus decided.

'Can we get another girl, try again?' Caiaphas asked.

O'Deamus shook his head. 'Jesus won't fall for that.'

'A boy then? Do his interests lie in that direction?'

'I don't think that's the way.'

'Well, what is? If he carries on like this, we'll have no control over the people at all.'

'I think we should watch and wait,' O'Deamus said. 'If he's not the Messiah, he'll trip up sooner or later.'

'And what if he is? The Messiah?'

O'Deamus shrugged. 'Then there's no power on earth can stop him.'

Caiaphas considered this. His worst fear. 'Where is he now, do we know?'

'Out in the countryside, the Dales.'

Caiaphas sighed. 'I don't suppose he can do much damage out there.'

✝

Near Horton in Ribblesdale, Northumbria.

John was nervous. Excited. He sensed in his spirit today's talk was going to be important and the many thousands who'd gathered in the Northumbrian Dales seemed to know it too. They were buzzing, the atmosphere electric. Same sort of atmosphere you sometimes got at a big football game. A night match, under floodlights. Leeds maybe, or one of the Manchester clubs. Or at the games in the Arena. But then, it was more like a music festival than a religious gathering. Gaily coloured tents stretched for miles. Flags of the kingdoms fluttered in the slight breeze, smoke from cooking fires and dope mixed, drifted. There was a carnival, party atmosphere.

Everywhere John looked, from his elevated position on the slope of Pen-Y-Ghent, groups of people gathered in the fields and the moorlands. Friends, strangers, mixed in together, chatting, animated, anticipating, waiting for Jesus to begin speaking. A Mexican wave started, rolling tide-like to the back of the crowd, cheering accompanied it, as it turned, swept back.

They had flocked from all parts of the kingdom, and not just Northumbria. People were here from all over the island. East Anglia, Mercia, Wessex, distant Cornwall, Scotland, Wales, all represented. The news of this gathering had gone viral and the people had responded.

The message was getting bigger, the ministry growing. Jesus though, was his usual, unassuming, affable self. He moved through the crowds, had time for everybody, a word, a prayer, a healing. He'd disappeared earlier, found a quiet place, and spent time with the Father. But now he was back, hugging the disciples, ready to make his entrance before the people, deliver his message. John hadn't a clue what it would be about. Didn't understand a lot of what Jesus said, just knew he was the way to salvation and eternal life.

It was time.

Jesus held up his hands. A silence spread, beginning at the front and rippling back to those who required binoculars to see him. It was amazing though, his words, without benefit of a sound system, could always be heard. John watched on the TV monitors as the camera zoomed in on his face.

Jesus waited for the silence, and then spoke, 'Blessed are those who have come to the end of themselves, for they will enter into His kingdom.'

Whistles, cheers, greeted this opening statement. John frowned. Why couldn't they just listen? Jesus smiled, continued. 'Blessed are those who mourn, are lonely and lost, for they will be comforted.'

Several shouts of, 'We love you Jesus.'

Jesus smiled. 'Bless you my child. I tell you the truth. There is a day coming when a greater understanding of love will be known.' He spread his arms wide. 'I love you all.' Wild cheers erupted. Jesus waited while the crowd settled, then continued. 'Blessed are the self-controlled and humble, for God will fulfil them with every good thing.'

John's nervousness evaporated. These were good powerful words. Jesus was on top form.

'Blessed are those,' Jesus paused, sipped from a

bottle of water, 'who passionately long for me and what is right in our land, for I will satisfy your souls.'

The crowd was silent before each statement.

'Blessed are those who show mercy through forgiveness, kindness and compassion, for they will receive mercy.'

Then, every statement was greeted with a cheer.

'Blessed are those who have a pure heart, for they will see God.'

Cheers.

Silence.

'Blessed are those who have been reconciled to God through me, and who take this message of peace to others, for they will be called children of God.'

Jesus paused again, took another drink. John sensed the statements were drawing to a close.

'Blessed are those who dare to live in righteousness and suffer persecution,' Jesus paused, 'for they will receive the kingdom of heaven.'

The crowd too, seemed to sense that this part was over. The cheering, whistling, hollering went on for many minutes. John looked round the others, exchanged glances, and shared smiles. He knew some disciples better than others. The first six called, Peter, Andrew, Jamie, Jim, Jude, and John himself had been augmented by other hand-picked followers, Matt, who used to be the pimp Levi, Tom, Phil, Nathan, Simon, and of course their treasurer, Judas.

There were scores of other followers, among them the former prostitute, Maggie. John glanced at her now. She was stood as usual with her friend, Poppy. Maggie gave him a shy smile before looking away.

Maggie thanked Jesus every day for the transformation in her life, knew she was blessed, knew she'd been touched by the son of the living God. Some other followers thought Jesus to be a good man, a great teacher, and philosopher. But she knew the truth. She'd been down in the pit of hell, her body, inhabited by seven demons. Addicted to Morph, reduced to selling herself in order to live. She smiled wryly at the thought of her dress slipping to the floor, inviting him to have her, his reaction, eyes fixed firmly on hers, telling her she was a beautiful woman. The way he'd hugged her in love, pure love, banished the voices, cured her addictions, and gave her new life. No mortal man could have achieved those things, not to mention all the other wonderful healings. The way he caused limbs to grow, gave life to the dead. God must be responsible for all those miraculous events.

She looked at him now, a warm glow flooded her body as she listened to him speak.

'You are the salt of the earth. But if the salt loses its saltiness, how can it be made salty again? It is no longer good for anything, except to be thrown out, trampled underfoot.'

'Salt is good precisely because it tastes different to other things, it improves what it's added to. In the same way you are going out into the world to make a difference. If you become like the world, you lose your value.'

The disciples looked at each other, out at the multitude hanging on Jesus' every word.

'You are the light of the world. A city on a hill can't be hidden. Neither do people hide a lamp under the table. Instead they leave it on, giving light to everyone in the house.'

This was so simple, so profound, Maggie realised, wondered why it hadn't been said before. Jesus glanced at her. She could almost read his mind, I haven't been before.

Jesus continued, 'In the same way, let your light shine before men, that they may see your good deeds and praise your Father in heaven. But take care. Good works should be seen for God's praise, not your own.'

Jesus paused, took a drink. The crowd was quiet, thoughtful, soaking in Jesus' words.

'Do not think that I have come to abolish the Law, or the Prophets. I haven't come to abolish them but to fulfil them. I am not talking here about individual laws, but the Law, the first five books of the ancient scripture. I tell you the truth, until heaven and earth disappear, not the smallest letter, not the least stroke of the pen will, by any means, disappear from the Law until everything is accomplished. Then, a new standard of righteousness will come into effect.'

✝

Matt lay back on the grass, eyes closed, for all the world asleep, but who could sleep through this? It was like Jesus was speaking a new language. The man was a genius, every word he spoke had to be weighed, considered. Did it mean this, did it mean that?

The way he'd approached him, bounding across the road, skipping through the traffic, Matt, thinking it was someone coming for him, reaching down, stretching for the pistol he kept under the seat. Jesus by the window, eyes locked on his, reading his soul, then, follow me.

Follow me. Two simple words. A choice to make. Follow, or stay in the old life. Time stood still, Jesus waiting, didn't matter how long. Traffic sped by, people moved past, lives continuing. Then Peter arrived. Look on his face. Priceless. Matt smiled, moved his hand, brushed a fly away. Tried telling himself he'd only said yes to annoy Peter, but knew that wasn't true. He'd said yes because he couldn't say no.

He tuned back into Jesus.

'In the Ten Commandments given to our greatest prophet, Moses, God said, "Do not murder, and anyone who murders will be subject to justice." People of the ancient faith, know this, they've been taught this, they know it to be a truth from the Father.' Jesus caught Matt's eye, smiled.

'But I say to you today, anyone who is angry with his brother, his fellow man, will be subject to divine judgement. Let me make it clear, you will be judged on your anger. If you have an urge to kill, or wish someone dead, you are a murderer in your heart, even if you don't carry out the act.'

'As you know, if you call your brother a foul name, you are answerable to the Sanhedrin, but anyone who says, you fool, will be in danger of the fires of hell.'

'Do not despise other people. If you are about to worship God and remember that your brother has something against you, leave straight away, go and be reconciled with your brother, then come back and offer your worship. Do not wait for your brother to take the first step, seize the initiative.'

'I tell you the truth, seek peace. That is the way of

true righteousness.'

Matt brushed his hand across his eyes, saw Peter looking. He smiled at his brother disciple, unashamed of his tears and glad of the second chance he'd been given.

✝

Peter had never felt better. Jesus coming along had transformed his life. He'd been dead and not known it. Jesus had restored him to life. His drinking was under control, the lust, the desire to have any woman, had been tamed. The effect Jesus had on people was amazing. Maggie, the former prostitute, was a follower now, her life changed for the better. Peter had felt uncomfortable when he realised the beautiful young woman who sought him out, hugged him, kissed his cheek, was the demon possessed, drug ridden addict, he'd once paid for sex. Maggie had been so gracious in modelling the behaviour Jesus spoke of.

Peter glanced at Matt. He seemed upset. He should speak to him, seek him out, apologise for his hostility. Okay, the guy used to be a pimp, a drug dealer, and for all Peter knew, a murderer, but Jesus had forgiven him, had called him, given him a fresh start. If he was good enough for Jesus he was good enough for Peter.

Jesus spoke again, 'You have been taught, do not commit adultery.' He paused. Let his words find a landing place. His eyes settled on Peter who inclined his head. 'I am telling you now that anyone who looks at another person lustfully has committed adultery in their heart. The old law says one thing, but true righteousness requires more, much more. If your eye causes you to sin, gouge it out, bin it. Likewise, if your hand causes you to sin, cut it off, bin it. It is better for you to lose a part of your body than for your whole body to end up in hell.'

Peter wondered how literally Jesus intended his message to be. He could envisage a long queue at the hospitals if folks took him at his word. He, for one, wouldn't have many body parts left.

'You might think I'm being extreme,' Jesus went on, 'to make a point. You're right, I am. Sin originates in thoughts and that's where the surgery is required.'

'It has been said, "Any man who divorces his wife must ensure she has a certificate of divorce." But I tell you, the man who divorces his wife for reasons other than unfaithfulness, causes her to become an adulteress, and any man who joins with the divorced woman commits adultery. God intended the joining of a man and woman to be a life-long commitment.'

Peter thought about his partner, Jayne, wondered where she was, what she was doing, knew it was his own behaviour that had driven her away. He missed her but doubted they could ever be reconciled.

†

'Again, you know it was said to the people in ancient times, "do not break your promise, but keep any promises you make to the Lord." But I'm telling you all today do not swear at all either by heaven, for it is God's throne. Or by the earth, for it is His footstool, or by York for it is the city of the great king. Just let your 'yes' be 'yes' and your 'no' be 'no'.' Nathan suppressed a smile, most of the crims he knew, their 'yes' was 'no'. Their 'no' was 'yes'. Everything else was 'no comment.' Far as his bosses were concerned, he was a crim himself now. He'd packed in his job, gone over to the dark side. It was the best thing he'd ever done. Keep it simple. Keep it honest. He loved it. Everything was simple and straightforward with Jesus, in theory anyway, the practice was challenging at times.

Nathan had waited a long time for Jesus to approach him since their first meeting on the beach at Whitby. He'd been content to follow along at a distance, on the periphery, was surprised one day when Jesus sought him out, said those words, follow me. Nathan agreed on the spot, handed in his notice, and became a disciple.

He'd often thought about telling Jesus about his time with the Polizei, but hadn't, on the basis that he'd know anyway. He'd heard Jesus speak many times, but this was different. This was setting a new standard, raising the bar.

'You have heard it said, "An eye for an eye, and a tooth for a tooth." But I tell you now, if someone strikes you on the right cheek, turn, offer him the left. If someone takes your coat, offer him your shirt. Do not resist an evil person.' Jesus paused, wiped his brow, 'my point is, do not take revenge. Respond in peace. Do not try to hurt others.'

†

Phil had written many songs about Jesus, wasn't often seen without his guitar in hand, but now it was laid aside on the grass. He propped himself up on one elbow, let Jesus' words soak in.

'Again, you will have heard it said, "Love your neighbour and hate your enemy." But I tell you, love your enemies and pray for those who persecute you. If you love those who love you, what reward will you get? Even the pagans do that. And, if you greet just your brothers, what are you doing more than others? Your love for others is to be complete, to extend to all people, at all times. I tell you the truth, be perfect, as your heavenly Father is perfect.'

'You've seen them. We've all seen them. People doing religion. They make sure they're seen doing good and they receive the admiration of many, but that is all they'll receive. Their good works are not done to serve God, but to serve themselves.'

'So, be careful not to do your acts of righteousness before men, to be seen by them. If you do, you will have no reward from your Father in heaven. So, when you give to the needy, do not announce it on Twitter, or broadcast it all over Facebook. Rather, when you give to the poor, do not let your left hand know what your right hand is doing, so that your giving may be in secret. Then, your Father, who sees what is done in secret, will reward you.'

'The focus should be on attitude, not appearance.'

'Again, when you pray, do not be like the hypocrites, who love to be seen praying in the synagogues and the Temple. I tell you the truth. They have received their reward in full. When you pray, go into your room, close the door, and pray to your Father who is unseen. And when you pray, don't babble like pagans, who think the more they say, the more they'll be heard. Your Father knows what you need before you ask him.'

'This, then, is how you should pray,

Our Father in heaven. Holy is your name. Let your kingdom come. Let your will be done on earth as it is in heaven. Give us today, our daily bread and forgive us our debts as we have forgiven our debtors. Lead us not into temptation. But deliver us from the evil one.'

Phil picked up his guitar, strummed a chord. Such beautiful words. He was sure he could set them to music.

EIGHT

Jesus, his face wreathed in sweat, came off stage to tumultuous applause. The message had been given and received. Peter handed Jesus a towel. 'That was great, Boss. Fantastic.'

'Jesus?'

Peter groaned. Not Brotherton again.

Jesus wiped his hands and face. 'Yes, Brotherton?'

'Why do you heal on the Sabbath?' The Pharisee asked. 'You must know it's forbidden.'

'My Father is always at work on this day and so am I.' Jesus replied, taking the drink Peter offered.

'You make yourself equal with God?'

'I tell you the truth. The Son can do nothing by himself. He just does what he sees the Father doing. Whatever the Father does, the Son does as well. The Father loves the Son and shows him all he does. And he will show him greater works than these and you will be amazed. For just as the Father raised the dead and gave them life, the Son also gives life to those whom He pleases.' Jesus paused, took a long drink of water.

'In fact, the Father judges no one, but has entrusted all judgment to the Son, so that all may honour the Son just as they honour the Father. Whoever does not honour the Son does not honour the Father, who sent Him.'

Go Jesus, Peter thought, looking on an interested

spectator. He loved it when the Pharisees or other zealots challenged Jesus.

'I tell you the truth,' Jesus continued, 'whoever hears my word and believes in him who sent me, has eternal life and will not be judged but has crossed over from death to life. Again, I tell you the truth, a time is coming and has now come when the dead will hear the voice of the Son of God and those who hear will live. For as the Father has life in himself, so he has granted the Son also to have life in himself. And he has given him authority to judge because he is the Son of Man.'

Do not be amazed at this, for a time is coming when all who are in their graves will hear his voice and come out. Those who have done what is good will rise to live, and those who have done what is evil will rise to be condemned. By myself, I can do nothing. I judge as I hear, and my judgment is just, for I seek not to please myself but him who sent me.'

Brotherton held up his hand. 'So, you're saying that you're the son of God?'

Jesus smiled. 'If I testify about myself, my testimony is not true. But there is another who testifies in my favour, and I know that his testimony about me is true.'

'Baptiste?' Brotherton sneered.

Jesus shrugged. 'You have asked Baptiste and he has testified to the truth. Not that I accept human testimony. But I mention it that you may be saved. Baptiste was a lamp that shone and gave light, and you chose for a time to enjoy his light.'

'Baptiste has been arrested. He's rotting in jail.'

'I have testimony weightier than that of Baptiste.' Jesus replied. 'For the works that the Father has given me to finish. The very works that I am doing testify that the Father has sent me. And the Father has himself testified concerning me. You have never heard his voice nor seen his form, nor does his word dwell in you, for you do not believe the one he sent. You study the Scriptures because you think that in them you have eternal life. These are the very Scriptures that testify about me, yet you refuse to come to me to have life.'

'What should I do? Bend my knee, fall on my face?' Brotherton mocked.

Jesus shook his head. 'I don't accept glory from human beings, but I know you. I know that you don't have the love of God in your heart. I have come in my Father's name, and you don't accept me. But if someone else comes in his own name, you will accept him. How can you believe since you accept glory from one another, but do not seek the glory that comes from the one God?'

Brotherton stared at Jesus for a moment, looked about to speak, but then turned, walked away.

'Boss?'

'Yes Peter?'

'Don't you get fed up with the Pharisees challenging you all the time?'

'This is just transient, Peter. Very soon the old order will be swept away.'

✝

Early evening at the campsite, the sun dipping towards the horizon, slight chill in the air as another glorious day played itself out. Thin wisps of smoke drifted from the fire. Phil was strumming his guitar, setting the words of what had become known as the Lord's Prayer to music. It was a happy, calm, peaceful atmosphere. It'd been a good three days Jamie reflected as he made tea, poured it into plastic mugs.

Most of the visitors to the gathering had left and the surprise was they'd taken all their rubbish with them. The disciples would strike camp tomorrow, move on. The rumble of a diesel engine as a local farmer, dog hanging out of the window, drove past in his battered Land Rover. He pipped his horn, waved. The disciples waved back languidly. Jamie handed out the tea and the talk turned to the Sermon on the Mount, as Tom, with his eye for a headline, had dubbed it.

'Not much of a mountain.' Peter declared he'd seen higher waves in the North Sea. The others had laughed, but it was good-natured. Tom didn't care, told them first titles often stuck. Pen-Y-Ghent might not be much of a mountain, but according to Wikipedia, it was one, and that was good enough for Tom.

'Where's the Boss?' Jamie asked.

'Out for dinner with a local Pharisee.' Andrew told him.

'I don't trust them an inch.' John said. 'I hope he knows what he's doing.'

'He must have a good reason.' Peter replied.

There was silence for a few moments, then Judas, the group's treasurer, said, 'I wonder what tomorrow will bring?'

Quick as a flash, Andrew responded. 'Don't worry what tomorrow will bring. Each day has enough trouble of its own.'

The others laughed. It was their new favourite

game. Quoting Jesus' words at each other.

'What shall we eat?' From John.

'What shall we drink?' Jim continued.

'The world runs after these things, but your heavenly father knows what you need.' Peter finished.

After a while, Jude said. 'Do not store up for yourselves treasure on earth.'

'Where moth and rust destroy,' From Simon.

'Where thieves break in and steal.' Phil said.

'But store up for yourselves treasure in heaven, where moth and rust do not destroy, where thieves do not break in.' Nathan completed.

'There are no thieves in heaven.' Matt declared.

Away to one side, Maggie and Poppy sat together. 'You fancy him, don't you?' Poppy said.

Maggie could feel her face burn red. 'What makes you say that?'

Poppy laughed. 'It's so obvious. You follow him round like a puppy.'

'No, I don't.' Maggie protested.

'Yes you do and it's not just because he rid you of those voices, cured your addictions. You love him, don't you?'

Maggie thought for a moment. Poppy was voicing what she knew anyway. 'Yes.' She admitted.

'Do something about it then. Let him know.'

'I can't.'

Poppy shrugged. 'You could. He's just a man, and you've had plenty of them.'

'Yes, he is.' Maggie replied, 'but then he isn't. He's more, much more.'

'He's very attractive.' Poppy said, with a wicked grin. 'If you're not going to make a move, maybe I will.'

'Don't Poppy. Please don't.'

Maggie hadn't told Poppy about her unsuccessful attempt to seduce Jesus, knew she should warn the girl not to risk making a fool of herself. But, would she? Jesus would let her down in such a way it wouldn't feel like a rejection.

The women fell silent, listened to the men talking. Jim was talking about the hypocrisy of making a fuss about a speck of sawdust in somebody else's eye while ignoring the plank in his own.

'Have you noticed how he uses his former trade as a basis for a lot of what he says?' Jude said.

'Yeah,' Jim laughed. 'That story about the wise and foolish builders. I've known a few of them.'

'Did Jesus used to be a builder?' Poppy asked.

'Yeah,' Jim looked across at the two women. 'Well, a chippie.'

'What's a chippie?'

'A carpenter, someone who works with wood. Have you ever seen his hands, all rough and calloused they are?'

'The poor love.' Poppy said. 'He needs a good manicure.'

Laughter erupted. 'You won't find many blokes going for a manicure, love.' Jim said.

'No?' Poppy replied with an innocent smile. 'You won't find many in nappies either, but I've known a few who've done it.

†

Skipton, Northumbria.

It had been a successful evening Simon decided. As a prominent Pharisee, he had a position to uphold in the community and getting Jesus to his dinner table wouldn't have done him any harm at all. He was relieved not to have been tripped up by any of the innocuous questions Jesus was known to ask from time to time. The main drawback, as far as he could tell, was the woman, Rebecca. She was of rough, common stock, who, rumour had it, was guilty of the most appalling behaviour. He was grateful she hadn't disgraced herself, or shown him up, and as the women were about to withdraw there was little likelihood that she would do so now. His wife must have invited her. Simon decided he must talk to her about her choice of guest.

His wife stood now and invited the women to join her. They began to drift out, but Rebecca seated herself at the side of Jesus, whispered in his ear. Jesus inclined his head, smiled. Simon watched in horror as Rebecca opened her bag, got out a nail file, began filing Jesus' nails. His wife, stood in the doorway, met his eye and shrugged.

Jesus reclined in his seat, watched as Rebecca shaped his nails, rubbed oil in his hands. Simon was aware that all his guests were watching. The women who'd left now crowded the doorway, watching the little scene out-play itself.

Amazed at the woman's audacity, Simon noticed tears trickle down her face, onto her hands, onto Jesus' hands. He seemed to be enjoying what was happening, but Simon was disappointed with Jesus. As a prophet, he must know the woman's reputation.

It seemed a good idea at the time when asked to host a dinner party of local worthy people with Jesus as the guest of honour. Now, it was beginning to seem like a big mistake.

'Simon, I have something to ask you.' Jesus said.

Simon, aware of all eyes on him, gritted his teeth, smiled. 'Yes?'

'Two people owed money to a payday moneylender.' Jesus said, 'One owed five hundred Euros, the other, fifty. Neither had the means to pay,' Jesus shrugged, gave Rebecca his other hand, 'the debts of both were written off. Which of them, do you think would be more grateful?'

Simon knew he'd either get it wrong and be humiliated or if he got it right, there would be a sting in the tail. It was a stupid question anyway. No self-respecting moneylender would ever cancel debts like that. Both debtors would end up in intensive care. But still, he doubted that was the answer Jesus expected.

'I suppose the one who had the bigger debt.' Simon replied, his eyes flicking to Rebecca, who was still massaging Jesus' hands.

Jesus smiled. 'Your judgement is correct.'

Simon felt absurdly pleased for a few seconds.

'I came into your home tonight, Simon,' Jesus continued, 'you weren't there to greet me, but you see this woman? She took my jacket, brushed it down, and hung it up. You didn't offer me a drink, yet she brought me one. When you came into the room, you didn't even shake my hand, whereas she filed my nails, wept tears for me, rubbed them in my hands along with a lotion.'

Simon blushed deep red. His humiliation was total. This would be round the neighbourhood in hours.

'I tell you,' Jesus went on, 'her many sins have been forgiven as her great love has shown.' He smiled at Rebecca, told her, 'Your sins are forgiven.'

Simon gave a tight smile. It was true then, he forgave sins.

'I tell you Simon, whoever has been forgiven little loves little.' Jesus turned to the room in general. 'The higher someone thinks of themselves, the less they will be able to love others, because they'll always be looking down on them, measuring them by their own standards. To grow in love and graciousness towards others, you need first to grow in your love for God. Grace can't be given until it has first been received.'

Silence greeted Jesus' words. Unperturbed, he turned to Rebecca. 'Go in peace, Rebecca,' he told her, 'your faith has saved you.'

†

Huddersfield, Northumbria.

Beaumont yawned, rubbed his eyes, looked out of the upper window watched some kids playing on scrubland.

Life had changed beyond all recognition. He'd left the school for good in July and wasn't working now. Mercer, the fat sweaty bastard of a Head Teacher had called him into the office a week before the end of term, told him not to bother coming back in September.

That had been bad enough, but when Beaumont

found out a young Saxon teacher, newly qualified at that, would be taking his place, he'd stormed into Mercer's office, told him what he thought of him, the Saxons and their shitty Union. Mercer hadn't seemed unduly perturbed. He'd listened in silence, then, when Beaumont ran out of steam, had advised him to take care about repeating the things he'd said. Had also gone on to say, Beaumont had blown any chance of a reference.

Beaumont should have heeded the warning he'd been given at their earlier meeting and gone of his own volition. Left high and dry, he had no chance of getting a teaching post. He supposed he could have found work in a menial capacity. Waiting on tables, stacking shelves, shovelling shit. He knew people had to do those sorts of jobs, but he was better than that.

When he'd told Bocus what had happened, the immediate offer to move in with him had been accepted. Beaumont intending it to be a temporary arrangement, while he got his act together. After a few months, an opportunity had arisen, through one of Bocus' shady resistance contacts. They were looking for someone to be the custodian of a safe house, look after men and woman, who, for whatever reason, needed to lay low.

Beaumont had jumped at the chance as he and Bocus were beginning to grate on each other. It gave Beaumont a roof, food, and a small income. It was boring, unexciting work for the most part, but relatively safe. The first time his contact, Slater, arrived with a brown envelope full of Euros, Beaumont had asked where the money came from. Slater gave him an old-fashioned look, told him tersely, the bank. The penny dropped, he was no longer a respectable teacher. He was a receiver of stolen money, a criminal. One of the kids, perhaps sensing he was being watched, looked up, stared at the house. Beaumont ducked behind the curtain, sweat breaking out on his brow. Had he been seen? Not that it mattered. He counted to thirty, chanced a peek. The kid was back playing with his mates.

Beaumont dozed fitfully on his bed for a while, and then went downstairs seeking company. Henderson, the only resident, was in the kitchen drinking from a can of lager. He popped the top on a fresh can, handed it to Beaumont who took it, tilted his head back, drained half the can in one go, then belched. 'Pardon me.'

Henderson laughed.

'What?'

'You're so polite.'

Beaumont frowned, what if he was, he couldn't help it.

'Cards?' Henderson suggested.

Beaumont sighed. Another afternoon of cards and lager beckoned. Henderson shuffled, dealt for three-card brag. The cards were dealt, hands played, the score kept. Beaumont, bored after five minutes, studied Henderson. A thin, small man, straggly air, but a quiet inoffensive manner. He held his cards close, flicking a look every few seconds, alternatively whooping with delight, or groaning with despair, telling Beaumont he was a right lucky sod. Henderson wasn't his real name, everybody on the run used false names. Beaumont was Carter.

Beaumont wondered what Henderson had done.

He never seemed jumpy or bothered if the doorbell rang. Not like others who passed through from time to time. First creak of the gate, they'd be up, out the back door and away.

'What's the point?' Henderson used to say. 'If your number's up, it's up. Polizei come knocking, put your hands up, and don't give them a reason to shoot.'

Beaumont got bored with cards after a while, told Henderson who shrugged. 'Dommies then, fives and threes?'

Beaumont nodded. He would have preferred chess, but Henderson found it too complicated.

Henderson packed the cards away, got the dominoes. It was a quiet, still afternoon. A fly buzzed aimlessly round their heads, Beaumont waved his hands every so often. Henderson though, didn't seem bothered by it.

The phone call when it came was unexpected, a moment of excitement.

Beaumont answered. 'Yeah.'

'Get out now.' The voice said. 'You've got five minutes. The Polizei are coming.' The line went dead.

Beaumont panicked, jumped up, the table toppled, dominoes scattering everywhere. He told Henderson what he'd just heard.

Henderson paused from picking up the dominoes. 'Who was it?'

'Don't know.'

'Man, woman?'

'Man.'

'Do you believe it?'

'How do I know?'

'Gut reaction, Carter. Do you believe it?'

'Yes.' He did. He believed the Polizei were coming to get him.

'Then go, now.'

In his panic, Beaumont ran to the front door, flung it open, and looked out. Everything looked the same, no snatch squad, no hovering drone, no dogs, just normality.

'Not that way dickhead.' Henderson hissed. 'Go out the back, over the fence, keep watch from the bushes.'

At the door, Beaumont paused. 'What will you do?'

'Open the door. Invite them in for tea and cake. Whaddaya think. Now, go.'

Beaumont scrambled over the fence, knew he should have stayed, bluffed it out. If anything, it should be Henderson panicking. He was the fugitive in hiding. Beaumont was the innocent tenant of a rented property.

He landed with a thud, his left knee gave way, the bones jarring, protesting. Beaumont scrambled to his feet, ignored the pain and hurried to the bushes. He prayed under his breath that nobody would notice as he limped his way to cover. The kids had all disappeared and apart from the faint faraway sound of sirens, it was quiet.

Reaching the bushes, he threw himself down, burrowed his way as deep as he could manage. He lay still, adrenaline pumping, his breathing laboured. The sirens became louder, stopped. Beaumont could hear sounds of activity, shouted commands. Two Polizei officers in black snatch squad uniforms appeared and taking up position by the back fence, waited. A few minutes later, a muffled shout came from the back garden of the safe house. The officers disappeared, and then a few minutes later were back, dragging Henderson between them. They forced him to his knees, not far from where Beaumont was hiding. A Polizei officer touched the barrel of the shotgun against the back of Henderson's neck.

The noise was deafening.

Beaumont watched in horror as Henderson sprawled full length, his head vanishing in a cloud of bloody mist. The silence broken by the sound of someone sobbing. One of the officers spun round, marched to the bushes, and pointed the weapon, called, 'Come out.' He hefted the pump action. 'Now.'

A small boy, seven, eight years old, emerged a few metres from Beaumont's own position. The boy stood sobbing, body shaking. Beaumont noticed a wet patch appear on the front of his trousers.

The officer lowered his weapon. 'Just you?'

The boy nodded.

'What's your name?'

'Alex.' The boy whispered.

'Okay, Alex.' The Polizei officer said, pacing his words. 'I want you to go home now, do you understand?'

The boy nodded again.

'Off you go then.'

The boy started backing away.

'Alex?' The boy stopped. Beaumont could see the terror on his face. 'Not a word, okay?' The officer said.

Alex nodded.

'Otherwise.' The officer the man made a gun shape with his hand pointed at Alex. 'BANG.'

Alex turned, fled, his legs pumping.

Beaumont watched as the Polizei stood over

Henderson's body. One of them radioed for a clean-up squad. The suspect had been shot whilst attempting to escape. Beaumont burned with righteous indignation as he listened to the lies, the laughter. Flies were already settling on Henderson's headless corpse when the Polizei left a short while later.

In the bushes Beaumont vomited, then realised as he gulped air down his burning throat that he too had wet himself.

✝

STATE SECURITY HQ, YORK, NORTHUMBRIA.

Swanger sipped her coffee, smoked a cigarette as she skimmed the article in the Northumbrian Times colour supplement.

SERMON ON THE MOUNT.

On the gentle slopes of Pen-Y-Ghent, a minor mountain in the Northumbrian Dales, near the small village of Horton in Ribblesdale, thousands of people gathered at a three-day festival to see the renowned prophet, Jesus. Over the course of the long weekend, many of those gathered were healed of their afflictions as Jesus moved among the people, blessing them, and forgiving their sins to the chagrin of the Pharisees, who insist that only God has the power to forgive sin.

The Pharisees are divided by Jesus. Some accept him as a genuine man of God, a great teacher of the law whilst others take the opposite view, accusing him of being sent by the devil. On one occasion over the three-day event Jesus cast out a demon from a man and was accused of having an impure spirit within him.

The prophet used his favoured device of a parable to respond, asking, 'How can Satan cast out Satan? If a kingdom is divided against itself, that kingdom can't stand. If a house is divided against itself, that house can't stand. So, if Satan opposes himself and is divided, he can't stand, and his end has come. Nobody can enter a strong man's house without first restraining him. I tell you the truth, all sins will be forgiven and every slander they speak, but whoever blasphemes against the Holy Spirit will never be forgiven.'

Many commentators believe this reference to the Holy Spirit is Jesus' way of acknowledging that he is the son of God. The long-awaited Messiah.

Another of the Pharisees complaints is that Jesus and his followers work on the Sabbath, which is forbidden to those adherents of the ancient faith. It is the practice of Jesus and his disciples to camp in the open fields, to cook over wood fires, and share their food among those in need. One particular Pharisee took exception to this, telling Jesus that cooking on the Sabbath was unlawful.

Jesus responded with refreshing candour. 'Haven't you read what David (an ancient king of the Jews) did when he and his companions were hungry? They entered the house of God, and ate the consecrated bread, which was illegal. If you knew what these words mean, "I desire mercy, not sacrifice" you would not condemn the innocent. The Son of Man is Lord of the Sabbath.'

There was more in a similar vein, but Swanger put the paper aside, drained her cold coffee. Lighting another smoke, she considered the article. She had no doubt the reporting was accurate enough, but it was all about the difficulties with the Pharisees, it didn't get to the essence of Jesus the man.

Swanger thought about Jesus a lot. He had a good gig going. This Son of God, Messiah thing, was a masterstroke. The healings, exorcisms, all looked good, all designed to trick the gullible. Handsome too, charismatic, Swanger reflected. But what was his angle? What was in it for Jesus?

†

LEEDS, NORTHUMBRIA.

The tapping on the door was so quiet Bocus thought for a second that he'd imagined it. He muted the sound on the TV, strained to listen. The three taps came again. Still quiet, but somebody was definitely at the door. The back door. Nobody came round the back. They came to the front door, rang the bell.

Instant, immediate thought, Polizei.

Bocus jumped up, his heartbeat moving through the gears into overdrive. Would the Polizei knock on the door, or come storming through? He thought about slipping out the front. No point, they'd have both doors covered.

There was no way out, he was trapped, was going to die.

He turned the lights out, stood in the dark, waited.

Tap. Tap. Tap.

It couldn't be the Polizei. They wouldn't keep knocking; they'd have been in by now, seconds after the stun grenades. If it was the Polizei he'd either be dead already or on the way to State Security HQ. Who then?

Who would come knocking on his back door gone ten on a Sunday evening? Those people he spied on in the woods. The earth worshippers who sacrificed that child. No, not them. That was months ago.

Bocus flung the door open, stepped back as a dishevelled figure pushed past, and closed the door. 'You took your sodding' time.'

It took Bocus a few wild seconds to recognise him. Beaumont looked old, haggard, worn out. His face was filthy, his clothes muddy, torn, arms scratched, the sole of one shoe flapped as he walked.

Bocus was shocked. 'What on earth has happened to you?'

'You don't know? You haven't heard?' Beaumont asked, surprised.

Bocus shook his head. 'No. Nothing. What's happened? I've heard nothing of you, or what you've been doing since I introduced you to my contact.'

Beaumont sighed. 'You got any grub? I'm starving.'

The story came out haltingly as Beaumont drank a pot of hot sweet tea. Bocus cooked eggs and bacon, listened as Beaumont told him about the safe house, the warning phone call, the raid, Henderson led outside, the summary execution. Leeds wasn't far from Huddersfield, thirty kilometres by road, but still far enough to walk on an empty belly, in fear of being captured.

Bocus placed the food on the table, watched as Beaumont wolfed it down. He made another pot of tea, poured them both a mug. Beaumont nursed his in grimy hands, looked at Bocus. 'You didn't know where I was. The safe house.'

'No.' Bocus sipped his tea, 'It's all done on a need to know basis. If you don't need to know, you don't get told. The less you know, the less you can tell.'

Beaumont sighed. 'Nice theory. In practice, the less you know, the more they torture you.'

'That didn't happen to you. You got away.' Bocus reminded him.

'Unlike Henderson, poor sod. Did you know him?'

Bocus frowned, the name meant nothing. 'We change names that often, I don't know who I am half the time.'

'Why would they do that? They brought him to the back of the house, blew him away.' Beaumont fell silent, remembering. 'His head just disappeared.'

'Because they can.' Bocus replied vehemently. 'That's why we're involved. That's why we're doing what we do.'

'I'm not sure I want to be involved anymore.' Beaumont said. 'I'm a history teacher, not a terrorist.'

Bocus snorted. 'You were a history teacher, now you're fighting for the freedom of the land you love.' He was silent for a moment. 'There's no escape. You know too much.'

'I don't know anything.'

'Like you said, who's gonna believe that?'

'That's what scares me.' Beaumont said.

They talked for a while longer, and then Bocus ran a hot bath, left Beaumont to get as clean as he could. He sorted some pyjamas, an old dressing gown, and made up the spare bed.

Once Beaumont was asleep, he stepped out into the garden, smoked a cigarette, and wondered what to do next.

NINE

STATE SECURITY HQ YORK, NORTHUMBRIA.

Heathersedge pushed a folder across the desk. 'What do you make of that?'

Swanger skimmed through the report of an operation to arrest a terror suspect. Should have been a routine job for the Ninjas. Something had gone wrong though, and the target, Henderson, had been shot while resisting arrest. Apparently, he was being led outside to the unit vehicle when he'd made a dash for it - with handcuffs on. Swanger raised an eyebrow. Whoever wrote this rubbish should be writing fiction.

She finished reading, laid the folder down. It was a classic of evasion and obfuscation and she didn't believe a word of it.

'Well?' Heathersedge demanded.

Swanger shrugged. 'It happens.'

Heathersedge snorted in disbelief. 'It shouldn't happen.' He picked up a pen, tapped it on the desk. 'Intel said there were two men in the house, Henderson, and another, name of Carter.'

'And he's gone to ground.' Swanger stated the obvious.

'Correct.'

'He'll be picked up sooner or later.' Swanger told

her boss, 'Most of these agitators, although cunning, are basically stupid.'

'I'm not so sure,' Heathersedge frowned, 'they're getting a lot better organised, the Four Kingdoms United lot, in particular.'

Swanger thought Heathersedge was making too much of it, but then, she didn't have the bigger picture.

'I want you on this,' Heathersedge continued, 'drop everything else you're working on.' He pushed the file towards Swanger. 'I want this Carter found and brought in alive. Okay?'

In her office twenty minutes later, Swanger lit a cigarette, thought about speaking with the Ninja team who'd fouled up, but they'd been withdrawn from front line duties and were now undergoing refresher training in Berlin.

Despite Heathersedge's gloom, Swanger didn't see that FKU were a big threat. Okay, so a few bombs had exploded in various places. Water facilities, railway yards. In remote places with poor security. Nobody had been killed or hurt. A minor irritation, nothing more. Still, Heathersedge wanted action, so that's what Swanger would give him and knew where to start.

Simon the Zealot.

Swanger stubbed out her cigarette, pulled the file on the twelve disciples, located the info on Simon, read,

Simon aka The Zealot. Age 25, dark hair, blue eyes. Hot head, easy to provoke. Quick to lose temper. Whisky drinker. Married to Samantha - see separate file - but known to have numerous concurrent heterosexual relationships outside of marriage. No children. Attractive to women, knows it, flirtatious, attention seeker. Stubborn bordering on arrogant. Self-employed mobile mechanic. Tenacious when faced with problems. Strongly suspected of being linked with FKU in an unknown capacity.

Swanger looked at the attached photo. It had been taken from a distance with a telephoto lens. He had dark olive skin, curly black hair. He was wearing a black leather jacket and Swanger could see how the man would appeal to women.

She put the file to one side, leaned back in her chair, smiled. Simon the Zealot might have seen the light, might have renounced his former ways, might even be a faithful husband to Samantha, but he had information that Swanger needed, and Swanger was going to get it.

✝

WHITBY, NORTHUMBRIA.

After Jesus had spoken to the faithful, a crowd gathered round him, wanting to talk, be healed, or just shake his hand. Jesus had a warm word for everyone. At one point during this session with people all around and hemmed in close, he spun round. 'Who touched me?'

Peter frowned, 'There's people all around you, Boss. It's hard not to be touched in this crowd.'

'No, Peter. This was a deliberate action. I felt power draining from me.'

'I'm sorry, Lord.' A woman stepped from the crowd. 'I meant no harm.' She was shaking, close to tears. 'I've been suffering with prolonged menstrual bleeding for twelve years which the doctors can't cure. I didn't want to bother you and thought if I just touched your shoulder I might be healed.'

Jesus smiled. 'I knew it. How do you feel?'

'I feel better, Lord.' The woman replied, 'the moment I touched you, I sensed a change in my body.'

'Go in peace, sister,' Jesus told her. 'Your faith has healed you. You are freed from your suffering.'

Later, at the end of the evening, Peter waited by the door. The meeting in the sports centre hall had been a great success. Scores of local people had turned out to welcome Jesus home. They were convinced Jesus was the Messiah and were proclaiming him as such. Peter screwed his eyes tight, yawned. He was knackered, needed his bed. It had been a hectic few weeks. The trip to the Dales, followed by a slow journey back through numerous towns and villages had worn him out. It wouldn't be long before they could get off. The lads were packing away, stacking chairs, sweeping the floor. Slumped against the wall, rattling the keys, he listened as some of Baptiste's followers questioned Jesus.

'How is it that we and the Pharisees fast often, but your disciples don't fast?' One of them asked.

Peter listened in fascination to Jesus' reply, 'How can the guests of the bridegroom mourn while he is with them? The time will come when the bridegroom will be taken from them. Then they will fast.'

Peter looked at the man, could see he was struggling, and wanted to call across, don't worry mate, take your time, you'll get it sooner or later. Although the meeting was over a few people remained. The ubiquitous Pharisees, led by Brotherton, who dogged their path round the kingdom.

'Is this where Jesus is healing people?' A blind man was at the door, complete with white stick and a black Labrador.

'The meeting's over, mate.' Peter said. 'Come back next time.'

'If I could just have a word with Jesus.' The man pleaded.

Peter sighed. They'd never get home at this rate. 'I'll see what I can do, come with me.'

Jesus listened as Peter explained. He looked at the blind man, who said, 'Lord, have mercy on me.'

'What do you want me to do for you?' Jesus asked.

'Lord, I want to see.' The man replied, a catch in his voice.

Jesus reached out, touched the man's eyes. The man blinked in surprise, opened his eyes, and closed them against the light. When he opened them again, tears trickled down his cheek. 'I can see.' He sniffed, and then caught sight of a vase of flowers. 'So that's what they look like. I've loved the scent all my life and now I can see how beautiful they are. Lord, I am so grateful to you.'

After Jesus had told the man to go in peace, John sat praying with him for a while.

Peter ushered the last of the stragglers through the door, was about to lock it, when a distraught man rushed in asking for Jesus. Peter recognised him as one of the elders of the synagogue. The man knelt at Jesus' feet. 'My daughter has just died.' He said. 'If you come and lay hands on her I'm sure she will live.'

'Don't be afraid,' Jesus responded. 'Just believe.'

At the man's house a crowd of relatives had

gathered, were comforting the girl's mother. The woman was bereft, weeping and wailing.

Jesus asked to see the girl.

'You're too late mate,' a man told him, 'she's dead.'

Jesus shook his head. 'Not dead. Sleeping.'

People looked at him in disbelief.

The man shrugged. 'I know dead when I see it, mate.'

'Show me the girl.' Jesus demanded.

The distraught father led Jesus upstairs and left him with the dead girl.

Five minutes later Jesus appeared in the main room. He was leading the bewildered girl by the hand. The stunned silence lasted a few seconds, but was then broken by hooting and hollering. Her father hugged her, and asked what had happened.

Blinking through her tears, the girl replied, 'He just told me to get up.'

Unnoticed, Jesus and Peter slipped out into the night.

✝

NORTHUMBRIAN MOORLAND OUTSIDE WHITBY.

Clear of the town, on the top moorland, heading west, Peter closed his eyes, snuggled into the corner of the seat, the recent trip to Whitby uppermost in his thoughts. A lot of goodwill had been generated, but some people, in particular, the Pharisees and Temple priests would never get it. Result, they'd been run out of town again, were now en-route to the opposite side of the kingdom. Blackpool of all places.

Again and again, Jesus had been challenged by the Pharisees dealing with all their objections and trick questions with ease. The doubts though, had trickled down to the ordinary people. Those who'd known Jesus as a boy, as a teenager, as a local carpenter in the family business.

Peter could see them now, their voices in his head,

Who does he think he is? A thin ferret faced woman.

Who gave him this wisdom? A fishmonger, known as the octopus among his female customers.

What are these miracles he's performed? Chain smoking local doctor.

Isn't that Mary's son. The carpenter?

He ought to stick to what he knows.

Jesus had told them straight, 'A prophet will never be honoured in his own town, among his relatives, even in his own home.'

His family proved him right as well. His mother, Mary, turning up with his sisters, various cousins trailing along in their wake, calling for him to come home, to give it up, find a wife, have a family. Following him round from meeting to meeting, they'd even threatened to have him sectioned at one point. Peter grunted, snuggled further down, and lulled by the steady swish of the tyres on the tarmac.

The Boss had put them in their place, though. At one gathering, someone had called out, telling Jesus his family were outside asking for him.

He'd spread his arms wide, gestured to the people before him, pointed at his disciples, 'Here is my mother, my brothers, my sisters. I tell you the truth, whoever does the will of God is my mother, my brother, my sister.'

Not long after that, it had been made plain that they should leave if they valued their safety.

Phil was strumming his guitar at the back of the minibus, a few of the lads joining in with the latest composition. Peter stopped thinking, gave himself up to sleep.

†

OUTSKIRTS OF MANCHESTER.

A steady stream of traffic headed out of Manchester. It was baking hot in the minibus. Jim squirted water on the windscreen, flipped the wipers, watched in disgust as the flies smeared across the glass. He pulled the lever, squirted more water, was mesmerised by the rhythmic swish of the blades as they struggled to clear the screen. He wondered when, if ever, it would rain again. It was slow going on the link road. Tempers were fraying. Horns blared in anger and echoed back in sympathy or derision. At one stage, a long continuous blast of a horn raised a laugh among the disciples. Jim glanced out, saw raised fingers, gesticulations. Anger everywhere. He could imagine the curses, sighed, wished he wasn't driving.

He turned on the radio for traffic news. It was the usual gloom, tailbacks and delays for the foreseeable future. Jesus and the guys were singing a rousing version of, 'One Man Went to Mow', as Jim negotiated a roundabout, a mile to the motorway. The flashing blue light, sirens, came as a surprise. The singing tailed off. Somebody growled. 'Trouble.'

Jim checked his speed, well within the limit. He signalled and pulled over into a desolate lay-by where a two man council team were fighting a losing battle. One of them litter picking, the other struggling to empty a bin. They paid no attention to either the minibus or the patrol car.

Jim watched as a Polizei traffic cop, menacing in his dark uniform, stepped out of the car. He looked around, adjusted his shades, walked the short distance to the minibus, and motioned Jim to wind the window down.

'I wasn't speeding.' Jim protested.

'I know that.' The voice, quiet, authoritative.

Jim frowned. 'Why the stop then?'

'You've got Jesus on board?' The officer asked.

Jim hesitated.

'It's okay,' the cop interjected, 'I'm not here to bring you trouble. I'd just like a word with Jesus.'

'Can I help?' Jim asked, wondering what it was about. The officer looked uncomfortable, out of his depth.

'It's a private matter.'

'It's okay Jim.' Jesus called. 'How can I help you officer?'

'Can we speak in private?' The cop asked, sticking his head through the open window.

'We're all friends here.' Jesus replied.

The officer looked at the disciples in turn. 'It's my buddy. My partner. He was shot - flesh wound, nothing too serious. He was recovering well.' The officer paused, sighed. 'But then he picked up an infection. MRSA.' he shrugged, 'he's in a bad way, and...' He stopped again for a second. Jim could see tears glistening in his eyes. 'He's maxed out on his medical insurance.' There was a catch in his voice as he said, 'I don't think he's gonna make it.'

'Where is he?' Jesus asked. 'Do you want me to come and heal him?'

The cop shook his head. 'I don't deserve you to do that, but just say the word and I know he'll pull through, I say this because I am a man under authority with men under me and they do as I say.'

Jesus looked round the disciples. 'I tell you lads, this man has great faith.' He turned back to the officer. 'Let him recover just as you believe he will.'

There was silence as the officer got back in his patrol car and drove away with a wave. Jesus got out of the back door and approached the two refuse collectors.

Jim heard him say, 'Thank you, guys, you're doing a great job.'

'Nah, thank you, mate.' One of them replied, 'We're invisible to most people. It's good to be appreciated.'

†

BLACKPOOL, NORTHUMBRIA.

The sun was high. The early haze burnt off. Matt picked his way through the crowds, smiled at two youngsters enthralled by a mechanical laughing Polizei officer in a glass case. Past an arcade, flashing lights, electronic noises, he walked on, his senses bombarded.

'...eighty-eight, two fat ladies...'

'...Mungo Jerry...'

'...Top o' the shop...'

'...in the summertime...'

'...two and three...'

Matt paused for a second, listened.

'...forget renowned prophet and healer, Jesus of Whitby, is in town today, so if you need a prophecy or a cure, head down to the Central Pier...'

He continued walking.

'...news on the hour...'

'Please mum...'

'You can't do that...'

'Go on then...'

Matt looked up, caught a glimpse of the soon to be demolished rusting tower. Saw a teenage boy waving his arms at a gull dive-bombing his chips.

'Just a quick one...'

'...there. Green bikini...'

'I said no...'

Past the usual deadbeats outside the Leg and Cramp. Same blank faces, day after day, too far gone to wave away the wasps circling their drinks.

Matt arrived at the pier and joined the other disciples in the small room where they were having a meeting before Jesus addressed the crowds. He caught Tom's eye. 'Have I missed anything?'

'Nah.' Tom shook his head.

Matt took a deep breath, tuned out the world, listened to Jesus. 'A farmer sowed good seed in his field, then, that night while he was sleeping his enemy came along and sowed weeds in the field. Months later when the wheat appeared, so did the weeds. One of the farmhands asked the farmer why he'd sown weeds as well as wheat.

'The farmer told him an enemy had done it.'

The farmhand asked, 'Shall we go and pull up the weeds?'

'No,' the farmer replied, 'because while you're pulling the weeds, you may uproot the wheat as well. Let both grow together until the harvest. Then, the harvesters will separate the weeds and the wheat. The weeds will be bundled together and burnt. The wheat will be stored in the barn.'

'I'm just a simple fisherman Boss.' Peter said. 'I know nothing about farming.'

'You'll have to tell us.' John said.

'The field is the world,' Jesus began, 'the farmer who sowed the good seed is the Son of Man, the good seed stands for the people of the kingdom.'

Tom held up his hand, Jesus nodded. 'Are the weeds the people who aren't of the kingdom?'

'Correct,' said Jesus, 'and the one who sows them?'

'The devil.' Jamie said.

'The harvest is the end of the age,' Jesus explained, 'and the harvesters are angels.'

'So the angels will gather up the people not of the kingdom,' John said, 'and throw them in a burning furnace?'

'You've got it.' Jesus said.

'And the people of the kingdom will live happily ever after.' Phil suggested, strumming a chord. 'There's got to be a song in that.'

†

DISCIPLES' CAMPSITE, LAKE WINDERMERE.

Simon didn't feel the prick of the needle, was just conscious of the swaying motion as he was hoisted over the Ninja's shoulder, and carried from the camp. It was dark inside the sleeping bag, hot, sweaty, stale air, and Simon, befuddled by sleep, and the effects of the drug, couldn't make sense of it. He decided it must be a dream, tried to turn over, and in his panic tried screaming for help, but couldn't.

His last conscious thought, I'm dying.

He knew he wasn't thirty minutes later when his sleeping bag was unzipped in the back of a black van three kilometres away and the duct tape was torn from his mouth. He winced with the pain, opened his eyes, and blinked as bright torchlight hit his face.

'If this is some kind o' flaming joke...' He tailed off as a voice told him to shut it. He closed his eyes, listened as the voice assured him it wasn't a joke. That he was in very serious trouble. That he would see out his days in agony in the bowels of State Security HQ in York.

Silence.

'What do you want?' Simon asked.

'A name.' The voice replied.

'What name, whose name?'

'Someone who's active in Four Kingdoms United.'

'What makes you think I'd know something like that?'

'Simon, why don't you stop pissing me about? You were active in FKU. You were part of a cell, you ran errands, conveyed messages. You might even have planted bombs...'

'No. Nothing like that.'

'But the other stuff, you did that?'

Silence.

'Then, when Jesus came calling,' the voice continued, 'you saw the light, whatever that means and became a follower.'

'I follow Jesus, yes.'

'A name.' The voice insisted. 'Give me a name.'

'And then you'll kill me.' Simon replied flatly.

'No.' The voice said. 'I'll check out the name. If I find you've spun me a tale, then I'll come back and kill you, okay?'

Simon gave her a name.

TEN

LAKE WINDERMERE, NORTHUMBRIA.

'Phil?'

Phil stopped strumming. 'Boss?'

'It's getting late,' Jesus said, 'no sign of anybody leaving. All these people,' he gestured, 'they must be starving. How many are there?'

Phil scanned the crowd. He'd seen more some days, but it was still a fair size. 'Dunno, Boss. Four, five thousand?'

'It's about that, isn't it?' Jesus said. 'How shall we feed them?'

Phil shrugged. Feed them? That's a new one. 'Meal deal from Asda. Sandwich, drink, crisps.' He paused, thought. 'Say, five Euros a head. That's twenty five thousand Euros.' He looked at Jesus. 'That's a lot o' money, Boss. I'm not sure we afford that. Speak to Judas, he'll know.' He'll know to the penny that one.

Judas looked up at his name and shook his head.

Andrew said, 'There's a lad here with a couple of cheese rolls and a packet of crisps.' He pulled a face. 'Won't go far though.'

Peter burst out laughing. 'Not even enough for me there bro.'

Jesus stooped and spoke to the boy in a low voice. The young lad handed over the rolls and crisps to

Jesus who put his hand on his head and blessed him.

'Peter, can you get me a basket for the sandwiches and a bowl for the crisps?'

'Sure thing, Boss.'

Jesus broke the bread rolls into pieces, put them in the small wicker basket, and held it before him. 'Father, we give thanks for your provision. For this bread and cheese.' Handing the basket to Phil, he then emptied the crisps into the bowl Andrew held. 'Father, we thank you for your provision, for these crisps.' Jesus looked at Phil and Andrew. 'Go and feed the people.'

†

Later, when the multitude had been fed, and the Lakeland scene was restored to its normal tranquillity, Jesus withdrew to spend time alone with the Father. The disciples sat around a small fire. They brewed tea and discussed the miracle of the never-ending food.

'I knew something was gonna happen,' Phil said, 'some miracle. I kept looking in the basket, trying to watch the rolls appear, but I didn't see it.'

'That's right.' Andrew agreed. 'Same with the crisps. People took handfuls, but the bowl never became empty.'

'What amazed me was,' said Jamie, 'we had just enough left for us to eat.'

'Is it always gonna be like this?' Jude wondered.

Brilliant, isn't it?' Peter declared. 'Just brilliant.'

It was a fine evening, the red-flecked sky help promise for the following day, although a light breeze rustled the leaves. Around eight in the evening, they made their way to the landing stage where their boat was moored. Jamie started the engine, called. 'All aboard the Skylark.'

The boat pulled away from the shore. Matt watched Andrew idly trail his hand in the water, envied his relaxed state. A flock of ducks glided low across the water, dropping their legs at the last moment and settled. It was idyllic but Matt was anxious, he'd be glad when they were back on dry land. He couldn't swim and hated water. It took under ten minutes to cross the lake, which was about 1.5 km at its widest point. He shut his eyes, concentrated on the rhythmic beat of the engine, listened as Jude tried to convince Tom the woods on the west bank were haunted, based on a conversation he'd had with a local.

'Rubbish.' Tom stated flatly.

'What he said.' Jude insisted.

'Nah, be some natural explanation.'

'Nobody's ever seen anything, but things disappear from garages.'

'Kind o' things?' Tom asked

'Packets, tins, food from freezers, that and bottles o' booze.'

'A ghost that eats and drinks.' Tom laughed. 'Be some homeless guy living in the woods.'

Jude shrugged. 'He's never been seen if it is.'

Matt looked towards the woods that covered the bank, where the disciples were camping. He sighed. Something else to worry about.

'Looks like we're in for a bit o' rain.' Peter remarked.

Matt looked up. The sky had turned black in a short space of time. As far as he knew, a storm hadn't been forecast.

'Here it comes.' John said.

Matt felt the first drops on his upturned face, turned towards the shore, couldn't see it. A light mist had rolled in obscuring the bank. The water now a bit choppy, not quite as smooth as before.

'You all right Matt?' Peter asked, 'you've gone a bit pale.'

Matt gave a tight smile, didn't reply, and fought his rising panic. The wind was blowing a bit stronger, water slopped over the side, soaking his trousers.

'It's just a drop o' watter.' Peter told him, his accent getting broader. Matt wondered if he was enjoying his discomfort. 'Don't worry we'll soon be on the other side. If you think this is bad, you'd never make it on the trawlers. Waves as big as mountains. Hey Andy, do you remember that time...'

The engine stopped. Apart from the wind, the rain, it was eerily silent.

Somebody laughed. It was a nervous sound.

Matt knew he was going to die. Retribution for his bad life. He looked to Jesus for reassurance, couldn't see him. Jesus wasn't on the boat.

Peter laughed. 'Nice one, Jamie.'

Jamie muttered something, tried starting the engine. The engine coughed, whined. Matt could smell burnt diesel. He felt sick.

Voices sprang up,

'What the...'

'Not funny.'

'Come on Jamie, it's gonna start lashing down any minute now.'

Jamie pressed the starter button again. More

coughing, whining, and spluttering.

'Stop pissing about Jamie.'

Jamie, white faced. 'It's not me guys.'

'You've run out of fuel.' Peter accused.

'There's plenty of fuel.' Jamie retorted, pressing the starter again. Nothing.

The rain became heavier, large drops exploded on the wooden boat. Matt, dressed in light summer clothing, soon became soaked. The boat started rocking from side to side with the force of the wind.

'It shouldn't be doing this,' Peter said, 'it's a lake.'

Andrew shrugged. 'It is.'

Peter dropped his hand on Matt's shoulder. 'Don't worry, it'll soon pass.'

Matt nodded, exchanged glances with a few of the others. They looked as scared as he felt. Why wasn't Jesus on the boat?

One or two of the disciples began praying. Simon joined Jamie in tinkering with the engine.

'Look.' Judas pointed out into the lake.

Matt couldn't see anything.

'It's a ghost.'

'Don't be stupid.'

'No such thing.'

'There is.'

'It is. It's a ghost.'

A scream.

A laugh.

A curse.

'Peter, look, there, on the lake.' Phil tugged his sleeve.

Matt stared through the driving rain, rubbed the water from his eyes, and could make out the figure of a man standing on the water. His shirt rippling in the strong wind. His immediate thought - the ghost from the woods. He closed his eyes, shook his head. This was a complete nightmare. He counted to ten, tried to remain calm.

The disciples, cowed by the howling of the wind, the rain lashing against the boat, the creaking of the timbers, huddled together. Matt opened his eyes. The figure, still there, seemed nearer.

'Who are you?' Peter called. 'What do you want?'

'Don't be afraid,' the response, 'it's me.'

'Lord?' Peter queried. 'Lord, is that you?'

'Yes.' The simple reply.

Relief washed over Matt. It was Jesus, everything was going to be alright.

'Lord, if that's you,' Peter shouted above the wind, 'tell me to come to you.'

Matt watched as Jesus, unaffected by the storm, held out a hand. 'Come.'

There was an immediate chorus from the disciples,

'Are you stupid?'

'Don't go.'

'You'll drown.'

'Crackers.'

Peter swung his legs over the side of the rocking boat. 'We have to step out in faith at some point.' He looked at his brother and shrugged. 'Why not now?' He said, before lowering himself down onto the water. Matt hesitated to look, but when he did, saw Peter a metre from the side, standing on the surface of the water.

'Come.' The figure called.

Matt watched in awe as Peter put one foot

tentatively in front of the other. If this was a film it'd be done with CGI, but it wasn't. It was real.

Peter turned. 'Hey lads, look at me. I'm walking on the chuffing water.'

'Sooner you than me, mate.' Nathan muttered.

The disciples were used to seeing Jesus healing the sick, raising the dead, banishing demons, but this simple act of walking on water had taken it to a whole new level. What Jesus and Peter were doing was impossible.

Matt watched Peter walking towards Jesus. He was, perhaps, halfway there, when he stopped, looked down, started sinking. 'Lord, help me.' He screamed in panic, the water up to his waist in seconds.

Jesus closed the gap between them, 'Oh Peter, such little faith.' Jesus steadied him, helped him back to the boat, where they both clambered aboard.

The disciples crowded round them both. Peter soaking wet, Jesus dry as a bone. Jesus stood in the middle of the boat, held his arms aloft. 'Stop.'

It was a sudden transformation. The rain stopped like a tap had been switched off, the wind dropped. The boat stopped rocking, and the lake became calm once more.

Jesus looked at his followers. 'Why are you so afraid? Do you still have no faith?'

He went and sat in the rear of the boat. Jamie tried the engine again. It fired and started at once.

†

Outskirts of Skipton, Northumbria.

Once clear of Skipton, in the depths of the countryside, it was totally dark. Too dark for Beaumont. Bocus was driving a stolen van, Beaumont happy to let him. They'd taped some false plates from the same make and colour of vehicle registered to a Manchester builder. In theory, with their false id, cover story of a late finish at a job in Bradford, they should be okay if stopped.

Beaumont had been panicking all the way from Bradford where they'd picked up the van, his unease abating now they were out in the sticks, away from the Automatic Number Plate Recognition cameras. He was still fearful of routine patrols. Could imagine the conversation, the questions.

Why come though the Dales, when you could use the trans-Pennine link road?

We got lost, officer.

Could you open the back doors please?

Followed by the puzzled looks at the plastic explosive, the realisation.

He looked out at the dark surroundings of the moonless night as they left civilisation, and swept through quiet villages. A city lad, Beaumont hated the countryside with a passion. When Bocus requested his help on a trip to blow up a water facility in the Northumbrian Dales, he'd tried unsuccessfully over several days to resist. In the end, he'd agreed just to shut him up. He still thought every day about what had happened to his life. He had no job and an uncertain future. He was beholden to Four Kingdoms United. A fact that Bocus reminded him of every day. The pressure of being on the run was getting to him. He'd once voiced to Bocus that he was thinking of walking into the Polizei building on Elland Road and give himself up.

Bocus had laughed, 'More fool you.'

Of course, he hadn't. The memory of Henderson was too fresh, too seared in his memory. Anyway, Bocus wouldn't let him. Beaumont wasn't allowed out of the house, couldn't answer the door, and had to stay clear of the windows. He was a prisoner. Always on edge, waiting for the Ninjas to storm through the door, end one nightmare, and start a new one.

Beaumont glanced across at Bocus. He was totally relaxed, hands light on the wheel. The radio was on low, Bocus humming along to the music. Bocus glanced across. 'Don't worry,' he said, 'it's always worse the first time.'

Beaumont exhaled air, wondered how many bombs Bocus had planted.

'Soon be there.' Bocus told him, swinging round a corner, heading down a single-track road, the headlights picking up scattering rabbits. A bump as the wheels went over one.

Bocus laughed. 'Supper.'

Beaumont felt sick.

The track ended at two-metre high steel gates.

'Is this it?' Beaumont asked.

'Yep.'

Beaumont frowned. 'We just drive straight up to the gates?'

'Yep.' Bocus smiled. 'The most secure part of the facility, the gates. The rest of it is just a crap chain link fence.'

'No cameras?'

'Not installed here yet.' Bocus said, opening the door, 'Stay here till I call you.'

Beaumont watched as Bocus approached the gates and pressed a button. He expected the gates to open automatically, and was shocked when they did to reveal a middle-aged man in a black uniform with a peaked cap. Beaumont caught a snatch of muffled conversation before the guard turned to push the gate wider. As he did Bocus swung his arm and caught the man a blow on the side of his head. It was like watching a film. The man's cap flew to one side as he dropped soundlessly to the floor. Bocus stood over him for a moment, and then came back. 'Come on, give us a hand.'

Together they taped a plastic carrier bag over the man's head, secured his hands and feet with cable ties. Bocus went inside the building leaving Beaumont with the body. He'd thought the man dead, was startled when he heard a groan, saw the bag suck inwards as he desperately struggled to breathe.

Bocus came back with a heavy chain, Beaumont pointed to the guard. Bocus shrugged, and fastening the chain round the man's waist dragged him inside the facility. Beaumont watched in silence. He felt sick, but followed Bocus and helped tip the man over the wall into the cold water of the reservoir.

Beaumont waited until Bocus brought the van inside the gates and closed them before speaking. 'Did you know there was a guard here?'

Bocus gave him a look. 'Of course.'

'You came knowing you were going to kill him?' Beaumont was appalled, stunned at this turn of events.

'Yes.' Bocus replied. 'We're not playing party games you know. We're fighting to rid the country, our country, of these Saxon bastards.'

'But he wasn't one of them.' Beaumont protested. 'He was just an innocent man doing his job.'

Bocus didn't reply, just set about unloading the explosive. If he wanted help, he didn't ask and Beaumont was in no mood to volunteer, instead he wandered off looking round the inside of the building. It was a small place. Apart from the plant room, where Bocus was placing the bomb, there was an equipment store, a toilet, a small kitchen with a kettle and a dog. A small, sad eyed spaniel that wagged its tail when it saw Beaumont. Must be the guard's he thought, stooping to pat it on the head. 'What are we gonna do with you,' he looked at the tag on the collar, 'Archie?'

Beaumont knew he couldn't leave it where it was, when the bomb went off the building would be flattened. He couldn't bear the thought of the animal being killed or injured. Knew also he couldn't take it, Bocus would never wear that, might even find another weight, drop it in the water.

The solution was simple. He took the dog's lead from a hook by the door, fastened it, led it outside, up the track, and let it go in a field. Archie seemed reluctant to go and stood looking at Beaumont with its watery eyes. But, after a few words of encouragement, it scampered off into the darkness. He hoped it wouldn't just have a piss and make its way back to the building.

Beaumont stood by the gate for a few minutes staring into the night. He'd been thinking about the prophet, Jesus. He'd toyed with the idea of leaving the house when Bocus was at work, seeking him out and joining his band of followers. A pipe dream, he knew he wouldn't do it. What would Jesus want with the likes of Beaumont anyway?

His phone buzzed, he answered. 'Hello?'

'Where are you?' Bocus demanded.

'I needed some fresh air,' Beaumont explained, 'back in a minute.'

'I'm done here, it's time to go.' Bocus cut the call.

Beaumont sighed and made his way back to the van.

✝

Disciple's campsite, Lake Windermere.

Simon turned the bacon on the grill and stirred the pan of baked beans. Sipping his tea, he stared into the dark greenness of the woods. He'd heard movement in there earlier, but had dismissed it as the wild boars that lived in the forest. He'd caught a glimpse of one yesterday. A fearsome looking brute, far bigger than a domestic pig. It had looked at him for a second, and then moved off. Jesus had appeared from the trees a few minutes later. He hadn't seemed bothered by boars, or beer drinking ghosts.

The weather looked set fair to be another glorious day, not that Simon had been enjoying life for the past few days. He'd been jumpy ever since his night-time abduction. After his encounter with the voice, he'd been given his sleeping bag, bundled out of the van, and warned to keep quiet. It had taken him three hours to walk back to the camp. Dawn was breaking by the time he'd arrived. He'd just had time to get his bag back in the tent he shared with Jamie when it was time to get up.

Simon was ashamed of giving that name to the voice. But as he kept telling himself, what else could he have done? He heard talking from the path. A few of the lads were up and about; he expected they'd been down to the lake for an early morning swim. They came trooping round the corner. Peter and John were having a heated discussion about a parable Jesus had told them. Jamie came over and asked if he was okay. Simon assured him he was, and told him breakfast would soon be ready.

'Need any help?' Jamie asked.

'Yeah, you can check the eggs.' Simon told him, lifting the grill from the open fire. He looked at the serving table. Everything was set and he was about to call out breakfast was ready when a news report on the radio caught his attention.

'...in the centre of Manchester causing major damage. The Governor responded by promising the perpetrators, when caught, would be shown no mercy. In other news...'

Simon wondered whether any of his old cronies were involved, thankful he'd left the nationalist movement when he had. The call from Jesus had come at the right time, he'd been on the verge of signing up for a bomb making course He hadn't hesitated, joining the disciples that day, leaving his old life behind. He shuddered as he realised that he must be on a list of suspects. He could have planted a bomb, thought he'd got away with it, and been arrested within hours. Jamie raised his eyebrows. Simon smiled a reassurance.

Later, plates emptied, stacked, ready for washing, Judas nudged Jamie's arm. 'Look.'

'Another ghost, is it?' Jamie smirked.

Everybody laughed.

'No. Look.' Judas pointed. 'That's no ghost.'

A man stood on the edge of the clearing just inside the tree line. He didn't speak, just stood and stared, his head bobbing up and down. It looked to Simon as though he was shaking. He could hear him muttering away to himself.

'Boss?' Andrew caught Jesus' attention.

'I've seen him, Andrew. I've been expecting him.'

'What do you think, Boss?' Peter asked. 'Can we help him?'

'He has to want help.' Jesus replied. 'He needs to come to me. Just ignore him. He'll come over when he's ready.'

The disciples chatted between themselves, glancing at the man from time to time. Simon studied him out of the corner of his eye. He was clean-shaven, his long hair tied back in a ponytail that swished from side to side as he moved his head. His jeans and T-shirt, although clean, were crumpled. Mid to late thirties at a guess. If he hadn't been muttering and jerking his head around, he would have appeared normal.

After a while, he approached and stopped a few metres away. Jim offered a hunk of bread, holding it until the man crept close enough to grab it, and wolf it down. Now he was close, Simon noticed the numerous cuts on both his arms, some fresh, others scabbed.

'He self-harms.' Simon pointed out.

Jim nodded. 'Yeah.' He filled a beaker with water and put it on a table. The man seized it. He drank the water and was about to move back into the trees when he noticed Jesus. He became agitated, jigging about from foot to foot, muttering all the while.

Jesus spoke in a low voice. 'Come out of this man, you impure spirit.'

The man dropped to his knees. 'What do you want with me, Jesus, son of the most High God?' He screamed. 'In God's name don't torture me. Help. Help.'

He looked at Simon. 'You'll help me, won't you?'

Simon, embarrassed, looked away, and was amazed to see half a dozen wild boars emerge from the trees. They stopped, looked towards Jesus, as though they were watching the scene, almost as if they could understand what was being said.

'What's your name?' Jesus asked.

'Legion.' The man answered, pronouncing it Lee-jon. 'For we are many.'

It seemed to Simon, every time the man spoke, it was with a different voice. A young man, old woman, young girl, uneducated, refined, they were all there. He looked back towards the trees. The boars were still coming. In small groups, they emerged from the woods. He nudged Jim, whispered, 'Look.'

'I've seen them.' Jim replied. 'Weird.'

The man was speaking again, this time in a small boy's voice. 'Please, Jesus,' he begged. 'Don't send me away.' He looked at the disciples asking each in turn if they would help him. He noticed the boars, who by now were too numerous to count, and seemed to have moved closer. 'The pigs,' he pointed. 'Send us into the pigs.' He turned back to Jesus. 'You can do that, can't you, Jesus. Let us go into the pigs.'

'Go.' Jesus said. 'Leave this man.'

The man moaned, and then slumped to the floor. There was a roaring noise like a tornado approaching, but no movement. After a moment, everything became still and silent.

Simon and Jim, at Jesus' command helped the man to his feet. They all moved away from the tables and gathered at the edge of the camp. Nothing happened for a few minutes, but then the animals began moving, grunting, squealing, and bunching together, they trotted forwards, their bulky bodies swaying. Picking up speed, they rushed straight through the camp knocking over tables and chairs, and demolishing tents. A rancid smell was left in their wake as they sped along the track around the bend, and rushed down towards the lake.

Jude and a few others followed, but most of the disciples stayed back, talking among themselves. Simon gave the man a mug of sweet tea. He smiled in gratitude, and told them his name was Dixon. He explained how he'd been living deep in the woods in a concealed shelter for fifteen years, surviving by breaking into people's garages and outbuildings, just taking what he needed to live a frugal life. He couldn't say when he first became demon possessed, but thought it was after he'd been living rough for a number of years.

Jude, Jamie, Phil and Tom returned and said they'd seen the wild boar plunge into the lake, thrash about, and then drown. Jesus, who had listened to Dixon's story in silence, blessed him and told him he was free of possession. Dixon wept tears of joy, and asked if he could join them.

Jesus shook his head. 'No, I'm sorry. You need to go back to your own people. Tell them all that the Lord has done for you, and how he has shown you mercy.'

✝

Lake Windermere, Northumbria.

A small group of men gathered by the lakeside. Todman looked at them with satisfaction. His group, his men. Todman followed Jesus, which didn't say much. He'd followed other prophets that sprang up from time to time. Those whose stars had flared for a time before darkness overtook them. He'd been optimistic that this guy Jesus was the real deal. He'd thought Jesus was going to make a difference. That he was the Messiah. That things would change because of him. Todman expected life to change for the better but was still waiting on real change. He was finished with promises. He'd been part of the crowd fed on scraps yesterday, but, despite the miracle of the food, he was wavering, on the cusp of leaving. Jesus often spoke in riddles and Todman found him difficult to understand. He resented being told to use his ears to hear. What else would he do with them? It didn't help that Jesus wasn't here this morning, where Todman and his group had expected him to be. It was mid-morning he should be here. The miracle of yesterday was forgotten. He wanted bigger, better miracles today. It was fair to say Todman was a lukewarm, fair-weather supporter. While the going was good, he followed and got out of it what he could, but he was always ready to jump ship.

He looked at his men. They followed Jesus because Todman followed Jesus. They were sheep and he was their shepherd. But even sheep became dissatisfied. They were grumbling at having to wait for the Messiah. Somebody mentioned that Jesus was still over the other side of the lake, at his campsite, where just the official disciples were welcome.

Well, bollocks to that.

He called for a boat, one of his men found one and they crossed the lake. Nearing the far shore, they were amazed to see the drowned bodies of wild boar. They nudged a course between them, pushing them clear with a boat hook. There must have been several hundred. His men were quiet and fearful, wondering what had happened to cause all the animals to end up in the water.

Tying up the boat, they made their way up the narrow track towards the campsite, Todman leading the way. Coming into the clearing, they were met with a scene of devastation. Tables and chairs had been over turned, tents torn down, clothing strewn about. It looked as though a tornado had swept through the camp, that, or a herd of wild boar, Todman thought and smiled wryly.

Jesus and his followers were in a huddle in the centre of the camp. Nobody noticed them and Todman seethed at being ignored. He was sure one or two of the disciples had noticed him, but nobody spoke, they just carried on with their meeting. Todman, determined not to mention the chaos in the camp, called out, 'You're still here, Jesus.'

Jesus turned and addressed the newcomers. 'I tell

you the truth,' he said, 'you are looking for me, not because you saw the signs I performed but because you ate your fill of the bread and the cheese.' He shook his head. 'Do not work for food that spoils, but for food that endures to eternal life, which the Son of Man will give you. For on him God the Father has placed his seal of approval.'

'What is this work that God requires?' Somebody behind Todman called out.

'The work of God,' Jesus replied, 'is to believe in the one he has sent.'

'What sign will you give,' another asked, 'that we may see it and believe it?'

Peter exchanged glances with Andrew, not another bunch wanting a sign.

'Yes.' A voice from the crowd called. 'What will you do?'

'The thing is,' Todman said, 'our ancestors ate manna in the wilderness, as it says in the ancient scriptures, "He gave them bread from heaven to eat."'

'Don't you find it amusing,' Tom muttered to Judas, 'When people quote the ancient scriptures at the Boss?'

Judas shrugged in reply.

Jesus smiled and said, 'I tell you the truth, the bread of God is the bread that comes down from heaven and gives life to the world.'

Todman bowed his head. 'Then always give us this bread.'

'I am the bread of life,' Jesus declared. 'Whoever comes to me will never get hungry, and whoever believes in me will never be thirsty. But,' he paused, and shook his head sorrowfully, 'as I told you, you have seen me and still you do not believe. All those the

Father gives me will come to me, and whoever comes to me I will never drive away.'

'I'm not quite getting that Jesus.' Todman said, with a puzzled look at his small group.

It's quite simple, 'Jesus replied. 'My Father's will is that everybody who looks to the Son and believes in him shall have eternal life, and will be raised up at the last day.'

A few in the crowd started muttering.

'That's ridiculous.'

'Who is he to say he's the bread of heaven.'

'Said on internet, he used to be a builder.'

'...from a poor family.'

'Come down from heaven?'

'I don't think so.'

Jesus held up his hands. 'Oh, stop grumbling.' He commanded. 'I am the living bread that came down from heaven. Whoever eats this bread will live forever. This bread is my flesh which I will give for the life of the world.'

The disciples listened as the crowd began arguing among themselves.

'How can this man give us his flesh to eat?'

'Bloke's a cannibal.'

'I bet they all are.'

'It's the end of the world.'

'Is it a parable?'

'Listen,' Jesus raised his voice above the clamour, 'I tell you the truth, unless you eat the flesh of the son of Man, drink his blood, you have no life in you.' He paused, looked at them all, included the disciples, 'Whoever eats my flesh, drinks my blood remains in me, and I in them. Just as the living Father sent me and I live because of the Father, so the one who feeds on me will live because of me.'

'Well, I'm right sorry about that.' Todman retorted. 'We've followed you without question for many months, but this is a step too far. All this talk of eating human flesh, drinking your blood.' He shook his head. 'I'm not having that.' He looked around at the nods of confirmation, 'We're not having it.'

Jesus sighed. 'The Spirit gives life, the flesh counts for nothing. The words I have spoken to you are full of the Spirit and life. If this offends you, it's better you go now.'

The disciples watched in silence as the crowd, led by Todman, walked away until they disappeared round the bend where the wild boar had gone not long before.

Jesus turned to the twelve gathered around. 'This is why I told you that no one can come to me unless the Father has enabled them. Do any of you want to leave too?'

Peter shrugged. 'Where would we go Boss? You're the man. You have the words of eternal life.' He looked round at the others who nodded, smiled their confirmation. 'We believe you are the holy one of God.'

'I chose you all individually.' Jesus said. 'But, I tell you now, one of you is from the evil one.'

†

'We need to get bread.' Simon told Jude on the boat back over to Bowness.

'No probs, buddy, I'll sort it.' Jude replied.

'Be careful,' Jesus told them both. 'Be on your guard against the yeast of the Pharisees and the priests.'

Simon gave Jude a puzzled look. Jude shrugged. 'No idea mate.'

A few of the others heard the conversation and joined in. Very soon, a heated debate about Jesus' meaning was going round the boat. The argument was still going strong when they arrived at the minibus.

'I expect it's because we're out of bread.' Peter suggested.

Jesus listened for a while to the various interpretations, and then said. 'You have such little faith. Why are you talking about having no bread? Do you still not understand? Don't you remember the two cheese rolls for the five thousand and how much was left? How is it you don't understand that I'm not talking about bread? But to be on your guard against the yeast of the Pharisees and the priests.'

'I think,' John said, 'That the Boss means to guard against the teaching of the Pharisees and the priests.' He looked at Jesus for approval.

Jesus nodded. 'Correct, John.'

Correct, John. Peter seethed within. He was the leader of the disciples, and second in command to Jesus. You need a skipper and he needs a deputy. He slumped into a corner seat, glad he wasn't driving. He groaned when he heard the hiss of the radio through the speakers.

'...flash. It has been announced that the death has occurred of the itinerant preacher, Baptiste. Details are sketchy at the moment, but unconfirmed sources are suggesting that Baptiste was beheaded whilst being held without charge at State Security HQ in York. More on this and other news at the top of the hour. Now, it's back to Mad Mike in the studio...'

Jim clicked the radio off, glanced over his shoulder and saw the others had heard.

'Bastards.' Tom exploded. Jesus moved seats, put his arm round Tom's shoulder and murmured a few comforting words.

The mood was sombre. Most of them knew Baptiste and were shocked by his death. Nothing of note had been given out on the main news, just the fact that Baptiste was dead. Beheaded, how did that happen?

'Who do people say the Son of Man is?' Jesus asked after a few minutes silence.

Peter resolved to stay out of this one as various answers were given by the others.

'Eliyahu.'

'Jeremiah.'

'One of the other prophets.'

Jesus looked across at Peter, 'What about you?' He asked. 'Who do you say I am?'

Peter hesitated for a second, then, 'You are the Messiah,' he replied. 'The Son of the living God.'

Jesus smiled. 'Blessed are you Peter, son of Jonah, this wasn't revealed to you by flesh and blood, but by my father in heaven. Your name, Peter. Do you know what it means?'

Peter shrugged. He was sure he knew at some point, but had forgotten. 'No, Boss.'

'It means rock in the Greek language.' Jesus took Peter's hands in his own. 'I tell you the truth, you are the rock, on which I declare, I will build my church, and the gates of hell will not overcome it. I will give you the keys of the kingdom of heaven. Whatever you bind on earth will be bound in heaven, and whatever you loose on earth will be loosed in heaven.'

Still holding Peter's hands, he looked round at the other disciples. They were all present apart from Judas who preferred to travel on his powerful motorbike. 'I tell you lads, this is a momentous day. But don't tell anyone that I'm the Messiah.'

The disciples looked at each other, promised Jesus that they wouldn't. One of the lads muttered something, the others laughed. Peter didn't care. He felt incredibly proud. Second in command. A rock on which a church would be built. Jim started the engine, pulled out of the car park, and headed north to Carlisle.

ELEVEN

CARLISLE, NORTHUMBRIA.

Andrew marched on, Peter trailed behind, wondered what had got into his brother.

'Not so fast Andy.' He said, catching up. 'There's no rush.'

They were in Carlisle. Jesus was in the shopping centre, walkabout and preach, healings, casting out of demons, usual stuff. Peter had volunteered to get camping site info from the local tourist information office. Andrew had tagged along.

Andrew stopped abruptly, turned, and waited for his brother to catch up. 'You gonna tell us then?' He asked bluntly.

'What?' Peter met his gaze impassively.

The day before, on the road to Carlisle, Jesus had called a halt. He'd set out walking across the fields, taking Peter, Jamie, and John with him, leaving Andrew and the others in the minibus. Intrigued, they'd watched the four men walk into the distance until they disappeared from view. Four hours later, they'd returned, got on the bus, and resumed their journey. Nobody said a word.

Andrew had been pissed off at not being invited along, further annoyed not to be told what had happened. He was still annoyed now. They were either in it together or they weren't.

'Don't play the innocent, Peter.'

Peter shrugged. 'Dunno what you mean.'

Andrew took a deep breath. He'd have to spell it out then. 'Yesterday. On the mountain.'

'Oh, that?' Peter smiled. He gave the same smile as a child when he knew something Andrew didn't. It still had the power to infuriate.

'What happened yesterday?' Andrew demanded.

Peter shook his head. 'Nothing much.'

'What, you three went up a mountain with the Boss and nothing happened?'

'I can't tell you. Simple as that.'

'Can't or won't?'

'Look, if you want to know, ask Jesus.'

'You won't tell me?'

'I can't. I wish I could, but the Boss told us not to talk about it.'

'You looked different when you came back.' Andrew probed. 'All of you. Like you'd had some kind of spiritual experience.'

That was it, Peter thought. A spiritual experience.

They'd left the minibus, crossed the fields, and climbed a narrow path up Helvellyn. Just short of the summit Jesus had stopped. Peter, Jamie, and John looked at each other, tried to work out what was happening. Peter would have found it difficult to put into words what happened next even if he was allowed.

Jesus' face had taken on a brilliant glow and his clothes had turned a radiant white. Then, if that wasn't disturbing enough, two people appeared, joined Jesus in conversation. A bright cloud appeared over Jesus and the two men, hiding them from view. A voice from the cloud proclaimed, 'This is my Son, whom I love. I am very pleased with him. Listen to all he tells you.'

That had been enough for the three disciples. They all hit the deck at the same time. Peter couldn't say how long they stayed like that, but after a while, Jesus tapped him on the shoulder, told him to get up. Peter had looked up. Jesus was alone and looking normal again. Jesus had told them not to mention what they'd seen.

Talking later with Jamie and John it transpired that all three of them had thought the other two to be Moses and Eliyahu and that the whole episode had been a confirmation of Jesus' divine status.

Peter held his hand out in a conciliatory gesture. 'Come on bro, you know I'd tell you if I could.'

Andrew shrugged. 'Yeah.'

They walked on in silence.

†

CAMPSITE, CARLISLE, NORTHUMBRIA.

'Boss?'

'Something troubling you, Peter?'

'I've been thinking about this forgiveness business.' Peter scratched his ear.

'And, you've reached a conclusion?'

Peter shrugged. 'I know it's a good thing to do. Everything you teach is good in that way.'

Jesus smiled. 'But you're unsure about something.'

'How many times should I forgive my brother or

sister who's done me wrong? Some o' the lads reckon two or three,' but, Peter frowned, shook his head, 'I reckon six or seven.'

Jesus sighed. 'I tell you the truth, Peter, not seven times, more like seventy-seven.'

'I'm way off the mark then.' Peter conceded.

Jesus nodded. 'It's like a king from bygone days. He was owed ten thousand bags of gold by this particular man. The man couldn't pay, so the king ordered him to be thrown in the dungeons and all his possessions sold to go towards paying the debt. When the man heard the verdict, he fell on his knees, begged for more time, and said he'd pay it all back. The king took pity on him and cancelled the debt on the spot.'

'The man was so relieved. He went straight out to celebrate. He bumped into somebody he knew who owed him a hundred silver coins. He gripped the man by the throat, demanded his money back. The man fell to his knees, asked for time to pay. The first man went off and had the second man thrown into prison until he could pay the debt.'

'Now, when other people heard what had happened, they petitioned the king. The king called in the first man, told him he was wicked, had him jailed, and reinstated his debt.'

'This Peter,' Jesus concluded, 'is how my heavenly Father will treat each one of you, unless you forgive your brother or sister from your heart.'

✝

SKIPTON, NORTHUMBRIA.

Swanger drank her tea, refused a biscuit, and looked around the living room. Letting the silence build, she took in the shabby furniture, faded curtains, and frayed carpet. Opposite her on the settee, the middle-aged woman tugged her skirt over her knees. She seemed nervous. A natural fear of authority, or something else?

'Your partner?' Swanger said after a few minutes. The woman avoided eye contact, licked her lips. 'When did you last see him?'

'I went through all this with the Polizei officers who came out.'

Swanger smiled. 'It's a pain I know,' she took a quick glance at her clipboard, 'Stella, but as his employer, we at Northumbrian Water need to be sure about what happened.'

Stella was silent. It was obvious to her what had happened.

'He was one of the family.' Swanger continued, 'We feel a measure of responsibility.'

'Will there be compensation?' Stella asked.

'Maybe,' Swanger conceded, but don't push it, love.

'I just want him home.' Stella whined.

'What do you think happened to him?'

'How would I know?' She shrugged

'Another woman?'

'Alan?' She laughed scornfully. 'I doubt it.'

'We've excavated the building where the explosion took place,' Swanger said. 'There's no sign of a...' She let it hang.

'Or Archie.' Stella reminded.

Swanger nodded. 'Or Archie.'

'Alan took that dog everywhere, company, like.' She sniffled into a tissue. 'He loved that dog.'

'Did Alan have any political affiliation?' Swanger asked.

'You what?'

'Could he have been involved in the planting of the bomb?'

'Alan? No. He was crap at that sort o' stuff. DIY, like.' She shook her head. 'Tried mending the toilet once, flooded the house.'

Swanger wondered if it was worth booking her in for a session in the basement of State Security HQ. She claimed not to know anything but most wives, in her limited experience, knew something.

'Happen he's at the bottom of the reservoir.' Stella sniffed again. 'Him and his blessed dog.'

Swanger nodded, didn't comment. She couldn't remember seeing anything in the report about an underwater search. Try that, first, she decided, leave the water boarding for now.

†

SHOPPING CENTRE, CARLISLE, NORTHUMBRIA.

They heard a commotion coming from within the shopping centre. The other disciples were surrounded by an agitated crowd. When Jesus and John approached, a cheer went up. 'At last.' A voice called out. 'The organ grinder.'

'What's the problem?' Jesus asked Peter who was arguing with a red faced man in his thirties.

'I'll tell you what the problem is,' the man retorted, 'I've brought my son to be healed. He's been possessed by an impure spirit who's robbed him of speech. It gets right violent at times, throws him to the ground. He's alright, one minute, next, bang, he's on the deck. Foaming at mouth, grinding his teeth. He's gonna hurt himself one day.'

Jesus listened, nodded understandingly.

'And if that weren't bad enough, this lot here,' the man swept his arm in an arc, encompassing the watching disciples, 'are complete rubbish.'

The disciples looked at each other. The guy was being unreasonable.

'You unbelieving and perverse bunch.' Jesus addressed the disciples. Peter opened his mouth, shut it again. 'How long shall I put up with you?' He paused. 'How long shall I stay with you?' Jesus turned back to the irate father. 'Is this the lad with you now?'

'Aye.' The man pushed his teenage son towards Jesus.

'How long has he been like this?' Jesus asked.

'Since he was a nipper, hardly out o' nappies.'

The crowd was silent now, watching expectantly. 'Please help us,' the man pleaded, 'if you can.'

'If you can?' Jesus seemed amused. 'Everything is possible for one who believes.'

'I do believe.' The man insisted. 'But please, help me overcome my unbelief.'

The crowd murmured.

Jesus placed his hand on the boy's head. 'You deaf and mute spirit,' he said, 'I command you to come out of this boy now.' As Jesus finished speaking, the boy convulsed, fell to the floor. The crowd groaned, and then backed away in alarm when a loud shrieking noise was heard. Wraith like wisps of smoke hovered over the boy for a second, and then vanished. The boy lay so still that Peter thought him dead, but Jesus helped him to his feet, shook hands with his father, and wished them well.

Later, when the crowd had dispersed, Peter asked, 'Why couldn't we drive it out?'

'Because you have too little faith.' Jesus replied. 'I tell you the truth. If you had faith as small as a mustard seed, you can say to this mountain, 'move from here to there,' and it will move. Nothing will be impossible for you.'

'Hey up, they're here again.' Jim called out.

Peter looked up and groaned. The small band of Pharisees that followed them around, questioning, criticising, had gathered together. Their ringleader, Brotherton, was first to speak. 'Why do your disciples break the tradition of the elders?'

'Which one?' Peter growled.

Jesus held up his hand, Peter fell silent. He knew the Boss didn't need his protection, but these people, they were hard to like, let alone love.

Brotherton ignored the interruption. 'They don't wash their hands before they eat.'

Peter groaned in annoyance. This was the ceremonial hand washing that the Scribes insisted upon before eating, whether one's hands needed it or not.

'And why do you break the command of God,' Jesus replied, 'for the sake of your tradition?'

Brotherton looked affronted as Jesus continued. 'God said, 'honour your father and mother,' and 'anyone who curses their father or mother is to be put to death.' But you say that if anyone declares that what might have been used to help their father or mother is 'devoted to God,' they are not to 'honour their father or mother' with it. So you nullify the word of God for your tradition.'

Brotherton was silent.

'You hypocrites.' Jesus said. 'Isaiah was right when he prophesied about you.

"These people honour me with their lips,

But their hearts are far from me.

They worship me in vain.

Their teachings are just human rules."'

Jesus called the disciples to him and said, 'Listen and understand. What goes into someone's mouth does not defile them, but what comes out of their mouth, that is what defiles them.'

Brotherton and his band, turned, stalked off.

Jamie said, 'I think you've upset them again, Boss.'

Jesus sighed. 'Every plant that my Father has not planted will be pulled up by the roots.' He shook his head in sorrow. 'Leave them. They are blind guides. If the blind lead the blind, they'll both fall.'

'Explain the parable to us.' Peter said.

'Are you still so dull?' Jesus demanded. The others laughed. 'All of you.' He turned, took them all in. 'Don't you see that whatever enters the mouth goes into the stomach, through your digestive system, then out the other end? You must know this from biology at school. But the words that come from a person's mouth come from the heart and they defile them. For out of the heart come evil thoughts. Murder, adultery, sexual immorality, theft, false testimony, slander.

These are what defiles a person, not eating with unwashed hands.'

Later, moving about the crowd, Jesus took a baby in his arms. 'Whoever welcomes a child in my name welcomes me,' He kissed it on the forehead, 'and whoever welcomes me doesn't just welcome me, but welcomes the one who sent me.' He blessed the child, handed it back to the beaming mother, and moved deeper into the crowd.

We could do with proper security Andrew thought, keep the crowds at a sensible distance. Jesus didn't seem to have any regard for his own safety, didn't mind who he spoke to, who he greeted. Andrew hated it when he was surrounded by people like now, any nutter could pull a knife. He'd confided his fears to the others and they were all in agreement. Jesus needed protecting.

Some hours later heading to the car park, a youth appeared in front of Jesus. 'You Jesus?'

'I am.' Jesus replied.

Andrew glanced at his watch, looked at Peter who nodded. 'Boss, we should be getting on.'

'Have you not been listening, Peter?' Jesus responded. He turned his attention to the youth.

'Jesus the prophet?'

'Yes.'

'Who's gonna be Messiah?'

Jesus confirmed he was.

'Well then,' the youth began, 'happen you can help with something.'

'If I can, I will.' Jesus told him.

'I do a paper round.'

Andrew sighed. This was ridiculous.

'I had a paper round when I was your age.' Jesus said, smiling.

Andrew frowned, he hadn't known that.

'Then you'll know what the trouble is.' The youth said.

'Apart from dogs, the biggest problem I had was letter boxes.'

'I'm alright wi' dogs, but letter boxes are a right pain. All different sizes, in different places in the door. It needs sorting.'

'And how can I help?' Jesus asked.

'When you're in charge, perhaps you can make a law that says all letter boxes have to be in the middle of the door, horizontal, and open automatically.'

A few of the disciples who were close enough to listen burst out laughing.

Jesus chuckled, ruffled the youth's hair. 'What a great idea.' Holding the lad's gaze, he said. 'I tell you the truth, from this day onwards you no longer just deliver the news. You are the news from me, to be read by everyone.'

†

DISCIPLES' CAMPSITE, CARLISLE, NORTHUMBRIA.

John and Simon dumped the shopping bags down, looked at the others. 'We've seen it all now, haven't we?' He looked at Simon for confirmation.

'What happened?' Andrew asked.

'This feller in the market place was driving out demons in the Boss' name.' John said, indignant.

'Cheeky git.' Peter responded. 'What did you do?'

'Told him to stop, o' course.' Simon looked at Jesus for approval.

'Don't stop him.' Jesus said. 'Nobody can do a miracle in my name one minute, and then say something bad against me the next.' He shrugged. 'Whoever is not against us is for us. I tell you lads. Whoever gives you a drink in my name because you belong to the Messiah will not lose their reward.'

The disciples looked at each other, shrugged.

'Anyway,' Jesus continued, 'I've decided to give the feast of tabernacles a miss. But,' he held up his hand to stop the disappointed clamour, 'you should all go as planned.'

'Your choice, Boss.' Peter said, looking around, 'but we think you should go. You'll miss a golden opportunity to show the brothers in York the good work you're doing.'

'Peter's right.' Andrew said. 'Nobody who wants to become a public figure can work in secret.'

'Boss, you're the Messiah.' John insisted. 'The people in York will expect to see you.'

'It's a big stage.' Tom remarked. 'Show yourself on it. Get some exposure.'

'Any time will do for you lads.' Jesus said. 'But, it's not my time. The world can't hate you, but it hates me because I testify its works are evil.'

'How will you know when it's your time?' Phil asked.

'Believe me, I'll know. The Son of Man is going to be delivered into the hands of men. They will kill him, and after three days he will rise.'

The Talbot, York, Northumbria.

Two in the afternoon, the pub was heaving. Bodies were packed five deep at the bar, music was booming, and dense cigarette smoke clung to the ceiling. Peter took a sip of his ale, glanced around, and knew full well they wouldn't be in the pub if the Boss was with them. Not that Jesus disapproved of people kicking back, enjoying themselves, it was more that, people thought he did, and that led them to modify their behaviour around him. He checked out the few disciples he could see. Keeping an eye, making sure they behaved themselves.

It was a good time to be alive, he reflected. Although still unsure about Jesus' exact mission, he knew that only good things would come from it. Jude caught his eye, mimed, did he want another pint?

Why not? His drinking was well under control, another one wouldn't hurt. He nodded, remembered the conversation he'd had with the Boss before leaving for York. The lads had put him up to it. He'd approached Jesus at a quiet moment. The Boss had known he was troubled and anxious. He always knew.

Peter had outlined the disciples concerns. All this talk of suffering at the hands of the priests and Pharisees, of being put to death and rising on the third day was having an unsettling effect. Sure, it might be mentioned somewhere in the ancient scriptures but, hey, you're the Son of God. There must be a better way.

Peter had told him straight. 'It's not gonna happen, Boss. We'll protect you. Me and the other lads.'

The response, Peter recalled, had been amazing,

totally unexpected.

Jesus held up his hand, stepped closer. 'Enough.' He'd said in a low voice. 'It is written, Peter. It will happen.' Jesus stepped back, searched Peter's face. 'It's like having Satan stood before me again. You are a stumbling block to me, Peter.' He softened his tone. 'I know you mean well, but you're pre-occupied with human concerns, rather than the concerns of God.'

Peter, embarrassed and chastened, with tears in his eyes, followed Jesus on to the minibus and heard him say, 'Whoever wants to be my disciple must deny themselves and take up their cross and follow me. For whoever wants to save their life will lose it, but whoever loses their life for me will find it. What good will it be for someone to gain the whole world, yet forfeit their soul? Or what can anyone give in exchange for their soul? For the Son of Man is going to come in his Father's glory with his angels, and then he will reward each person according to what they have done.'

Peter shook his head, cheeks burning at the memory. He looked up at his name. Jude handed him a pint. Peter took it, nodded his thanks, and tuned into a conversation at the next table.

'...believe the things Jesus does...'

Peter turned his head, looked at the speaker. 'Did you say Jesus?'

The man, tattooed arms, shaved head, an air of menace, looked at Peter. 'Aye, what of it?'

Peter grimaced. 'Nothing. A shame he's not here.'

'But he is, my friend.' Tattoo man assured. 'I heard him preaching in the Temple courts a short while ago.'

Peter frowned. 'Is he still there?'

'Dunno pal. There was a bit o' trouble, a few rowdies tried grabbing him, but he got away.' He shrugged. 'He might have gone back. You know what he's like.'

Peter sighed. Had it been Jesus' intention all along to come to the festival in secret?

The tattoo man finished his pint. 'That's me done. Be seeing you pal, nice talking to you.'

Peter turned to his brother. 'Did you hear that? Jesus is here, preaching in the Temple courts.'

Andrew pulled a face. 'That's odd. He definitely said he wasn't coming.'

'Scared he'll spoil your fun, Peter?' Judas called across the table.

Peter looked at him, felt Andrew's hand on his arm. You and me in a dark alley, pal. He wondered what the Boss saw in the creepy accountant. Rumour had it among the lads that Judas was fiddling the books, skimming a bit off the top for himself. He'd love to find out it was true. 'Whatever, Judas.'

Peter turned back to Andrew. 'I'm gonna nip down there, see if I can see him.'

Andrew nodded. 'Want me to come with you?'

'Nah, stay here with the lads. Let Judas entertain you with his wit.'

Minutes later, swamped by the thick crowd, all Peter could hear was talk of Jesus.

'He's back then?'

'Is it true they tried to kill him?'

'Nah, arrest him.'

'He needs to be careful...'

'Messiah, my arse'

'He slipped away.'

'He's a good bloke, that Jesus.'

Peter pushed on through the crowd, anxious now. He should have been with him, protecting him, watching his back. What on earth was he thinking of, coming alone.'

'Temple guards tried to arrest him.'

'Aye.'

'Blasphemy.'

'...happened.'

'They didn't.'

A burst of laughter washed over Peter.

'...runs rings round 'em,'

'When's he gonna take over?'

'Aye, he needs to make his move.'

'...ripe for the plucking.'

Then, Peter heard Jesus, 'I am with you for such a short time, and then I'm going back to the one who sent me.' Peter listened, tried to get his bearings.

Jesus again, 'You will look for me, but you will not find me.'

Like now, Peter muttered, pushed his way through a complaining crowd.

'And where I am, you can't come.'

How did he manage to make himself heard all over the area?

'What's he mean?'

'...short time.'

'Thought he was Messiah?'

'Why can't we go?'

A gap appeared in the crowd, Peter squeezed through, and there he was. Stood on a box, blue jeans, white T-shirt, looking for all the world like an ordinary man. He was talking to the people surrounding him, as though holding a conversation, but his words carried to the distant parts of the courts.

Jesus noticed Peter, gave a small smile, carried on. 'Let anyone who is thirsty, come to me and drink. As the scriptures say, whoever believes in me will find rivers of living water flowing from within.'

The crowd cheered.

'This man is a living prophet.'

'Jesus for Messiah.'

A chant started.

'Jesus.'

'Jesus.'

'Jesus.'

'Jesus.'

'Jesus.'

✝

THE TEMPLE, YORK, NORTHUMBRIA.

'Jesus.'

'Jesus.'

'Jesus.'

'Jesus.'

'Jesus.'

Caiaphas motioned with a flick of his hand. One of the attendants closed the window, the sound from outside dropped to a faint whisper.

Caiaphas looked at the selected members called to the impromptu meeting. 'Can you hear that?'

Nobody answered. O'Deamus took the question as rhetorical.

Silence.

'This needs sorting.' Caiaphas said. 'I've seen Pilate. No help whatsoever. He demands proof that Jesus is involved with FKU before he'll act.'

'That doesn't seem too unreasonable.' O'Deamus murmured.

Caiaphas shot him a look, chose to ignore the comment. There was no sense in falling out among themselves.

'What happened to the Temple guards?' A Scribe asked.

Caiaphas snorted. 'They stopped to listen, decided Jesus was speaking a lot of sense, and decided not to arrest him. Needless to say I've decided they're unfit to hold the office of Temple guard.'

Caiaphas picked up a sheet of paper. 'Apparently, Jesus claims to be the light of the world,' he paused. O'Deamus could feel the indignation coming off the man in waves. 'And whoever believes in him,' Caiaphas continued, 'will have the light of life.'

He looked round the small gathering. 'The Sanhedrin decides religious matters in the kingdom. It is not determined by that rabble out there.' He waved towards the window. 'This situation cannot be allowed to continue. Jesus doesn't call the shots, we do.'

O'Deamus smiled to himself. It seemed as though Jesus was firmly in control of the situation. The question was. How long would he wait before making his move?

TWELVE

ONE YEAR AGO.
LEEDS, NORTHUMBRIA.

The TV flickered in the corner of the room. Scenes of burning buildings, vehicles, youths running amok, crowds looting, came and went in quick succession. They told their own story, but the scrolling text gave words to the pictures, Violence has once again erupted in the major cities of the kingdom.

Bocus stubbed his smoke out in the ashtray, popped the top on another can of lager. 'Don't know what the world's coming to.'

Beaumont watched the pictures in silence, thought it rich that someone responsible for planting bombs, killing innocent people should complain when others ignored the rule of law.

'It'll be martial law next, troops on the street corners.'

'Isn't this all part of the campaign?' Beaumont asked.

'This?' Bocus gestured at the TV. 'Anarchy in the streets?'

'I would have thought anything that put pressure on the authorities could only help.' Beaumont said.

'It's playing into their hands.' Bocus replied. 'Too much of this and Pilate will put a curfew in place. That could screw things up for us.'

On the screen, high pressure jets from water cannons knocked protesters over. Snatch squads darted in, and despite a hail of bricks and petrol bombs, dragged them away.

'Poor buggers.' Beaumont said.

Bocus snorted. 'It's their own fault, they deserve everything they get. You can't tackle the State head on. You have to wear them down. It's a war of attrition.'

'Like we're doing?'

'Exactly.' Bocus declared. 'Don't underestimate the work we do.'

'Planting bombs?' Beaumont said.

Bocus gave him a look. 'Every bomb that goes off reminds the Saxons that we're still around, we're not going away. We're a major irritant.'

Like wasps at a picnic, Beaumont thought, that's how irritating we are, and as dangerous.

Some time later, when NBC had tired of the riots, a picture of Jesus came onto the screen. Bocus groaned. 'Not him again.'

'Do you think he might have a point?' Beaumont asked.

'Jesus?'

'Yeah.'

'Maybe, if you're a lame brain who can't think for yourself.' He opened another beer. 'Do you?'

Beaumont shrugged. 'I don't know.'

'Bloke was a builder in Whitby.' Bocus held the can to his mouth. 'What's he know about anything?'

'He seems to talk a lot of sense.'

'Yeah,' Bocus shook his head, 'sounds good on paper. Love the Lord your God, love your neighbour as yourself.' He belched. 'I'll love my Saxon neighbour once he's buggered off home, left us to rule ourselves.'

'Not gonna happen, is it?' Beaumont sighed. 'We're just wasting our time.'

'Don't be so negative.' Bocus replied. 'The Saxons will soon have had enough. They'll piss off home, leave us to it.'

'Do you reckon?' Beaumont was sceptical.

Bocus swigged from the can, belched again. 'Bound to.' He wiped his mouth on his sleeve. 'Course, this Jesus, this Messiah, he might just be waiting for the right moment to make his move.'

'And if he does?'

'Fair play to him. If he has a plan to overthrow the Saxons, unite the kingdoms, bring peace and prosperity.' Bocus shrugged. 'What's not to like?' sudden grin, 'It'll bloody well save us the time and effort.'

†

SUBURBAN STREET, SHEFFIELD, NORTHUMBRIA.

Sheffield, down near the southern border with Mercia, was almost a foreign land. The minibus had broken down, and Jesus, not wanting to be delayed, had set off walking. He was due to speak at Meadowhall, the vast shopping complex, just off the main route north and south through the kingdom. They were moving through a poor deprived area. All around street after street of terraced houses, broken bikes, abandoned toys left in the gutter, the air of neglect palpable. The disciples moved as a close knit group, eyes to the side, front, rear, checking, always checking.

The burnt out cars seemed to be the norm round here, and nothing to do with the recent riots. Should have been demolished years ago, Jim thought, as they passed another street end, mangy dog in the road chewing a bone.

Peter called a halt, checked the map on his phone. He frowned, held it aloft. 'No flaming signal.'

'Again?' Andrew questioned.

Peter shrugged, showed him the display. 'Or it's being blocked.'

'Why block a sat nav signal?' Andrew frowned.

'So we get lost?' Jude suggested.

'Where's the Boss?' Peter wanted to know.

Jim pointed back the way they'd come. Jesus and John had stopped, were talking to an elderly couple. The disciples looked about uneasily. Peter sniffed the air. It was quiet, almost peaceful, but not quite. There was something intangible in the air, a feeling that it might kick off at any moment, a thought not dispelled by the faint, faraway sound of a siren. He frowned, tried to concentrate, wished Jesus wouldn't keep stopping.

Peter was too far from the sea. He wanted out of this warren. 'Come on.' He set off in the direction they'd been going. A few of the lads were grumbling about their feet, he ignored them, checked that Jesus and John had left the old couple and were catching up.

'Hey up, Peter?' Tom called in a low voice. He'd stopped, was looking down another identical street. 'Something's happening.'

A crowd had gathered a hundred metres down the

street. Thirty or forty people on the narrow pavement, spilling onto the road. The people in the crowd were quiet, too quiet.

Tom wanted to be there in the thick of it. 'What do you reckon?' He asked.

Peter shrugged. 'Dunno, some sort of vigil?'

'It doesn't feel right.' Tom replied.

'Leave it.' Peter decided.

'We should check it out.'

'No.' Peter was insistent. 'Leave it.'

'Why?'

'I don't want Jesus getting involved in any trouble.'

'Could be a story in it.'

'There's more to all this than you getting another story.'

They stood arguing for a few minutes, the other disciples chipping in from time to time. When Jesus arrived he asked what the problem was. The disciples fell silent. Tom, ignoring the look from Peter, explained what they'd seen.

'Come on then,' Jesus decided, 'let's go.'

Peter sighed. Just what he didn't want.

As they got nearer Tom realised the crowd weren't silent. There was a low buzz of angriness. He asked a woman with two small children clinging to her hands what was happening.

One of the children, a boy, piped up. 'A naughty man lives there.'

The woman pulled her children even closer. That's right, darling.' She shrugged and pulled a face at Tom. 'Just come out of prison and they dump him back in our community. He's either coming out, or this lot are going in.' She looked at Jesus. 'I know you, don't I?'

'Come on Boss,' Peter urged, 'let's go. We can't do anything here.'

Jesus ignored him.

A few other people turned, studied the strangers.

'Hey up, it's that Jesus feller.'

A few people split off from the main crowd, surrounded Jesus and the disciples, asking questions, wanting healings, miracles, anything. A shout came from near the house. 'There he is, dirty bastard.'

Tom looked up, saw a pale face at the window. A white flash, then it was gone.

Jesus made his way through to the front, Peter followed pushing people aside. A line of glass bottles on the pavement, rags coming out of the top, strong smell of petrol. Why wait, he thought. Why don't they just do it?

A man at the front, holding a snarling dog on a straining leash, looked at Jesus, looked again, grinned. 'Hey up, Jesus mate, how ya doing?'

Jesus bent down to the dog. The man jerked the lead. 'Wouldn't do that mate, he'll have yer.'

Ignoring the advice, Jesus reached out, spoke to the animal. Those near enough were convinced they heard him say, 'Come out.'

In any event, the animal became calm, docile. It lay down, exposed its belly, and allowed Jesus to stroke it.

The man looked on in amazement, and offered his hand. 'Ackroyd.' He laughed as he pumped Jesus' arm. 'That was amazing. He's allus been a vicious bastard.'

Jesus nodded, didn't speak.

'Come to give us a hand,' Ackroyd asked, 'have yer?'

Peter wondered if he was serious, then watched in amazement as Jesus dropped to his haunches, and moved his finger across the footpath. The words, I AM, appeared, etched into the stone pavement.

Tom held his phone up to his face, pressed RECORD. The buzzing of the crowd which had died down at Jesus' arrival, increased in volume.

'Sorry feller.' Ackroyd said. 'No filming.'

Tom nodded. 'Shame.' He lowered the phone, slipped it in his pocket.

'What do you intend doing if he comes out?' Jesus asked.

Ackroyd nodded at a rope hanging from a lamp-post. 'We string him up.'

'Once we've cut his knackers off.' A woman called from the crowd. A nervous laugh rippled round. A child started crying.

Jesus, eyes blazing, shook his head. 'No. No, no.'

Ackroyd squared up to Jesus. 'We've got our own way o' doing things round here, Jesus. By all means give us hand talking him out, but don't interfere otherwise, okay?'

Jesus ignored him, stooped to the floor again. Peter moved closer, eased Ackroyd to one side, saw Jesus' finger move. The words, YOU SHALL NOT, appeared.

Jesus stood, stretched. 'So, you want the man inside to come out?'

'Yes.' The crowd roared.

'Boss.' Peter said. 'We need to leave.' He jerked his head at the baying crowd. 'This could get ugly. Now would be a good time to go, leave them to it.' He looked to Andrew for support. His brother, white-faced, tense, nodded.

Jesus heard him out in silence, then. 'Peter, my

friend. Don't you see, forgiveness is for everyone.'

Jesus turned, addressed the crowd of people. 'Who amongst you has never done anything wrong?'

The crowd shuffled, muttered among themselves. They could have had this done by now, been home in time for tea, feet up, telly on.

'Who among you is guilt free?' Jesus called. 'You, Ackroyd? Are you guilt free? Have you always been faithful to your wife, never slept with another woman?'

Ackroyd blushed, stammered. 'No.' As a denial it was less than convincing.

The crowd jeered.

A woman stood by his side looked mortified. His wife, Peter assumed.

'You?' Jesus pointed at a thin, rat faced woman, roll up hanging from her mouth. 'What about your husband, convicted for robbing post offices. Taking something that belongs to someone else is both shameful and sinful.'

The woman looked away.

'This bloke had stuff on his computer.' A voice called out. 'That's worse than being unfaithful or robbing a post office.'

'Who are you to judge the law,' Jesus retorted, 'All sin is sin, and as you well know, the penalty for sin, according to ancient scriptures, is death.'

The crowd listened in stony silence as the disciples exchanged nervous looks. Get this wrong and they'd all be hanging from lamp-posts.

'So,' Jesus picked up a petrol bomb and continued, 'let anyone who has never sinned pick up a petrol bomb or a brick and throw it through his window.'

There was silence, then gradually, over the course

of ten minutes, the mood changed. People began to drift away, and the excitement was over. Ackroyd's wife took him firmly by the arm, pulled him away. Fifteen minutes later, Jesus and the disciples were alone on the street. Peter breathed a sigh of relief, wanted to speak, found he couldn't. He looked down at the pavement where Jesus had carved in the stone with his finger. The words had vanished, the path smooth once more.

Jesus knocked on the door. After an age it opened a minimal amount. The terrified man peered out. When he saw Jesus he fell to his knees sobbing uncontrollably. 'Oh, Lord, please forgive me. I know I've done wrong.'

Jesus helped the man to his feet, embraced him, and then said, 'Where is everybody? Do any of them condemn you now?'

The man took a deep breath. 'No, sir.'

Jesus placed his hand on the man's shoulder. 'Then, neither do I. Go in peace and sin no more.'

✝

GOVERNOR'S OFFICE, YORK, NORTHUMBRIA.

Pilate looked at the embossed invitation. Signed by the Fuehrer's own hand no less.

'Was that Caiaphas I saw leaving?'

Pilate looked up. 'What?'

He wished his wife wouldn't just appear at his side like that. 'Yes, yes. Complaining about Jesus again.'

Claudia sighed. 'How annoying. He reminds me of a vulture.'

Pilate smiled at his wife. 'A vulture in robes.'

They both laughed.

'What does he expect you do about him?'

Pilate shrugged. 'Arrest him, throw him in the dungeons.'

'You won't, will you?' Claudia frowned.

'What's it to you?'

'Nothing.'

'You're not a follower are you?'

Silence.

'Are you?' Pilate was not amused.

Claudia looked at her husband. 'No, I'm not a follower.'

'What then?'

'I've been to one or two meetings.'

'I didn't know that.' Pilate met her eye. 'Don't you realise how that might look?'

Claudia shrugged. 'A few meetings, that's all. I don't think anybody recognised me.'

Pilate sighed. 'Don't tell me you've bought into this whole Messiah, son of God business?'

Claudia clicked her tongue. 'No, of course not. He's a good man, a just man. He teaches people the difference between right and wrong.'

'It's all relative.' Pilate was scathing.

'Wer Macht hat, hat recht.' Claudia replied and moved to the door. She turned and shrugged, 'It's no big deal.'

'All the same, it might be as well if you didn't go again.' Pilate advised.

'Why?'

'You never know.' Pilate said with a half-smile. 'I might have to sign his death warrant one day.'

'You'd better not.' Claudia left and closed the door a little too firmly.

Pilate sighed again, pressed the buzzer twice. No sense in falling out over it now. It might never happen. Anyway, he had more important things to think about. Like this invitation to the conference at the Wannsee Centre in Berlin. Just one item on the top secret agenda, The Jewish Question.

'Come in.' Pilate called in response to a light tap on the door. Winston, his tall, black, shaven headed, slave cum bodyguard set his coffee down on the desk and waited to be dismissed.

Pilate looked at him. 'What do you think of this Jesus character, Winston?'

'Nothing, sir.'

'Nothing?'

'He seems like a good man, sir.'

'Anything else?'

Winston was silent for a moment. 'No, sir.'

'Do you believe he's the Messiah?'

Winston, uncomfortable at being questioned, shook his head. 'I don't know, sir.'

'If he was coming at me to cause me harm, what would you do Winston?'

'I would stop him, sir.' Winston replied. Pilate waved his hand in dismissal. Winston paused at the door. 'Wouldn't happen though, would it, sir?'

†

BARNSLEY, NORTHUMBRIA.

'When do you think he'll make his move?'

John frowned. 'What move?'

'March on York, Berlin.' Simon the Zealot looked at John. Was he stupid? 'Overthrow the Saxons.'

'What makes you think that's the plan?'

Simon shrugged. 'Gotta be. Hasn't it? The way I see it. He's building up popular support. The message is spreading across the Union. Ask Maggie about the hits we're getting on the website. He's even got Pharisees and Polizei officers coming for healing.'

'So?' John shrugged. 'They're just opportunists. I don't see too many declaring their allegiance.'

'You don't think they could be persuaded to join a popular revolution?'

'And if they could,' John snorted, 'what then? You think the Fuehrer is going to let that happen? Let a bunch of Jews take over part of the Union? I don't think so.'

'We could join with FKU, time it so we take power in the four kingdoms, unite under one flag.'

'Dreams, my friend.' John replied. 'Anyway, I can't see Jesus getting involved with that bunch.'

'I used to be involved with that bunch.' Simon retorted.

'Yeah, but you saw the light, saw that following Jesus was the way.'

Simon sighed. 'It's all peace and love, though.' He cracked his knuckles. 'I'm not against peace and love, but it's gonna take a lot more than that to dislodge the Saxons.'

'It's bigger than that.' John replied. 'You don't think Jesus has come just to get rid of the Saxons, do you?'

'No?' Simon looked disappointed.

John shook his head. 'I believe that God loves the

people of the world so much that he's sent his son to die for us, and that whoever believes in him will never die, but have eternal life.'

'That's big.' Simon said, and thought for a moment. 'In fact, that's immense.'

†

State Security HQ, York, Northumbria.

Swanger sank into her office chair. She needed a drink, a smoke, and a good night's sleep. Fresh from another progress meeting with Heathersedge she was considering her options. It was a joke, an insult. Senior operatives like herself, used to working alone, following their noses, should not be saddled with junior agents fresh out of training school.

A JFDI from the very top, Heathersedge had claimed, over Swanger's clamorous protest. All the field operatives were being partnered up. Trouble was the pensions were crap, you had to keep working till you dropped otherwise retirement was a long drawn out decline into poverty. Some managed better than others. The ones who'd managed to line a little nest egg along the way. That had never been Swanger's way, couldn't see herself starting now.

She poured another drink, lit a cigarette, pulled the smoke deep, held it, and then blew a thin plume towards the ceiling. The effects of the nicotine and alcohol calmed her down. After a while she pushed her sense of injustice to one side, considered the two files on her desk.

Operation Raven, the investigation into the Four

Kingdoms United bombing campaign was stalled. The bombings continued, but there was no lead on who was responsible. Swanger wasn't working alone on Raven. Scores of State Security agents and hundreds of Polizei detectives were sweating blood to no avail. The Governor had promised a large reward for any officer who provided the breakthrough. Swanger couldn't see any realistic prospect of it being her. Although the hunt was intelligence led, Swanger knew that luck played a part. The way it was going it would be some plod stumbling across the solution by accident. The case of the serial killer who'd been caught when he'd pissed over a copper's boots in a doorway was legendary. She stubbed out the cigarette, rubbed her eyes, and idly flicked through the mass of information. Although the data was computerised and cross referenced, Swanger liked to have a print out on her desk that she could touch.

The one tangible lead, the missing guard, had come to nothing, when a body, wrapped in chains, had been found at the bottom of the reservoir. Alan, the guard, had been identified by his dental records, and his wife left alone to grieve or otherwise. No sign of Archie the dog, though, she noted with a wry smile.

Swanger looked at the other file out of curiosity. Operation Gosling, the surveillance on Jesus and his band of merry men, as Swanger thought of them. The file had been updated with a new set of photos. She skimmed through them. The one of Jesus, in front of an angry mob, petrol bomb in hand, caused her to smile. She wondered what the story was behind that.

Thinking about Jesus brought Simon the Zealot to mind once again and the name he'd given up the night he'd been lifted.

Bocus.

Swanger said it again. She was reluctant to confront the guy yet, but knew the time was fast approaching when she'd have to eyeball him. See what he was made of. Bocus worked for Northumbrian Water in some kind of project management position. He'd been responsible for checking out the security at all the company's facilities, including the sites that had been attacked in the past few months. Coincidence? Maybe. Who better, though, Swanger reasoned, than such a man, to be behind the recent phase of bombings.

She studied the photo. Average looking guy, straight black hair, regulation cut, brown eyes. Looked a decent, honest citizen. Not married, wasn't seeing anybody, man or woman, didn't, as far as was known, visit NorPro. Went to work, came home. Lived a boring, solid life. That bothered Swanger. Nobody in their thirties had that reclusive a lifestyle unless they were hiding something.

She stared at the photo, willing it to tell her something, anything, about the man.

What are you hiding Bocus?

Swanger pushed the file away, lit another cigarette, paced round the office. Heathersedge wanted results. The Governor was on his back, and he was feeling the pressure. Swanger didn't want to alert her target, force him deeper underground, but the situation needed a shake.

Bocus had been under a light surveillance regime for the past few months, his telephones wired, his internet usage and emails, monitored. Result, nothing. He'd been followed from time to time, but apart from going to work and back, and the occasional visit to his local pub, where he made two pints last an hour, there was nothing. The guy was apparently clean. Swanger knew she needed to eyeball the guy, see the whites of his eyes. She knew if Bocus was up to anything he wouldn't be able to hide it from a seasoned investigator.

How to get up close though, without alerting him?

An hour later, ashtray overflowing, whisky bottle two thirds empty, Swanger thought she had the beginnings of a plan. It would be expensive, and it would need Heathersedge to sign it off, but it might, just might, reveal something.

THIRTEEN

LEEDS, NORTHUMBRIA.

It was a time of teaching and anointing.

Seventy-two apostles had been recruited. Their initial training completed, they were being sent out for a three day final assignment. Like the twelve disciples who'd undertaken a similar exercise they would operate in pairs, travelling to all parts of the island.

Jesus, flanked by Peter and John, addressed the new recruits.

'I am sending you out like lambs among wolves.' Jesus began. Peter caught John's eye, winked. These lads were in for a treat. 'Do not take food, money, cards or phones,' Jesus continued, 'just the clothes you stand in. Do not greet anybody on your travels. Wait until somebody speaks to you. When they do, wish them peace.'

'When you enter a town or a village and are welcomed by the people, take what hospitality is offered to you. A bed, food, drink, and be thankful. Heal the sick that are there. Tell them the kingdom of God has come near to them.'

A buzz broke out. The apostles murmuring to each other. Jesus waited a few moments, held up his hand, waited for the chattering to die down.

'But,' he continued, 'if you enter a town or a village,

and are not welcomed, wave it goodbye, and leave at once.' Jesus paused. All eyes were on him. 'Whoever listens to you, listens to me. Whoever rejects you, rejects me. But whoever rejects me rejects the one who sent me.'

Silence.

Each pairing of apostles had been decided by drawing lots. Slips of paper pulled from a bag by Jesus. A small group gathered at the door as the apostles left. Jesus greeted each man by name, shook hands, and embraced them as they left, as did Peter and John. Maggie on a rare excursion from the office was handing out the return rail tickets, the destinations, like the pairings, picked at random.

The line dwindled until the last pair stood before Jesus, a mixture of excitement and apprehension clear on their faces. Jesus stepped forward. 'Carl.' They shook hands, embraced. He greeted Carl's younger companion, Ben, in similar fashion.

Maggie smiled at the two eager apostles, handed them their tickets. 'Wolverhampton.' She told them.

Peter checked they hadn't any money, cards, food, or phones. They assured him they hadn't.

'Then go.' Jesus commanded.

†

The seventy-two had departed. The disciples, drinking tea, coffee, munching biscuits, came into the hall, and settled down on chairs that had been set up in front of a white screen. One or two finished mobile phone conversations, others watched with interest as Jude set up a laptop and went through the starting procedure.

He negotiated a menu, and highlighted a video. He turned to Jesus. 'All ready, Boss.'

Jesus thanked him, checked all phones were on silent, and waited till he had full attention.

'Jesus?' A voice called from the back of the hall.

Peter groaned, looked at John. 'Thought you'd locked the door.'

John insisted he had. At the front, Jesus was asking Brotherton what he could do for him.

'As it happens, Jesus,' Brotherton replied, making his way to the front, 'you can tell me how to inherit eternal life.'

A collective groan sprang up from the disciples. They were all sick of Brotherton and his questions.

'He knows Boss.' Peter growled. 'The guy's stubborn, he refuses to accept it.'

Jesus held his hand up for silence. He asked Brotherton, 'What is written in the law? How do you read it?'

Brotherton considered the question. 'Love the Lord your God with all your heart, with all your soul, all your strength, and your entire mind...'

'And love your neighbour as yourself.' Peter jumped in, ignoring Brotherton's glare, and basked in the cheers of the disciples.

Jesus grinned. 'That's right. Do this Brotherton and you'll live.'

'Like I said, Boss. He knows.' Peter pushed his chair back, stretched his legs. 'No excuses.'

Brotherton ignored Peter. 'But Jesus, who is my neighbour?'

'Ah, that's easy.' Jim declared. The disciples muttered their agreement.

'We'll see, shall we?' Jesus said. 'Today lads,' he paused, 'we're going to watch a video.'

Ragged cheering met this announcement. It's like being back at school, Peter thought. Teacher showing a film on a rainy afternoon.

'What's this film, Jesus?' Brotherton again.

Jesus didn't answer. He turned on the big screen. 'Who's heard of The Shades and The Rench?' He asked.

Who hadn't?

The Shades and The Rench were by far the two biggest criminal gangs jostling for position and eminence in the kingdom. Both gangs were into drugs, pimping, protection, and a host of minor crime. They often clashed over territory, vicious beatings were commonplace, and any gang member who fell into the hands of the rival outfit knew it wouldn't end well.

The hall descended into a hubbub of noise as the disciples swapped horror stories of what they'd heard about the two gangs. After a few minutes, the noise died down and Peter asked Jesus why he wanted to know.

In reply Jesus pressed play on the laptop. 'Watch this.'

Jude dimmed the hall lights as the screen flickered into life.

The film was put together from CCTV images taken in a city centre. It opened on a man, mirror wrap round sunglasses, walking in a busy pedestrianised shopping centre. A large, four-wheel drive vehicle appeared in shot following behind the man. Shoppers looked, nudged each other and moved out of the way. Mothers gathered children, held them close. The doors on the car flew open and three men, each holding a baseball bat, jumped from the slow moving vehicle. They moved into position behind their unknowing victim.

The violence, when it started, was all the more shocking for being silent. One of the assailants struck the Shades man behind the knees. As he fell to the floor, the others started laying into to him, the bats rising and falling in hypnotic rhythm as they struck him time and again. Peter counted over twenty sickening blows, then, almost as soon as it had begun, it was over. The three men jumped back into the vehicle, it turned off into a side turning, and was lost from sight. The camera remained focussed on the victim lying motionless on the floor.

A few of the twelve shifted uncomfortably. Okay the guy was a member of a criminal gang, but he didn't deserve to be beaten like that.

On the screen, life in the city centre was continuing as normal. Shoppers continued shopping, none spared a glance for the stricken man. A Polizei officer walked towards the man on the pavement. It was obvious he hadn't seen him, but when he did he stopped, turned and walked the other way.

A priest, robes flapping behind, hurried past. 'He's seen him.' Jim said, indignant.

Minutes passed, the disciples continued to watch. A man, with a baseball cap, wearing a dark blue hoody, walked up to the injured man, stooped, and spoke to him. As he dropped to his knees to help, the yellow TR, signifying The Rench, came into view.

What now, Peter wondered. Stiletto to the ribs, finish him off?

The Rench man helped the Shades member to a sitting position. He took out his phone, made a call, and then walked away. Jesus forwarded the video. An estate car, blue flashing lights on top, appeared. It stopped, a paramedic got out, and started attending to the injured man.

The screen went blank. There was silence in the hall.

'Which of these was a neighbour to the victim Brotherton,' Jesus asked, 'the Polizei officer, the priest, or the Rench member?'

Brotherton squirmed in his seat, caught between a rock and a hard place.

'Yeah, come on Brotherton.' Nathan called out.

'The one who helped him.' Brotherton muttered.

'That's right.' Jesus replied. 'Go and do likewise.'

✝

Maggie, back from the sending out of the seventy-two, opened the door of the Ops centre, and scanned the room. The office was dotted with work stations, four to a pod, desks facing inwards. Everybody here was a committed follower of Jesus, all engaged in advancing the kingdom.

This was the place where Maggie spent her time. Long hours coordinating the schedule, making sure Jesus and the disciples had the most up to date info. She hovered for a while, monitoring conversations. Could Jesus, open a fete, visit a school, a retirement home, a prison, and speak at a business conference?

Calls came in from the press and TV stations. Everybody wanted an interview with Jesus. If he wasn't available one of the disciples would do, at a pinch. The media beast needed feeding on a regular basis. This was where social network feeds were monitored, staff searching for #Jesus or #Messiah, and then posting replies.

Maggie caught Poppy's eye as she moved to her desk. She watched as her old friend wrote the number, 34, next to the legend, DMP - Daily Marriage Proposals. She always had a slight pang at this figure. All those lonely women who wanted Jesus for themselves, believing he would make the perfect husband. She sympathised with them all, but knew it would never happen. Maggie recalled the conversations she'd had with him about marriage. How he'd told her about the church that would be built in his name, that he would come back one day as the bridegroom, claim the church as his bride. Not that she'd understood what he'd meant, but realised that if she wanted a husband, kids, it would be with somebody else a little less perfect than the Son of God.

At her desk in a corner of the large room, she switched her computer on, sighed when she saw the number of emails in her inbox. It was so different to the early days when most of her time was spent on the road with Jesus and the lads. She checked Jesus' online diary and making a call to Peter, confirmed that Jesus had arrived for the civic lunch at Wakefield Town Hall.

†

WAKEFIELD, NORTHUMBRIA.

Jesus shook his hands, turned from the hot air dryer and held the door for Tom, who frowned as Brotherton forced his way into the gap, blocking the exit.

'I notice you didn't wash before eating?' Brotherton said. Tom wondered why he still bothered. Trailing round after them all the time, chipping in, sniping away. It didn't seem to bother him how many times he got knocked back, he'd still be there trying his best to undermine Jesus.

Jesus threw back his head, laughed. 'You Pharisees, you crack me up.'

'Why?' Brotherton frowned.

'You wash the outside, scrub it clean, but inside,' Jesus sighed, shook his head, 'inside, you are full of greed and wickedness. You are foolish people. Didn't the one who made the outside make the inside as well? But what is inside you now? I tell you the truth, Brotherton, be generous to the poor, and everything will be clean.'

'Now hang on a minute.' Brotherton blustered.

Jesus held up his hands. 'Woe to you Pharisees. You give a tenth of your income to the Temple, but you neglect justice and the love of God. You should do both.'

Brotherton was silent.

'Woe to you Pharisees.' Jesus continued, 'You love the most important seats in the synagogue. You revel in the respect shown to you. Woe to you Pharisees. You are like unmarked graves, which people walk over without knowing it.'

Another of the Pharisees came in at that moment. Tom couldn't recall his name, knew him as an expert in the law. He joined Brotherton in condemning Jesus. 'When you say these things, Jesus, you insult us.'

'And you experts of the law,' Jesus replied, 'Woe to you as well. You load people down with burdens they can hardly carry, and you don't lift a finger to help. You have taken away the keys of knowledge. You have not entered the kingdom, and you hinder those that want to enter.'

†

LEEDS, NORTHUMBRIA.

The seventy-two apostles had all returned without incident, which Peter thought amazing. He'd been expecting a few casualties. Thought one or two might have been seduced by the bright lights of the world. He pursed his lips and looked them over. They didn't seem much the worse for their experience. The fact was, a few days after their return, they were still full of it, still bubbling over with enthusiasm. He called the gathering together, thanked them for their obedience, made sure they were rested, and then began the meeting in prayer before handing over to Jesus.

'It is so good to see you all back safe and well.' Jesus said. 'I'm sure you've all had amazing adventures for the sake of the kingdom of God.' He continued with a twinkle in his eye, 'And now it's time to share those adventures.' Jesus looked round the room. 'The last to go were Carl and Ben. I think it fitting that they be the first to share with us.'

The two young men were met with thunderous cheering as they took their place in front of the room. Carl took stock of his fellow apostles, the disciples and Jesus. He waited for the applause to die away, and then said, 'Lord, even the demons submit in your name.'

More applause, cheering, and echoes of appreciation greeted this remark.

'I saw Satan fall like lightning from heaven.' Jesus replied. 'I gave you authority to trample on snakes and scorpions, and to overcome all the power of the enemy. Nothing will harm you. However, do not rejoice that the spirits submit to you, but rejoice that your names are written in heaven.'

Carl considered this, then said, 'We had an amazing time. Like you, we had nothing apart from the clothes we wore. No money, no food, no phone. Just the two of us and a bag o' nerves.'

Ben nodded his agreement.

'And as you know,' Carl continued, 'the idea was simple enough, preach the good news about Jesus,' he smiled, 'heal the sick.' He paused for a moment. 'Simple enough, eh, lads?'

Silence.

'Anyway,' Carl continued, 'we arrived in Wolverhampton on Friday evening, and headed out into the city to get our bearings. I must admit I was half expecting someone to meet us at the station with our names on a board. They'd whisk us away to a five star hotel with hot food, shower, warm bed, and clean sheets - the works.' He paused, laughed. 'Nah, didn't happen.

'We got talking to a few people on the streets. We prayed for them, we prayed for the healing of the sick.

While we were walking round, I stumbled, fell over, and hit the deck, hands and knees job. It would have been embarrassing if anybody noticed, but, nobody did.'

'We spent the night in a shop doorway. We were cold and too hungry to sleep. At one stage a couple o' drunks peed in the doorway. We had to move on, find a dry place.'

'My faith was low, I'm sure Ben was feeling the same, but I could hear him whispering to himself, "God is good, God is good." After a while I joined in. The angels didn't come down to save us, fire from heaven didn't appear to warm us, but God was with us, and hope returned.'

'The next morning we were up early after an hour's sleep. We prayed, walked around for a while to get warm. We were both very hungry and light-headed with it.'

'For the rest of Saturday we wandered around the city. We met many homeless people; difference was, they weren't playing at it, like us. I felt challenged to try to get some food for them. We went into lots of places, burger bars, and kebab shops. Nobody wanted to know. We kept being told, get a job, and feed yourselves. After a lot of searching, we found one place, Subway, where they gave us two free sandwiches. We wandered round looking for somebody deserving to give them to. I have to confess, I was hoping Ben suggested we ate them, but he didn't.'

Ben laughed. 'I was hoping the same, mate.'

'Then we met these two homeless guys, Derek and Steve. Originally from Scotland, they'd been working down in Wessex, but their contract had come to an end sooner than expected. They'd been left adrift without any money, and were hitch hiking back up north when they'd washed up in Wolverhampton. They were grateful for the food. While we were standing chatting with these guys a group of lads out on the town wandered past. One of them pulled out a wad of notes, flashed it, taunting us. I asked Derek if that happened a lot. He told me it happened every day. After a bit more chat, they wandered off to find a place to sleep.'

'Then Ben started talking to this man, Stuart. We asked if he'd heard of Jesus. He told us he was part of a group who met on a Sunday morning to talk about Jesus and what he means for the world. Stuart was amazed when we told him who we were and who'd sent us. He invited us back to spend the night at his house, before the meeting on Sunday. We spent the night with Stuart and his family, chatting, watching the latest uploads on the Boss, and what was happening. We each had a sleeping bag on his living room floor. We were warm, we had hot food, but you know, I couldn't stop thinking about the two Scottish lads who were trying to get home.'

'We woke early on Sunday morning, had breakfast, and made extra bacon and egg rolls, then set out to find Derek and Steve. After what seemed like ages, we found them huddled together in a shop doorway. We gave them the food and invited them along to the meeting.'

'At the meeting there were about twenty or so people, men and women who wanted to know about the Boss,' Carl nodded at Jesus, 'we had to tell them all we knew, what he was about, what he'd come to achieve. Derek and Steve shared their stories, and were amazed when Stuart and his friends had a whip round. It made them enough money to get a train back to Scotland. They left with tears in their eyes. To them, after months of living rough, existing on what other people had thrown away, such generosity was unbelievable.'

'After the meeting we went back into the city centre with Stuart and his group. We approached the lovely people at Subway, and asked for more food for the homeless, which we got, and then we spent the afternoon distributing it. When we left, they were talking about setting up a permanent soup kitchen to feed the homeless on a regular basis.'

The hall was silent. The disciples as enthralled as the new recruits.

'You never realise,' Carl continued, 'until you're in a position to see them, just how many people are living down there,' he pointed at the floor, 'in the gutter.

'We were doing this for the weekend. Friday night through Sunday night, then we came home, back to civilisation. There are people out there, good people, men, women, children,' Carl took a deep breath. 'It's their way of life. They exist on the streets, in the shadows. They're invisible, and when we joined them, we became like them. Invisible. Anonymous.'

There were nods of recognition from the other apostles, the disciples. They knew too well just how bad it could be for people on the margins of society.

FOURTEEN

LEEDS, NORTHUMBRIA.

Once the woman had rung the bell, Beaumont couldn't settle to anything. He interspersed pacing the floor with surfing the afternoon TV channels. It was the standard fare. Old films, shopping channels, glamorous girls selling you stuff you didn't know existed, much less wanted. He lingered for a while in horrified fascination over a studio filled with a baying audience as two women fought over a smirking young scrote. Worn out by watching, he switched off in disgust, smoked a joint, drank two cans of lager, and convinced himself the black clad Ninjas would be through the door any second. It took all of his will-power not to rush out in the street and give himself up.

The gate creaked. Beaumont took up his position at the back of in the living room near the kitchen door, saw the woman as she approached the door again. The bell rang loud and shrill. Beaumont waited for her to realise there was nobody home. After a minute she wandered down the path, looked back at the house, and closed the gate.

Through the open window, he could hear the noise of the machinery, the pneumatic drill, the diggers, the clash of shovels, could imagine the men, stripped to the waist, glistening with sweat. He pulled the settee away from the wall, grabbed cushions, and wedged himself into the space.

†

Despite the heat of the day the car windows were closed, engine running, air con going full blast. Swanger watched as the road crew, stripped to the waist, dug holes in the street. Her young colleague, Barnabas, out in the field for the first time, fidgeted in the passenger seat. For Swanger, used to working alone, being anonymous, it felt like she had somebody surgically attached. Every time she turned round the kid was there. At her elbow, under her feet, asking questions, complaining, moaning. It was too hot, it was too cold. The air con was too loud.

'You want to try lying in a ditch for a week, drinking water from a tube.' Swanger told him.

Barnabas considered this, 'What about toilet facilities?'

'Piss yourself.' Swanger replied tersely, and turned on the radio. These surveillance jobs could get downright boring. Infinite patience was needed, and she wasn't sure Barnabas had what it took. It was a mystery how he got through training.

'Hey.' Barnabas turned up the volume. 'It's Jesus.'

So chuffing what?

'...Jesus speaking earlier to his disciples, told them, "I tell you, do not worry about your life, what you will eat or drink. Or about your body, what clothes you will wear. Life is more than food, and the body more than clothes. Consider the pigeons. They do not sow or reap, they have no storerooms, yet God feeds them. And how much more valuable are you than birds. Who of you by worrying can add a single hour to your life? Since you can't do this simple thing, why worry about the rest."

"Also, consider how the wild flowers grow. They do not labour or spin. Yet I tell you, not even the richest man who ever lived was dressed like one of these. If that is how God clothes the grass of the field, which is here today, gone tomorrow, how much more will He clothe you?"

"Do not be afraid, for your father has been pleased to give you the kingdom. Sell your possessions and give to the poor. Provide wallets for yourself that will not wear out. A treasure in heaven that will never fail, where no thief comes and no moth destroys. For where your treasure is, there will be your heart..."

'Amen to that.' Barnabas said.

Swanger turned the radio off. Gave him a look. 'You follow Jesus?'

'Is that a problem?'

'It might be for you.'

'How?' Barnabas frowned.

Swanger sighed. Where did they get these people? 'Part of our job is to keep an eye on Jesus and his main associates, the so called disciples. Peter and that bunch.'

'So?'

Swanger laughed. 'Could be, one day they're brought in for questioning. You might be involved in the interviews. How do you feel about that?'

'Don't we have specialist teams to question suspects?' Barnabas queried. 'I thought we just gathered the information.'

'You're right, son. We do. But sometimes we monitor the interrogation, make sure the right questions are asked,' Swanger shrugged, 'suggest further questions. How would you feel if it was Jesus being questioned?'

'I don't know about the twelve disciples,' Barnabas chuckled, 'but you won't find Jesus breaking the law.'

'How's that then.' Swanger wanted to know.

'Simple. Jesus is without sin.'

Swanger, stunned into silence by this naivety, settled back to wait for their target to appear.

†

Approaching Northumbria International Airport.

Pilate was buzzing. Even the bumpy flight back from Berlin hadn't dampened his enthusiasm for what he'd learned. Now, nearing home, he closed his eyes, prayed to a god he didn't believe in, and hoped for the best. The aircraft banked as the pilot lined up the final approach to Northumbria International. Pilate licked his lips, tried to relax, but the undercarriage clanking down startled him for a second. He looked out of the window at the fast approaching ground, knew it would be a good landing.

Thirty minutes later in his official limousine, even the latest news of the riots, relayed to him by Winston, couldn't take the edge off his excitement. It was a stunning idea, even if it'd been presented by that odious creep, Heydrich. Pilate fingered the lock on his attaché case, thought of the slim red folder with the bold black letters on the front, the Wannsee Protocol, Top Secret. When Heydrich had talked them through the plan, it'd been one of those, why has nobody thought of this before moments?

But then it turned out, they had. Wannsee was a resurrection of an old plan first mooted in the time of the first Fuehrer and named for the Wannsee Conference centre on the outskirts of Berlin, where the idea had first been discussed. In essence and somewhat simplified, Wannsee offered Jews and other undesirable people groups the opportunity of living in their own settlements in various locations throughout the Union. These would be self-contained, walled, gated communities, where they'd be able to lead happy comfortable lives with their own kind. They would be offered favourable terms to move and, once they did, would have to remain there for the remainder of their lives. It was hoped that the vast majority would take the Fuehrer's kind offer.

When one brave soul had asked about those who might not want to go, Heydrich had turned his dead eyes on the man, told him refusal wasn't an option. They could either go of their own accord, all expenses paid, or go kicking and screaming, but, go they would.

What was the timescale, somebody else wanted to know.

Plans had been drawn up for these new towns and villages, Heydrich explained. Building work had already commenced at Auschwitz, Belsen, Buchenwald and Ravensbruck. The names meant nothing to Pilate, but the layout of the settlements, the plans for the buildings, looked good on paper.

The Fuehrer hadn't been present of course. She was a busy woman with a Union to run, and Pilate had been disappointed and relieved in equal measure by her absence. As much as he loved the Fuehrer, he found her unpredictable with her ferocious tempers that would blow up out of nowhere.

One thing puzzled Pilate though. There seemed to be another level to Wannsee, but nobody spoke of it. He'd just heard whispers of something called, Endlosung, The Final Solution.

✝

LEEDS, NORTHUMBRIA.

Bocus needed a drink. It'd been another tough day in the office. His boss, Schultz, had been a complete arse over some figures. The drive home, always slow, was worse than ever today. A shunt on the ring road had delayed him for thirty frustrating minutes. The utility companies were taking turns to dig up the roads, cones and red barriers blocking off major sections, diversions in place. The traffic news on the radio accurate as usual, but no use when you were already jammed. Two lines of vehicles were merging into one. A white van jumped the queue, out muscled Bocus into the next available space.

Bastard.

In the mood for a ruck, he leaned on the horn in anger, willed the driver to get out, but amidst the answering chorus of blaring horns the man raised his arm in a conciliatory gesture. Bocus let it go, his anger draining away. He thought back to work. It went through his mind that he was being targeted. He'd caught Schultz giving him a speculative glance more than once, the Saxon looking away when Bocus caught his eye.

The traffic was now moving in a single file, it was steady progress. Bocus tried to push his anxiety aside, told himself he was too sensitive. His paranoia not helped by the coffee machine gossip, the persistent low level buzz going round the office that the spate of bombings at Northumbria Water sites was an inside job.

Bocus had joined in with the chatter to begin with, enjoyed the vicarious thrill of knowing he was talking about himself and Beaumont, but soon tired of it once the speculation of who it might be had started. He didn't feel in any danger. There were plenty of other candidates on the list of potential suspects within the company, engineers were always in and out of these places, not to mention the long list of disgruntled ex-employees let go in the recent round of redundancies. Now, not wanting to tempt fate, he kept his own counsel when the talk turned to Four Kingdoms United.

Once out of the city, away from the road works, the traffic eased. Bocus relaxed, imagined the ice cold lager in the fridge, his name on it. He turned off the main road into his estate, his feelings of negativity almost gone. They soon returned though, when he was met by a barrier blocking his street. Beyond that workmen, diggers, noise, chaos.

†

Beaumont opened his eyes, blinked. He wasn't sure where he was. He eased his way to his feet, became aware of Bocus stood in the doorway, an amused expression on his face.

'What you doing behind there?' Bocus asked.

'Trying to get some peace.' He massaged his temples.

'Beer?'

Beaumont shook his head. 'No thanks.' He had a raging headache and a cricked neck. He told Bocus about the woman at the door.

'It'll be a clipboard Charlie.'

Beaumont frowned. 'Who?'

'It's what we call the people who knock on doors and explain what's happening.' Bocus explained. 'Keeping the customer informed. I expect the gas board do the same. It's good PR. Cuts down the number of complaints.'

In the kitchen Beaumont swallowed three headache tablets and drank a pint of water. 'Is it genuine?'

'Is what genuine?'

'Whatever they're doing, digging up the road.'

Bocus shrugged. 'Looks genuine to me. There's a strong smell of gas out there.'

Beaumont thought for a second. 'Could it be faked though?'

'Anything can be faked,' Bocus laughed, 'but why?'

Beaumont shrugged. A gesture that irritated Bocus. He drained the can, crushed it. 'Do you think all that,' he waved towards the street, 'has been set up just to annoy you? Faking a gas leak, digging up the street, just to wind you up?'

'No, of course not. But it would be a good way to

get in the house, have a look round.'

Bocus stared at Beaumont, wondered whether to laugh, or play along.

The doorbell rang. Beaumont jumped. 'Don't answer it.'

Exasperated, Bocus said. 'Don't be daft. She'll have seen me come home.'

'You could be in the shower, on the bog, anything.' Beaumont sounded desperate.

'She'll come back. Look, I know these people. I know how they think. It's better to answer the door, let her give me the spiel.'

'Don't invite her in.'

No, course not.' Bocus took his friend by the arm. 'Get yourself upstairs, out the way. Let me handle it.'

From a position on the landing Beaumont heard Bocus open the door, heard the woman say in her ordinary voice that there was nothing to worry about. The leak would be repaired soon, but would it be possible to do a quick meter check while she was here.

†

STATE SECURITY HQ, YORK, NORTHUMBRIA.

Swanger rubbed her eyes. Knackered didn't do it justice. Against the dark outside the computer monitor was unnaturally bright. She switched on the small angle poise lamp on her desk. A quick glance at the clock, it was gone eleven. She knew without checking that she was the last one from the day shift still in the building. She drained her cold coffee, poured a whisky, and lit another smoke. Okay, one last play through the video, then she'd go.

Double clicking on the icon, she watched the feed from the body cam as the front door approached. Her finger snaked out, rang the bell, waited. Was there movement behind the door, a hurried panicked conversation, and then a scuttling up the stairs?

The door opened. Bocus stood there, open expression, friendly, smiling. No surprise though. He's expecting somebody to ring the bell. She paused the video.

Why would that be? He's just got in. Because, she told herself, somebody had warned him.

She thought back to those first impressions. There was a strong smell of cannabis. Nothing wrong in that of course. All drugs were legal, as long as they were bought from registered outlets, and the tax paid. She knew too well though, from her days in the anti-smuggling department there was always somebody who could supply it cheaper. Knew too how successful they were at it. The open borders policy of the Union meant no restrictions on the southern border with Mercia. The Union's relations with Scotland being friendly, there were hardly any checks on entry and exit. In any case there were plenty of unmanned crossing points. And that was before you considered the sea routes, the small dark coves, the relatively short distance across the water to the Isle of Man, Eire, and beyond that, the Combined States of America, with all the decadence of that Dark Continent.

Swanger sighed. Smuggling had gone on for centuries, it was the second oldest profession. She poured herself another shot, pressed play, immersed herself in the video, and tried to concentrate.

'Good afternoon, sir. Northumbrian Gas.' On the screen Swanger flashed her genuine Northumbrian Gas id card.

Bocus glanced at the card. 'About the leak, is it?'

'That's right, sir. This is just a courtesy call to keep you up to date. All the details are on the website, but we believe it's important to see our customers face to face at times like this.'

Bocus smiled, nodded, not at all impressed by Swanger's faux corporate bull. 'Be long will it, before we're back on?'

'About an hour, I'd say.'

'Okay, thanks.' Bocus moved to shut the door.

Swanger resisted the temptation to put her foot in the way. 'There is one other thing.'

'Oh?' Bocus held the door half open, looked ready to slam it.

'Yeah.' Swanger consulted her clipboard. 'We'd like to take this opportunity to check the meter against our records.'

Bocus laughed. 'Make sure your precious customers ain't fiddling the system.'

'No, sir.' Swanger can hardly restrain herself from laughing. 'It's for your benefit as well as ours.'

Bocus opened the door. 'Cupboard under the stairs.'

The camera moved into the cupboard. Swanger flicked on her torch, wrote down the serial number, read the display, backed out, switched off the torch. 'That all seems to be in order, sir.' Swanger paused, pen poised. 'Just to complete the records, is it just yourself living here?'

And there it was. The tell, the giveaway. Bocus' eyes

flicking to the stairs, back to Swanger. 'Yeah, just me love.'

Swanger leant back in her chair. An expensive operation, yes. Also, lots of disruption for ordinary law abiding citizens. But, she'd put money on Bocus being involved in something dodgy and there being somebody hiding upstairs.

FIFTEEN

BURNLEY, NORTHUMBRIA.

It had been a busy time. Jesus and the disciples travelled throughout Northumbria teaching in towns and villages, keeping away from the larger venues. Attempting to keep a lower profile, the disciples assumed. Not that it worked. Massive crowds appeared wherever Jesus went, all asking, pleading, and persuading him to heal them, bless them, and even arbitrate in their financial disputes. Like the money grabbing git who called out at the last event, Phil recalled, just as Jesus was reaching a critical moment in his talk.

'Jesus, tell my brother to share his lottery winnings with me. We had a deal and he's broken his word.'

Jesus had paused, turned to the man who'd interrupted, telling him, 'Who appointed me a judge between you? Watch out. Be on your guard against all kinds of greed. Life is not about the size of your wallet.'

He'd then carried on with his address.

Then there were the constant concerns about the future. Folks always asking who would be saved.

Jesus advised people not to worry about others, but to make every effort to enter through the narrow door, telling them, 'Many will try to enter on the basis that they know me, but that's not enough. They will not be allowed access. Once the owner of the house gets up and closes the door, you will stand outside in vain knocking and pleading for entrance.'

'There will be much upset,' he'd warned, 'people will come from all over the world to take their place at the feast in the kingdom of God. Those who are last will be first, and those first will be last.'

The venue was filling up. Phil could hear an excited buzz in the hall, so many packed in, jammed together, trampling on each other. Why couldn't they just sit still, wait in patience, then hear what the Boss had to say. He looked round for Jesus, wanting to share his latest song. He couldn't see him, then remembered he'd withdrawn for quiet prayer and reflection before speaking.

He thought back to the recent Festival of Dedication when Jesus, walking in the Temple Courts had been surrounded by tourists, priests, Pharisees. Questions flying in thick and fast.

'How long will you keep us hanging on, Jesus?'

'All this suspense.'

'If you're the Messiah, tell us.'

Jesus had stopped walking, stood firm in the midst of the crowd surging and swaying against him. 'I've told you many times.' He'd told them, 'but you're a stubborn people. You don't believe. The works I do in my Father's name testify about me, but you don't believe them because you're not my people. As sheep listen to their shepherd, my people listen to my voice. I know them and they follow me. I give them eternal life, and they shall never perish.'

He'd paused, waiting for further dissent. The

crowd, silent and hostile, waited.

Then, 'No one will snatch them out of my hand. My Father, who has given them to me, is greater than all. No one can snatch them out of the Father's hand.'

This response enraged a few people in the crowd. They booed, hissed, a few clenched their fists.

Jesus addressed them firmly. 'For which of my many good works do you object?'

One of his tormentors replied, 'We're not attacking you for the good work, but for blasphemy. You're a man, yet claim to be God.'

Another called out, 'Piss off now, before Caiaphas gets his hands on you. He'll sort you out.'

Jesus had laughed at that one. 'Go, tell that fox, I will keep on driving out demons and healing people today, tomorrow, and on the third day I will reach my goal.'

The hostility soon reached a level where Peter, concerned for Jesus' safety, quickly organised a protective shield around the Boss. With the aid of decoys they'd managed to slip away through the crowds and avoided a possible attack.

Jesus was back in the dressing room. One second he wasn't around, the next his presence filled the room. Phil knew he was back without seeing him, or hearing him speak. He always told the others he could feel the energy.

Jesus gathered the disciples close around him, told them, 'Be on your guard against the hypocrisy of the Pharisees. There is nothing concealed that won't be disclosed, or hidden that won't be revealed. What you say in the dark will be heard in the light of day, and what you have whispered in secret will be proclaimed from the rooftops.'

The disciples had glanced round, grinning at each other. They loved these impromptu teaching sessions. Every one revealed a nugget of gold.

'I tell you my dearest friends,' Jesus continued, 'do not be afraid of those who kill the body,' he shrugged, 'after that they can do no more. I will show you whom you should fear. Fear him, who after your body has been killed, has the authority to throw you into hell. Yes, fear him. Are not five rabbits sold in the market for a few Euros? Yet not one of them is forgotten by God. Indeed, the very hairs on your head are numbered. Do not be afraid. You are worth more than many rabbits.'

Silence.

'I tell you, whoever publicly acknowledges me before others, then I will acknowledge before the angels of God. But whoever disowns me before others will be disowned before the angels of God. And everyone who speaks a word against the Son of Man will be forgiven, but anyone who blasphemes against the Holy Spirit will not be forgiven.'

Peter gave the disciples a quick look. This was serious stuff. He prayed they were taking it in. Hard times were coming and they'd all need to be on their guard.

As if reading his thoughts, Jesus continued. 'When you are brought before the authorities, before the priests, the magistrates, the judges,' Jesus shook his head, spread his arms wide, 'do not worry about how you will defend yourself or what you will say. The Holy Spirit will teach you at the time what you should say.'

State Security HQ, York, Northumbria.

Heathersedge was annoyed. Swanger could tell by the way he kept picking up his pen, putting it down, lining up the notepad, moving his coffee mug, squaring everything off. His desk, neat and precise, like the man. He put down the report he was reading, glanced at Barnabas, and then locked eyes with Swanger. 'The Governor is not happy.'

'We're doing our best.' Swanger responded mildly.

'In fact,' Heathersedge continued, 'he's very unhappy. These people. These FKU people are planting bombs with complete impunity. Under our very noses it seems. It used to be that these bombs were planted out in the sticks. Water treatment plants, railway yards, motorway bridges. But now it seems they're getting bolder.'

He pushed that morning's copy of the Northumbrian Times across the desk. Swanger read the upside down headline, BOMB OUTRAGE IN YORK.

'He's talking about calling in the army, martial law, complete lockdown.'

'That won't be popular.' Barnabas ventured after a quick glance at Swanger.

'Popularity doesn't come into it.' Heathersedge told him. 'He's under pressure. Berlin is becoming increasingly interested in what's happening in their northern outpost. We're not some tin pot little shithole in the back of beyond. This is Northumbria. An important component of the Union. We can't let this situation continue.'

Swanger shrugged. 'Like I say...'

'Yes.' Heathersedge cut in, voice icy, 'you're doing your best.'

Swanger said nothing. Barnabas looked uncomfortable.

'Well,' Heathersedge said after a moment's silence. 'Your best isn't good enough.'

Swanger was content to ride out the storm. Hoped Barnabas had the sense to do likewise. The silence stretched, until Heathersedge tapped his pen on the pad, 'So, Where are we? Have you got anything for me at all? Any titbit I can feed the Governor? Are you out there shaking the trees, seeing what falls?'

Swanger wondered idly which question to answer first, couldn't treat them all as rhetorical.

'This Bocus character, for instance.' Heathersedge demanded. 'What about that expensive operation you convinced me would work? Digging up the road, pump the smell of gas everywhere. Piss off a load of citizens. For what?'

'Having seen the guy, I'm convinced he's up to something.' Swanger shrugged. 'He claims to be living alone, but his body language told me there's somebody else there. But, as yet, there's no proof he's involved with the bombings.'

'He's under surveillance?'

'Of course.' Swanger had increased the surveillance to full-time round the clock.

'Phones, internet monitored?'

Swanger nodded.

'Have you considered pulling him in? Handing him over to the interrogators,' Heathersedge laughed, 'two hours with them, he'll confess to screwing his grandmother. I wouldn't fancy being water boarded by those crazy bastards.'

'To what end?' Swanger wanted to know. 'We both know that innocent men will confess to anything if they're tortured. We need solid proof that he can't deny.'

'Then flaming well get it then.' Heathersedge said, raising his eyebrows as one of Swanger's many mobiles started ringing. 'Would you like to get that?'

Swanger sighed, pressed the green symbol. 'Hello?'

'I don't know if you remember me...' The voice on the end of the line tailed off.

Woman's voice, uneducated. 'If you could refresh my memory.' Swanger prompted, conscious of Heathersedge tapping his pen.

'You came to see me.'

'Did I?' Swanger was bored.

'When my husband died in the bombing.'

Pause.

'At the reservoir.'

Silence.

Swanger dug deep. 'That's right.' She had her now. A shy, nervous woman. She dug deeper. 'Stella, isn't it?'

'You remembered.' Swanger could picture her, seated on the shabby sofa, in the shabby room, tried to recall what she'd told her. It came back. Swanger had been from HR, expressing concern for her missing husband. Telling her what a wonderful employee he'd been, how he'd be missed.

'If it's about the compensation, I'm afraid nothing's been decided yet.'

'No, no, it's about Archie.'

'Archie?'

'He's back. Archie's back.'

The dog, Swanger remembered, wondered why Stella had thought it worth calling the HR operative from Northumbria Water. Still, better play along. 'That's brilliant. I'm pleased.' She stifled a yawn. 'Well, thanks for letting me know.'

Stella carried on as if she hadn't spoken. 'And the camera's still attached.'

'Camera?' Swanger queried. 'Tell me about the camera, Stella.'

†

BURNLEY, NORTHUMBRIA.

After the meeting, people lingered, all desperate to meet Jesus. He moved among them. Bringing light into dull, grey lives, Phil thought.

He hovered by a group as the Boss recounted another parable. This one was about a farmer who'd been blessed with an abundant harvest.

'This left him with a problem,' Jesus said, getting eye contact with his audience. 'His barns weren't big enough to store all his crops. He had a light bulb moment, decided to start again. He got the contractors in, tore down the old barn, built bigger, better, storage facilities. Happy days. Time to take it easy, put his feet up, eat, drink and be merry.'

'But,' Jesus paused, grinned, 'God had other plans. That very night, the man died.'

Jesus let the silence stretch. 'What did he profit from his greed? This is what will happen to those that store things for themselves but are not generous towards God.'

Jesus moved away from the small group, leaving them to discuss the parable. Phil smiled. Yet another tale about money or possessions. The Boss had a lot to say about those subjects. He watched as another group laid claim to Jesus.

After much prompting, head shaking, and cajoling from Peter, Jesus re-joined the disciples and together they boarded the minibus. Once on the road, heading for their next stop, Jesus spoke, 'Be ready at all times,' he said, 'be dressed, keep a watchful eye, like teenagers watching for their parents returning from work.'

'Also,' he paused, waiting until Tom who was driving had joined the motorway, 'also, watch for the thief who comes in the night. If you know what hour the thief comes, you will not be robbed. You must also be ready and watchful for the Son of Man who will come at an hour you do not expect.'

'Is this for us, Boss,' Peter wanted to know, 'or everyone?'

Jesus gave him a look, shook his head. 'I tell you the truth, Peter. From everyone who has been given much, much will be demanded and from the one who has been entrusted with much, much, much more will be asked.'

Peter frowned. There was so much of what Jesus said that he didn't quite get. He looked at John, who seemed, as usual, to have no problem with the Boss' words. He sighed, knew full well he'd be asking for an explanation later.

Jesus continued with a quiet, fierce intensity, 'I have come to bring true life on earth and how I wish it were already here. But,' he sighed, 'I have a baptism to undergo. I'm under constant restraint until it's completed.'

Again, Jesus lapsed into silence as Tom pulled out and limped past a massive truck. He waited until the minibus was back in the inside lane before saying, 'Do you think I come to bring peace on earth? I haven't. I bring division. From now on there will be five in a family divided against each other. Three agin two and two agin three. Father agin son, and son agin father. Mother agin daughter, and daughter agin mother.'

There was silence for a while. John watched the parched fields slip by. Then the faint sound of sirens came could be heard. The disciples looked at each other uneasily. John looked back, could see a patrol car zooming up the outside lane, blue lights, headlamps flashing. Jesus met his eye, gave a quick shake of his head. 'Not yet,' he said, his voice low, almost inaudible. 'Soon, but not just yet.'

The car sped past, nobody daring to look.

John settled back in his seat, wondered if Jesus was feeling the strain as much as the disciples.

✝

STATE SECURITY HQ, YORK, NORTHUMBRIA.

'That dog deserves a medal.' Barnabas said, for the third time.

Swanger nodded, smiled in confirmation. She was happy again. The pressure was easing.

The call from Stella had changed everything. She'd found Archie the Spaniel sitting on the front door step when she came back from the shops a week ago. Considering the animal had been wandering around the Northumbrian wilderness for several months it was a wonder it was still alive, Swanger thought, never mind able to make its way home.

After making a huge fuss of him, she'd taken Archie for a check-up. The vet noticed the small camera on Archie's collar. Stella hadn't thought much of it, but remembered that Alan had put it on for amusement, so he could see what Archie had been up to when he let him off the lead for a run. Without any great expectation, Barnabas had been despatched to Skipton, to retrieve the camera.

Despite her eagerness, Swanger had sent the camera for immediate analysis by the technical department, who'd declared it genuine and retrieved the footage.

Swanger pressed play, and watched as a man, tall, thin, miserable looking, came into view. He bent down, patted the dog, looked at the collar tag, stepped back, and mouthed something.

There was no sound on the camera, but lip reading experts had studied the video and pronounced the word to be, Archie. This made sense Swanger thought, and continued to watch. The real gem though, came next. The man retrieved a lead from a hook on the wall, clipped it on the collar, and led the dog outside, through the gates, up a track. They arrived at a farm gate, which the man opened. He unclipped the lead, stood by the open gate, tried to usher the dog through. Archie must have been reluctant, the camera staying on the man's face for a while as he tried to persuade the dog to go. Swanger watched as the mystery man spoke to the dog. Thanks to the lip reading expert, she knew what was being said and spoke the words aloud.

'Go on Archie.'

'Off you go.'

'Look, sod off, or Bocus will have you.'

The dog moved past the man into the field. The man closed the gate and the playback stopped. Swanger looked at Barnabas, big smile on her face. 'He did say Bocus, didn't he?'

Barnabas, too excited to speak, grinned.

The drones had been making regular sorties over the house. The heat-seeking camera had definitely confirmed another human presence in the house at a time when Bocus was known to be at work. Heathersedge had given the go ahead for a stealth team of Ninjas to make an entry, bring back what they found.

✝

DONCASTER, NORTHUMBRIA.

Another day, another gig.

Phil strummed his guitar, looked at the door from time to time, and wondered if anyone would join him. Ignoring the frowns and muttered comments, he'd decided to stay backstage for this gig, wanting to work on his new song in the peace and quiet of the dressing room. He couldn't expect the others to understand. Fishermen and builders, what did they know about creating art?

Jesus hadn't minded though, smiling at Phil before going on stage. Was that because the song was about him? But then, all Phil's songs were about the Boss. He smiled at the thought, dismissed it. Jesus was bigger than that. He was the star of the show. The others, Phil included, were just members of the support act, noise in the background.

Phil tried to concentrate. Once he'd nailed the chorus, the rest should be easy. He looked at the scribbled words on the scrap of paper, pulled a face, made an alteration. Was about to start singing when he heard Jesus' voice coming through the tinny speaker.

'...anyone comes to me and does not hate their father, mother, partner, children, brothers, sister, and even their own life,' Jesus paused, waiting. 'Such a person cannot be my disciple.'

Phil could imagine the silence in the hall as the implication was considered. A few people would drift out. Jesus, his heart heavy, watching them go.

'Suppose one of you wants to build a house,' Jesus continued. 'Won't you sit down first, estimate the cost, make sure you have enough money, go to the bank, and arrange a mortgage. Imagine starting, laying the foundations, running out of money. Everybody laughing, pointing the finger.'

Phil could hear the laughter in the hall. Jesus had perfect timing. Had it not been for this Messiah thing, he could have made a good career in the business.

'In the same way, those of you who do not give up everything you have cannot be my disciples.'

Phil strummed a chord, started to sing,

'I believe that no one can. Show me love like the son of man.'

A heckler had started calling out. A few others were shouting him down. Jesus' voice strong, clear over them all, 'You Pharisees are the ones who justify yourselves in the eyes of others, but God knows your hearts. What people place a high value on, is detestable in God's sight.' Amen, thought Phil, continuing.

'Jesus, you're the one. The only one.'

There never seemed to be any structure to the meetings though. That bothered Phil. He liked order, a well-run show. Jesus would speak, pray, heal, bless, in any old order. Now, it seemed as though he was speaking with somebody who'd arrived with a swollen body.

Phil listened as the man's friends explained the situation. They were concerned that Jesus wouldn't be able to heal because it was the Sabbath. Phil grinned as Jesus called out, 'Any of our Pharisee friends still with us?'

There was no response, but Phil knew they'd be there. Brotherton and his mates most like.

'So,' Jesus asked, 'is it lawful to heal on the Sabbath?'

Silence, then a great cheer came through the speakers. Phil could feel the vibrations as people stamped their feet in approval. He guessed the man had been healed.

'Tell me,' Jesus challenged, 'if any of you has a child that falls into the river on the Sabbath day. What would you do, pull it out, or let it drown?'

Silence.

The meeting continued. Phil went back to his song for a while, half listening to Jesus' words. He broke off to answer a ringing mobile. It was Jesus' phone, name on the display, Martha calling.

He answered the call, listened to the anxious voice, and then said, 'I'll tell him the first chance I get.'

†

Peter, first through the dressing room door, holding it open for the others, saw Phil slumped in a chair, head back, snoring. He nudged Jim who grinned, was about to tip the chair over when he caught Jesus looking his way. He shrugged, put the kettle on to boil, and sorted the mugs while the others talked about the meeting.

Jim poured the tea, passed it round.

'Sorry lads, no biscuits.' He stared at Judas, raising an eyebrow.

Judas shrugged. What did he care if he'd forgotten to stock up? He had more on his mind than biscuits.

Amidst the moaning and groaning, Jesus began another parable.

'There was a manager of an engineering company.' he began, 'accused of fiddling the books. He was called into the office by his boss, asked to account for his actions. Now the manager was scared of losing his job. He had a family, mouths to feed, bills to pay. He'd worked hard to get where he was, didn't want to drop back onto the shop floor.'

Phil opened his eyes. 'Wouldn't get another job though, would he?' He pointed out. 'Not without a reference.'

Peter stifled a grin. He didn't think Phil had ever had a proper job in his life. But then everybody knew Judas was on the fiddle. Was the story aimed at him?

'Good point, Phil.' Jesus replied. 'And it wasn't just his salary he stood to lose, it was the whole package. The pension, company car, health insurance. He had to get some money in from somewhere, so he spoke to those who owed the company money, told them he'd accept a reduced amount for immediate payment. They agreed, and he was able to bring in half of what was required.'

'Did it work?' Jim asked. 'Did he save his job?'

'No, he didn't.' Jesus replied. 'Even though he was commended for the shrewd way in which he dealt with the situation, he lost his job.'

'Serves him right.' Jim stated. He looked at Judas who met his gaze with a smile.

'The thing is,' Jesus explained. 'No one can serve two masters. Either you will love one, hate the other, or you will be devoted to one, despise the other. You can't serve God and money.'

Later, on the way out to the car park, Phil passed on the message from Martha. Jesus smiled and thanked him.

SIXTEEN

LEEDS, NORTHUMBRIA.

It'd been a busy few days. Bocus, glad to be home, filled the kettle, called upstairs to Beaumont. He dropped tea bags into mugs, added boiling water, milk, and sugar. Rummaged in the cupboard for biscuits. Tea made, packet of chocolate biscuits to get through, he wandered into the living room, called to Beaumont again, then slumped into his favourite chair. Half a dozen biscuits later, tea down to the dregs, he realised what had been bothering him since he stepped through the back door.

It was quiet in the house. Too quiet. Five minutes later, a rudimentary search told him that Beaumont was gone, although his few meagre possessions remained. Bocus stood on the landing, considered for a moment that it might be an elaborate joke on Beaumont's part. That he could even now be hiding in the loft, sniggering. Was that possible? He'd been fretting for days about Bocus having to go away for work.

'Why do you have to stay over?' He'd moaned.

'It's my job.' Bocus had told him. 'It would look suspicious if I insisted on travelling each day.'

'Newcastle's a mere a hundred kilometres up the road. You'll be there and back in a couple of hours.'

'It's more practical to stay over. Relax. There's nothing sinister about it.'

But now, Bocus was beginning to wonder. There had been no real need for him to be there. The local guys were more than capable of handling the situation.

Would Beaumont go as far as hiding himself away, getting his own back for being left home alone? Knowing it was stupid, Bocus got the pole, lowered the loft hatch, climbed the ladder, thrust his head into the dark space, and flicked on the light. Nothing, apart from the stuff he'd put there when he'd moved in.

Of course, Beaumont could have gone for a walk, but it seemed unlikely, afraid as he was of being picked up by the Polizei. Bocus looked at the kitchen clock, just after 18,00. He'd been home less than an hour. Give him two hours before panicking, he decided.

Bocus spent the time going through the house searching each room at a time. There was no sign of a forced entry. Doors, windows, all intact. Four hours later the conclusion was unavoidable. Beaumont had gone. Whether by choice, was harder to determine. The one thing that jarred was the tidy duvet. Beaumont never made his bed. He had to assume the worst. That Beaumont had been arrested, either on the street when he'd left the house for some reason, or the Ninjas had been here.

This new situation left Bocus with a difficult decision. By rights, he should go himself. Leave. Walk away, without a second thought or a backward glance. Wouldn't that be just a bit over the top? It would mean leaving his job, going underground. All it would take was a phone call using the mobile hidden under the floor in the spare bedroom. One call, then away into hiding until the regime had changed.

Did he want that? He wasn't sure.

Another thought struck him. If they had got Beaumont, they'd be watching the house. Soon as he showed any sign of flight, they'd swoop. If that was the case, he was done for either way. Sleep on it, he told himself, decide in the morning.

✝

LIVERPOOL, NORTHUMBRIA.

Peter scanned the room, all the while listening to the phone clamped to his ear, muttering a word when he could, which wasn't often. His eyes locked onto Phil, he watched as the musician placed his guitar to one side, stood and stretched. He said something to Jude who laughed in response. Tracking the musician as he left the room, he assured the caller he'd get back to them as soon as he knew more. He cleared the call and followed Phil.

Andrew, watching from a corner, followed Peter. He'd recognised the expression on his brother's face. He was in time to see Peter enter the gent's toilet. He wasn't in time to stop Peter grabbing Phil by his shirtfront and push him up against the tiled wall.

Phil blinked in surprise, tried to speak, but couldn't stem the torrent of words spewing out of Peter.

'You took a call from Martha?'

'Few days ago?

'Message for the Boss?'

Silence, apart from the automatic flush of the urinals.

'Well?' Peter demanded.

Phil realised it was his turn to speak. 'Yeah.'

Peter relaxed his grip. 'You pass it on?'

'Yeah, course I did.' Phil wriggled free, backed away. 'Why, what's wrong?'

'What was the message?' Peter again, insistent.

Phil frowned. 'That her brother, Laz, was sick, could the Boss come soon as?'

'Did she say how worried she was? That Laz was very sick?'

By now, there was a crowd in the doorway. Men came in, stood, did their thing, and went. A few of the disciples stayed, and watched. They looked at each other and smiled. It was just Peter having a strop.

Phil, happy to see friendly faces, shrugged. 'I told the Boss.'

Peter shook his head, frustrated. 'Didn't you think to let me know?'

'Nah, why?' Phil shrugged. 'Like I say, I told Jesus.'

'What's the problem, bro?' Andrew asked.

Peter explained the situation. 'She's concerned that Jesus hasn't been in touch.'

'Hardly Phil's fault, is it?' Jim said.

'She thinks he'll die.' Peter, anger draining away, sighed. 'She sounds desperate. She's convinced Jesus could heal him.'

'Yeah,' Judas chipped in. 'What's the point of having influential friends if they don't help?'

Peter glared at Judas.

'I told the Boss.' Phil repeated, appealing to the others. 'I did what I was asked to do.'

Andrew smiled, patted his shoulder, and assured Phil he'd done nothing wrong. Typical Peter. Up like a rocket, down like a stick, as their old man used to say.

A toilet flushed. The cubicle door opened and Jesus appeared.

The disciples watched in silence as he washed his hands at the sink. He looked at them all in turn. 'Our friend Laz won't die. It's for the Father's glory, that the Son will be glorified through this situation.'

He thrust his hands under the hot air blower, further words cut off by the noise, although Andrew thought he heard Jesus mutter something about lack of faith.

†

LEEDS, NORTHUMBRIA.

Swanger sat in her car, smoked another cigarette, and blew a thin plume of smoke through the gap in the window. Waiting was the worst part. Even though there was no need to be here, she had a compulsion to be around, wanted or not. The Sergeant commanding the six-man team of Ninjas had made it clear.

'Keep out the way.' He'd warned.

Though he looked young enough to be in the sixth form, Swanger knew appearances were deceptive. She smiled nonetheless.

'Well out of the way.' He gave her a hard stare, maintained eye contact until Swanger blinked first, and nodded her agreement.

It was coming up to three in the morning. They should be moving in soon. Shame that Heathersedge wanted to delay the interviews for a few days. Swanger could see the benefit of letting the guy stew in a holding cell for a while, but she wanted to get stuck in. Confident of her own abilities, she expected a signed confession within the hour.

She could hear drunks squabbling somewhere close and a plaintive voice singing 'Are you lonesome tonight?' floated in on the night air. Swanger sighed. Every night buddy, she thought, every night. Closing her eyes for a moment, she was startled by a rap on the glass.

Embarrassed, she lowered the window, hoped the Sergeant hadn't heard her little squeal.

'Scare you?' He asked, broad smile.

Swanger looked at him. 'Problem?'

He shook his head. 'Nah. All good. The target's on his way to York as we speak.'

'You've done it?'

The Sergeant grinned, amused at her surprise. 'They don't call us the Ghost Squad for nothing.' He turned to go. 'Night.'

†

NEWCASTLE, NORTHUMBRIA.

The queue of children, mothers' holding their hands, stretched a long way. Just like the winter solstice, Judas thought sourly, visit of the Holly King bringing his gifts. A total load of rubbish. Most kids stopped believing soon as they could think for themselves. He sighed. This wasn't going as he'd expected. When would Jesus make his move? Seize the capital, overthrow the Saxons?

Peter joined him, scanned the line of children.

'We'll be here all day at this rate.'

'Shall I start turning them away?' Judas asked, eager to start.

Peter shook his head. 'You're joking. Remember the last time we tried that.'

'Yeah.' Judas smiled.

Jesus had been so annoyed at catching one of the disciples turning children away from seeing him, telling them all, 'Let the children through. The kingdom of God belongs to such as these. I tell you the truth lads, anyone who doesn't receive the kingdom of God like a little child will never enter it.'

Later in the day, when the children had gone, Jesus and the disciples were enjoying a rare break. A moment of peace after the tumult.

After a while, a well-dressed man who'd been hanging around most of the day approached the group. Jesus noticed him and asked what he wanted.

'What must I do to inherit eternal life?' The man asked. 'I'm a good person, and never intentionally done harm to people.'

The disciples looked at each other. Were there still people who didn't know?

'Remember the commandments.' Jesus told him. 'Do not murder, do not commit adultery, do not steal, do not give false testimony, do not defraud, and honour your father and your mother.'

Peter finished his sausage roll, sipped his coffee, and looked at the man incuriously as he told Jesus that he'd kept all the commandments from childhood. You'll be alright then sunshine, he thought. You're in.

Jesus drained his mug of tea. 'There is one more thing.'

'Oh?' The man looked eager to know.

'Sell everything you possess and give it to the poor,' Jesus shrugged, 'you'll have treasure in heaven. Then, come and follow me.'

Peter smiled as he watched the man's face change from anticipation to grievous disappointment. He muttered something, turned, and walked away.

'He won't do it, Boss.'

'I think you're right, Peter.' Jesus said ruefully. He glanced round all the disciples. 'You see lads. It's easier for a camel to go through the eye of a needle than for a rich man to enter the kingdom of God.'

'Who can be saved then?' Jim asked.

'With man, impossible.' Jesus replied. 'But with God, all things are possible.'

'Boss, we've left everything to follow you.' Peter protested.

'Ah, Peter.' Jesus looked at him. 'No one who has left family, partners, mothers, fathers, businesses, jobs, for me and the gospel, will fail to receive a hundred times as much as this present day. Along with,' Jesus paused, looked at them each in turn, 'persecutions, and in the age to come, eternal life. But remember, many who are first will be last, and the last first.'

✝

'Jesus?'

Jesus and the disciples were packing their equipment away after the meet and greet in the shopping centre when Brotherton and his gang arrived.

Jude hoped Jesus would ignore them for once.

'Jesus?'

Jesus paused. 'Yes, Brotherton?'

'This kingdom of God,' Brotherton gave a sly glance at his friends. 'When will it come?'

'The kingdom of God is not something that can be seen.' Jesus replied. 'You can't say, here it is, or there it is. The kingdom of God is already here, now.'

As Brotherton and his band of Pharisees went away moaning at never getting a straight answer, Jesus gestured to the disciples and drew them close. 'Listen lads, the day is coming when you will long to see the Son of Man, but you won't be able to.' He paused. The disciples were attentive, listening. 'People will tell you, there he is, or here he comes. I tell you the truth. Don't go chasing rumours.'

'When the Son of Man comes back, he'll be like lightning that flashes and lights up the sky from end to end.' Jesus spread his arms wide.

'And we all know what comes after lightning.' John said.

Jesus nodded. 'But, before any of that, before any talk of coming back, he will, he must, suffer a great deal and be rejected by this generation.'

The disciples stirred uneasily. They weren't too keen on the suffering aspects, preferring to concentrate on the destination rather than the journey.

Jesus waited for them to settle again. 'Back in the day of Noah, people were eating, drinking, having a good time, then,' Jesus snapped his fingers, 'the flood came, destroyed them all.'

Silence, then Jesus continued. 'It was the same back in the day of Lot. Eating, drinking, planting, building, but on the day Lot left Sodom, fire and sulphur rained down from the sky, destroying them all.'

'It will be like this on the day the Son of Man is revealed. On that day, no one who is outside should go back into their homes to get their belongings. No one who is at work should go home. Remember Lot's wife? She turned, looked back,' another snap of the fingers, 'and became a pillar of salt.'

'I tell you the truth, whoever tries to keep their life will lose it. Whoever loses their life will be restored. On that day, two people will be talking in the street, one will be taken, the other left. Two people in bed together, one will be taken, the other left.'

'When, Lord?' John asked. 'When?'

Jesus looked at him. 'Where there is a dead body the vultures will gather.'

✝

RICHMOND, NORTHUMBRIA.

Although tired, Judas knew he wouldn't be able to resist turning on the laptop, logging on to the poker site. He hoped to win back some of his recent losses. He knew full well he had debts to service. Also knew he couldn't keep dipping into the accounts for which he had full responsibility. With a bit of luck a winning streak would sort that out. He'd be able to pay his debts, have some left over.

With the bike on the stand and his helmet off, he had a sense he wasn't alone in the garage. He half turned to the door that he'd left open. It was closed. Even then, the blow was totally unexpected. A feeling that his left ear had exploded in a confusion of bright lights. Totally bewildered, he crumpled to the floor, instinctively drawing his knees into his chest as best he could. A pair of trainers came into his eye line, one pulled back. The kicking started. Blow after blow thudded into his body. Ribs, chest, stomach, taking the brunt. His assailant circling, landing kicks at any and every exposed part. Judas tried to cover his head with his arms, could hear the quiet breathing of his attacker. Judas thought he was going to die, but then, save a final kick to the face, it was over.

The man bent low over him. 'That's just a taste. You've three days to find the money. Otherwise it's a hospital job next.'

Judas wanted to protest, say he didn't know what money, that they must have got the wrong man, but didn't. Self-preservation kicked in. he remained silent as the man left, even then he didn't vomit until he'd heard the car on the street move off.

SEVENTEEN

TADCASTER, NORTHUMBRIA.

Peter pushed his half-eaten breakfast to one side. Looking round the tables it seemed the others were suffering a similar lack of appetite. Andrew and John were deep in conversation. Phil was staring aimlessly out the window, guitar for once left on the minibus. Matthew scribbled notes in his journal. It was odd to think he used to be a drug dealing low life called Levi. Nathan and Tom exchanged the occasional word. Jude had a phone glued to his ear, no doubt organising some deal. Simon was at the counter paying, Jim was filling up with fuel. Jamie was making his way back from the toilet, which left Judas.

Peter scanned the cafe. No sign of Judas.

It'd been a shock to a few of the lads. Judas turning up like he'd gone fifteen rounds with a heavyweight champ. Reckoned he'd tripped, fallen down the stairs at home. As if, Peter snorted, looked around. Jesus, sitting a little apart from the others, had cleared his plate. He either hadn't realised there was an atmosphere or was ignoring it. Peter watched as Jesus poured the last of the tea from the pot, buttered more toast. He looked up, caught Peter's eye, smiled. Peter nodded, looked away.

Peter was puzzled. Jesus had promised Laz

wouldn't die, but he had. No wonder the lads were quiet, feeling let down. Betrayed was too strong a word, but it'd been a severe jolt. Up until now the Boss had delivered on everything he'd promised. He'd even said, in front of witnesses, that Laz wouldn't die.

But Laz had died.

It wasn't even as if Jesus had tried and failed. He just hadn't bothered. All the people he'd healed over the last three years, would one more have been beyond him? His mate at that.

'What time is it?' Nathan asked.

'Ten thirty.' Peter replied, 'we should be going.' He pushed back his chair, stood. The funeral in an hour's time was going to be a big, lavish affair. Peter was worried at the reception they'd get.

The other disciples shuffled to their feet. Dreading the coming ordeal as much as Peter.

'Wait a moment, Peter.' Jesus said.

Here it comes, Peter thought, the explanation. Why it had been necessary for Laz to die.

Jesus sipped his tea, finished his toast, pointed to the TV on the wall. The reporter was talking about a recent court case where workers had challenged the validity of zero hour contracts. The court had found in favour of the employer, to the widespread dismay of workers.

'A manager of a business needs six staff for the day.' Jesus told them. 'He calls them up, offers them 50 Euros, they agree.' He looked at the disciples who shrugged. So what? Most businesses did the same. Get a call on the day, you worked. No call, no work. It was the way of the world, it wouldn't change anytime soon.

'Later on,' Jesus continued, 'at lunchtime, it's getting

busy. He needs more staff, so he calls another couple of people. They came in for the afternoon shift. Same again mid- afternoon, and again about six.'

Peter sighed, knew there was a point to this parable, but disappointed that Jesus hadn't addressed the real issue.

'At the end of the day,' Jesus went on, 'the manager paid them all a day's wages of 50 Euros. Those that were first in grumbled about this. They thought they should have been paid more because they were there first and worked the longest. They complained that those who came at six had worked two hours for their pay. It wasn't fair.

The manager listened for a while, and then told them, 'I'm not being unfair. You agreed to do a day's work for 50 Euros, that's what you've got. If I want to pay the ones I hired last the same as you, don't I have the right to do that? Are you envious because I'm generous?'

'So,' Jesus gave the disciples a broad smile, 'as I keep telling you lads, the last will be first, and the first will be last.'

Nobody spoke. If Jesus was surprised at their silence, he didn't show it. The minibus pulled up outside the door. They boarded in silence.

Judas was already on the bus, Peter noticed, phone clamped to his face, talking in a low tone. The bruises from his recent accident still were still vivid. When the disciples crowded on, he frowned and turned his head to one side, his voice dropping to a whisper. He finished his call after a minute, closed his eyes and pretended to sleep.

State Security HQ, York, Northumbria.

Beaumont opened his eyes, blinked, tried to move, but couldn't. He was on his back, which was unusual. He stared at the ceiling for a few moments. The familiar crack in the plaster shaped like a donkey's hind leg had changed and moved a bit further towards the middle. The plain beige light shade had gone, replaced by a bare bulb.

Other familiar cues to the morning routine were also different. He couldn't hear the Breakfast Show on Radio Northumbria. Bocus always left the radio playing in the kitchen when he left for work.

Today, it seemed he hadn't. A bleeping noise had replaced the music. Beaumont didn't want to turn his head, but forced himself. First to the left. The clock on the bedside cabinet had gone, as had the cabinet itself. A plain white wall had replaced the garish orange and brown wallpaper. He closed his eyes, took a deep breath, expelled it, and told himself not to panic, there'd be a simple explanation. He turned his head the other way, knew before he opened his eyes that the wardrobe would be gone.

It was.

He closed his eyes, tried to make sense of it and told himself it was a dream, a vivid one for sure, but a dream nonetheless. If it wasn't a dream, then he must have gone mad. Beaumont refused to accept the possibility that he'd been arrested and thrown into a cell. He'd know, wouldn't he? He'd remember the Ninjas storming through the door, the windows blown out and smoke grenades exploding. He wouldn't have blocked all that out, would he?

He tried once again to get out of bed, and once again found he couldn't. His muscles ignoring the command to move. He was immobile and didn't know why. He puzzled it over for some time and when the solution came it was simple. He'd had a stroke. He was in hospital and a nurse would be in soon, to explain the situation.

Minutes, hours passed, no way of knowing.

He was about to call out when he heard the door open, someone came in, stood just out of his eye line.

'Hello?' He called, his voice was timid, weak and under used. 'Who's there?'

Swanger and Barnabas stood back from the bed. They regarded the patient with interest. Beaumont was lying still. IV lines ran into his body, various monitors giving visual feedback on his condition. Swanger hadn't a clue what any of them meant. 'At least he's awake.'

'What happened to him?' Barnabas asked.

Swanger gave him a look. 'You've heard of locked in syndrome?'

'Yeah. Conscious, aware,' Barnabas shrugged, 'but can't move, paralysed.'

Swanger nodded. 'That's what we have here. Artificially induced locked in syndrome. He can open his eyes, move his head a little and speak. Everything else is shut down.'

'That's horrible.' Barnabas shuddered.

'Yeah.' Swanger agreed. Her worst nightmare. 'Just make sure it never happens to you.' She reached for the bed control unit, pressed a button. The bed started raising Beaumont into a semi upright position. 'It's time for a little chat with our friend here.'

TADCASTER, NORTHUMBRIA.

Ouch.

That must have hurt.

Martha stepped back, her eyes round, her mouth opened and closed. She had no words. Jesus, the handprint visible on his cheek, was silent. He looked at Martha for a second, and then reached towards her, arms open. Martha stumbled, her eyes blinded with tears, and fell into the safe embrace. The disciples looked at each other in shock.

Martha, mumbling apologies, recriminations, allowed herself to be comforted by Jesus. The other mourners, the priest, the empty grave, waited.

'You're upset, Martha.' Jesus said.

'You've noticed.' Martha snorted through tears and snot.

John shuddered. He hated anything to do with death at the best of times.

'He would have lived if you'd come sooner.' Martha gulped. Far as she was concerned that was a given. In her opinion Jesus could have saved her brother. 'But, even now,' she stopped, her throat tight, constricted. 'Even now God will give you whatever you ask.'

Was it that simple, John wondered. Say the word, click of the fingers? He caught Martha's eye, gave her a half smile. She ignored him, continued letting Jesus know that she blamed him for her brother's death. Jesus listened in silence as Martha poured it all out, laid it at his door. What was it he'd once said, come to me all who are weary and burdened, and I will give you rest.

Martha, without doubt was laying her burden down,

but then, John knew she could be a bit like that. A right moaning Minnie. Last time they'd seen her, she'd been banging on about having to do all the work while her sister, Mary, sat at Jesus' feet, hanging on his every word. Jesus had put her straight on that occasion. John wondered how he'd handle her this time.

Jesus waited until Martha ran out of steam, took her hands in his. 'Martha, your brother will rise again.'

'I know that, Jesus.' Martha sobbed. 'I know he'll live again on the last day when the resurrection of all the dead takes place.'

'I am the resurrection and the life,' Jesus said, 'the one who believes in me will live, even though they die.' He paused. 'Do you believe this?'

'Yes, Lord.' Martha sniffed. 'I know you're the Messiah who has come into the world.'

Amen to that John thought, and wondered where this was going. A short distance away, a crow, perched on a gravestone, seemed to be watching the proceedings. It moved its head, fixed a beady eye on John. He shivered, wanted to shoo it away.

Jesus spoke to Peter, who in turn spoke to the funeral director who frowned. A muttered conversation took place. The undertaker shrugged and spoke to a pallbearer. Tools were brought, and, ignoring the protestations from the wider family, the coffin lid removed.

Martha gripped John's arm, pulled him closer, and forced him to look at the dead man. John stared down into the coffin, was amazed just how little room there was. Laz hemmed, almost forced, into the small space. Laz, in his best suit, white shirt, dark blue tie, hands resting on his chest, with his pale waxen face, didn't look like Laz anymore. It was him, but there was something missing. The essence of the man had gone.

Didn't I tell you,' Jesus said, 'if you believe, you'll see the glory of God.'

John squeezed Martha's hand. Conscious of his pounding heart, he forced himself to breathe.

'Laz,' Jesus said in a clear voice. 'Wake up. Wake up now.'

John looked at their dead friend, glanced at Peter, who stared resolutely at Laz in his coffin. Had a little colour returned to his cheeks. Did his face seem a little fuller. Was that little sigh the wind through the trees, or the breath of life?

Laz opened his eyes.

John closed his eyes and crumpled to the floor as the crow took off with a noisy screech.

†

STATE SECURITY HQ, YORK, NORTHUMBRIA.

Swanger lit a cigarette, blew a stream of smoke, and regarded Bocus with interest. There was more anger in his eyes than she'd encountered with Beaumont. He'd been a pushover, leaf in a gale. She'd blown, he'd fallen over, spilled it all out. His words a jumble until she'd told him to calm down, then, the relief tangible, he'd told her everything.

Bocus eyed the cigarette as she brought it to her mouth. She inhaled, drew the smoke deep, held it for a second, and then released. 'Want one?' She offered the packet, saw the spark of anger.

'Like I can get one.' Bocus whined.

Swanger put a cigarette between his lips, helped him smoke for a while before he told her he'd had enough. She popped the lid of her Styrofoam coffee cup, blew on the top, and sipped it. After a minute or two Bocus said, 'the gas board woman. Clipboard Charlie.' His eyes narrowed. 'Bitch.'

'This is just an informal chat,' Swanger said. 'No tape, no video.'

'I want my phone call.' Bocus demanded.

Swanger was amused. 'Who ya gonna call? You've got no mates, oh,' She snapped her fingers, 'well, apart from Beaumont, but, guess what, he's here as well.'

Bocus regarded her in silence.

'Bocus.' Swanger shook her head in sorrow. 'You're in deep shit. I have everything I need to take you before a court, get the death sentence. This time tomorrow you could be nailed to a cross.'

'I want a lawyer.'

'A lawyer?' Swanger, incredulous at the man's cheek, laughed out loud. 'You've no chance, son. We're detaining you under anti-terror legislation. No lawyer for you my friend.'

'I've got rights.'

'Wrong. You've got no rights. You've put yourself beyond the law.' She smacked the bedside table with her fist.

Bocus flinched at the sudden movement.

'It's not a game anymore.' Swanger told him. 'You're on your own. Nobody is coming to save you. I've got Beaumont next door crying like a baby, begging for forgiveness.'

'No comment.'

Swanger sighed. 'All you're doing by not talking is

making it worse for yourself. You're a dead man walking. Answer my questions, and I'll see to it you get a swift exit.'

'No comment.'

'Your mate's booked a nice clean exit.' She touched an IV line. 'We turn the tap on full. He goes to sleep, never wakes up. He won't feel a thing. It'll be peaceful and dignified.' She sighed, 'You, on the other hand, are heading for a nasty, messy, degrading, painful death.'

'No comment.'

'All I want is the names of all your contacts in FKU.'

'No comment.'

'How many?'

'No idea.'

'Bocus, believe me, you will talk. We have trained staff. They use all the latest techniques. They have a one hundred percent success rate.'

'No comment.'

'You won't win.' Swanger promised.

'Neither will you.'

Swanger sighed again. 'You will talk, you will die. By the time those lads have finished with you, you'll be begging for death. Do yourself a favour, think about it,' she pushed back her chair, stood. 'I'll drop by later, see if you've changed your mind.'

†

TADCASTER, NORTHUMBRIA.

The impromptu party was in full swing, wine, beer, flowing liberally. People, still marvelling at the earlier events, stood around in groups. Flushed with success they talked at length about the miracle of Laz's resurrection. Those who'd been graveside, seen it themselves, in most demand, repeating their story to anyone who'd listen. TV crews had been and gone, interviews with Laz were playing on all the major channels. Every time his face appeared on the big screens dotted around the house, cheers erupted. The story had exploded across the internet. Social media alive with the buzz, #Jesus, #raisedfromthedead, the highest trending topics.

Martha followed Jesus from room to room, apologising all the while for her lack of faith, her doubts. She stroked his cheek where her handprint was still faintly visible, and begged his forgiveness. Her sister Mary, more pragmatic, hugged Jesus once, kissed his cheek, promised him a formal celebratory dinner in a few days' time, then left him alone. Laz himself, tired after all the excitement had taken himself off to bed.

The disciples and Peter in particular, were feeling humbled and chastened by the experience. He'd seen the Boss raise a dead girl before he told himself, he should have known better. He vowed never to doubt Jesus again. Had told him he'd follow him unquestioningly to the ends of the earth. Jesus had accepted the assurance with a smile, but Peter was again left with the feeling events were beyond his grasp.

A cloud had lifted, everything, everybody was okay again. Jesus hadn't lost it. He'd known what he was doing all along. All they'd needed was faith. In short supply when most required, now, it was abundant.

Later on in the evening, with people drifting away,

Jesus called the disciples together. 'Lads, as you know it will soon be the Passover,' he told them, 'when we go to York, the Son of Man will be delivered to the Chief Priest and the Pharisees. They will condemn him to death, hand him over to the Saxons, who will mock him, flog him, and kill him. Three days later he will rise.'

Silence greeted Jesus' words. The disciples looked at Peter, willing him to speak. Stunned, he shook his head.

Jamie and John took Jesus to one side, leaving the others to discuss Jesus' prophecy. 'Boss,' Jamie said, 'we want you to do something for us.'

'What is it?' Jesus replied.

'In your glory, Lord, let one of us sit at your right side, the other to your left.'

Jesus frowned. 'You don't know what you're asking.' He looked round them all. 'Can you drink from the same cup as me? Can you undergo the suffering I will undergo?'

'We can, Boss.' John replied.

'And you will. I tell you the truth, you will.' He paused, and then said, 'But to sit at my left and right is not for me to grant. These places belong to whom they have been prepared.'

†

YORK, NORTHUMBRIA.

As Caiaphas watched the silent TV, he seethed with a cold dark fury. Although the high priest believed in the concept of Messiah, he didn't believe for one moment that Jesus was the chosen one. More like he was an agent of darkness, sent by the evil one. Every time the man's name was mentioned, or he heard his voice, his stomach knotted, his blood pressure soared. It was personal. How dare this man, this imposter, appear in their midst proclaiming the kingdom of God, upsetting the faithful, and stirring up trouble. He had to be stopped and it would be Caiaphas who would step up to the mark.

A picture of Jesus appeared on the screen, shrank, and swirled into the top corner. The female anchor, Michelle, appeared.

Caiaphas pressed the mute button.

Michelle pursed her lips, lowered her voice. 'Signs of divisions are beginning to appear in the camp of Whitby prophet, Jesus. Our religion correspondent has the full story.'

Caiaphas increased the volume.

The scene changed to a man in shirtsleeves standing outside the Temple in York. He touched his ear, and then spoke into the microphone he was holding. 'That's right, Michelle. Sources close to Jesus have told me that at a recent meal given in his honour at the home of Mary and Martha...'

'If you could just explain who they are...' Michelle broke in.

The reporter frowned, changed direction flawlessly.

'Mary and Martha are members of a wealthy Tadcaster brewing family who are known to support Jesus in his ministry to make the kingdom of God known to a wider audience. You may recall the astonishing scenes last week when their brother, Laz, who had died from a viral infection, was brought back to life by Jesus in spectacular fashion, during the burial service.'

The reporter paused, sensing further questions.

'The meal.' Michelle prompted. The resurrection of Laz was old news.

'Yes, the meal. The meal was being held to honour Jesus and the part he played in raising Laz from the dead. During the meal, Judas, one of the disciples, objected when Mary anointed Jesus with a jar of expensive perfume.'

Michelle, 'On what grounds? Couldn't it be viewed as a gracious act?'

Reporter, 'It seems that Judas objected on the grounds of cost. Judas is the financial adviser for the group and he thought the money could have been better spent on feeding the poor.'

Michelle, 'What was Jesus' reaction?'

Reporter, 'According to my source, Jesus came to the defence of Mary, telling Judas and other objectors that they would always have the poor among them, but that he, Jesus, would not always be with them. He then went on to praise Mary for her act of worship in anointing his body for burial.'

Michelle, 'For his burial?'

Reporter, 'Michelle, It's not always easy to decipher the words of Jesus. He employs the use of parables in many of his talks and his public statements are viewed by many as cryptic, but in this case my source made it clear that Jesus seemed to be referring to his own death and burial.'

Michelle, 'Interesting.'

Reporter, 'Indeed. And when you consider that Jesus and his disciples will soon be making their way to the Temple here in York for the feast of the Passover, it could get more interesting. As you know Michelle, The Temple in York is the heart of Judaism, where many of Jesus' fiercest critics are based. With these latest reports of friction among his disciples it remains to be seen how he gets on when he arrives here.'

Michelle, 'Yes, thank you for that update on the prophet Jesus and his activities.' She turned back to the camera, composed herself, 'You can get the latest update on this story from our website, the address of which is on the bottom of the screen.'

Pause.

'There is still time to watch our special report on the hidden world of child sacrifice in the modern age. This can be accessed by pressing the red button on your remote.'

'And of course, I should point out that other spiritual advisors and alternative lifestyles are available.'

'And now, over to Gary for a full round up of all the day's sporting action...'

Caiaphas muted the sound. Closing his eyes, he thought about the next step. Victory was close, very close, but it would need careful handling.

EIGHTEEN

THE FINAL WEEK.
WHITBY, NOTHUMBRIA.
MONDAY.

The clock radio clicked on.

'And now the Shipping Forecast, issued by the Met office at 05, 05 today...' Andrew lay still, listening. He hadn't been to sea for years, but old habits die-hard. Marje stirred, murmured in her sleep, but didn't wake. He could feel her, warm and soft against his body, knew he needed to be up soon, but didn't want to move.

'There are warnings of gales in all areas.'

Today was the day Andrew would meet up with the other disciples and Jesus. Together they'd make their way to York for the Passover. It had been a lovely few days back with his family, but now it was back to work.

'The general synopsis follows.'

He waited until the weather report had finished, was about to get up, when Marje touched his arm. Much later than he'd expected Andrew made his way to the bathroom, showered, shaved, and made ready for the day.

†

Peter hadn't slept well, knew he was keyed up, excited. Curled up on his side, eyes closed, he recalled the days when all he needed to be happy was the wind through his hair, salt spray on his face, and a full cargo of fish. Not forgetting a warm, loving wife to lie beside in bed. Those days gone, he forced himself out of bed, and went to the bathroom.

He'd just finished shaving when the text came through. Andrew he thought, checking I'm up, ready to go. It wasn't Andrew. The message, from a number he didn't recognise, read, I'm so sorry.

Jayne.

Had to be.

Me too, love.

The funny thing was, he'd been thinking about her a lot in recent days, didn't know why. Months could go by when she didn't enter his thoughts, then, for no apparent reason, she was there, muscling her way in.

Another message beeped. Can we talk?

Why now?

She must have seen him on the media a lot over the past few years. Happen her new relationship had gone wrong. He sighed, knew he'd forgiven her, but wasn't sure they needed to talk about the past, rake it all up. It would be like taking a stick to a crystal clear pond, stirring the mud at the bottom, spoiling the water.

Beep.

It's Jayne.

I know love. Peter blinked away his tears and threw the phone on the bed.

†

RICHMOND, NORTHUMBRIA.

Judas looked out the window again, for the third time in ten minutes, and wondered what the day would bring. Bit o' luck and they'd be set up in the Governor's residence this time tomorrow, Northumbria, theirs for the taking. Once Jesus was in charge, Judas would be Chancellor of the Exchequer. He was the logical choice. He'd be able to pay off his debts, repay the beating he'd received as well. Bastards. They'd been no need for that. He would have paid what he owed.

But what if Jesus didn't take over. What then? What if it all turned to dust? How would he pay his debts without access to the treasury of the kingdom? He'd have to make a run for it, he thought, one option, Scotland. Another, Mercia. Lie low for a while.

A horn beeped in the road. Jim, come to collect him. Peter had insisted they all travel to York together. Judas locked the door before joining Jim in the car.

✝

YORK, NORTHUMBRIA.

Crowds, six deep in parts, lined the route into the capital. For the most part, they were content to wave little plastic Northumbrian flags, but at intervals, helium balloons bearing the face of Jesus bobbed above their heads. The vast crowd was kept in check by goodwill and the occasional Polizei officer who cheered along with the others. Drones hovered overhead, the pictures fed back to State Security HQ.

'Jesus, Jesus, give us a wave...' The crowd sang as the open topped bus crawled towards the city centre. Jesus, front centre, upper deck, waved back, prompting a fresh wave of flowers to be thrown, some reaching the bus itself.

'This is alright, isn't it?' Phil said, waving back.

Jude the Dude grinned back. 'They love him. They absolutely love him.'

The closer to the centre, the thicker the crowds, the bus now moving at a walking pace. The disciples, led by Peter, waved to the crowd, who responded by chanting their names in turn, followed by three quick claps.

'It's like we've won the cup.' Tom laughed, when he heard his own name.

'Here we go, here we go, here we go.' The people sang. The disciples grinned at each other, basked in the reflected glory, and joined in with the singing and chanting.

'What happens when we get in?' Andrew asked his brother in a moment of relative quiet.

'We storm the Temple, Governor's residence, take over, proclaim God's kingdom on earth.' Peter replied with a big grin.

'You're joking?' Andrew, sceptical. 'The Temple is God's house. It can't just be stormed like an ancient castle.' He looked around for support.

John smirked. 'I think your brother's joking.'

'Are you?' Andrew asked Peter.

'Yes, brother. Of course I am.' Peter ran his hand through his hair, 'This is all surreal. It's down to the Boss what happens next, but I somehow doubt he'll be mounting a takeover. Not his style. Anyway, we might be met by a load o' uniforms and ordered to disperse. This could be as good as it gets. Enjoy it while you can.'

He'd wondered whether he should tell Andrew or the Boss about his text from Jayne. Decided not at this stage, he didn't want to spoil the occasion.

An impressive red carpet was waiting when they pulled up outside the Temple. A small Polizei presence along with Temple security guards in their distinctive orange Hi-Viz jackets held back the screaming crowds as Jesus and the disciples disembarked. A small girl presented Jesus with a posy of flowers. He took it, ruffled her hair, and blessed her while her mother beamed.

Followers based in the capital came forward, greeted Jesus. 'Blessed is the king who comes in the name of the Lord,' one said, 'peace in heaven, glory in the highest.'

Pharisees in the crowd took exception, and rebuked those speaking in favour of Jesus.

Jesus paused on the Temple steps. 'I tell you the truth, if they keep quiet, the paving stones along this road will call out.'

For a second it looked as though the security guards would refuse access, but they parted at the last moment. Jesus entered the Temple courts followed by his disciples while the Pharisees muttered among themselves.

†

THE TEMPLE, YORK, NORTHUMBRIA.

The small but powerful Sanhedrin sub-committee was in session. Jesus the topic of discussion. There was consternation among the priests and Pharisees. The would be Messiah had rocked up to the Temple with his disciples, assorted hangers on, and done his usual trick of overturning tables and driving out the money changers. The honest traders selling doves were complaining. According to the account given by one of the security guards, Jesus claimed the Temple was being turned into a den of thieves.

Caiaphas waved the guard away. He waited till the door closed behind him. 'Have you witnessed the crowds greeting him?' He said after a long moment. 'Lining the streets, shouting, cheering. A vulgar spectacle.'

O'Deamus, doodling on his pad looked up. 'He stopped on the way into the city, healed a blind man, and restored his sight.'

'And?' Caiaphas demanded.

O'Deamus shrugged. 'Just saying.'

'Isn't that good?' Brotherton wondered.

'Not if the power to heal comes from the devil.' Caiaphas retorted. 'This is the second time he has violated the sanctity of the Temple. This situation cannot be allowed to continue. He needs stopping. He needs stopping now. Any suggestions?'

'We could have him killed.' One of the Pharisees said.

'An excellent idea.' Caiaphas laughed.

'You are joking?' O'Deamus looked appalled.

Caiaphas shrugged. 'Would it be such a

catastrophe?'

'If he was the Messiah it would.' O'Deamus said.

'But he's not, is he?' Caiaphas snarled. 'Hasn't that been a major plank of our opposition to him these last three years?'

Silence, then O'Deamus asked, 'Do we need to go that far?'

'Yes, I think we do.' Caiaphas said. 'Here is this man performing signs and wonders. He even raised his friend, Laz, from the dead. Sooner or later the Saxons will come to realise this man is hell bent on taking over, becoming the ruler. The people will support him. The FKU idiots will jump on the bandwagon. Then,' he paused, looked at them all in turn, 'then they'll be a terrible crackdown. The Saxons don't like us Jews at the best of times. We're tolerated. We don't need to give them further reason to find fault with us.'

A few people agreed, their voices strident, others were still undecided.

'It seems so extreme.' O'Deamus objected.

'Better that one die than the whole nation perish.' Caiaphas said.

'That's right,' Brotherton jumped in, 'Who knows what might happen if the Saxons decide to crack down on us because of this man Jesus.'

Caiaphas nodded. 'Look at it in a positive light.' He glanced round the table. 'As you know, Northumbria is by far the biggest population of Jews in the world. If Jesus dies, it will be for the good of the people, it might even be a rallying call for the scattered children of God to come home. Just imagine, the scattered tribes making their way across Europe, here to Northumbria.

There was silence while they considered this prospect.

'I vote we do it.' Brotherton said.

Caiaphas nodded his approval. "Are we all agreed?'

Of the nine members, seven voted in favour, O'Deamus, along

with a man called Joseph, abstained.

'Anyway,' Caiaphas concluded as the meeting broke up, 'if he's the Messiah, God won't let him die, will he? What father would stand aside, let his son be put to death and not intervene. It will be a good test. If God saves him, I'll acknowledge him as Messiah, and submit to his authority.'

NINETEEN

THE TEMPLE, YORK, NORTHUMBRIA.
TUESDAY.

Jesus and the disciples were back in the city early the next morning. Peter was amused to see the moneychangers and other traders had set up business outside the Temple walls. If Jesus noticed, he didn't comment. Once the gathered throng realised Jesus was in their midst, they surrounded him and he was soon teaching the pilgrims. A few of the disciples spent time talking with the many visitors to York. People who'd journeyed from all parts of the kingdom for the Passover, which was fast approaching. It was getting on for mid-morning when the Temple doors opened. A deputation of Pharisees and teachers of the law appeared. Jesus was speaking with a young woman when the group, led as usual by Brotherton, approached.

Brotherton was about to speak when a glare from Peter silenced him. He waited until Jesus had blessed the woman, and then said, 'By what authority are you doing these things, Jesus?'

'I will ask you one question,' Jesus replied, 'answer me, and I will tell you by what authority I act.'

He looked at Brotherton and his followers.

Brotherton nodded his acceptance.

'John's baptism,' Jesus said, 'was it from heaven, or of human origin?' He looked at them expectantly.

'We need to confer.' Brotherton replied. The disciples chuckled as he withdrew his group a short distance away while Jesus waited.

'If we say from heaven,' a Scribe explained, 'he will ask why we didn't believe him.'

Brotherton nodded in agreement. 'Whereas, if we say of human origin the people who did believe will kick off, because they believe Baptiste was a prophet sent by God.'

The disciples watched with interest as the debate raged among the small group. After a fierce discussion, they made their way back to Jesus.

'We don't know.' Brotherton admitted.

Jesus smiled. 'Then neither will I tell you by what authority I act.'

Apart from Peter, the disciples jeered as Brotherton and his band withdrew. Peter had been watching Brotherton. The guy didn't seem at all put out by Jesus' refusal to divulge his authority. If anything, he seemed pleased. He had the air of one who knew secrets others don't know. 'Hypocrites.' He growled.

'Watch out for the teachers of the law,' Jesus warned, 'they like to walk round in fancy sharp pressed suits. They expect to be greeted with respect wherever they go and have the most important seats in the synagogues and places of honour at the civic events.'

'Like I say, Boss. Hypocrites.' Peter repeated.

✝

GOVERNOR'S OFFICE, YORK, NORTHUMBRIA.

Pilate was amused. He shook his head. 'Not my problem. He's one of yours, Caiaphas.'

The high priest sighed. He knew it wasn't going to be easy.

'Jesus,' Pilate continued, 'is a religious concern, not a civil one.' He shrugged. 'He talks of spiritual kingdoms, not earthly ones. Anyway, I've got bigger concerns.'

'FKU?' Caiaphas suggested.

Pilate nodded, knew he had to be careful. The arrest of Beaumont and Bocus didn't diminish the threat posed by the terrorist organisation. There would be others to take their place. And there was the Wannsee Protocol to consider. It wouldn't be wise for Caiaphas to get a sniff of the plan to repatriate the Jews. It would be a massive undertaking, army units from Saxony would be required to help keep order. 'The FKU are a concern. They're stepping up their activities and the Fuehrer is getting agitated.'

'If...' Caiaphas hesitated, continued, 'if Jesus was found to be involved with FKU, would you act?'

'Of course.' Pilate spread his arms wide. 'But he's not, is he? We're not stupid, Caiaphas. Jesus and his followers have been security vetted. They preach a message of love and peace. As much as you don't like them, they're not terrorists.'

'If there were proof?' Caiaphas offered.

'Bring me proof,' Pilate said, standing up, 'and I'll act on it.' He showed the high priest to the door, knew full well that proof would be found, and wondered what he'd do then.

THE TEMPLE, YORK, NORTHUMBRIA.

Later in the day, Brotherton and his coterie were back.

'Jesus?'

'Yes, Brotherton?'

'I know you're a man of integrity,' Brotherton gave his companions a sly look. 'And that you teach the way of God in accordance with the truth. You aren't swayed by others, because you pay no attention to who they are.' Peter thought about hitting the man, knew he shouldn't, and resisted the temptation. He smiled at Jim who was miming vomiting. 'Tell us then,' Brotherton asked, 'is it right to pay taxes to the Union?'

Jesus shook his head. 'You hypocrites, why are still trying to trap me?' He took a Euro coin from his pocket. 'Whose image is shown on the back?'

'The Fuehrer's.' Brotherton replied.'

'So give to the Fuehrer what is the Fuehrer's, and to God what is God's.'

Peter grinned at the expression on Brotherton's face. The Pharisee had been outwitted again.

'Okay then, which is the greatest commandment in the law?' A Scribe asked.

Peter had the distinct impression the Pharisees were getting desperate. They must know this stuff. Jesus had been preaching the same message for the last three years. He didn't seem to mind repeating himself, though. Maybe he thought it would stick sooner or later.

'Love the lord your God with all your heart, with all your soul, with all your mind.' Jesus told his questioner. 'This is the first and greatest commandment, 'the second is, 'love your neighbour as yourself.'

The small group of Pharisees clucked among themselves for a while, but soon disappeared. Jesus gathered the disciples a short distance away from the Temple doorway. He told them to watch the bowl where people placed their offerings of money. The disciples watched in interest as a steady stream of well-dressed, prominent people, dropped a Euro or two into the bowl. All of them looked to John as if they could afford more than they gave. There weren't many notes given.

After thirty minutes or so a small, hunched back woman, dressed in rags, dropped two small cents into the collection, and limped away. 'You see that woman,' Jesus said, 'I tell you the truth, lads. That woman has given more than all the others. They gave out of their wealth. She gave out of her poverty and all she had to live on.'

TWENTY

THE TEMPLE, YORK, NORTHUMBRIA.
WEDNESDAY.

Brotherton stared out the window high on the front of the Temple. Down below a group of people clustered round Jesus and his band of followers. Brotherton seethed with righteous indignation. Caiaphas was right. He had to be stopped. Turning away from the window, he looked at Caiaphas. 'This plan of yours.'

'Ours, my dear Brotherton.' Caiaphas smiled. 'This plan of ours.'

'Yes, yes, ours.' Brotherton conceded. 'When will it be done?'

'Soon.'

'It needs to be done before the Sabbath begins. That means Friday at the latest.'

'Of course.' Caiaphas soothed. 'It's all in hand.'

'He'll need to be arrested.' Brotherton fretted. 'We've tried that before, and he's always slipped through our hands.'

'God will deliver him to us.' With a little help, Caiaphas thought, didn't say.

'And then?' Brotherton wondered.

'Then what?'

'How will he die?' Brotherton fretted. 'Who will kill him?'

Caiaphas laughed. 'The Saxons will do it for us.'

Brotherton frowned. 'Why would they do that?'

'You need to stop worrying, Brotherton.' Caiaphas said. He was getting annoyed with the snivelling Pharisee. 'It's all taken care of. God will deliver him. The Saxons will dispose of him. That's all you need to know.'

Brotherton nodded. It was better he didn't know the details.

✝

A small group of tourists were admiring the Temple building, taking photos from every angle. One of them approached Jamie as the disciples were leaving the Temple courts, asked him to take a photo of him and his wife with the Temple in the background.

'It's a lovely building,' Jamie remarked on re-joining the others, 'best looking building in all Northumbria.'

'Best looking building in the four kingdoms.' Andrew protested.

'The Union.' Simon chipped in.

'I tell you what, lads,' Jesus interrupted, 'lovely building or not, not one stone will be left on top of another. Every one will be knocked down.'

The disciples stopped joshing with each other, looked at Jesus, and realised he was serious.

'When will this happen, Lord?' Peter asked.

'And what will be the signs of your coming, and the end of the age?' Nathan added.

They gathered round Jesus as he began speaking in a low voice. 'Watch out that no one deceives you.' Jesus told them. 'Many will come in my name claiming to be the Messiah. Many will be deceived. You will hear of wars, rumours of wars, but don't be alarmed. There will be signs in the sun, the moon, and the stars. On the earth, nations will be in anguish. Such things must happen, but the end is still to come. Nation will rise against nation, kingdom against kingdom. There will be famines and earthquakes. These are the beginning of the birth pains.' He fell silent as a drone, silent, sinister, appeared a few metres away. It hovered above them, the black eye of the camera visible underneath. Music from the fun fair could be heard in the distance. 'I tell you the truth,' Jesus continued, 'this generation will not pass away until all these things have happened. Heaven and earth will pass away but my words will never pass away.'

The drone moved off, watched by the disciples. Despite the warmth of the day, Andrew shivered.

'Then, you will be handed over to be persecuted and put to death. You will be hated by all nations because of me. At that time, many will turn away from the faith. They will betray and hate each other. False prophets will appear and deceive many people. Because of the increase of wickedness, the love of most will grow cold, but the one who stands firm to the end will be saved. And this gospel of the kingdom will be preached in the whole world as a testimony to all nations, and then,' Jesus snapped his fingers, 'the end will come.'

A clamour of voices broke out.

Jesus held up his hands. 'Don't ask me when. The day, the date, the hour, yes, even the hour is unknown to all but the father. The angels don't know, the son doesn't know.' He looked at them each in turn. 'Just the father, he knows.

'So,' Jesus smiled, 'keep watch, be ready at all times for the return of the Son of Man. Be careful, or your hearts will become weighed down with good living, and the anxieties of life, and that day will close on you like a trap.' He clapped his hands. 'It will be at the time you least expect him.'

†

Campsite, York, Northumbria.

The disciples were camping, again. There'd been a few moans, an assumption that a stay in a Travelodge was well overdue. The tents, motor home, had been set up in a half circle, all the doors, and entrances facing each other. In the middle of the communal space, the fire was blazing. Simon was preparing the evening meal, after which a visit to the funfair was planned.

Judas, bored, not on the food rota, listened idly to the talk around the food prep table.

'If the Boss is right.' Jim said.

'He's always right.' John insisted.

'Yeah, I know that,' Jim retorted, 'but if he's right about being arrested and put to death by the authorities, it could happen at any moment.'

'I can't see it.' Peter said firmly. 'The people love him. They wouldn't stand for it. There'd be a riot.'

'They love him now.' John replied. 'That could change in a matter of hours.'

'Hours?' Nathan snorted. 'People are fickle, change with the wind. Go against him in an instant.'

There was a brief fierce discussion threatening to

get out of hand.

'Listen lads,' John said, raised his voice to be heard, 'when has the Boss ever said something would happen, and then it didn't? Think about it. If the Boss says it's gonna happen, then it will happen. We need to remain vigilant, assess the situation at the time, and take our lead from Jesus.'

Bored with the talk, Judas walked round the site, came across Jesus and a few of the guys having a kick about. He watched in amusement as Tom commentated on the game.

'That's a lovely through ball from Jamie, right to the feet of Phil, who swerves, crosses the ball into the area. Matt dummies the defender, shoots low into the corner, he's certain to score, but no, Jesus saves.'

Judas expelled air through his teeth. He can't save me. His phone vibrated in his pocket. He pulled it out checked the message, I have the solution to your problem. Number unknown. He looked up. The guys were engrossed in the match. Nobody was taking any notice.

What problem? He sent back.

The reply was instant. Your financial problem.

Tell me more. He typed, sent.

The reply named a service station on the York ring road, gave a time of 22:00.

The next one said, 'Just down the road from where you're staying.'

Judas looked up in alarm, there wasn't a soul looking his way. The campsite was full. Caravans, tents, motor homes filled a vast field. Music from the fairground over the road drifted across. Nobody seemed to be paying him any attention, but somebody knew where he was.

†

FAIRGROUND, YORK, NORTHUMBRIA.

Screams, bells, whistles, shouts, laughter, threats, curses, music, above all, music. An explosive cacophony of noise filled the air. Thin streams of green light pierced the night sky, pulsated in time with the music from the Waltzer. The acrid smell of burnt diesel from the generators intermingled with fried onions. People of all ages packed into the fairground. Pensioners to toddlers, most having a good time.

The disciples were huddled in a tight group near the food outlets waiting for Jesus and Matt to return from the burger van. Judas checked his watch, fidgeted, wondered how and when he'd be able to slip away. He caught Tom's eye, gave a half smile, looked away, and took the burger that Matt offered.

After they'd eaten, Jesus said. 'Come on, I want to show you something. He led the way into the hall of mirrors. The disciples looked around, staring at the myriad images of themselves. Tom became disoriented as the others disappeared further into the maze of reflections. Everywhere he looked, he could see multiple versions of himself. Andrew appeared at his side, Tom turned to speak, but he was gone, vanished round a corner.

'This is what life is like for most people.' A voice whispered. 'You're all too absorbed by yourselves, too busy looking in the mirror to notice what else is happening. This is the me generation.'

Tom watched as Jesus moved away. Then John appeared. Tom wasn't sure if he was real or just a reflection. 'He's right, you know.' John said, 'we should be looking to him, not ourselves.'

Tom felt ill. A sheen of sweat pricked his forehead. He was lightheaded and claustrophobic. He turned, backtracked, got lost. Then saw the familiar figure of Judas. He seemed to know where he was going, so Tom tagged along behind.

Back out in the night air, Tom felt a little better. Judas, a little way ahead, seemed to be heading for the exit. Tom assumed he was heading back to the camp, decided he was ready to turn in, and followed. Judas disappeared into the dense crowd. A group of youths clutching cans of lager lurched past. One stopped, vomited, and girls, giddy with excitement laughed. Parents pulled their children to one side as Tom sidestepped the stricken youth. He ignored a beaming young man presenting his girl with a large teddy bear. In his haste, he bumped against a small boy carrying a goldfish in a plastic bag. He muttered an apology, moved on, oblivious to the glare of the boy's mother.

At last, he was free of the fairground, but not the music. It followed him down the road. He could feel the vibrations in his chest. He could make out a figure some way ahead, and assumed it was Judas. But was less sure, when the figure didn't turn into the campsite, but instead continued walking. Another time, Tom would have been nosy and followed, but not tonight. Tonight he just wanted his bed.

✝

Service station, Ring Road, York, Northumbria.

The service station was a kilometre down the road. Judas peered back into the darkness, he was sure Tom had been behind him earlier, and half-expected to see him come into view, ask what was happening. A few cars passed by, their headlights slicing through the night. None turned into the empty car park. Judas decided Tom must have been going back to the campsite. He moved across the forecourt, he peered through the window of the small cafe, but couldn't see anything. Taking a deep breath, he pushed his way through the door. There were no other customers. Harsh fluorescent lights did nothing for the ambience, or his mood. Keyed up, excited and apprehensive, he wondered if this was the right response to an anonymous text. It could even be a ruse to separate him from the safety of the pack.

He waited at the counter until the teenage girl, pre-occupied with her phone, noticed him, and with a sigh, asked what he wanted. Judas ordered coffee, and made his way to a table by the emergency exit, as far from the entrance as possible. It would give him longer to assess anybody approaching. He knew if it came to flight or fight, he was already running. Taking cautious sips of coffee, he kept a close eye on the door.

Just as he was beginning to relax, a hand clamped on his shoulder. Judas jerked upwards, the coffee went over, dripped onto the floor. A man, wearing a suit and tie, who could have been an office worker, took a wad of paper towel from a cleaning cart, wiped the table dry, and sat down. 'Want another?' He offered.

Judas, not trusting himself to speak, shook his head. Toilets. He'd been waiting in the toilets.

'That's the thing, friend,' the man said with a half-smile on his lips, 'you think you're safe, looking for trouble in one direction, it comes from another.'

'You sent me a text?' Judas asked, anxious to recover his poise.

'You're Judas?'

Judas nodded.

The man took something from his pocket, slid it across the table.

'And you are?' Judas asked, keeping eye contact.

He received a smile in reply. They looked at each other for a long moment, until Judas could take no more. He glanced down at the table, at the exclusive Silver Euro Express card bearing his name. The card of choice for the filthy rich. You couldn't apply for one. You were invited to join the elite.

'What's this?' He couldn't control the tremor in his voice.

'That my friend is your salvation.'

Judas looked at the card, knew if he picked it up it would be game over. He would be this man's property, would never know peace again.

'Pre-loaded with thirty thousand Euros.'

Judas picked up the card, turned it over between his fingers, felt the power of the money. There was a thumping sensation in his chest. His heart, or was it the bass from the fairground music? This was a fortune. It would pay off his debts and then some. He'd be able to start over.

'You want something in return.' Judas said, a statement not a question.

The man grinned. 'Of course.'

Judas listened in silence while the man outlined the price of his salvation.

TWENTY-ONE

YORK, NORTHUMBRIA.
THURSDAY.

They left the campsite and made their way into the city on foot. The streets of the old town were packed, bodies spilling out of pubs and bars. Male and female on parade, more flesh than the meat stalls in The Shambles. Packs of young people drifted from pub to pub, moving in waves, settling for a drink, then at an unseen signal, moving on. Just like one of Attenborough's documentaries, Tom thought. The warm evening magnified the smells coming from the fast food outlets. Kebabs, fried onions, fish, chips, candyfloss.

Peter led the way, checking the route on the map on his phone. Many people recognised Jesus. Some stared, and pointed. A few went as far as approaching, wanting selfies, or a chat, but these people were deflected by Peter. Jesus, who loved to stop for conversation, resisting all attempts to hurry him along, on this occasion allowed himself to be guided through the crowds. The majority of people though, unaware of their presence, were only intent on achieving oblivion through the time honoured means of alcohol and drugs. Big screens on the street corners gave out public information, warnings of pickpockets, and the address of NorPro. It urged citizens to take care if driving, suggested walking as the better choice, and then wished everybody a pleasant and safe evening in York, before looping round again in a never-ending cycle.

There were a few uniformed Polizei officers dotted about in little groups. Safety in numbers. Helmets were on, visors were up, but the eyes were watchful, wary. They scanned the crowd for troublemakers, agitators, signs of dissent. Other eyes too, were alert. Plain clothed officers lurked in shadows, mingled with the crowds. And always the ever-present lenses of the ubiquitous security cameras turned this way and that. Drones hovering above head height, able to follow anybody anywhere underlined the message. There was no hiding place.

Senior officers would be monitoring the situation from the control room, ready, at the first sign of trouble to move in the reinforcements waiting in vans parked in side streets. Fresh officers, bored witless, would be more than ready to break a few skulls.

Trouble though, if it came, would be later in the evening, when enough drink had been consumed, and the agitators had done their work. For now, the people were happy, boisterous but calm.

'We eating then or what?' One of the group asked. With all the noise on the streets, Tom didn't hear who it was. A few others asked the same question.

'Relax brothers, it's in hand.' Jude told them. 'I've booked us a private room at a recommended restaurant. It's not far now.'

'As long as it's not Indian.' Simon muttered.

The sound of sirens drew closer, strobing blue

lights flashed past. A loudhailer could be heard, warning the crowds to move back. Jeering, shouting, football chants, all in the mix. Despite the carnival atmosphere, the tensions were rising. They continued through the narrow streets. As far as Tom could tell, they were heading for the river. It was quieter here, the main streets left behind. It became easier to move.

There was a moment of confusion at the Ganges Indian restaurant, no record of the booking, according to the dinner-jacketed waiter on the door. Judas slipped him a few notes and everything was fine. They were led through a crowded room, tables crammed with diners enjoying their evening. One or two looked up as the thirteen trooped by, but didn't seem that interested. Up a narrow staircase, past the gents. Peter peeled off, not hesitating to take advantage of a proper loo, the rest entering the room where a long table was laid with cutlery, glasses, napkins, candles in small dishes.

As the group settled at the table a waiter appeared, handed out menus, took orders for drinks, and had a brief conversation with Judas before departing. Jesus seated himself in the middle of one side of the table, leaving space for Peter to his left. John was to his right, then the others crowded in, squabbling to get as close to Jesus as they could. Tom for his part was content to sit on the end. Judas, he noticed was at the other end nearest the exit. Andrew opposite Jesus was flanked by Matt and Jim.

A few minutes later, Peter came in moaning about the state of the toilets. 'Typical, first chance I get to use a proper toilet and they're filthy.' He took his place next to Jesus. 'Have we ordered yet?'

Jesus didn't reply, just pushed his chair back, stood, eased his way past the chairs and left the room. 'I wouldn't use the bogs here, Boss.' Peter called after him, 'they're in a right old state.'

The disciples studied the menus, and chatted until a lone waiter appeared struggling with a tray of drinks. Peter waited until the drinks were on the table then asked him if he'd seen Jesus.

'Coming now, mate.'

They watched, bemused as Jesus came back carrying a bowl of water, flannels and soap. A diminutive dinner jacketed waiter trailed behind carrying a stack of towels. Jesus cleared a space, set the bowl down in front of Peter, and asked for a foot.

'You what, Boss?' Peter didn't like the look of the bowl of water. Jesus was on another mission.

Jesus slipped the Crocs off Peter's feet, and soaped a flannel, the scent of lemongrass filling the air.

'No, Boss.' Peter pulled his feet away. 'My feet are clean, thank you. I had a shower earlier.' He looked at the others. 'We all did.'

'Unless you let me wash your feet you can't be a follower of mine.' Jesus replied.

Peter shook his head sullenly. 'It's not right.'

'Peter, my friend, you don't understand what I am doing now, but some day you will. Let us prepare.'

'In that case Lord, do my hands and hair as well.'

'A person who has had a shower does not need to wash all over again. They are clean except for their feet.'

Peter looked at the others who pretended not to notice his discomfort. Peter knew he wouldn't win so lowered his head in submission. 'Okay Boss, do it.'

Jesus washed the grime and dust from Peter's feet before towelling them dry. As a final act of service, he dipped his head and kissed them.

After Jesus had washed the feet of all his disciples, he said, 'Do you realise what I've just done for you?' The disciples looked at each other. 'You call me teacher and Lord,' he continued, 'and you're right to do so, for I am your teacher and Lord.' He paused, took a sip of his drink, 'But if I, your teacher and Lord, have washed your feet for you, you must be ready to do the same for each other. Do you understand? The messenger is not greater than the one who sent him, and now you know this, you will be greatly blessed if you do it.'

There was silence as everybody tried to take in what Jesus was saying, then the waiters came back to take the orders and the moment passed. Tom handed his Smartphone to one of them. They bunched up together, smiling for the photo.

Simon, who had been quiet for a while, said, 'Why can't we have good traditional food?'

'Like?' Nathan asked.

'I don't think you can go wrong by going back to the ancient writings.'

Groans all round.

'Not the ancient writings.' Jim sighed.

'You don't expect that we should butcher our own meat do you Simon?' Peter, already on his second pint, a touch of belligerence in his voice. 'Sitting round the camp fire, roasting freshly killed lamb on a spit?'

Simon shrugged. 'Nothing wrong with that.'

'It's the modern age.' Andrew said. 'We have butchers for that sort of thing.'

'Perhaps he'd like some manna.' Phil suggested.

'What was manna?' Matt asked.

'Are we ready to order?' Jesus asked.

'Maybe you could miraculously produce some spit roasted lamb for Simon?' Peter suggested with a sly grin, to laughs all round.

Jesus smiled. 'Not tonight, Peter.'

'Good,' Peter said to more laughter, 'I like Indian.'

†

STATE SECURITY HQ, YORK, NORTHUMBRIA.

Swanger yawned, stretched. It was late, another twelve-hour shift ending. She ought to get off home, not that she had a lot at home, just Max the tabby. She sighed, poured another whisky, lit another cigarette, and looked at the mound of paperwork on her desk. It might be a technological age but the paperwork never diminished. She picked up the uppermost file. Operation Raven had been a stunning success. Swanger was still basking in the afterglow. Heathersedge was delighted and the Governor had passed on his congratulations. Somebody suggested that the Fuehrer knew that she was the agent responsible for breaking one of the terror cells associated with FKU, but Swanger discounted this possibility.

And broken it was. The two terrorists had spilled everything, as Swanger knew they would. Her technique, a mixture of good cop, bad cop, never failed. Of the two, Bocus had been the tougher character, holding out for a couple of days, but in the end, aided by his inability to move, he had broken. Tears streaming down his face, he gave her the name of his controller who, despite going on the run had been tracked to a safe house in Wessex and brought back by the Ghost Squad. He in turn was giving names and a further part of the FKU network was being rolled up. Beaumont had given up the house in Huddersfield and the locations of all the bombs they'd planted.

One more session with each of them should wrap it up, Swanger thought, then, as a reward for their co-operation, Beaumont and Bocus would be extinguished without ceremony. The chemicals running down the lines into their bodies would be changed. It would be a slow descent into nothingness. Swanger shuddered, conscious of her own mortality, she didn't like to think about death. She couldn't imagine anything after this life, couldn't imagine not existing anymore either.

Swanger stubbed out the butt end of her cigarette, rubbed her eyes, drained the glass of whisky. She knew full well she smoked and drank too much, the doctor at her last medical had advised her to cut back at once. She turned on the TV for a final glance at the news before leaving. A familiar face appeared on the screen. Jesus. He was seen arriving in York on the open topped bus. The crowds going wild. Swanger watched with amusement. Most politicians would sell their souls for a reception like that. A montage of shots followed showing Jesus schmoozing the crowds, healing the sick and breaking bread with the poor. What was he about?

The picture changed. Caiaphas the Jewish high

priest looked disapproving, the camera tracking him as he arrived at the Governor's residence. The picture changed again. Jesus once more at the fair this time, on the Waltzer, on the Dodgems, laughing, joking with his disciples, hanging out, having a good time and enjoying life.

Why hadn't he harnessed the power of the people? Swanger wondered. Stormed his way into power. He had the looks, the popularity. The people would follow him anywhere. Because, she realised, he'd never intended it that way. If he was a king, then he was a different kind of king. A type never before experienced on earth.

✝

After the meal, Jesus called for silence, said, 'This will be the last meal we share together.'

There were concerned looks among the disciples, and conversation stopped. Jesus produced a wooden drinking bowl from his pack, poured wine, took a piece of leftover naan bread, looked up, and gave thanks. He broke the bread into pieces, handed it round the twelve. 'This bread is my body given for you, eat it, and remember me.'

Mystified, they all ate a piece of bread.

Jesus again looked up, gave thanks, and pouring wine into the bowl he passed it round the table, 'This is the new covenant made with my own blood, which is shed for you. Drink and remember me.'

They all drank from the bowl. Tom noticed that Jude the Dude who drank last slipped the bowl into his own pack.

Jamie said, 'what is happening Jesus, why you are saying these things? We're not giving up now, are we?'

Jesus looked troubled. 'You don't understand, but soon it will become clear.' He looked at each of the disciples in turn. 'I'll tell you the truth. One of you around this table will betray me tonight.'

'No.' Peter jumped to his feet. 'Never. That's impossible.' Feeling awkward, he sat down, noticed John leaning in towards Jesus. He beckoned to him. 'Go on John, ask him who it is.'

Jesus looked at them both. 'Watch.' He said, and breaking a piece of naan, dipped it in some curry sauce, and gave it to Judas. 'It's time Judas, to do what you have to do. Go, and be quick about it.'

Judas took the bread, stood, muttered something about needing a pee and left, throwing the piece of bread into the corner.

After Judas had gone, Jesus once again bemused the remainder with his words. 'Brothers, we have travelled far and wide these past three years, but I'll be with you for just a short time now.'

They looked at him in silence as he continued, 'Let me give you a new command, Love one another. I ask that you love each other in the same way I have loved you. In this way people will recognise you as my followers.'

As the power and simplicity of these words settled on the room, Peter blurted out. 'Lord, where are you going?'

'I am going,' Jesus replied, 'where you can't follow now, though you will follow me later.'

'Why can't I follow you now?' Peter demanded.

'You will look for me and want to join me, but I tell

you now, where I am going you will not be able to follow.'

There was much muttering and confusion until Jesus held up his hands. 'Tonight though, every one of you will lose faith in me. As it says in the ancient scriptures, "I will strike the shepherd and the sheep will be scattered".' He looked at them all. 'Believe me, it will happen.'

'I would lay down my life for you Lord.' Peter stated.

A sad smile creased Jesus' face. 'The truth, Peter,' Jesus said, 'is that before the cockerel crows tomorrow, you'll deny me three times.'

Peter, speechless for once, looked at the other disciples, dared any to speak. Nobody met his eye. Nobody spoke.

Jesus, unconcerned by Peter's annoyance, held his arms wide. 'Lads,' he implored, 'why the long faces? Don't let your hearts be troubled. You believe in God. Believe also in me. My Father's house has many rooms. I am going there to prepare a place for you. I'll come back and take you with me.'

Silence.

'You know the way to the place where I'm going.' Jesus assured them.

'Lord,' Tom shook his head, 'we don't know where you're going. How can we know the way?'

'I am the way and the truth and the life,' Jesus answered, 'no one comes to the Father except through me. If you know me, you will know my Father as well.'

'Lord,' Phil said, 'show us the Father and that will be enough for us.'

'Don't you know me, Phil?' Jesus responded. 'Even

after I've been with you such a long time.' He looked round them all. 'Anyone who has seen me has seen the Father. Don't you believe that I'm in the Father, and the Father is in me? The words I say to you, I don't say on my own authority. It is the Father, living in me, who is doing his work. Believe me when I say that I'm in the Father and the Father is in me. Or at least believe in the evidence of the works themselves. I tell you the truth, lads, whoever believes in me will do the works I've been doing, and they'll do even greater things than these, because I'm going to the Father. And I will do whatever you ask in my name, so the Father may be glorified in the Son. You may ask me for anything in my name, and I will do it.'

The disciples were quiet as they took in Jesus' words. 'If you love me,' he went on, 'keep my commands. I will ask the Father to send you another advocate to help you and be with you for all time. The Spirit of Truth. The world can't accept him, because it neither sees him nor knows him. But you know him, for he lives with you and will be in you.' He smiled. 'I will not leave you as orphans.'

Peter, still smarting from being told he would betray Jesus, didn't take in a lot of what Jesus was saying. John was busy writing it all down. At least he could read it later, he thought.

After a short while, Jesus concluded by saying, 'Come on, lads, it's time to leave.'

†

The Garden.

Peter paced up and down.

It was a beautiful evening, mild for the time of year. T-shirt weather, not that Northumbrians needed mild weather to wear next to nothing. He remembered the lasses in the city earlier. The acres of flesh. It was a long time since he'd known a woman, too long. He remembered with shame the man he used to be, and the women of whom he'd taken advantage. Taking out his phone, he read again the texts from Jayne. Did he want her back? Could they make it work? He'd meant to ask Jesus what he thought, but now didn't seem the right time. He sighed, and walked some more.

The moon, pale, and low in the sky, provided little light in the depths of the park. He could just about hear noises from the river Ouse, pleasure boats, blaring music, carousing. He looked around. It seemed quiet enough, no danger.

It had been a good evening until Jesus had started talking about betrayal. What was that about? Peter recalled Jesus' words, 'One of you will betray me.'

He knew Jesus was an excellent judge of character but to say that, and then point the finger at Judas. Okay the bloke could be a wazzock at times, but betrayal, to the authorities? Peter found that difficult to accept. No wonder Judas had rushed off in a huff.

And then, to come out with, 'And you Peter, will deny me three times before the cock crows.'

That had been hurtful. If anyone else had spoken like that, they'd be still picking up their teeth. But Jesus was another matter. You couldn't help loving the guy.

Peter stopped by the bench, suppressed a burp. He

rubbed his eyes. That third pint had been a mistake. Neither Jamie nor John responded. Peter looked at them with contempt. Jamie was slumped on a park bench, half curled up, arms wrapped round his body. His eyes were closed, and he twitched every so often. While John, the beloved John as he liked to call himself, was seated on the opposite end of the bench, one leg on the bench, one on the floor, head back, snores rasping.

Pillocks.

Both of them.

He peered into the shadows. Could just make out the form of Jesus on his knees praying. Peter couldn't hear the words but it sounded urgent, desperate almost.

Well he wouldn't let the Boss down. He was certain of that. He would stay awake, keep watch, and show these two he could be relied upon. Still, it wouldn't harm to sit down for a minute or two. He pushed John's leg from the bench, and slumped down.

It was so peaceful here. It was hard to believe they were in the middle of a metropolitan city, the capital of Northumbria. He could almost believe he was out in the Dales. Peter closed his eyes, breathed in the night air. Life was good.

✝

THE TEMPLE.

The Temple, illuminated by discreet lighting, as magnificent at night as during the day was both welcoming and forbidding. The main gates were closed. Anybody wanting entry had to convince the security guard of their credentials. Judas could see the guard inside the booth. He looked to be making tea.

He stood in the shadows over the road turning over in his mind the step he was about to take. He couldn't back away now. The man he'd met the previous night had made it plain. He'd been committed from the second he'd picked up the Silver Euro Express card with its weight of money, blood money. First thing he'd done was check the balance on the card. It was there alright. Thirty thousand Euros, his escape route.

This was it though, the ultimate betrayal. He was giving up the man he'd lived side by side with for the past three years. There was no real alternative, Judas realised, not if he wanted to live, anyway.

But to betray Jesus.

Judas sighed, a deep heartfelt groan that came from the depths of his being. It was almost as if Jesus knew what was going to happen, who it was that would betray him. The way he'd looked at him, the way he'd said, 'It's time Judas, to do what you have to do. Go, and be quick about it.'

Perhaps Judas was part of some cosmic plan. He'd never been convinced that Jesus was the Son of God, the Messiah. In his head, yes, but not in his heart, not where it mattered. He wasn't alone in that, the mood of the people seemed to be changing. There'd been grumblings of discontent since their arrival in the capital on Monday. They wanted a king to defeat the Saxons. Love and peace was all well and good, but it would never overcome the bomb and the bullet.

But just supposing Jesus was the Son of God, the Messiah, then Judas would be betraying God himself.

That would put him on the side of the devil, the evil one. He wasn't sure he could live with that, the end result might be the same, no matter what he did.

He shivered uncontrollably, looked around, there was nobody watching. Quick look at his watch, decision time.

Judas, mind made up, crossed the road, entered the warmth of the security booth, gave his name to the guard, and was led into the Temple complex.

†

THE GARDEN.

Jesus looked at the sleeping disciples on the bench. His closest companions, sleeping like innocent children. He sighed, shook his head. 'Peter, Peter.'

No response. Jesus shook Peter's arm. 'Peter.'

Peter opened his eyes, saw who it was and struggled to his feet. 'Sorry, Boss. I just closed my eyes for a minute.' He shook Jamie and John awake. 'Hoy, you two, you're letting the Boss down, falling asleep on the job.'

The other two roused themselves. They stood before Jesus, repentant. 'Your spirit is willing but your flesh is weak.' He told them.

John and Jamie mumbled their apologies as Jesus continued. 'I need you three to keep awake, to keep watch. All of you pray that you don't have to face temptation.'

With a final look, Jesus moved back to where he'd been praying earlier. Falling to his knees, he lowered his head until his forehead was touching the dry earth, said, 'Father, if it is not possible for this cup to pass from me then let your will be done.'

Silence.

Minutes passed, Jesus remained in the same position for a short while, and then went back to the disciples, who once again were asleep.

More hurt than angry he left them, and knelt in prayer.

He needed to be sure.

He stood a few minutes later. There was no room for doubt.

Silence was the affirmation.

The time had come.

He returned to the three disciples, shook them awake. 'Can you not keep awake for ten minutes? In a minute, you will see the Son of Man betrayed into the hands of evil men. Look,' he pointed, 'here comes my betrayer.'

Peter exchanged glances with John and Jamie. He could tell they were as perplexed as he was. Peter looked at Jesus who was staring towards the park entrance.

'Let's go meet them.' Jesus said and walked towards the gates.

John and Jamie looked to Peter for direction. He shook his head in annoyance and frustration. They could stay or follow. He was tempted to stay. 'Come on,' he said after a second's hesitation. 'We can't leave him.'

They hurried along the path after Jesus. 'Where are the others?' Peter asked.

'Around. Here and there.' Jamie replied.

'Round them up, meet us at the entrance.'

John and Jamie hurried off to find the other disciples. If there was going to be trouble, there'd be safety in numbers. This is ridiculous, Peter thought. There's nothing happening and nobody's here. But still, something had alarmed Jesus, and Peter, after the earlier criticism, wasn't taking any chances.

It was the distant thrum, thrum, thrum of the helicopter seeping into Peter's consciousness that alerted him to the possibility of trouble, that and the flashing blue lights coming down the road. It was eerie seeing the lights penetrating the black of the park. Quiet too, no sirens to excite the good citizens of York. By the time Peter caught up with Jesus, he was waiting just inside the entrance looking at the gates. Peter stood by his side. They watched in silence as the convoy of vehicles came to a halt outside the park. The helicopter arrived overhead, took up station, its searchlight piercing the night air, lit up a wide circle around the two men.

Peter touched Jesus' arm, leant in towards him, struggling to make himself heard above the rotor blades. 'There's still time to get away.' He said, but knew in his heart there wasn't.

Jesus, staring as the Polizei officers began to disembark, said, 'I have to drink from the cup my father has prepared.'

Uniformed officers formed up outside the gates. Peter could see they were armed but not expecting any trouble. This was a routine operation for them, an easy lift of a bunch of rebels. It was too late to get away now, they should have fled the moment Jesus sensed trouble. What was he playing at?

The chopper with its spotlights and heat seeking

equipment could follow them without any problems. There was no escape. Peter decided it would be better to go with the authorities and bluff it out. The others led by John, with Jamie bringing up the rear, arrived. He told them his thinking, was rewarded with nods of agreement. They formed up alongside Jesus, solidarity in action.

A senior officer made his way through the gates. He was flanked by a sergeant and the rest of his squad, hands resting on their stun guns. Peter was amazed to see Judas trailing a step behind, the dog returning to its vomit.

So Jesus was right after all.

The inspector spoke to Judas who nodded, then stood in front of Jesus.

Jesus smiled. 'Judas, my friend, you've returned.'

'Boss.' Judas acknowledged, leaned in, kissed Jesus on the cheek, then looked away, not meeting anybody's eye.

'Are you Jesus?' The officer asked.

'I am.' Jesus replied.

'You're under arrest, on suspicion of sedition against the state.'

'So, you've come with your helicopter and your armed police to arrest me like a common bandit,' Jesus shook his head, 'yet day after day I've been teaching in the Temple and you never laid a finger on me.'

'Are you coming or not?' The officer asked.

'It is done like this in the night to fulfil the prophecy of the ancient scriptures.'

'Let's go.' The sergeant spoke for the first time.

'This is your hour.' Jesus replied. 'The power of darkness is yours.'

Peter stirred. 'We'll come with you, Boss.'

'They don't want you Peter, or the others.' Jesus told him.

'He's right.' The sergeant said, an amused smile on his face. 'The rest of you can piss off. A chicken without a head will run around for a while but it's still a dead chicken.'

Peter swung his fist, heard the satisfying crunch as it connected with the sergeant's face, and smiled as the man slumped to the floor in agony, his jaw shattered. He rubbed his knuckles ruefully.

Jesus gave him a scathing look, stooped, touched the man's face, and helped him to his feet, his jaw healed. 'Keep your fists to yourself,' he told Peter, 'shall I not drink the cup the Father has given me?'

Peter, silent, looked round for the other disciples but they'd gone, scattered like sheep. He watched in impotent frustration as they handcuffed Jesus and led him away.

TWENTY-TWO

THE GARDEN.
FRIDAY.

Peter, sick to his stomach, watched as the vehicles moved off. The searchlight from the helicopter vanished. The pitch of the engine changed, noise from the rotors beating a farewell. Apart from intermittent pools of street lighting, he was left in darkness.

What would Jesus do, he asked himself. Helpless as a baby torn from its mother's breast his response was to break down and cry. Weeping uncontrollably he realised this was the first time in three years he'd been deprived of the wisdom of Jesus, and crushed by a paralysing fear he raged against the injustice of the situation.

Tired, exhausted by fear, he lapsed into silence, staring down the empty street at a complete loss. For how long he didn't know. It was as if he'd sunk into a trance that was only broken by a low voice calling his name. He spun round, stared into the blackness of the gardens. 'Who's there?'

A figure emerged from the bushes.

'You been there long?' Peter needed to know how much of his distress John had witnessed.

John shook his head. 'Nah. I was hiding in the gardens. I thought it was time to come out for a look and saw you standing there. You alright?'

It was a stupid question, Peter thought, but didn't say. Now wasn't the time. He shrugged, mumbled an affirmative, asked about the others.

'Dunno. I'm surprised they didn't take us all.'

'They don't want the headless chickens, mate.' Peter told him. 'Look how we scattered when trouble came.'

'You didn't.'

'Over too quick, John. I was rooted to the spot.'

They discussed the night's events, speculated where Jesus might have been taken.

' State Security HQ.' John suggested.

'It'll be the Temple.' Peter said. 'Pilate won't want anything to do with it. It'll be Caiaphas up to his tricks.'

'It was the Polizei who came for him.' John reminded.

'Means nothing.' Peter declared. 'C'mon, let's go.'

'Go where?' John didn't want to admit he just wanted to go home.

'Temple.' Peter gave him a look. 'We need to be there when the Boss is released.'

John looked at Peter. Had he lost it? Was the strain proving too great, had he not heard a thing Jesus said last night? This is my body. This is my blood. Eat, drink, and remember me. He couldn't see Jesus coming out of this alive.

Peter moved off down the street. 'C'mon.'

John sighed, followed.

†

Inside the Temple.

Early hours in the Holy Place. The flickering light from the candle gave Caiaphas just enough light to see where he was going as he paced from the door to the curtain. Every time he reached the curtain, he stopped and gazed upon it with awe. To think that the living presence of God was behind the thick material screen, and that he, Caiaphas, high priest of the Jews, was the one man alive allowed to venture into the most holy place. And that was only permitted on one day a year; Yom Kippur or the Day of Atonement. He looked at the curtain now, at the fine linen, at the angels embroidered in blue, purple, scarlet yarn, and marvelled.

He sighed, turned, and paced the short distance to the door, turned, and repeated the journey. As he walked, he worried if he was doing the right thing. He'd asked God, but God was silent on the subject. He would have to decide for himself. It was a heavy burden. The future of his faith depended on getting it right. He glanced at his watch. They must have detained Jesus by now, or had he wriggled free like so many previous occasions? He resisted the temptation to contact the officer in charge of the squad. Radio silence had been agreed, the fewer people who knew about the nights work the better. Time enough for the world to know.

On and on he paced, the minutes ticking by. Caiaphas mentally prepared himself for the forthcoming chat with the so-called Messiah. His aim, get Jesus to condemn himself through his own words, to provoke the man into discretion that could be viewed as blasphemy. He'd need the backing of the Sanhedrin, but they would follow where Caiaphas led. There would be no option other than to convict Jesus, and that would mean one outcome, death.

†

OUTSIDE THE TEMPLE.

Speaking little, Peter and John moved through the darkened streets. Reaching the Temple, they were surprised to find a small group of people gathered, with others arriving in dribs and drabs. They eased their way through the knots of people, trying not to draw attention to themselves. Peter heard the name Jesus mentioned a few times.

'They know.' He whispered to John.

John nodded.

Up against the closed gates, Peter stared at the Temple complex, wondered where Jesus might be, how he might be feeling. Lights shone from some windows and high above the ground he could see a figure at a window.

†

INSIDE THE TEMPLE.

The waiting was over.

Jesus, to Caiaphas' relief, had been arrested by the Polizei and handed over to the Temple guards. They would bring him upstairs to be questioned. It wouldn't be long now, Caiaphas thought. He could hear the low buzz of excited, nervous chatter from the large meeting room next door, where selected members of the Sanhedrin, summoned from their beds amidst much grumbling, were beginning to gather.

Waiting in the anteroom, Caiaphas looked out of the window. A silent crowd gathered by the gates. It seemed to be swelling as he watched, people pouring down the streets to join those already assembled. As he continued to watch large vans bearing the logo of Northumbria Broadcasting pulled up, technicians dismounted, started assembling camera equipment. Caiaphas sucked his teeth, realised it was bound to happen. Nothing could be kept secret in the present age. He turned from the window, shook his head in amusement. What was it about this Jesus that attracted so much attention?

There was a light tap on the door. It opened on Caiaphas' command, and then, there he was, the man who'd brought so much grief into his life, Jesus.

Caiaphas looked at him, savouring the moment. It had taken a long time, but now, the pendulum had swung the other way. The months, years, of Jesus setting the agenda, were over. The rightful order had been restored. Caiaphas slowed his breathing, tried to quell his mounting excitement, told himself this was the right course of action. He couldn't think of a better way to preserve the integrity of the Jewish faith.

Jesus, blindfolded, wearing light coloured trousers, a short-sleeved blue shirt, stood before him, silent. It looked as though he'd been struck in the face. A mark on his jaw, a cut lip. He looked at the guards holding Jesus by the arms. They stared back, giving nothing. He should have realised one of them would get carried away. Still, it should make it easier now he'd been softened up. He smiled to himself, with luck this would be the end of Jesus and all this Messiah nonsense. He turned and led the way through to the meeting room where his handpicked court waited.

†

OUTSIDE THE TEMPLE.

The roving news reporter drifted through the crowd, cameraman a pace behind. Nothing much was happening. He was bored, tired and annoyed he'd been dragged out of bed for this non-event. He stopped every so often, stuck his fluffy microphone under a fresh nose, asked for an opinion on, what they thought was happening. Had Jesus been arrested? What would happen next? Had he been charged? Anything to keep the news machine churning.

Peter and John kept out of his way. Whenever it seemed he might get close, they moved position, turned their faces away. He seemed to ghost through the throng, Peter thought, popping up when least expected.

'What does Jesus mean to you, are you a follower?' He asked a man a few metres away. Peter shifted his balance, didn't wait for the answer. He slid round a large woman, and raised his eyebrows at John who shrugged.

The dark of the night was fading, the sun lurking just below the horizon. It might be his imagination Peter realised, but it seemed as though a number of people were looking at him with recognition. He moved through the crowd avoiding eye contact. They should get away while they had the chance, save themselves. They couldn't do anything to help Jesus. He was lost, trapped in the machine, at the whim of forces beyond their control. Just because the disciples hadn't been arrested yet didn't mean it wouldn't happen. He was just about to suggest leaving when a woman whispered to her companion who stared at the two disciples. He nodded in confirmation. The woman hesitantly approached Peter. 'Do I know you?'

'No.' Peter frowned, turned to John for support but he'd vanished into the crowd.

'I do.' The woman insisted. 'You're one of the disciples.'

'I can assure you, I'm not.' Peter replied forcibly.

The woman looked puzzled as Peter moved away. He searched for John as he walked but couldn't see him. The crowd by now had swollen to a vast number. No chance, Peter thought. John would have to fend for himself. He abruptly cannoned off a man who staggered backwards. 'Watch where you're going, mate.'

Peter muttered an apology, moved off. The man grabbed his arm. 'It's Pete, isn't it? One of Jesus' disciples. What's happening, mate? Any news?'

'You've got me confused with somebody else.' Peter told him, pulling his arm free. As he moved off, the man insisted to anybody who'd listen that the disciples were in the crowd.

It was getting lighter all the time. The crowd was getting anxious, bored, agitated. In the absence of news, rumours started. Jesus was free, was talking to the TV people. Jesus was dead, shot while trying to escape. Jesus had taken over, was established in the Governor's residence. Peter heard the rumours, ignored them. He just wanted away.

At last, the crowd thinned, it became easier to move, and a side street appeared. He was about to turn into it when a black fluffy microphone was thrust under his nose. 'And here we have Peter, right hand man of Jesus for the last three years. You were there, I understand, Peter, when Jesus was arrested. Can you tell the viewers what happened?'

Peter looked beyond the reporter into the unblinking eye of the camera. 'It wasn't me. I wasn't there.' He turned, and ran down the empty street. As he fled, heart pounding, the first cockerel of the day began to crow.

†

INSIDE THE TEMPLE.

Caiaphas registered the faint crowing of a cockerel as he began outlining the case against Jesus. Dawn already. They needed to move fast. He cleared his throat, and addressed the court. 'Here is Jesus. Take a good look at him. This self-proclaimed Messiah. The son of the living God.'

He paused for effect, taking a sip of water. 'Ask yourselves, would God allow his son to be arrested, bound, blindfolded and brought before you in this condition? Where are the angels to protect him, to guard him? Don't you think God's son could summon legions of angels for protection?'

There was murmuring from the assembled

Pharisees, and teachers of the law.

Caiaphas let his words settle for a few moments. He crooked a finger at a guard, whispered in the man's ear, watched with a smile as the guard slapped Jesus hard across the cheek.

Shocked, the court fell silent.

'Jesus,' Caiaphas mocked, 'shouldn't you now turn the other cheek?'

Caiaphas felt a burning rage as Jesus turned his head to one side. He lashed out, striking Jesus. 'So, Jesus, son of God, famed prophet of Whitby, who struck you?

Silence.

'Can't speak, won't speak.' Caiaphas turned to the court. 'We've never known the man so silent, have we?'

Somebody laughed.

'Three years he's been travelling around Northumbria, proclaiming this new kingdom,' Caiaphas went on, warming to his task. 'God's kingdom. It's here. It's now.'

'Well gentlemen, it's not either of those things. God is in heaven. He hasn't sent his son to be with us, this man is no more God's son than Brotherton is.

More laughter. Brotherton acknowledged the recognition with a little bow.

'No,' the high priest continued in a lower tone. 'This man is an imposter. For reasons best known to himself, he's come along to trap the unwary. Well he's done plenty of that these last three years. He's played us all for gullible fools. Well enough is enough.'

'Excuse me?'

Caiaphas looked at O'Deamus.

'Yes?'

'Is it possible for the blindfold to be removed? I think at least Jesus should be able to see his accusers.'

Caiaphas snapped his fingers and waited while a guard removed the blindfold.

Jesus blinked in the harsh lighting of the committee room, focussed, and looked at O'Deamus, who looked away.

Caiaphas drank more water. This was going well. He had most of the members with him, O'Deamus the possible exception. It was time to introduce the first of the two witnesses. He'd decided not to over complicate the case. The more charges, the more witnesses, would mean more room for doubt, more wriggle room. A simple conviction for blasphemy would suffice.

Caiaphas drained his glass, signalled for more water and ordered the guards to produce the first witness. He paced up and down while he waited for the man to be summoned. Once the witness had been sworn in, Caiaphas asked him to repeat what he'd heard. It should be simple. He'd been told the exact words to say, was being paid well enough to say them.

The witness, a middle-aged man, avoided looking at Jesus. 'I heard this man say, "I will destroy this building with my own hands and in three days will build another, not with my own hands."'

'"This building?"' Caiaphas frowned. 'Which building?'

'This building, sir. The Temple, sir.'

Caiaphas nodded. The cretin had got there in the end. 'What do you say to this testimony against you, Jesus?'

Silence.

'Are you not going to speak?' Caiaphas shook his head in amusement. 'You always have so much to say, but when it's important to speak, you remain silent.'

Silence.

'Are you sure?' Caiaphas goaded. 'This is your opportunity to defend yourself.'

Jesus remained silent. Caiaphas would have expected the Messiah to speak, at least in his own defence. 'Very well.' He dismissed the witness, called the next and last witness.

There was a short delay while the witness was located in the toilets. He stood before the court now, and was asked what he'd heard. He replied confidently. 'This man said, "Angels would destroy the Temple and everybody in it, and then three days later he would rebuild it from the ruins."'

Caiaphas thanked him, told him he could leave. 'What do you say, Jesus?'

Silence.

Caiaphas sucked his teeth. He needed Jesus to speak, to condemn himself with his own words. It was one thing having witnesses, video evidence, recordings, but the court needed to hear it from Jesus himself. He pushed his frustration aside, the last thing he needed was an acquittal, or not proven verdict. He could feel the eyes of the court on him. He was so close. Perhaps he hadn't asked the right question. He turned, addressed Jesus. 'Are you the Messiah, the Son of God?'

'I am,' Jesus spoke for the first time. 'And you will see the Son of Man sitting at the right hand of the Mighty One and coming on the clouds of heaven.'

Caiaphas nodded, and smirked in triumph as he

addressed the court. 'And there we have it. Do we need any more witnesses? I think not. You have heard this blasphemy.' He paused, savouring the moment. 'What is your verdict?'

There were several shouts of death, and crucify him. A show of hands was taken and despite a few abstentions, there were more than enough votes for the death penalty. Caiaphas called for silence, and addressed Jesus. 'It is the sentence of this court that you be taken from here to a place of crucifixion and nailed to a cross until you die. May God have mercy on your soul.'

Caiaphas tried not to let his triumph show. His outward persona calm, inside he was doing back flips. Calm down, he told himself. Pilate still had to be convinced to ratify the decision of the Sanhedrin.

Jesus, who was silent throughout the voting, was blindfolded again and led out. The more belligerent members of the court formed two lines through which he was forced to walk while they kicked and spat on him.

†

ASKHAM BRYAN, NEAR YORK, NORTHUMBRIA

Swanger pottered around her tiny kitchen, the radio playing in the background. She'd just finished her second coffee of the day, and was beginning to feel human when a change in pitch on the radio, something akin to excitement, caught her attention.

'...ing news. We're receiving reports that the renowned prophet, Jesus of Whitby, has been arrested, and is being questioned in connection with the recent terror campaign mounted by Four Kingdoms United. We've tried speaking with his inner circle of followers, the disciples, but nobody is available for comment at present. A Polizei spokesperson wouldn't be drawn on the reports either. So, stay tuned and we'll keep you updated with the latest reports as we get them.

Now a quick weather summary before we return to the studio, it's hot and sunny all the way. And remember, the hosepipe ban is still in force.'

It was a surprise it had taken so long, Swanger thought as she washed, dried, put away her breakfast things. It must be a Polizei operation, she decided, the SS had long since lost interest in Jesus.

Leaving the house her phone rang. It was an upset, indignant Barnabas, wanting to know if she knew, or worse, had been part of the operation to arrest Jesus. She assured him she didn't know beforehand, had not been involved. He wanted to talk more but she told him later. Right now, she intended wrapping things up with Beaumont and Bocus.

TWENTY-THREE

STATE SECURITY HQ, YORK, NORTHUMBRIA.

Beaumont studied his face in the mirror. He didn't think he looked too bad considering he'd been in a vegetative state less than twelve hours ago. He needed a shave but that could wait. He blew air through his teeth, was surprised, amazed to be alive. When the white clad officials had entered his room the night before and started messing with the IV lines, he'd assumed the worst. Couldn't believe it when they removed the needles from his arms, unhooked all the equipment. The lead nurse had patted him on the cheek, told him to get a good night's sleep. Tomorrow was a big day.

Well, yesterday's tomorrow was today, and he felt good. As good as could be expected. In truth he hadn't slept that well, he'd been far too wired. As far as Beaumont was concerned, the big day was the day of his release. Why else, he reasoned, would he have been allowed the use of his body again? If they were going to kill him, they could have done it at any time by just pumping the chemicals into his body. Anyway, that woman, Swanger, had promised if he talked, he would die humanely. So, it stood to reason, he was either being transferred to prison to await trial or, his preferred option, he was being released.

He finished towelling himself dry, put on the orange coveralls that had been left out. There wasn't any underwear, which felt a bit strange, but nothing could diminish his joy at being alive. The door opened, a guard stuck his head in. 'You ready?'

Beaumont nodded and followed him out, down a corridor, where he was placed in a holding cell with other prisoners. He tried talking to one or two, but was met with blank indifference. After a while he gave up, was content to sit in silence and wait.

✝

GOVERNOR'S OFFICE, YORK, NORTHUMBRIA.

'I wasn't aware my dear Caiaphas that you Jews had the right to pronounce the death sentence.'

'A recommendation, Excellency.' Caiaphas assured.

'Hmm.' Pilate glanced at the slip of paper offered by the high priest. He pushed it to one side. 'On what grounds have you convicted him?'

'He claims to be the king of the Jews.' Caiaphas shrugged his disdain. 'He comes from lowly stock. His father was a builder, wasn't even married to the mother when she bore him.'

'A bastard?' Pilate laughed. 'Not exactly crime of the century, is it?'

'Of course not Excellency, but he does make rather extravagant claims...'

'I'd quite like to meet this Jesus.' Pilate interrupted.

'You want to see him. Jesus?'

'Why not?' Pilate smiled thinly, 'or have you

bumped him off already?'

'No, of course not.' Caiaphas said, moving to the door. 'I'm sure it can be arranged.'

†

STATE SECURITY HQ, YORK, NORTHUMBRIA.

The custody official, portly, middle aged, florid complexion, fondness for ginger biscuits, didn't have to look in the custody book. 'Not here, love.' He pronounced with finality. Swanger frowned. She should have known about this. The official, sensing her confusion, was more than happy to gossip. 'Yeah, surprised you didn't know.' Another biscuit disappeared down his throat. He reached for his mug of tea. 'Booked out an hour ago.'

'Who booked them out?'

The official sighed, drew the book towards him, and ran a nicotine-stained finger down the page. 'Name of Heathersedge.'

'In person?'

'Naah.' The man closed the book, reached for the biscuits. 'He wouldn't lower himself to visit this level. His name on the chitty is all.' Two more biscuits vanished.

'But they couldn't walk.' Swanger protested.

'They could this morning, straight out the door they walked.' He mimed two fingers walking across the desk to the biscuits.

Swanger wanted to take his head and smack it on the desk, instead forced herself to remain calm. 'Where have they been taken?'

The man shrugged. He'd lost interest in the exchange. 'Like I'd know something like that. Once they've gone through that door, my involvement ends.' He picked up the empty biscuit packet, made a funnel, tipped the crumbs into his mouth.

Swanger hoped the fat jobs-worth would choke.

✝

GOVERNOR'S OFFICE, YORK, NORTHUMBRIA.

A crowd had gathered outside the Governor's residence. In the main, they were ordinary people who earlier had been massed outside the Temple, but were now seeded by agents of the Pharisees. The Polizei held back those by the gates, as two cars either side of a secure van, flanked by motorcycle outriders, swept through the gates, and parked out of sight at the rear. Sirens, flashing lights stopped.

A short time later Jesus was led into Pilate's office. The guards withdrew and the Governor regarded Jesus with interest. He seemed unlike any criminal or king he'd ever seen before. 'I've heard a lot about you, Jesus. My wife's a fan of yours.'

Jesus inclined his head.

'I understand you're the king of the Jews?' Pilate said.

'Is that your own idea,' Jesus asked, 'or did others talk to you about me?'

'Am I a Jew?' Pilate replied. 'Your own people, the high priest, Caiaphas, sent you to me. What have you done to upset him?'

'My kingdom is not of this world.' Jesus replied. 'If

it were my followers would fight to prevent my arrest. Even now, they would be making plans to free me. My kingdom is from another place.'

'You are a king, then?' Pilate said.

'You say that I'm a king,' Jesus answered. 'In fact, the reason I was born and came into the world is to testify to the truth. Everyone on the side of truth listens to me.'

'Truth.' Pilate retorted. 'What is truth?' He crossed to the big window leading to the balcony. 'If you're a king, these must be your subjects out here.'

Chants from outside could be heard. Crucify, crucify.

Jesus shrugged, didn't reply.

Pilate tried again. 'Where do you come from?'

Silence.

'Do you refuse to speak to me now? Don't you realise I have power, either to free you, or have you crucified?'

Jesus said, 'You would have no power over me if it hadn't been given to you from above. The one who handed me over to you is guilty of a greater sin.'

Pilate tried several more times to get Jesus to speak but he remained silent. Pilate became irritated by Jesus' silence. He picked up the phone, and asked for the sergeant of the guard to come to his office at once. He replaced the receiver, told Jesus, 'You won't like this, but it might just save your life.'

A uniformed sergeant appeared a few minutes later. Clicking his heels, he stood to attention. 'Excellency?'

'Take this man, Sergeant Blake,' Pilate told him, 'this king of the Jews and flog him severely.'

The sergeant looked at Jesus. 'Just a flogging, sir?'

'That's what I said, Sergeant. I want him brought back to me when you've finished.'

'Yes, sir.'

'Alive, Sergeant.'

✝

STATE SECURITY HQ, YORK, NORTHUMBRIA.

'The person you are calling is unavailable.' Swanger pressed the red button, and then the green, same result, Heathersedge was unavailable.

She'd called round a range of contacts. Nobody knew anything about Beaumont and Bocus, or if they did, they weren't saying. They can't just have disappeared, Swanger reasoned. Been released? No, that's impossible. They were confessed terrorists. She could understand if someone had terminated them by mistake - wouldn't have been the first time - but this was premeditated. For them to be able to walk out this morning, the medication keeping them immobile must have been stopped last night. Which means, Swanger concluded, they've been taken somewhere for some reason. And the one person who could tell her was Heathersedge, and he was unavailable.

The lift powered up to the top floor. It was deserted. Considering this was the headquarters of State Security, there was a distinct lack of security. She walked down the corridor as far as Heathersedge's office, and entered confidently. The outer office was deserted, the secretary nowhere to be seen. Swanger listened with her ear up against the door of the inner sanctum. Total silence. She opened the door, expecting a challenge, none came. No sign of Heathersedge. The guy had a nose for trouble, could sense it coming over the horizon and vanished. A red folder lay on the desk, black lettering in bold, Wannsee Protocol. She flicked open the outer cover, revealing a buff folder. Swanger took in the skull symbol, the Saxon words, Streng Geheim, Endlosung.

Top Secret? Final Solution to what though? Swanger about to pick up the folder, read further but hesitated. Some things were better not known. Under the folder, two sheets of paper were revealed bearing the names of Beaumont and Bocus. She eased them out, and read in disbelief.

†

GUARDROOM, GOVERNOR'S RESIDENCE, YORK, NORTHUMBRIA.

Guard room duty, important, but boring. The six-man squad, without exception, were taking a break from routine duties - watching TV, making tea, reading papers - when Sergeant Blake led Jesus through the door.

'Aye, aye, Sarg. What we got here then?' Private Gledhill asked.

'What we have here lads,' Blake replied, 'is a king. To be specific, this is Jesus, king of the Jews.'

'A king, eh?' Gledhill wisecracked, 'and there's us thinking it was someone important.'

'Why's he here, Sarg?' This from Lance Corporal Varley.

'He's to be flogged.'

'Flogged, eh?' Private Flint walked round Jesus, thoroughly inspecting him. 'What you have been up to then, you naughty king?'

The others joined in the game, walking round Jesus, sharks circling a lone bather.

'If he's a king, Sarg, he'll need a crown.' Gledhill stated.

'Good point.'

'And a robe.'

Blake nodded his agreement. It all added to the fun of the occasion, relieved the boredom.

Flint stood to attention. 'Permission to leave the guard room, Sarg.'

'Where you going?'

'Room, Sarg, get something of interest.'

'Don't be long, Flint, you'll miss the fun.'

Private Oldham found an old purple robe in a box of theatrical costumes the Governor's wife had brought in for disposal. Together, he and Varley stripped Jesus of his shirt, and dressed him in the robe while Blake watched with amusement. Gledhill had found a short length of barbed wire and was busy shaping it into a makeshift crown. He jammed it firmly on Jesus' head and twisted. The barbs cut deep. Gledhill could feel them grind into the king's skull, watched as blood ran in rivulets down his face, into his eyes. Jesus blinked at the sticky warmth, said nothing.

Flint came back carrying a lethal looking object, saw Jesus dressed in the purple robe, crown on his head, smiled, and nodded his approval. 'Nice one. Feller looks like a king now.'

The others crowded round him. 'Whatcha got there, Flinty?'

'Flagrum, mate, got it on my last posting in Tuscany. Never used it, mind.'

'I should hope you haven't, lad.' Blake laughed.

They passed the object round, examined it. There was a short wooden handle with three leather thongs, each a metre long. On each of the thongs sharp, rough pieces of metal were attached.

'Are you suggesting we use this on the king here?' Blake asked. The cat o' nine tails was the traditional method of flogging. Painful, but not usually lethal.

'What the Romans used to use, Sarg.'

'Genuine, is it?' Oldham wanted to know.

'Nah, repo mate. Do the job though.' He looked at Blake. 'Fit for a king, that is Sarg.'

Sergeant Blake turned the evil looking object over in his hand, felt the weight, the balance. He grinned at Jesus who looked back impassively. 'Let's do it then. The old man wants him flogged, so flogged he will be.'

They led Jesus outside, stripped the robe from his shoulders, and cable tied him half naked to the metal rings set on the top of the stake outside the guard room, where generations of recalcitrant soldiers had been flogged.

'Who's administering the punishment, Sarg?' Gledhill asked, looking at Flint who held the flagrum and showing no sign of relinquishing it.

'I think Private Flint should have the honour.'

'Thank you, Sarg.' Flint grinned. He was going to enjoy this. 'How many lashes, Sarg?'

'What do ya think, lads, forty?'

'With that?' Varley stated bluntly. 'You'll kill him.'

'I expect you're right, private, let's say thirty-nine then.'

Laughter from the soldiers.

'Count the strokes, Varley. Carry on Flint.'

Flint, his feet apart, positioned himself behind Jesus. He had a practice swing first, and then brought his arm down in a swift movement. The flagrum, doing its job, ripped into bare flesh. The effect of the leather thongs and metal was soon apparent. A deep, painful laceration appeared on Jesus' back.

'One.'

'That's a tasty bit o' kit.' Oldham nodded approvingly.

Flint grinned, raised his arm and struck again.

'Two.'

Jesus flinched. His face contorted with every stroke, but he didn't make a sound. His unwillingness to cry out spurred Flint onto to greater effort. His pride dented, he was determined to get a reaction out of this king who'd been provided for his entertainment.

'Three'

Flint carried on, grunting with effort, wiping the sweat and blood spatters from his eyes every few strokes. The soldiers crowded round, cheering his every stroke. Varley keeping meticulous count.

'Seven.'

Jesus' back soon became a torn twisted mass of scarlet, hideously butchered beyond recognition as something human.

'Fifteen.'

Still, Jesus made no sound. Flint continued, Varley counted, the others now counting with him.

'Twenty Two.'

Jesus' bladder gave way, the front of his trousers and the robe, were soaked. The soldiers jeered, spat on him. 'King's pissed himself, Flinty.'

Flint grunted, continued, his arm rising, falling, rhythmically.

Eventually it was over, the thirty-nine strokes completed. Jesus was untied. He slumped to the ground and lay still. Sergeant Blake, privately worried at Pilate's reaction, bent over Jesus and checked his condition. He was amazed this king of the Jews was still breathing. 'He's a tough nut, Flinty.'

Flint, breathing hard, agreed.

A telephone call summoned Blake to the guardroom where he was informed Pilate wanted Jesus back in his office, pronto. Jesus was hauled to his feet, held upright between Oldham and Varley, and then, still wearing the robe and the crown, he was led back to Pilate.

†

GOVERNOR'S OFFICE, YORK, NORTHUMBRIA.

Caiaphas was back, waiting in the outer office where the Governor's secretary shot him hostile glances every few minutes. He checked his watch, looked at the woman, and was met with an indifferent shrug. 'He's a very busy man.' She told him.

I'm a very busy man Caiaphas wanted to tell her. I've got a Messiah to crucify. He smiled at the thought, and forced himself to remain calm. It should be okay, he thought. If the Governor signed in the next fifteen minutes there would be enough time to get Jesus on the cross and hopefully dead before the start of the Sabbath which commenced just before sunset, which today was at 19:43.

He could have done without that tiresome scene with Judas who'd arrived at the Temple snivelling that it had all been a big mistake, could he give the money back, and have Jesus released? When told he couldn't, he'd snapped the Silver cash card, flicked it on the floor, and then slunk off. Another problem to sort, he thought, as he massaged his temples. What would he now do with thirty thousand Euros? It couldn't go back in the Temple treasury. It was tainted. Blood money.

Startled, he realised the secretary had spoken. She was looking at him. 'Pardon?'

'His Excellency will see you now.'

Pilate met him at the door, ushered him in, told his secretary to take an early lunch, and not to rush back.

'Look,' Pilate said, 'here is your king. I've had him severely flogged, but in truth I find no basis to carry out the death sentence.'

Caiaphas glanced at Jesus standing by the desk. Jesus stared back impassively. Caiaphas took in the purple robes, barbed wire crown and dried crusted blood on his face. He looked half-dead already. He wouldn't last long on the cross. Caiaphas tried to hide his elation, turning his snigger into a cough. He turned his attention back to Pilate. 'He has to be crucified.'

'I've had him flogged.' Pilate repeated. 'Isn't that punishment enough? Look at him'

As if on cue, voices floated in through the open window, crucify, crucify. Caiaphas opened his arms wide as if to say, you've heard them, what can I do?

'You crucify him.' Pilate said. 'As for me I find him not guilty of any charge.'

'What about his claim to be king of the Jews?' Caiaphas asked.

'What about it?'

'And his claim to be the Son of God,' Caiaphas continued, 'sent by the Mighty One to set up his kingdom here on earth. Such blasphemy is punishable by death in our law.'

Pilate sighed. 'We've had this conversation before Caiaphas. It's a matter for you Jews.'

'There's also the matter of his civil disobedience,' Caiaphas said. 'He opposes the payment of taxes to the Union.'

Pilate yawned.

'His kingdom will be set up here in Northumbria.' Caiaphas went on, 'He intends to overthrow the civil authorities, proclaim God's kingdom here in York.'

'Proof man, where's your proof?' Pilate wanted to know.

Caiaphas shrugged. A slight movement. 'Would the Fuehrer require such proof?'

Pilate studied Caiaphas with distaste. Was it possible that this arschlock of a priest was attempting blackmail? He narrowed his eyes, tried to gauge Caiaphas' manner. The priest met his gaze impassively but was that just a glint in his eye?

Pilate went through a range of contrasting emotions. Annoyance, amusement, bemusement, and settled on cold fury. 'Shall I crucify your king?'

'We have no king but the Fuehrer.' Caiaphas assured him.

You won't be quite so keen on the Fuehrer in a few months, Pilate thought. 'Very well, Caiaphas.'

'You'll sign?' Caiaphas placed the crucifixion order

on the desk and slid it towards Pilate.

In reply Pilate took his pen, signed the paper, pushed it back. 'He's all yours, but I warn you, I'm washing my hands of this matter. I'll provide the facilities but it's your show.'

Caiaphas took the order, slipped it in his attaché case. 'Thank you.'

Pilate watched in silence as the high priest left. Caiaphas might have won the battle, he thought, but he sure as hell would lose the war. He'd make sure this accursed priest would be on the first transport leaving for the camps. Cattle class.

TWENTY-FOUR

UNION BAR, YORK, NORTHUMBRIA.

Swanger, second whisky chasing the first, perched on the edge of a stool. The TV behind the bar was showing the News24 special report on the trial of Jesus. The ticker at the bottom of the screen showed the breaking news. Jesus condemned to death - crucifixion today.

Michelle, the news anchor, rose from behind her desk, walked across to a different part of the studio, and looked at the camera. Why do they do that? Swanger wondered. Although the sound on the TV was low, the bar was quiet. Swanger could just about make out what was being said. '...take you now to the Governor's residence, and our reporter on the spot.'

A solitary bored looking reporter outside the white marbled, palatial building, pressed his ear piece, straightened abruptly, and spoke to camera, 'Jesus, the prophet from Whitby, has had his appeal for clemency turned down. Governor Pilate speaking a short while ago announced he was washing his hands of the whole affair, and if the Jews wanted to crucify their king, who was he to stand in their way. The crucifixion of Jesus will take place at twelve noon today. And now it's back to the studio.'

Michelle was back behind her desk. 'While many

people have decried the decision to crucify Jesus, others have welcomed the news. One man who is said to be pleased with the verdict is the high priest of the Jews, Caiaphas. Here he is now, speaking to our reporter at the Temple.'

The view changed to outside the Temple. Caiaphas, looking stern, and surrounded by Pharisees, was answering questions. Swanger signalled for another drink, ignored her phone on the bar when it rang, she'd already rejected a number of calls from a distraught Barnabas. She couldn't cope with his loss right now. Had no idea how to comfort a weeping colleague.

On the screen, Caiaphas was explaining it was nothing personal against Jesus, who he was sure, was a good man, who meant well, but at the same time couldn't be allowed to get away with calling himself the Son of God. It was blasphemy he explained, and that was punishable by death. Her drink came. She sipped it, savoured the taste, and lit a cigarette. Hypocrite, she thought, blowing smoke in a thin stream.

Her phone rang again. She sighed. Heathersedge calling.

At last.

'Hello.'

'You've been trying to reach me.' Voice smooth, oily.

'One question.'

'Go on.'

'Why?'

'I didn't have a choice.' No pretence, no denial. He knew what he was being asked.

'We all have choices.'

'Not if you want to keep your job, which I do,' pause, 'and I assume you do as well.'

Did she? Swanger blew more smoke, wondered if she could carry on after this.

'I gave them my word.'

'That was rather naive.'

'You knew. You backed me.'

'I know. I know.'

'Then why?'

'Orders from the top.'

'Pilate?'

'Higher.' Pause. 'Much higher.'

The Fuehrer. He had to mean the Fuehrer.

'Oh.' She stubbed the cigarette out.

'Precisely. Look, you've been pushing yourself. Why don't you take a few days off, have a holiday, get some sun.'

She mumbled a reply and, with no more to say, the call ended. Swanger, surprised she hadn't told him where to stick his job, turned her attention back to the TV and Michelle. 'Jesus, who first came to prominence in the coastal resort of Whitby three years ago, has long been a thorn in the side of the Temple authorities because of his radical statements. More controversially though, it was his claim to be the Messiah, the long awaited king of the Jews that has led to his downfall.'

Swanger shuffled off the bar stool, drained her glass, and walked unsteadily to the door. It was like a furnace outside after the cool of the bar. Sunny all the way, eh? Not for Jesus, it wasn't, she thought, as she climbed into the nearest cab.

✝

STATE SECURITY HQ, YORK, NORTHUMBRIA.

When he was led into the holding cell, Bocus didn't see Beaumont at first. He stood by the door and scanned the small area. Too many prisoners all looking the same, a mass of orange covered humanity. It was only when he spotted a gap on the narrow benches and squeezed his way between two young adult males that he saw his former comrade in arms seated on a similar bench on the other side of the room. He didn't attempt to attract his attention, he could see Beaumont was in a world of his own, sat there with a silly smile on his face. Oblivious to his fate, there was no point in Bocus putting him straight. He wouldn't be thanked.

There was no conversation. Anybody who attempted speech was given a look that said don't bother. From time to time, somebody would stand in a vain attempt to relieve numb buttocks. They stood, stretched, sat down again. There were no windows in the cell, the air was stale. All they needed to do was pump some gas in here, Bocus thought, job done in five minutes. Time dragged. Bocus had no way of assessing how long he'd been inside the cell, didn't bother trying. This was where he was now, after weeks of being immobile at least he could move.

Sometime later, there was noise and movement outside. A key turned in the lock, all eyes turned to the door as it opened. A uniformed guard with a clipboard stepped into view. Bocus wondered if it was his imagination but the majority of prisoners seemed to shrink back against the walls.

The guard ran a pencil down the list. 'Beaumont?'

The other prisoners looked around, breathed a sigh

of relief. Bocus looked at Beaumont.

Silence.

'Come on, Beaumont, I know you're in here.' He scanned the room, looked behind the door. 'Unless he was hiding behind here, sneaked out.'

Nobody laughed.

'Beaumont?' The guard asked again, edge to his voice, losing patience.

'What?' Beaumont looked towards the door. 'That's me.'

The guard ticked his list, cocked his head. 'Outside.'

Beaumont stood. 'Am I being released?'

The official smiled, mouth a tight line, no humour in his eyes. 'You could say that.' He scanned his list again, 'Bocus.'

Bocus looked up. This was it then. As he stood, he thought he heard someone mutter Skull Hill. Like I need to be told, he thought, as he walked out in to the corridor.

✝

THE ARENA, SKULL HILL, YORK, NORTHUMBRIA.

The black cab pulled up outside the Arena, deposited Swanger on the footpath. 'Must be mad.' She muttered, paid the cabbie, waited until it moved away before turning her attention to the big screen outside the building. It showed a man wearing a black top hat, swinging a walking cane. He was leading a procession of people out of the city to where Swanger was waiting. Someone in the crowd is beating a drum.

Swanger can hear it, both on the screen, and faint, in the distance.

It reminded Swanger of a funeral procession, and in many respects, it was. Above, the sky was black with drones. Some hovered stationary, others kept pace with the procession. The screen showed the battered, bruised, figure of Jesus limping near the front. A man behind carried the heavy wooden crossbeam. Not carrying your own cross, Jesus? There wasn't any sign of Beaumont or Bocus. Swanger wondered if that was good or bad.

The picture changed to an overhead view from one of the drones. It picked out Mary, Jesus' mother, eyes red rimmed, tearful, other followers of Jesus in support. Swanger recognised the former prostitute, Maggie, who'd been allegedly delivered of demons and had come to be one of his closest followers outside the inner circle. Other prominent women were present, but apart from John, the disciples were absent. Gone into hiding, she assumed. Apart from the booming of the drum, which provided a soundtrack to the images, the procession was silent.

A change of view. A few dissenting voices, protesters hurling insults at Jesus were tracked by a cameraman walking backwards. A commentator interjected a comment from time to time, voice deep with gravitas. '...just leaving the city now. Jesus, too weak to carry the cross beam, has it carried for him by a stranger plucked from the crowd.'

There was a break for adverts. Swanger, undecided for once on what to do, lit a cigarette, then turned her attention back to the screen and the soothing voice that announced, 'Welcome back to coverage of

Northumbrian TV's crucifixion special, sponsored by Property Parts, for all your DIY needs.'

Michelle, the news anchor, appeared on the main part of the screen. In a corner, the procession wound its way up the hill. The drum was getting louder, closer. Michelle was speaking, 'This is Northumbrian TV with our special broadcast of the crucifixion of the prophet, Jesus. Bringing you all the coverage from first nail, to final breath. And don't forget, after the crucifixions, the games will commence.'

'We're going now to our reporter with the procession, and he's talking to one of Jesus' twelve disciples.'

John appears on the screen. He looks terrible, eyes bleary, puffy. There's a man who hasn't slept well, Swanger thought as she listened to the brief exchange.

'Jesus is a good man.' John said. 'He hasn't done anything wrong. He doesn't deserve this.' Youths appeared behind him, waving, gesticulating. The camera went in tighter, blocking them out. The reporter ignoring the interruption, asked, 'John, is Jesus the son of God?'

'I believe he is, yes.' John replied.

Boom, boom, boom, the drumming was getting heavier, closer, louder. The reporter was struggling against the noise. 'Will he save himself? Will God save him?'

John shook his head. 'It's not that simple.' he broke down in tears. 'I'm sorry,' he said, 'this is too upsetting.'

The image cut to a reporter standing outside the main gates. Swanger can see him talking to camera. '... one of Jesus' disciples breaking down as speaks about the prophet soon to be crucified in the Arena, behind me here at Skull Hill.'

The picture from a drone shows Skull Hill from above. The reporter speaking over the picture, 'Skull Hill named, of course for the topographical representation of a skull shape as seen from above.'

The reporter came back on screen, 'The procession should be coming into view very soon, but before that a short break.'

Swanger looked away from the screen. Already the crowds were massing. Fast food vendors were doing a brisk trade. The smell of fried onions and candyfloss made her feel sick. The beer tent was bulging. She thought about another drink, decided it wasn't a good idea and set off towards the Arena.

It was a circus, Swanger realised, as she eased her way through the crowd, dodging the magicians, the stilt walkers, the fire-eaters, the sword swallowers. Making her way past the betting booths with electronic displays giving the latest odds on how long it would take Jesus to die, she arrived at the VIP entrance, confident her State Security credentials would get her in. She presented her badge to the card reader, half hoping it would turn red, refuse entrance. The green LED glowed, the gate clicked, and swung open. She was in, access all areas.

✝

The Arena, Skull Hill, York, Northumbria.

Swanger made her way through the bowels of the arena, through the dense crush surrounding the bars, up the steps that led to the terracing, the glorious cloudless blue sky beckoning. She stopped, looked around. The crucifixion arena was set out like a Roman amphitheatre, banks of tiered seating above an interior parched of grass. A steward asked if he could help. She flashed her badge, told him what she wanted. He gripped her elbow, pointed down to the front. 'The steward down there will let you through.'

Swanger thanked him and clumped down the steep steps, past the rows of banked seating, filled with excited, anticipatory spectators. At the bottom of the steps, Swanger spoke to the official. Her pass was examined, the gate opened and she was ushered onto the track that ran round the dusty arena. Here, between the seating and the exclusion zone where the crosses stood, was the most expensive viewing area, where families brought picnic hampers, made a day of it.

Swanger had never been to a crucifixion. Seen plenty on screen, but never up close and personal. Hangings, yes, plenty of those. But that was about carrying out the sentence of death expeditiously. A good hangman and young Pierrepoint was as good as they came, could have the prisoner dead on the end of the rope ten seconds after entering the condemned cell. Hangings though, were carried out in prisons, not out here in the full glare of publicity, viewed by TV cameras, and spectators with their picnics. Crucifixions were something else. They sent a different message.

As a VIP, she was able to walk along the small service strip in front of the crosses, and stand within a few metres of the victims. All she had to do was keep showing her badge, which she did now to guard after guard, all wearing the ubiquitous Hi-Viz jackets.

The crucifixion area, rebuilt in recent years, was a model of its kind. The upright posts were permanently positioned in a thirty-metre long concrete strip. Set on hydraulic jacks, they could be lowered and raised at the touch of a button. The cross beams, usually carried by the prisoners on the walk of shame, were attached shortly before the nailing took place. Now though, the post in the middle had a crossbeam attached, and was lower in the ground.

Knowing she couldn't put it off any longer, she raised her gaze upwards, past the feet, the naked torso, until she made eye contact with Beaumont. Her eyes pricked with tears and not able to bear his reproachful stare, she looked towards Bocus who had also registered her presence.

'Come to gloat?' He asked. His voice still strong.

She had given these men her solemn promise, and had let them down. She felt totally bereft, and wondered again why she'd come. 'No.' Swanger whispered and shook her head in denial.

A massive cheer came from the seating opposite the tunnel, spectators all around the arena came to their feet, stamping, whistling, hollering and cheering. Time for the main event, it was too late to move, she'd have to wait for Jesus to be nailed to the cross before she could leave. She looked towards the tunnel, saw Jesus limp into view. He was flanked by the three-man crucifixion squad. The doctor, to administer a sedative if required, and later, to pronounce death, trailed behind.

Close up, Jesus was a more pitiful sight than he'd appeared on screen. He had a blackened eye and a bruised face. Fresh blood seeped from old wounds. Jammed on his head was a woven ring of barbed wire. A grotesque parody of a crown. The crucifixion party reached the waiting cross, a short distance from where Swanger stood. For some reason Jesus wasn't wearing the obligatory orange coveralls but was instead draped in a purple robe. Two of the squad slipped the robe from his shoulder.

Swanger winced as she saw his back, a torn reddened mass of flesh. Once naked they spun him round, pushed his pale body up against the rough wood of the cross, and held his arms aloft in position. The squad leader positioned the heavy-duty nail gun against each wrist in turn. The crowd held their breath as the trigger was pressed twice. Thump. Thump. Jesus flinched with the pain. The crowd groaned. Then cheered. The squad leader ducked down to nail Jesus' feet while the other two bound his arms with cord, and then did the same to his calves.

Nobody spoke. It was a well-rehearsed established routine, as quick as a hangman, Swanger realised. It was just death that took far longer. The squad leader checked everything, hung a sign above Jesus' head, stepped back, and pressed a button on his remote keypad. The hydraulic machinery clanked below the ground. Swanger watched as the cross began to rise, heard Jesus say, 'Father, forgive them. They don't know what they're doing.'

Trouble is Jesus, Swanger thought, watching the cross rise to its full height, you're a mouse in a world of cats. She watched in silence as the crucifixion squad withdrew. They were replaced by the guards and stewards who would ensure nobody got too close. Jesus' mother, Mary, other family members and supporters were led into the family area. None of them looked her way.

She thought of the pistol in her bag, wondered if she had the guts to get it out, put Beaumont and Bocus out of their misery, knew she hadn't. She sighed; it was time to go, she could do nothing here. Swanger looked at Bocus, mouthed, 'I'm sorry.'

'Screw you.' He replied, closing his eyes as a spasm of pain racked his body.

She looked at Beaumont and gave the same apology. He nodded and maintained eye contact until Swanger was forced to look away. She took a last look at Jesus, at the sign above his head that read, JESUS, KING OF THE JEWS, then turned and walked away.

†

Soon after Jesus had been crucified, Caiaphas and an Arena official had a brief spat. They were arguing about the sign above Jesus' head while the crowd cheered in support, not knowing what they cheered.

'I am not lowering the cross to change a sign.' The official told him.

'It should say he claimed to be king of the Jews.' Caiaphas protested.

'That's the sign that came with him. If you want it changing, speak to the Governor. I'll change it on his authority.'

John was the sole disciple at the crucifixion. He looked at the others who'd come to witness the death of Jesus. Most prominent among them was his mother, Mary. She was weeping on her sister's shoulder.

According to the signs that hung on their crosses, the two men on either side of Jesus were terrorists. As bad as crucifixion was, at least they'd done something to deserve this fate. Both men had their eyes closed. One of them was muttering profanities. Apart from the short, overweight woman, nobody had come to see them die, and even she hadn't stuck it out.

John looked beyond them, at the row upon row of spectators. The families with their picnic baskets. The fast food vendors. At the three clocks on the main stand showing how long each man had been nailed to his cross. He took it all in, and felt overwhelming sadness for humanity. To think Jesus would die for these zombies was more than he could bear. Tears streaked his face. Maggie put her arms round him, and urged him to be strong. He told her he'd try his best. He wanted to go, but knew he couldn't. He felt compelled to stay and witness Jesus' death.

The afternoon wore on. The crowd silent and boisterous in turn as they waited for someone to die. Betting slips were thrown down in disgust as the allotted time passed, others were bought. Spectators in the VIP area hurled insults at Jesus. One came across now, and stood metres from the foot of the cross shouting at Jesus. 'You're gonna knock the Temple down, are ya?' he called, 'build it back up in three day, eh?' Worse for drink, he stood swaying. 'You need to save yourself first, lad.'

He was joined by Caiaphas, Brotherton, and some Pharisees. 'King of the Jews? Once he's come down from there, I'll believe it.'

'If you're the Son of God, get yourself down.'

'He saves others but can't save himself.'

'Happen God will rescue him.'

One of the terrorists joined in, calling across to Jesus, 'Aren't you the Messiah? Can't you save yourself? And us, save us, if you can.'

John was pleased when the rebel on the other side called over to rebuke him. 'Don't you fear God, Bocus? We're being punished for what we've done. But this man has done nothing wrong.'

'Screw you, Beaumont.' Bocus lapsed into silence.

'Jesus,' Beaumont called across, 'will you remember me when you come into your kingdom?'

Jesus turned his head, looked at Beaumont. 'I tell you the truth. Today you will be with me in paradise.'

Later in the afternoon, John heard his name being called. He looked up at Jesus who beckoned him closer with a slight movement of his head. Jesus' mother, Mary, noticed, and joined him. Together they got as close as they could before the guards stopped them.

'What is it, Jesus?' Mary asked.

'This is now your son, mother.' Jesus said. 'And John, this is your mother. Look after her.'

'Of course, Jesus, of course.' John assured. 'Anything.'

About six in the evening blackness came over the arena. After years of hot weather, there was an unexpected cold bite in the air. John, surprised by the sudden descent of darkness, looked up. From his narrow view of the sky he could see the sky was devoid of clouds. We're in for a right old storm, he thought, trying to remember the last time it had rained.

At that moment Jesus cried out in a loud voice, 'My God, my God, why have you forsaken me?'

'He's calling Eliyahu.' A voice called.

'Happen he'll be down to save him.'

'That'll be a laugh.'

'It'll not be long now.'

'Aye up, he's talking again.'

John had moved near to the cross at Jesus' first call, and was close enough to hear him say, 'It is done.' Then a few seconds later, 'Father, into your hands I commit my spirit.' His head slumped on his chest.

The moment Jesus died, screams of panic filled the air, as rain, propelled by fierce winds, drove across the arena. There was no hiding place and within seconds everybody was soaked to the skin. A loud sonic boom of noise cascaded round the concrete Arena, bouncing off the walls, reverberating, echoing. The earth shook, John staggered like a drunken man. He looked skywards, expecting to see military jets scream into view, but beyond the rain there was nothing to see. An earthquake, he realised, and wondered if the world was coming to an end.

Ten minutes later, the storm had passed and the sun was shining in all its glory. The fear had lifted from the crowd and the carnival continued. The leader of the crucifixion squad appeared, followed by the doctor. There was a whoosh of dispelled air as the hydraulics lowered the cross. The doctor placed his stethoscope on Jesus' chest. There was a brief pause as he listened for a sign of life. He spoke to the official, who then lifted his right arm to the crowd, his thumb extended. He turned in a full circle giving everybody the chance to see his signal.

The crowd, silent with anticipation went wild, as the stadium erupted with cheers and whistles from all sides. John buried his head in hands and wept uncontrollably.

†

Union Bar, York, Northumbria.

Swanger couldn't remember how many whiskies she'd drunk in the day. She'd either have a monumental hangover in the morning or would, like Beaumont and Bocus, be dead. It was early evening. The bar packed with a sophisticated theatre-going crowd. Drinks and snacks before curtain up. Everybody ignored the crying woman at the bar.

The TV special of the crucifixion was drawing to a close. The volume just audible above the buzz of conversation. Michelle, sombre expression on her face, appeared on screen. She paused for effect, and then said, 'Jesus is dead.'

Apart from Swanger, nobody in the bar took any notice.

'The death of the prophet, Jesus, was confirmed a few minutes ago. He was crucified at twelve noon and pronounced dead six hours later at six pm this evening.'

The screen showed Jesus, head on his chest, hanging lifeless.

What about Beaumont and Bocus, Swanger

thought, don't they deserve a mention?

The screen changed back to the studio and Michelle. 'According to reports from Jodrell Bank, the unexpected eclipse at the exact moment Jesus died was caused by a comet passing in front of the sun. This in turn led to the earthquake which struck the region at the same time. A spokesman for the Union Geological Society commented, "it was a natural phenomena and not a spiritual event caused by the death of one man."

'Damage caused by the earthquake is thought to be slight, however we can confirm that the heavy curtain in the Jewish Temple was torn in two, from top to bottom around the same time. Temple officials are at a loss to explain how or why this happened, but have been quick to rule out any connection with the death of Jesus.'

Michelle shuffled her papers. 'Two other men, identified as terrorists by State Security, were crucified alongside Jesus.'

Swanger nodded approvingly. 'Better late than never.' She thought, and beckoned the barman for another refill.

'Jesus was the first to die, followed by Beaumont, then Bocus. Apparently, Beaumont and Bocus were encouraged to die by the simple procedure of breaking their legs.'

The news anchor went on to explain that victim's legs were broken on the cross to allow their bodies to slump causing suffocation. 'Although, this wasn't necessary in the case of Jesus as he was already dead.'

'Lucky Jesus.' Swanger paid for her drink, told the barman to keep the change. She raised her glass, drank a toast to Beaumont and Bocus, then left to find a taxi.

THE TALBOT, YORK, NORTHUMBRIA.

Peter drained his pint, waved his glass in the general direction of the barman, and watched disinterestedly as the glass was filled. He grunted his thanks, pushed some coins across the counter, and sipped his beer moodily. Past three years they'd been living the dream, fooling themselves they were making a difference, but now with Jesus gone, what had it all meant?

He'd been part of the massive crowd outside the arena, had watched the procession coming up the hill. He'd been within a metre or two of Jesus as he'd passed, followed by his mother, then Maggie, John, and a few others. He hadn't known many of the people in the procession. Fierce tears stung his eyes as he remembered Jesus being led out for crucifixion. His battered, broken, bloodied body, nail-gunned to the cross. The howls, the jeers of the crowd. He hadn't been able to stay and watch Jesus' ultimate degradation. His lonely, public death.

Peter drank more beer, and thought about Jesus. The Messiah who couldn't save himself. The son of the living God hung naked to die on a wooden cross. A life touched by Jesus, Peter realised, was irrevocably changed. And to think that God was in all this. That he witnessed, condoned his son's public execution.

'Why?' Peter whispered.

He screwed his eyes tight. Too many questions, too few answers.

He had half a mind to follow that bastard Judas' example. A tree, a rope, and step into oblivion. He wept uncontrollably, knew he didn't even have the guts to do that. Jesus was dead, but Peter, having denied him three times, wanted to live. Suppose I'll creep off back to Whitby, he thought, get a job as a deckhand, and go back to sea. He groaned. It was a deep desperate sound. A few people looked round at the noise, but most ignored him. Embarrassed, Peter kept his head down. He thought about making his way to the campsite. See if any of the others had turned up. Trouble was, as Jesus' right hand man, he should have stuck it out, even if it meant his own death. It would be difficult to face the lads.

There was a movement at his side, a bar stool was pulled out. 'I've been in all the pubs in York looking for you.' His brother's voice whispered in his ear.

'You've found me.' Peter replied, 'want a drink?'

'Don't you realise how dangerous it is for us now. We need to keep our heads down.'

'Dangerous, yeah. Beer, Scotch?'

'The rock, eh?'

'You what?'

'What he said. What he called you, "The rock on whom I'll build my church."'

'And your point is?' Peter demanded.

Andrew shrugged. 'You need to start acting like a rock.'

'You don't understand...' Peter began, then broke off and drained his glass. He signalled to the barman for a refill.

Andrew caught the man's eye, gave a quick shake of his head. The man shrugged, carried on polishing glasses, watched the TV news, yet another rehash of the day's events.

'I'm no rock,' Peter shook his head, a grave, slow motion, his lips tight. 'How can I be with Jesus dead?

He was my rock and without him I'm sinking in the sand.'

Andrew pulled a face, he didn't have time for introspection. He gripped his brother's arm. 'C'mon, bro. Let's get to the safety of the camp site, get some rest.'

'He's dead, Andy.' Peter pulled his arm free. 'Jesus is dead.'

'I know.' Andrew sighed. 'I saw.'

'You were there?'

'Nah, watched it on TV. In a pub.'

Peter shook his head, tried to clear the fuzziness. 'Hey, pal?'

The barman avoided eye contact, and disappeared into the other bar.

'Do you think he'd want this?' Andrew asked. 'The Boss? Would he want us all sat around mourning him?'

Peter blew air through his teeth. 'It's gonna be so hard without him, Andy. The last three years have been brilliant. The best years of my life.'

'Yeah, me too.' Andrew agreed.

'Will we be allowed his body, for a funeral? A proper funeral, worthy of a king?'

Andrew nodded. 'Maggie's on it. She's made contact with the Governor's office, been told she can collect the body on Sunday.'

Peter nodded. 'That's good.'

'So,' Andrew asked, 'shall we go?'

'I don't know, Andy.'

The brothers sat in silence for a moment, and then Peter remembered he had some news. 'I had a text from Jayne, she wants to come back.'

Andrew asked how Peter felt about reconciliation.

'Yeah,' Peter replied. 'I think it might work.' He paused, 'I've missed her.'

Andrew smiled. 'Why don't you tell her that?'

'First chance I get, bro. I'm on it.'

Andrew looked at his brother, and took a deep breath. 'She's at the campsite, Peter. When she didn't hear back from you, she texted me. I gave her directions. She arrived earlier this afternoon.' He stopped. 'You don't mind?'

'No, I don't mind.'

Andrew placed an arm round his brother's shoulder and helped him to his feet. Together they walked to the door, then stopped, and turned back to the TV as the studio anchor said, '... the last word on Jesus to one of his disciples, John, who we reached by phone earlier.'

The screen showed a picture of John.

'This is what he had to say,'

John's voice came on air, 'Apart from the things the world knows about Jesus, he did many other things as well. If every one of them were written down, there wouldn't be enough room in the world for all the books that could be written.'

'Amen to that, brother.' Peter said, as they left the pub and walked out into a world that would never be the same again.

AFTERWARDS

PRISON MORGUE, YORK, NORTHUMBRIA.
SUNDAY.

The uniformed guard on the door looked at Maggie with a quizzical expression. Praying there wouldn't be a problem, she offered the permit provided by Pilate's office. He took the sheet of paper, inspected it, then handed it back. 'You have transport?'

The transport had been provided by Joseph, a rich man, one of the few members of the Sanhedrin who hadn't wanted the Lord dead. On Friday, having made himself known to Jesus' family and supporters, he'd offered space in the family burial vault, and provided linen for wrapping the body. He'd even supplied the oils that Maggie would use to anoint the Lord's body and make him ready for burial. That would be a difficult task but one that she was determined to accomplish, knowing it would be the last time she saw the man who'd restored her to life.

Maggie assured the guard she had transport. She was told to step through the airport style metal detector, where she was searched by his female colleague, before being ushered towards a reception desk. The receptionist, a middle-aged man, motioned for the paperwork. He studied the permit, glancing at Maggie over his glasses. Satisfied, he stamped the permit, gave it back. He spoke into the microphone on his lapel. 'She's here.'

An enormous guard appeared out of a door marked, SECURITY. He gave Maggie an appraising look then set off down a long corridor, calling over his shoulder, 'This way.'

Maggie followed a pace behind. Arriving at the morgue, a second guard unlocked the double steel doors and pushed them open. He stepped inside, Maggie followed and came to an abrupt halt as she cannoned off the stationary official.

'Oh shit.' The guard exclaimed. He pushed Maggie to one side and ran off down the corridor. The second guard pulled his pistol and edged into the room. He was back within seconds. He ordered Maggie to remain outside, and set off in pursuit of his colleague.

Maggie entered the room, and looked at the rows of steel drawers. They were all closed apart from one. The one with the label that read, Jesus. Knowing it was futile she looked in the open drawer. It was empty.

She looked round in desperation. Sunlight streaming through the window bounced off a stainless steel table in the centre of the room. Maggie, shielding her eyes, saw on the table, the neatly folded linen cloth that she had wrapped around Jesus' body on Friday evening.

Feeling faint, she took a deep breath, closed her eyes, told herself when she opened them the Lord would be there, and that none of the last five minutes would have happened. She opened her eyes, Jesus wasn't there, but two men clothed in brilliant white outfits had appeared from nowhere.

She gasped, took a step backwards, and decided she

was hallucinating. She wondered if, now the Lord was dead, the demons had returned. Not demons, she decided, but not humans either. This was just too much to bear. She burst into tears.

'What's wrong?' One of the men asked. He had an ordinary voice, Maggie decided, but there was something different about him.

'They've taken the Lord away, and I don't know where he is.' She babbled on about the funeral and collecting Jesus' body while the two men looked at her with puzzlement.

A hospital porter looked in. 'Is there a problem?' He asked. 'Why are you crying?'

'I'm looking for Jesus,' Maggie sobbed, 'He should be here.'

The porter smiled. 'Maggie, it's me.'

'Oh, Lord.' She cried out, and opened her arms to embrace him.

'Don't hold on to me,' Jesus said, 'for I haven't yet ascended to the Father. Go now to my brothers, the disciples. Tell them you've seen me. That I live, and will be with you all soon.'

ABOUT THE AUTHOR

A 'Northumbrian' at heart, Christopher has been writing for over 40 years. Originally from the city of Leeds, he now lives in the county of Warwickshire in the middle of England.

Fuelled only by freshly brewed coffee and a copious supply of biscuits, the writing of Arrival was a tenacious endeavour; the majority of the book being penned on an old laptop by the light of a battery operated head lamp, while seated on a hard wooden chair.

ACKNOWLEDGMENTS

A heartfelt thank you to everyone who made this book possible including family and friends for inspiration, encouragement, laughter, feedback, and prayer, especially my wife and father. Craig Walford for scriptural guidance. Carl Brown and Ben Rogers for their account of a '72' journey. Dawn Coleman and Natalya Miles for initial proof reading. Pauline Scatterty for final proofreading and editing. Beta readers – Hazel Bowden, Jane Read, Amanda Wymer, and P.G.

And finally, thanks to God, who gave me the idea and trusted me to write Arrival. All the glory is His, all the mistakes are mine.

JESUS WILL RETURN

Printed in Great Britain
by Amazon